Rucksack Jumper

Moss Croft

Copyright © Moss Croft 2023

The moral right of Moss Croft to be identified as the author of this work has been asserted by him in accordance with the Copyright, Designs and Patents Act of 1988.

All rights reserved. No part of this publication may be reproduced, transmitted or stored in a retrieval system, in any form or by any means, without permission in writing from Moss Croft, nor be otherwise circulated in any form of binding or cover other than that in which it is published and without a similar condition being imposed on the subsequent purchaser.

ISBN: 9798378816033

The Novels of Moss Croft

Rucksack Jumper

Boscombe

Raspberry Jam

Ghost in the Stables

Stickerhand

The Flophouse Years

Crack Up or Play It Cool

God Help the Connipians

About the Author

Moss Croft is a pen name. That means he is really someone else.

Contents

Chapter One:
Oujda — Page 7

Chapter Two:
Al Aricha — Page 65

Chapter Three:
Oran to Ghardaia — Page 119

Chapter Four:
Trip to Bury — Page 193

Chapter Five:
City of Bridges — Page 227

Chapter Six:
Nuoro, Sardinia — Page 283

Chapter Seven:
Heavy Rain in Tunis — Page 349

Disclaimer

This is a work of fiction, any resemblance to real persons or events is the result of unforeseen coincidence. Except for Presidents Bendjedid and Bourguiba who both looked as miserable as depicted.

Dedication

For Alban.

Chapter One

Oujda

1.

This is unexpected. As I climb down the three steep steps of the clammy bus, awaiting me on the red and dusty kerbside stands the tallest man I have ever seen.

'Hello, sir,' he says, and I wonder if he has mistaken me for someone else. A famous poet perhaps, for that is what I would wish to be. Nothing published and no poem read out in public since I left school nearly four years ago. For the time being, I am but a visitor in this country, a tourist with a hole in my shoe. 'Welcome. Welcome to Oujda,' he beams.

I cannot help myself from doing it, I smile back at him, whether it is right or wrong to behave so. The enormous man waves away the beggars and street urchins. Perhaps it is his size or it might be that he is known to them; he smiles as he hisses. 'Tsch-tsch.' I think the sound discourages them from gathering around, tugging on my clothing as has happened when I alighted in other Moroccan cities. The two others I have visited before today. The dirham-seeking children leave, a sorry-looking blind man sits back down on the scalding ground, dirty white robes folding beneath him as he lowers himself into a crumpled and cross-legged posture.

'I am here to greet you, to make your stay a fine one,' says the man. He is nearer seven feet tall than he is to six. I have no tape measure with me but I would swear to it. Bet my rucksack.

I cannot act as if I'm famous—don't try—no reason on Earth why he should fete me as he does. I feel a bit embarrassed; the man is drawing attention to me which I did not ask for. I have dealt with beggars on my own before now, the kids who try to pull on a sleeve. Mostly I avoid eye contact, say, 'Non,' if I think it will help. My experience of the country to date has been one long standoff. Nothing nasty but those who talk to me are angling for a cut of my money. Nine times out of ten. This chap is different: charming and courteous. If he is significantly different, that will be the surprise.

What a funny sight he is. A brown suit, a jacket when the sun is burning hot—which it always is in Morocco— beneath a small hat of the Arab type, round, shaped like a very fat disk. It sits plum on top of his head. He wears no tie despite the suit. And the top button of his shirt is clasped shut. I don't think men down here can be doing with all that flopping and knotting; I've not seen a tie in five days on the continent. Inscrutable Africa. Can't say I blame them; I wore a tie when I worked for an insurance company and that was a mug's game. They make us look important when none of us really are. There, you see, I'm virtually a philosopher. I don't suppose this fellow is actually seven feet tall. Is anyone? Easily six-nine, six-ten, he really is. My eye level is lower than his Adam's apple, he converses with me as if we are old friends.

'Please,' he says, 'don't be reticent.' He uses that exact word: reticent. His English is terrific and he is a Moroccan. His clothes, the little hat, coffee-coloured skin, all testify to that. He is older than I am—older than twenty that is—but probably by only five or six years. And most notably, he is very, very tall. 'I am not seeking money. Your money is your money.'

Oujda

I am pleased to hear it although his words do not tempt me to trust him. Not yet. Is that my shortcoming or a harbinger of his? As I have said, I'm just five days in the country. The continent. My impression is that everyone wants something. My loose change will do but I'm down here on a shoestring. Fathoming them—the Arabs—who to trust and who to avoid, that's a trick I have yet to master. It is the crux of the matter. Misunderstandings arise easily and inexplicably. In just a few days in North Africa, that much has become clear to me. Maybe if I just keep travelling—go with the flow—I will discover that I have gathered more about people than I yet realise. My French improves the more I use it, perhaps my capacity to judge people will grow likewise. I can fathom everyone in Lancashire, where I come from. It's dead easy up there. Right now, I cannot read Moroccans, their expressions or intentions. What does a smile, a nod or a shake of the head really mean among people of another culture?

'What are you after?' I ask the towering man. It feels disrespectful, requiring him to explain himself. He is making an effort, speaking in English where French is the more widely accommodated. And Arabic is surely his mother tongue. Still, I choose to put him on the spot, do so exactly because he says he doesn't want my money. I dislike myself for doubting him, do it nevertheless. Can't quite find the trust.

In these last five days, in Tétouan and Fes, I have seen children run up to travellers alighting from buses. 'Dirham!' they shouted. Money was exactly what they wanted. 'Dirham!' They called it to my face, tugged upon my sleeve. Perhaps they intended only to attract my attention; snatching and stealing felt likely to me. If this notion does them a disservice, I can plead only ignorance. It is my first time here. I like Moroccans in general, or if not in general, then in principle. Letting it show is the difficulty. If I appear too keen to meet them, will they infer concurrent gullibility on my part. I always shunned their outstretched hands. Thieves? Probably not, possibly yes. What is thieving when you get to the bottom of it? We've kept Gibraltar, the Spanish keep Ceuta; it all looks like it belongs to someone else if we quit playing spoof with history. Kidding ourselves. I don't engage them, the little street urchins. Never took a tour of Fes. Haggling over prices unnerves me. With smiling children, I think it quite unbearable. I should be grateful to this tall man; he clearly wants to help me. I don't trust him; however, one tall Arab should be easier to deal with than a whole throng of little ones. And I am not miserly; my father exhibits that trait, the man whose outlook I diametrically oppose. If I have learnt his Lancashire ways it is happenstance. I am not an advocate of fixed prices—on matters of economics I am quite open-minded—my difficulty is much more fundamental. I expect the cost of a thing to be immutable. Questions need answers; how much is each item worth. A verbal arm wrestle does not determine value: might is not right. If the tall chap doesn't want my money, there can be no misunderstanding. We are not there yet.

From his lofty viewpoint, he smiles down at me. 'I am from the tourist information service. I am at your service. The city of Oujda welcomes you. I am overjoyed that you have come.'

And this conversation is not the only one he currently conducts. While he engages me, he is similarly speaking with a tall blond girl. Fishing with two lines if my hunch is correct and his line about not wanting money is a bluff. The other conversation swings between French and English. I only eavesdrop because at the start of each phrase—before its content becomes clear—I think it might be me he speaks to. I note, with wry amusement, that the girl, who is taller than me but nothing like as tall as this self-proclaimed tourist information officer, is more overtly sceptical than I. Her demeanour is one of hostility. She comes across as thin-skinned, ever so slightly paranoid. Not having a happy holiday as far as I can tell. In Morocco people come up to you and sell you shit: that's just the way it is. I do not know why she is getting so hot under the collar about it. Hot under the T-shirt. Her attitude might derive from experience; I can imagine that lone female travellers have the harder time of it. In my five days here, most of the Moroccan women I have seen have been drably attired oldies, sitting behind a clutch of live chickens at a market stall. That sort. Covered from head to toe in the wraparound garments they all wear. Female flesh—visible and plentiful in Spain—is a collector's item here. In Morocco. Girls and ladies from my own culture, European countries, fall into my eye as if it were a magnet. It's the way they dress, I'm sure. Not that Moroccan girls are so different, simply not on display. Arab men must see them as I do, the European girls. And those who wear shorts and T-shirts might be signalling much more than their clothing implies back in their own countries. I expect Moroccans can no more read western body language, facial expressions, or penetrate dress codes, than I can those of the Arabs. This tall girl wears jeans—a sensible choice—but they show more of her shape than the potato sacks which the Moroccan women wear. I don't imagine her time here has been hassle-free. It is worse for women than it is for us men, I've seen it with my own eyes. Touched and prodded, spoken to with an insistence that I've never had to endure. Men can say no. Today, April sixth, nineteen-eighty—I denote the year in the Christian calendar, uncertain of its Islamic equivalent—this tall blond girl is undertaking a bold course. A lone female in this strange country. And her suspicion of this well-mannered and altitudinous tourist official could be the wisest course. I rather like him, wet behind the ears as I may be. We are in the land of the unpredictable.

I feel a certain protectiveness towards the blond girl. She is at sea and my assistance may smooth her passage. She ignores me, I suspect she has misconstrued my interest in her. If we were alone, I could explain to her my theory about culture shock. It is misinterpreting the scope and intent of the smallest of human interactions which unsettles us. I dare not give a thumbs-up sign here for fear it has a sexual connotation. The meaning of a raised eyebrow or a small tsch-tsch sound emitted from clenched teeth does not signify the same here as it did in Bury, Lancashire. My home before these travels began. Signs I once thought familiar have become a language as foreign as Babylonian. The universal language of smiles and winks turns out to be no more than a dialect. I adjudge that I should tell her none of this within earshot of the tall Moroccan. He might take offence and I intend none.

Instinctively, I step closer to the girl. In my mind it is an act of solidarity. Together we face the improbable tourist information guy, make sense of him collectively. Share notes. Travellers are really code-breakers, with a deeper interest in those whose land it is than the sun-seeking tourists. We hope to get beneath the skin of the new country, won't settle for the state of ignorance in which we first arrived. The girl's sunburnt face makes no turn in my direction, reciprocates no common feeling. She shifts her shoulder—a ninety-degree angle—warding me off in the manner used on a rugby field. Without a word passed, I have become another encroaching male.

We are waiting, the blond girl and I, for the bus driver to return our belongings. They are within his vehicle, a large side compartment beneath the seating, he accesses the luggage hold from here, from the roadside. The tall man—he has told me his name is Abdul—waits with us.

Talks all the while. I listen discreetly to the half of the conversation which he directs at the girl. She wishes to speak in French. To my ear, English is her superior language. Neither is her first. I think Abdul is a joke name. Perhaps uncouth tourists call him by it, and he uses it ironically; I haven't asked. Mild of manner when speaks to the girl; he has told her that he doesn't seek her money. My French stretched that far. The girl's sombre face looks at the bus, the now-open side. She has few words for the man who has welcomed us to Oujda. In two languages, the giant suggests where she might secure a reasonably priced hotel room. He has made this pitch to me also. I smell commission, it is no more than a guess. I am confident that he is not trying to get into my bed and—the girl might disagree with this—I do not think he is actively trying to get into hers. If my commission theory is incorrect, then I have no idea why Abdul—if that is indeed his name—is taking this proprietorial interest in either of us. He's got about fifteen inches on me and he comes across as rather pleasant.

'Are there two single rooms available at the Gafait Hotel?' I enquire, presuming responsibility to secure overnight accommodation for the frightened girl as well as for myself. It is the only name of many he has spoken which has stuck in my mind.

The girl gives me a blue-eyed glare for my troubles.

'Yes, yes, and you may both see many hotels. Stay in the same hotel; stay in separate hotels. Uptown, downtown. Here in Oujda, we have many, many choices for you, young visitors.'

The girl says something to me very quietly. In French. I think she is getting very muddled. Why address me in that language, Abdul's stronger, if the intent is to cut him out? I don't understand her phrase. The word, pension—which I know to mean hotel—is in it. Her voice has an unusual lilt, the oddest accent.

'Are you Swedish?'

'Norwegian,' she replies.

'We need rooms for tonight. Why not look at the hotel he suggested?'

Abdul looks away as we speak, he is not pushy at all. My distrust of him is based not on the strangeness of his interaction but its familiarity. This is the first time since Spain, since I left Europe five days ago, that I have been assisted without being simultaneously divested of cash. It could take a little getting used to.

'We try it,' hisses the girl.

* * *

We must look a strange caravan, walking up the main street under the intense afternoon sun. There are market stalls on both sides of the road and a few shops displaying fixed-price signs. We walk in the middle of the road; we are the traffic. As we come to a square, our leader takes a left turn which we duly follow. It is Abdul in front, my well-worn rucksack perched upon his gargantuan shoulders. He offered to carry the large suitcase that the Norwegian girl has with her and, if I understood his French correctly, her small rucksack too. She declined. Then he offered to carry my rucksack. Ridiculous. I have but a single item, and I am a man. This girl, though tall and tanned, looks strangely broken, by the heat and the peculiarity of her surroundings. I thought it cruel that she should have to stagger further with both case and rucksack. I passed my own tightly packed rucksack to our willing guide and said to the girl that she should pass her case to me. Initially she resisted my flawless plan to share our burdens. Relented only after three whispered exchanges, and this with a shrug of displeasure. She walks behind me on our trek across Oujda, her smaller rucksack enough to stoop her stature by a couple of inches. The top of her head is now no higher than my own. Even the swing of her blond ponytail lacks enthusiasm.

Why am I here? A northern lad, tanning, peeling a little, under the fierce African sun. Stepping stones and staging posts. My declared intention is to hitchhike to the Sahara. Into the desert. My secret wish is to write a volume of poetry inspired by the journey. There are two snags: Africa has unnerved me, I have hitched no rides at all since Spain, hence the bus; and my pen has run dry. Not literally, I could write a postcard. Could but don't. I do not believe the lack of verse represents any shortage of subject matter. I am overstimulated. I feel it with every step I take in this extraordinary land. A third reason drops into my mind: the verses I write can be a bit crummy, often as not. Can't understand half of it myself and that is a very poor show.

The man who I am sceptically calling Abdul sets quite a pace. His stride, I suppose. I try to keep up; Every few steps I must pass the enormous suitcase from hand to hand, such is its heft. I think to myself that the distrustful Norwegian girl is lagging at the rear so that she can assess the hotel from a distance. If she concludes that Abdul plans only to sell her into a house of ill-repute, she is far enough behind to simply take off. Leg it. Perhaps the burdensome case which she has passed to me contains house bricks: a plausible theory, say my sagging arms. I think it is just ballast, something that she was always prepared to jettison should the need arise. In fact, I realise that letting someone else carry it may have always been her plan. She might be disappointed that Abdul failed to be as insistent as I, her reluctance to let him take it a bit of overly clever psychology. The bluff that failed. And should she arrive at an acceptable destination, find no reason to flee, then with these bricks she shall a homestead build. Or perhaps it contains hair products, three or four pairs of shoes and a two-month supply of trashy Norwegian romance novels. It is the more likely but guessing is not knowing.

* * *

At the Gafait Hotel a room is to cost—currency conversion is a mental reflex for me—just under four pounds. The bedrooms are without running water; a hot shower beckons us just along the corridor. The girl begins to haggle, wants it for half the offered price. She argues unnecessarily in my view. The hotel proprietor glances at Abdul—a name I never hear him address towards the tall man—and then at the girl. He speaks in Arabic, requiring maybe-Abdul to interpret his words. He simply repeats the price he has already told us, says it warmly in French and English.

I advise the Norwegian girl that a fixed-price sign adorns the door of the hotel. It is four pounds or look elsewhere, the man will not budge. I hear what I guess to be a short Norwegian swear word emit from her lips. Despite her misgivings, we take adjacent rooms.

Abdul smiles, pleased that we are to stay in a hotel he has sourced for us. 'I will see you at seven,' he says, 'when I have finished working.'

'Where do you work?' I ask.

'This. I am the head of tourism for the city of Oujda.'

I want to laugh. At what, I am quite unclear. Is he a hustler masquerading as an official, taking a small cut for each hotel room booked? Or is it really the strategy of the local tourist board to meet every westerner off the bus, securing a bed for each and every one? Either seems funny but I keep my face as straight as I am able. His height is quite intimidating.

Before the hotel proprietor—an ageing gentleman whose hairline is a tidemark of sweat—can allow us to take up residence, he requires that we each fill in a lengthy form. I imagine that the girl, like me, has had to do this at previous hotels in Morocco. The paperwork demands that we write down our countries of birth, the address of our habitual place of residence. The proprietor transcribes our passport numbers into a book of his own, although he will also take the said documents from us, retain them in the hotel safe for the duration of our stay. Each time this occurs, I ask myself if I am a guest or a hostage. A little of each, I suspect. In a box upon the form labelled "Occupation", I enter the ubiquitous term, student. I am a student of life; however, unemployed would be a more truthful rendering. I receive no grant, enrolled as I am in no place of higher learning. I write poetry, most of which even I consider unpublishable. Not a penny has come of it. These travels—my quest to hitchhike into the Sahara Desert— might become the education my father has denied me. It is occupation enough.

My date of entry to Morocco I accurately record to have occurred five days ago. Another box requires me to predict my date of departure from the kingdom. The day after tomorrow, I write. I will cross into Algeria from this border town. I will do so very soon.

The Norwegian girl seems unmoved by the tedium of the task. She purses her lips, completing the exercise as though putting the final flourishes on a biology O-level examination. Her Norwegian test required her to dissect an auk. She is currently naming its many body parts in each of the proffered boxes, finishing her final paper. It strikes me that, for her, this interminable paperwork is all part of a strange holiday. Her comportment suggests she never intended to enjoy it. Never a thought that she might. I wonder if this girl is a new breed of misery seeker but choose not to raise the matter. Apart from pointing out that the hotel has a fixed-price sign in the window, she and I have not spoken a word to each other since we came inside.

When my medley of truth and half-truth, and the girl's

auk-related missive, are complete, the concierge gives us our keys and we climb a single flight of stairs together. The girl again—and despite a half-hearted offer of mine—carrying her own cumbersome luggage. We enter our respective rooms.

* * *

I unpack a few things, lie on my bed, stand up, then lie down again. Let a little time elapse. And then I step out of my room. Lightly, I knock on the door of my neighbour. There is no sound arising from within, neither of movement nor in reply. I knock again. 'Only me,' I call. To use the Norwegian girl's name might be the proper way to attract her attention; however, she has yet to divulge it to me. I fear that I continue to frighten her. How absurd. I am young, my hair is long but I keep it out of my ever-smiling face. In contrast, she has three inches on me and a hell of a frown.

Without any evidence of the coming presence, the door opens and the girl stands before me. She wears the same jeans as before; a sleeveless T-shirt now upon her. It is white, looks like a vest. Its narrow fabric on her shoulders intermingles with navy-blue bra straps. She has a healthy tan, rich blond hair, never smiles. It is a disconcerting mix.

'We may be the only Europeans in Oujda,' I tell her although I know it is fairly improbable. She looks back at me with her unwavering stare. Lips closed. 'Are you okay?' This is plainer speaking but I fear I may offend her if she believes I am implying she is not. No one wishes to be thought a defective tourist. 'Travelling alone is difficult.' I do not expect her to dispute my observation.

'You may come in to talk.' These are the first words she has directed my way since confirming I could carry her house bricks from the market place.

I do as she suggests, see on stepping inside that hers is a near-identical room to my own. 'Are you going on to

Algeria?' I immediately regret posing the question. I am not seeking a companion. She cannot hitchhike—some girls do but surely not in North Africa—and this sullen Scandinavian has limited appeal. Doesn't speak freely enough for my liking. I'm a go-with-the-flow kind of guy and I fear traveling with her would be onerous. For more reasons than just the house bricks.

'I will go south by train. The bus was a mistake.'

'South?'

'Marrakech. That is why we come to Morocco. It is not for Oujda.' I understand the point she makes although I have elected not to visit her chosen destination. For me, Morocco is a way station. I want to enter the true desert. Not that I have prepared well for my journey, there are few signposts in Bury for a trip like mine. I have looked at an atlas, half a plan inside my head.

'The man is coming back at seven,' I remind her.

'We should be out.'

She doesn't wish to meet Abdul and I am not surprised. Her distrust was written on her face throughout our time in his company. I concur, felt a little uncomfortable in the shadow of one so tall. To be fair, he has found us a decent hotel. 'Can I take you to dinner?'

She answers my question with laughter, a scathing not a joyous sound. Her first snicker since Norway, I suppose. If I am the cause, at least it has found pleasing lines upon her face. 'We can share a table but please do not take me on a date. You are a boy.'

That I am the younger of us has not escaped my notice. I adjudge that she is at least as old as the towering Moroccan. My reason for inviting her is primarily an act of charity. She appears fearful simply as a result of being here; my presence will alleviate the stress she might feel alone on the streets of Oujda. A little appreciation for the offer would have been nice. Her motive for accepting, I suppose, is to avoid Abdul. Nothing more. The not-a-date specification strikes me as wise. Re-entry into our separate rooms at the end of the evening will pass off without embarrassment.

2.

While showering, it comes to me that I have still to learn the name of the girl I will be taking to dinner. I try to think what it might be. I don't know any Norwegian names. Heidi would suit her, although I think it is Swiss. They are not so tall in that country, I believe. Guessing is not knowing but it is fun. If she ditched the ponytail for two plaits and shrank to half her current size, she could be Heidi of the children's books.

Abdul, who we are conspiring to avoid, has been as good as his word. Brought us to a fine hotel. The water here is hot, very hot. In Fes, I paid more for a room with access only to a cold shower. I used it but gleaned no pleasure from doing so. Here, I dwell in the stream of water. Seven sweaty hours on a bus, plus the dust from our trek across town flow from me, wash onto the shower tray, gurgle down the plughole. After a good soak, I turn the water down to a trickle, enjoy shaving the soft growth from my chin. Couldn't do this in Fes, there's no shaving to be had with cold water. Then I step from the stall, dry and dress, while contemplating my source of joy. Hot water. It has taken me five days without, to spot how much I love it.

When I leave the shower room the Norwegian girl is in the corridor. She wears a fluffy light-blue dressing gown with nothing beneath it. At least, it looks that way to me. Nothing visible, and she is on her way to the shower. As I return to my own room, I think about her, almost naked in the hotel corridor. A far cry from the frightened girl who alighted the bus onto the town square. I was unaware that

Oujda

she was on the same coach as I, all the way from Fes to Oujda. Funny that I should not see her, tall and blond as she is. Her presence eluded me until we were already off the bus, being assisted by Abdul. Or accosted by Abdul. A little of each, and I am unconvinced by his name. I looked up and down the bus all journey while talking with a couple of young Moroccans. Never saw her. She must have been cowering below the top of her headrest, reading a guide book or examining her own fingernails. I consider this carefully as I close the door to my room, take a two-minute lie on my bed. Perhaps the promise of my presence at supper tonight has helped her to relax, enabled her to take to the corridor in next to nothing. A blue dressing gown. This seems unlikely: I am a little guy from her vantage point—she has said as much—too young even for a date. It could be that she was in the grip of hashish earlier, a touch of paranoia that has now worn off. Plenty available in this country, yet I recall no other signs. And Heidi seems far too uptight for this second theory to fly. I suppose she is just following her longstanding showering routine, doing as she has always done since her fjord-side childhood. Keeping to the familiar is surely the antidote to the travel which she is clearly not enjoying. There you go, I roll the riddle around in my head until the knot comes loose. If I could understand Abdul, the Moroccans, Africa, as easily as I can my European cousins, I would get back hitchhiking instead of clambering on and off their stinking buses.

* * *

A little after six o'clock in the evening, the girl—Heidi until I learn better—and I walk out of the front door of the Gafait Hotel. We go back down Oujda's main street in search of cooked food. The detail of our quest we have not discussed; couscous or couscous has been my North African experience to date.

Rucksack Jumper

I scour the road ahead. No seven-foot giant on the horizon.

Heidi has not enquired what my name is. It amuses me to think she has decided I am Jim or Terry, a name of that ilk, done so for some tongue-in-cheek reason living only inside her mind. She is Heidi of the fjords. By day she works as a sub-post mistress in the busy and diligent postal service of that most serious of countries, Norway. The day job is a front. By night, throughout the long dark evenings in her northern coastal town—aurora borealis, all that jazz—she takes on a different persona. Heidi, the lady wrestler! Her art is entertainment masquerading as conflict. She has the height, of course, and, surprisingly, the strength too. She has acquired well-toned muscles by obsessively carrying a suitcase full of house bricks wherever she goes. She enters the wrestling ring as she earlier did the hotel corridor. A nice blue dressing gown. Beneath it, unseen by me today, for no bout was in the offing, she sports a black and sparkly leotard. I expect she attaches small gold caps to her most prominent teeth. Not here in Oujda—this is a wrestler's vacation—but when she applies them, her smile becomes as scary as her scowl. Just the ticket inside the roped-ring. Wrestling is not a sport for which Norway is known, a far cry from cross-country skiing or even bobsleigh. It is the underground sensation of the fjords. I've never been but I really think it might be. Headlock Heidi could be their most coveted starlet. In Tromsø, or thereabouts, her posters may adorn the walls of fjord-dwelling teenage boys. Her long legs arrowing down from her sparkling leotard. I would envy those boys so compelling a sight to greet their morning, had I not struck luckier still. I am on a date with the pro. Not a date-date but a boy can pretend. The posters probably smell of fish, it is the way of all Norwegian merchandise. I am grateful to be in the company of the real thing, to be spared the stench of herrings. She even showered. I can only imagine the sight of Heidi mid-bout, a knotted pair of matching pig-tails swinging from side to side. In Scandinavian female-wrestling circles, they are an accruement...

'I'm not very hungry.'

This interjection from the girl I call Heidi inside my own head breaks the chain of my mental fabrication. I still wonder when she will ask me my name. Or we may have waited too long for such normalcy to peek through. 'Shall we just walk?'

On this April evening, Heidi wears neither dressing gown nor leotard. Her voluminous luggage gave me pause for thought as I lugged it across Oujda to the Gafait. Bringing a dressing gown on holiday strikes me as excessive, and I can only speculate what other home comforts have made the journey. This lady wrestler must be an infrequent traveller. I could give her some travel tips and, in return, she might demonstrate a few holds. Heidi is in black jeans, a contrast to the blue ones of earlier in the day, and the third different T-shirt she has worn in my presence. This one sports a pink and red swirling pattern in its centre, trendy in nineteen-sixty-seven. Today it looks like spilt paint; thirteen years since the summer of love and Heidi is not a natural hippy. She wears a jacket too. Grey, casual. I like the jacket, it suits her. She looks good when she drops the frown.

As we walk, a man standing beside a small restaurant—the outside tables already set—comes forward and puts a hand on Heidi's arm. 'Vous aimez manger,' he enquires in French: You like to eat? I wonder if Heidi will repel him as she would if she were inside the ring in Tromsø. She might even tag me, requiring that I wrestle the restauranteur to the ground in her stead. To my surprise, or at least the surprise of my day-dreaming self, she flinches and mutters something unintelligible in Norwegian. The restauranteur then places the hand with which he'd held her arm onto the small of her back.

'Off me!' shouts Heidi.

I want to usher her away. Know better than to put an arm around her shoulder. I offer a hand to hold and, in keeping with her behaviour thus far, she ignores it. 'Let's press on,' I try.

She moves forward and then looks back over her shoulder, scowling at the man she clearly considers to have molested her. I would be a poor witness in any attempted prosecution of this case. Even in Bury, I have known shopkeepers and café owners touch a customer with a similar level of intimacy. It is friendly, not aggressive. Coming out of their shops and onto the street to touch a potential customer is a sequence which, outside of Morocco, I haven't witnessed. A hard sell but not a rape.

'These men!' Heidi exclaims.

I presume we are discussing the recent assault and nod my head, not wishing to deny her experience while hoping she does not press me to comment further. I wonder if I can get through the evening without trying a similar or even greater level of physical intimacy myself. I didn't feel this in the market square, yet now I find myself developing a sneaking physical appreciation for this agitated wrestler. And we are on a date.

'Arab men!'

I worry that her attitude towards the host country is not conducive to an enjoyable stay. I recognise that I have, so far, experienced no harassment beyond the children begging for dirham and the extortionate first haggle of every shopkeeper. For Heidi, the little contretemps I have witnessed may be only the tip of an iceberg. A big and sandy iceberg.

'Why does every-one want to touch me?'

A-ah! This one I can explain. If you imagine Heidi in a

leotard, all sparkly and lovely, and wearing long white sports socks, then wanting to touch her follows quite naturally in red-blooded men. I elect to keep her in the dark on this timeless truth. Change the channel on my fantasy television set. 'Sales,' I say. 'They try to sell. Get custom. It's pushy but it must work. Win more than it loses.' Heidi looks at me blankly. I am not sure she really cares to hear what might motivate a vendor to touch a prospective customer. 'I read,' I continue, 'that in supermarkets—not here but in America, probably across western Europe too—sales go up if the cashiers make eye contact with the customers and place the change skin on skin, directly into the customer's palm. The longer they take, let the touch linger, the more the customers like it.'

'Men like it!'

Heidi has her own bespoke analysis of the market research I paraphrase. It was the basis of an article in Time Magazine. 'I think it works. The problem is, it might hack off the ten per cent who feel it is over-intrusive; if ninety per cent like it, then it still works. That's capitalism.'

'In the village where I am living, the shopkeeper may place coins in my hand. I know him, his name, his house. I went to school with his son. There is trust. Here, these Arab men grabbing me, to put jewellery and teapots and their silly little souvenirs in front of my nose, they should not touch me. We have not a pinch of trust.'

It is no good; I am still thinking how Heidi bares her golden teeth while grappling with other leotard-clad Norwegians, each looking like Wonder Woman. Village! She said she lives in a village, so there really must be weekly wrestling in the village hall. What else can a body do in rural Norway through those dark winter months.

* * *

As we talk, we find ourselves sauntering away from the

town. We pass shanty houses, small and precariously built. Made from what is to hand, put together by the poor souls living within, I assume. Old pieces of wood, narrow sticks and thin snappable branches, bits of cardboard, woven together into a home of sorts. The smell of cooking wafts around the sub-shed constructions. A child's shriek here, the cackle of a radio sharing Arabic music there. There are piles of junk in front of every dwelling place. Barely clothed children play beside their makeshift houses. It is mesmerising to me. I see women in headscarves taking large pails to a nearby hydrant, filling them with water. And I understand that no other water enters these homes. The infrastructure for this entire neighbourhood is comprised of that single tap. The poorest of these dwellings look as if a modest wind could finish them. My Lancashire climate would be a wrecking ball. We come to an uninhabited plot. Something of that nature may have already taken place. A fallen house of cards, the sticks and slats all lie horizontally in the dust. A lone bicycle wheel and an inexplicable paint pot rest on top of the folded house.

Daylight is fading, dusk upon us.

'I don't feel safe,' says Heidi.

I think her cowardly declaration is proof that wrestling is fake. Not a true sport at all. I am not afraid of the poor. They must have far more to fear from us, from those with the means to crush them. 'I'm here,' I reassure her.

'Ha!' sniggers Heidi. She seems unconvinced by my worth as a protector. We head back to town. Just a few hundred yards and we are again passing houses of greater substance. Electric lights shine out from the homes; the absence of a street tap indicative that each has piped water. As we turn a corner, we see a very tall man standing beside one of these soundly constructed houses. He is beckoning us forward, inviting us into his home. I am sure that we both recognised him on sight. The near-seven-foot-tall man sports a fez hat which must tip him well over that imperious mark. A red jacket over a white T-shirt, black trousers, all beneath the fez. He could be a circus ringmaster, so striking is his pose.

'On time, right on time,' he announces, tapping his wrist although I see no watch strapped to it.

His pronouncement puzzles me. I thought Abdul—if that is his name—was going to come to the Gafait Hotel at seven. We, Heidi and I, never learnt where he lived. Not as I heard, and I cannot believe her short exchanges with him in French set this up. That she would do it unbeknown to me. I glance at my Norwegian companion. She looks perplexed although, in my limited experience, that is quite simply her look. It is possible that she thinks I have secretly cooked up this not-so-chance meeting with the friendly giant. I shrug and with this gesture communicate my non-complicity.

I am a polite guy, not argumentative at all. In this I contrast immeasurably with my father. It is not in my nature to refuse Abdul's hospitality, to be so rude to the man who took us to the hotel with its plentiful hot water. I nod to my Norwegian companion and start to walk towards the door. I hear Heidi sigh, a cross and frustrated breath of surprising duration, after which, shoulders slumped yet again, she follows me inside.

* * *

The house is dark within. Not pitch black, just gloomy. A naked light bulb gives a little illumination in the furthest corner of the room where a man—Abdul's father is my guess—reads from a hand-written piece of paper. A letter, perhaps. And there are many more spread out haphazardly across the table at which he sits. The lightbulb hangs from the ceiling on an exceptionally long flex, hovering just inches above the table on which the man works. It is strange that a light should dangle so low. Perhaps it is an improvised table lamp; if Abdul is electrically proficient, he will have modified the ceiling connection without need of a chair to stand on. The bare bulb has the imperceptible swing of a latent pendulum. Movement seen only in the sway of the ethereal shadows nudging the sides of this large and mysterious room.

'Have you eaten in our fine city? In the best restaurant, I hope.' says Abdul. I shake my head. I am about to lie and say I am not hungry but he speaks first. 'I am sorry. I had not meant to imply that you eat with me. My mother is assisting a sick neighbour. She would have cooked for you but I neglected to ask her to prepare a meal.'

I do not follow his logic. Never anticipated meeting him, nor held a corresponding expectation of being fed.

'We do not want your food.' Heidi is no charmer.

Abdul says something to her in French. I resent this a little. He must have spotted Heidi's proficiency in English, and even he cannot stretch his tongue to Norwegian. Speaking French simply excludes me.

The sullen girl answers him, also in French, and he laughs. Not that there is enough levity in the exchange to bring a change to Heidi's lingering frown.

'Come into the kitchen, my grandfather is a man you should meet.'

I follow Abdul, while Heidi remains standing in the shadowy front of the family's living room. She has ventured no more than two paces across the threshold.

In the back room a very old man—a thousand wrinkles crisscrossing his face—sits at the kitchen table. He has soup and bread in front of him, looks through rheumy eyes upon an open newspaper. It is in Arabic. I cannot understand its cursive type, I do recognise a face or two in the accompanying pictures. They are footballers, vaguely familiar to me. Their all-white football strips corroborate my hunch that they play for Real Madrid.

Abdul speaks only to me. The old man is for seeing, not talking with. 'Guess how old?'

My mental maths is efficient, Abdul twenty-six—a guess but surely close enough—plus thirty each for dad and dad's dad, that would be eighty-six. Then I take a little off. It is my understanding that parents have their children young in Morocco, in poor countries the world over. 'Eighty,' I hazard. My margin for error will be high; guesses are fun, not true. My wrestler improbable.

Abdul shakes his head, smiles at me as though I should try again. I do not, I wait for him to tell me. 'A hundred and ten,' he enunciates after the longest pause.

The man studying the football pages is a sight. His deep wrinkles appear as a Māori tattoo, grainy and something to which he is so accustomed he no longer notices how people scrutinise him. Maybe he is a hundred and ten, it will be the women who have children young here. Who knows how old the fathers of their children are? In Tétouan and Fes, boys of my age, even Abdul's age were hustling for dirham at the bus station, hardly the vocation from which to start a family. The old guys—when they have begged and bartered enough—may get the pick of the young girls who are, in turn, pleased to take leave of their carpet factory jobs. Happy to bear children to old men with a stash of hustled dirham. Plausible, I don't know it for a fact. I nod at the grandson. A hundred and ten is an impressive age.

'Amazing man,' continues Abdul. 'When Grandfather was a boy Hassan the First was king, now many kings later we have Hassan the Second. We tell him, "Grandfather, you have waited for another Hassan to return before departing this life." Grandfather dislikes our teasing, doesn't laugh when we tell him it is so. "Hassan the Third, Hassan the Fourth, let them all reign, I'm not going anywhere." That is what he says. So funny, don't you think? The Imam, most respected man in all Oujda, says, "This old man will not die. His heart booms with love for his family." Grandfather tells us of his mother who died one hundred years ago, his brother and four sisters, long passed on to heaven. Two dead sons. We can feel all these relatives still with us because he tells us their stories. Speaks of them often. Death is an inconvenience for our family; it does not keep us apart.'

Abdul talks about the old man, points at him, as though he is a picture hanging on the wall. And Grandad Oujda just keeps reading the sports pages. He might only look at the pictures; I don't know if he can read. Don't ask for fear of sounding patronising. The old man has turned the page of his newspaper and I no longer recognise the players pictured. In two adjacent photographs I see tall black men, basketballs in hand. They are American, I presume. I ponder the Arabic script reporting Spanish soccer, American basketball. What sports do Moroccans play? Abdul has the physique for basketball; it could be his picture in the paper but for the buses arriving in the square, the paucity of practice time with all those hotel rooms to fill.

Suddenly the old man shouts, not loudly, barked words. All in Arabic: I assume he is telling Abdul something important about a dead relative, or once more turning away the grim reaper.

Abdul puts a hand on my back and guides me out of the kitchen, back to the ill-lit front room. When there is a closed door between us, he turns to me and says, 'So funny. So, so funny. Grandfather thinks that you are another German come to pillage our country.'

Behind the closed kitchen door, we hear him still. Shouting—not at volume—throaty, phlegmy Arabic spewing angrily from the ancient man as his dulled eyes stare blankly at highly paid sports stars from far away countries. I like funny, do not see this exchange as Abdul has done. His grandfather's anger. I would apologise to the old man but this country is not one that the British have messed up, plundered. We did the others.

Heidi has remained in touching distance of the door ever since entering the house. The man I assume to be Abdul's father has risen from the table but wisely remained behind it. He either had no wish to approach the girl, or correctly read the lack of invitation in her non-existent smile. I see that he is almost as tall as his son. He speaks gently in French and Heidi listens attentively. Her hostile demeanour has abated a fraction. About two percent.

The father says something quickly to his son, the Arabic cutting out Heidi and I. Abdul shakes his head.

'Father wishes to offer you tea. Unfortunately, our water is not purified. Your stomachs are not ready for it. Far better that you drink in our fine restaurants. Use only restaurants with signage in French, menus in French. Please do as I ask. The city of Oujda wishes to take good care of its visitors.'

I use this as a cue and say to Heidi that we need to go and eat. She concurs and Abdul does not try to delay us. It strikes me—as we withdraw from the gently pulsating shadows of his living room—how odd it is that we even stumbled upon him. The tall, well-spoken young Moroccan has taken our impromptu visit in his stride. It is as though he arranged it. Him or fate: I could toss a coin.

* * *

We walk back towards the centre of Oujda. I navigate carefully, keep us on the opposite side of the road when passing the restaurant at which the over-enthusiastic proprietor and Heidi had their spat. To my way of thinking, it occurred mostly inside the Norwegian girl's mind. She has recalled it, blow by blow, as we made our way back here.

He is waiting, smiling proudly from the door of his establishment. Ready for round two. The girl turns her chin away, diverts her eyes. Nothing short of gunpoint could persuade Heidi to accept food from the man she has already adjudged a sex pest.

We step inside a small eating place situated diagonally opposite his. Immediately the proprietor of the establishment looms towards us. 'Cette table, merci,' I say, pulling a chair out for my girl. Giving this restauranteur no chance to molest her. He keeps coming closer, so I take hold of the shoulders of her well-cut jacket, pulling gently. 'Let me take this for you.'

She turns her face towards me, the scowl is back. 'I keep it on.'

She smooths the garment upon herself and I recognise that I erred in my actions. Feel pleased, nevertheless. I find Heidi, the feisty wrestler of my fantasy, far more attractive than the dull Norwegian girl who could not explain to herself why she has chosen to travel alone to so remote and baffling a place as Oujda, Morocco. The proprietor looks amused. He might think we have had our first tiff. I was going for the coat solely to prevent him from making the same mistake. I remove my sweatshirt; it is a warm night. Steamy in this enclosed space within which the aromas of mint and lamb mingle with cooking oil. He nods at me, takes my eye as he places two menus before us. I think to myself how much smarter he is than the guy across the road. Doesn't engage with women, just with their chaperones. My diversion was in vain but Heidi and I are only sharing an evening of mutual suspicion, not so much as pooling our respective names.

After a lengthy silence I ask, 'What did Abdul's father tell you?' I have atoned long enough for the touching of her shoulder.

'He had money advice but I didn't need it.'

'Money advice?'
'How to buy Algerian currency. I think he deals.'
'I need it. I'm going to Algeria.'
'He can get four times as much for your pounds as a bank will give. Or for my kroner but I don't want any. I shall not be going to that country.'
'Four times? Brilliant! How do I get it?'
'Black market shit. You shouldn't touch it.'

I order the couscous royale, only to hear Heidi snigger as I do so. She has plumped for a cheaper tagine. I consider myself to be an independent traveller, I have hitchhiked from Bury in the north of England to Algeciras, which sits at the bottom of Spain. I shall use buses only until I become familiar with North African ways. Then I will strike out again with my felicitous thumb. Heidi clearly imagines me a typical tourist, a notion based exclusively on the meal I have ordered from a limited menu. It is an elaborately titled dish, pitched exclusively at Europeans. Over-priced mixed meats on a bed of fluff. Her snort of derision is unwarranted. It is Heidi who has failed to lend herself to the travelling experience. In her cumbersome luggage she might have brought a Norwegian village. She views all that she sees with suspicion and then imagines that ordering a lamb tagine compensates for the cold shoulder she has turned on Morocco. We are a chance couple, not the main event. I don't even fancy her unless I dwell upon a backstory of my own making.

The signage and menus in this small restaurant are in French as Abdul advised us to seek. The lighting is as limited and shadowy as was his home. There are several other occupied tables and I guess that some of our fellow diners are European and others Moroccan. I cannot see clearly at all. They could be rich tourists, hitchhikers like me, or the local Imam. The outline does not disclose the core. They have shape but no more character than were they peripheral figures in a dusty oil painting. When the food arrives, the smell is enticing. We eat and as we do so Heidi surprises me, she praises the cuisine. Her first sign of satisfaction with a darned thing in Oujda.

* * *

After eating, we walk back to the hotel. I am careful to ensure my hands stray not an inch onto the Norwegian's flesh. I grapple with no corner of her clothing. The wrestler, who I do love a little, is only intermittently evident. Heidi told me, over dinner, about some of the characters who live in her home village. She spoke of them warmly. Her English is excellent, it was as if she brought to the table her older sister who has married the harbourmaster. She also spoke of the local penchant for whisky as we sipped only mint tea. Heidi conjured up memories of drunken evenings spent in her coastal village in northern Norway. If it even is up north: she neither named it nor directed me how I might get there. It is her village and she is not a girl who chooses to share. It crossed my mind that these were made-up stories, bravado to sound as reckless and carefree as any normal young traveller. On balance, I will presume them true. In the security of her fjord home, her frown may upturn; she may unclasp the ponytail, let loose her blond hair. She would never recreate such revelry here in Oujda. She drank not so much as a single beer, never stopped flaunting her suspicions as a protective armour. The village girl—Heidi at home—must trust herself implicitly, while the other girl, the discommodious traveller, trusts no one. Nothing. Not me; not a glass of cheap wine. I concurred with her sobriety, drank water with my couscous. I knew that sober I could contain myself, remain the dull and predictable company she sought. I never once asked about the wrestling.

When we are back on the corridor of the Hotel Gafait,

she says, 'Can we shower at this time?' In my mind the phrase she has used implies a degree of invitation, I decide not to test it. Her wording is surely a linguistic oversight.

'You've showered already,' I remind her.

'But I feel dusty and dirty.'

'I'm sure you can.'

I have the key for my door, collected at reception and as I put it in the lock, Heidi astonishes me. A hand on the back of my head. 'Thank you for dinner,' she says, although I paid nothing towards hers nor she for mine. She stoops for a quick kiss on my lips and then she is gone. To her room and a second shower.

I go into my own, unsure whether I should prepare for bed. I pick up the novel that I carry with me but my mind is not in it. I wait for Heidi to knock on my door, showered and wishing to go beyond the kiss. I wonder if I should shower similarly; if my failure to do so puts her off taking it to the next level. I could knock on her door and ask how the land lies. Contemplation is not action. I pass a night of only little sleep, accepting with easy stoicism that I will never again see my nameless wrestling amazon.

3.

The Gafait is the most comfortable African hotel in which I have ever stayed. It is my third. Even without the benefit of sleep it is apparent, and thoughts of the nervous Norwegian are not the sole cause of my insomnia. As the night draws on, I mull over my trip so far. Mentally, I have drawn a line under my journey from Bury to the bottom of Spain. Hitchhiking went well, it is my forte. There were incidents, of course, but nothing to write home about. Well, a chance meeting with a girl in Madrid might have been worthy of correspondence. The detail is not for my parents. I have no intention of writing them a single word.

The sea was rough, wild, at the Straits of Gibraltar. The crossing—Algeciras to Ceuta—takes little time. In the seating area, indoors, many Moroccan passengers were sick. The stench of it was most unpleasant. I took myself to the deck. Fresh air helped me combat my own queasiness. The view of Ceuta, of Africa, was intriguing. It has an air of not really belonging. The aridity and the sand-coloured stone of its buildings are similar to that which we left behind in Europe. It was the notion of Africa that stirred me, not the sight of another washed-out Mediterranean town.

My night at the youth hostel in that little Spanish enclave was a quiet one. However, the talk of my fellow travellers put me in a fearful frame of mind.

'Tétouan is a nest of thieves.'

'The people in Tétouan will steal your money…snatch your passport.'

'Tétouan is too dangerous for you English…for you Australians…for you Americans.'

This may have been an exaggeration, a half-truth, or the denigration of a fine city. Before leaving Spain, I had never heard of Tétouan, now I heard only stories of theft and peril. Knew no other narrative with which to counter the talk. I considered it a den of thieves by word association. I spent the following night in that vilified city, never leaving my cheap hotel room. I kept my money belt around my midriff all night for fear of intruders breaking down my door. Why would they not? They had their fearsome reputation to maintain. I tucked my rucksack under the thin blanket, raised my feet upon it. Imagined the world a safer place if all of the little I owned was in contact with my person.

I always believed that travel would change and inspire me. For a moment there I became quite unhinged. And my subsequent experience contradicted the fearmongering.

Tétouan and its inhabitants did me no harm. Apart from the fitful sleep, my stay there comprised only the passage between the bus station and the hotel. I never took a proper look. Of the boys and men, hustlers and beggars, congregating around the bus station, offering services to western travellers, none did anything untoward beyond speaking French more quickly than I could yet interpret. They turned away when I shook my head. Disinterest more than respect but I cannot complain. My gestures those few short days ago were worthy of Heidi. I have since reappraised the lack of return so timorous an outlook can elicit.

The hotel in which I spent my only night in Tétouan was dire. My room had a stone floor, no rug. A stained and worn-out mattress. It cost next to nothing and even that was poor value.

In my rucksack I had retained a sandwich, wrapped in brown paper, purchased at a roadside stall before boarding the bus in Ceuta. I intended to eat it hours earlier, two bites determined that it was spicier than I enjoy. That evening, without alternative, I consumed it alone in my room despite its hours of ill-storage in my rucksack which itself had journeyed from Ceuta in the amniotic warmth of a bus's undercarriage. I guessed that eating the sorry thing after all this time might precipitate some kind of indigestion. I know many of the travellers' names for stomach upsets from around the world. Delhi Belly or the Kathmandu Quickstep. Morocco may have some illness-related nomenclatures of its own; I knew none. In that hotel room in Tétouan, I tried to imagine what they might be. Came up with the Rif Retch and thought my designation highly amusing until it unfolded itself within me. In the event I only retched a little, floored principally by spasms of diarrhoea. Whatever edification may be gleaned from squatting on the footmarks of a bowl-less toilet in the basement bathroom of a squalid hotel evaded me. The establishment was without lavatory paper. I tore pages out of my French-English dictionary, cleaned myself as best I could. I don't think I will miss the bespoiled book. My greatest incomprehension is not of words spoken but of gestures made. I see men wave their arms like windmills on the roadside, girls staring blankly from the circle of their headscarves. The kohl-laden blinks of one or two older ladies confuse me. Eyes that reach into my soul. Dictionary, my arse, one might say. It is a stronger stomach which I need. And generally, I must hold my nerve. Go with the flow. This was the advice of the Australian girl I met in Madrid almost two weeks ago. A Tasmanian girl, no less. She had only made her way across Europe and Australia, not Africa but good advice travels well. This evening, just watching Heidi struggle, taught me the inordinate value of being trustful, not its opposite. But I am only an unemployed northern lad, still getting the hang of how going with the flow might work. Trying it on for size.

I liked Fes far more than I did Tétouan. Loved it. The smells that pervaded the streets in the old walled town were astonishing. Leather; spices; uncooked meat enduring the morning's rising heat; and sandalwood turned upon a foot-propelled lathe. Farmers and artisans, craftsmen and cultivators all displayed their wares. Each occupied a tiny covered stall lining the walkways. The city is timeless. I drifted across it in a daze of wonder. Shopkeepers accosted me, wanted to sell to me, while making it clear that the cash was but oil in the machine. The haggling formed the core, the raison d'être. Their wares were mostly tat.

Slowly I learnt to barter. When I challenged a high price by suggesting far lower, the vendor laughed at me—or even cried—such was the insult my offer suggested. I apologised the first time this happened, second too, then came to see that such a course is an admission of defeat. The histrionic reactions of vendors are quite simply a form of testing the water. It is a game in which I have no skill. I do not enjoy being toyed with. If the vendor suggested a price, I offered no more than ten per cent in reply. A worldly Dutchman had already advised me that this is normal. Expected. The vendor would tell me what hardship accepting such an offer would be to him. His contorted face expressing visible pain. When I followed this overstated objection with a second derisory offer, upped my bid by just a few centimes, it necessarily implied that I couldn't give two hoots if the vendor and his family ate or starved. That is not the person I care to be. Being a bastard in Morocco is not a big deal, it arises incidentally from the absence of price controls.

I saw disabled beggars, limbs twisted askew as they sat on dusty pavements or hauled themselves onto buses by their arms alone. In high-pitched voices, they asked for dirham. For money. I learnt, from that wise Dutch traveller, that these people are not the unfortunate victims of fate which they might appear. Their parents have twisted them into disability from a young age. Tied them up, done whatever it takes. Begging is not remunerative for the able-bodied. Their parents have rendered them this way to garner the sympathy of western onlookers. The more deformed, the deeper will they reach into their pockets. This way, their parents have mapped their children's futures. Their careers. Tourists—in contrast to an enquiring traveller such as I—never learn that the hard-earned, or not-so-hard-earned, cash they pass to the beggar furthers the logic behind this abuse. I found myself dwelling upon those parents, ones who might restrict their children's capacity for movement in the grossly mistaken belief that it could improve their life chances. I decided that my father, through his renunciation of my education, has done the same to me, then just as quickly rejected the thought. My woes are nothing compared to the emaciated beggars I watched pulling themselves up the steps of buses and across town squares. Arms dragging their useless legs, changing their painful wince to a grateful smile whenever a coin was passed to them.

I made friends entirely of the superficial variety. In public spaces, I found many young Moroccans who were keen to talk to me, to befriend me. They asked about rock concerts and football matches and I have been to both. Bury FC is not Manchester United but I have watched football in Greater Manchester: they were impressed. Many asked about London, a city I have yet to visit. Initially I told them of my nonattendance; however, by the third or fourth ask, I realised it was easier to report how grand Buckingham Palace is, to confirm that Harrods sells coats and perfumes that cost a year's wage. I do not like to disappoint.

One of these chanced-upon friends asked me to accompany him to his house. His eyes held my gaze. To me he seemed trustworthy. A year or two my junior, and my pre-existing wish to see a Moroccan family home made my acceptance inevitable. Getting closer to Arabs of my own age would yield a greater understanding of them, I believed. For I sought insight into our similarities and differences: it is why I travel.

In the event, Mohammed—the name of the boy—took me not to his house at all but to his father's carpet factory. There he showed me the weaving room and I saw how very young many of the workers were. Terribly young, far too young. Possibly they were ten years old and small for their age. My best guess is that some were no more than seven. Few of the children in that factory were teenage. It was five in the afternoon, I wondered if they had earlier been in school. Guessed not; the dust-filled factory floor might be their education.

A slight child, a girl of eight, I'd say, left her loom

momentarily to hiss the word, 'Dirham,' at me with outstretched hand. 'Dirham, dirham,' she pleaded. It was evident to her that I had a surfeit of them and she had not enough. I was unsure if failing to give anything might be an affront to my host. Before I'd decided upon a course of action, the decision was taken from me. A girl three or four years her senior stepped forward and slapped the girl hard across the head. Sufficient to leave a red weal on her cheek and send the child back to her loom. The violent supervisor shook her head at me in apology. I briefly hated Moroccans for living this way but quickly began to assimilate all that I had seen. The absolute poverty of those involved is at its core. Both assailant and victim have been bled of any choice in their conduct. It is pitiful and I felt guilty. My curiosity caused the slap, inflicted pain. My presence motivated the behaviour of both girls. That is the truth.

When Mohammed's father gave me mint tea and advised of the various payment methods by which I might purchase a carpet, I made an excuse to leave. I own no house so his efforts were always going to be futile. And more specifically, I do not subsidise violence to children. I didn't say it and perhaps I should have. No sale and that was that.

At night, the café life in Fes is vibrant. Not with music or revelry like Manchester city centre or even Bury on a warm Saturday night. And yes, even my home town does occasionally enjoy warmth of a summer's evening. Fes is different. Quieter in decibels; exclusively for men although a few western women were conspicuously present. In contrast to Manchester, all ages are in the mix. Side by side. There are bars, and many more tea rooms. Ageing Arabs puff on various pipes respiring tobacco, scented infusions and hashish.

An old man—not as creased and remote as Abdul's grandfather—white haired, stick in hand, very old to my eye, spoke to me as we shared hashish.

'This is not something we do in England,' I said. Rendered it in French as best I could. 'Not openly smoking like this. In my country we drink pint after pint of beer. Surely that is no better and no worse?'

He admonished me with great severity. A finger wagged. I should not drink alcohol, should not because the doing of it is wrong. I did not gather if he used the word sin—how that concept sits in the religion of Islam is unknown to me—but establishing the evil of alcohol was his broad intent. I—ignorant of North Africa, rooted too firmly in my own culture—found his comments ridiculous. I tried to tell him, in good humour, that we are brothers, the pipe smoker and the beer drinker. Apparently, it is not so. By my conciliatory words I became an offence to him. He was as adamant about the evils of alcohol as my own father is in his condemnation of recreational drugs. Of all who touch them.

It was only my third or fourth time smoking the stuff, and I have to say, I feel safer on beer. But I do take going with the flow seriously. Try to immerse myself in the host culture.

* * *

After those few short days and nights in Fes, I came by bus to Oujda. Came to the square in which Abdul met me as I alighted. The bus was hot and slow; travelling thus is of limited enjoyment for a hitchhiker such as I.

Before we had so much as set off, there were many food vendors hawking their wares through open windows. The beggars with their deformed limbs climbed on board, waving an expectant hand at all passengers. Lingering longest beside those from furthest away.

I chose to sit at the rear of the vehicle. Two boys, sporting the wispy beards of teenagers who have not once shaved, were already sitting on the long back seat. They dressed as I do, jeans and T-shirt, clearly Moroccan, and they looked pleased when I joined them.

'Hey, Johnny,' said one, and I allowed him to substitute that name for my own throughout the journey.

The boys' English was poor. They may have thought similarly of my French. A language dictionary would have helped but not one in the state in which I had disposed of my own. They were both students, studying in Fes, both engineers. Engineers to be. They laughed a lot, not at jokes I ever fathomed nor, to the best of my knowledge, at my expense. I thought them immature. Perhaps this was because I did not understand the precise source of their laughter. It can disturb.

Throughout the ride we passed mile after mile of red and dusty scrub. A few small towns, ramshackle, dirty, but with the odd building of splendour. Archways adorned with Arabic lettering.

One of the boys asked me if I had a girlfriend. I indicated that I did not and they seemed disappointed. When I confirmed that I had previously enjoyed such an association, they became animated again. What had I done with her, they wished to learn. Their hand gestures suggested some of the answers I might choose to give, and their interest was not with her character or pastimes, but her anatomy. I allowed them to indulge their fantasies while being less than vague in all I divulged. I would never be disrespectful to Sharon, the girl I used to date. We broke up in January of this year; she is a better person than I. On that bus, passing brown fields and red stony outcrops in the east of Morocco, I think I was kidding myself. Sharon MacDonald was no part of the conversation, however easily thoughts of her may fall into my mind. I communicated no sense of her to those boys, nor were they seeking such reification. They were thinking only of what they—yet to acquire a single girlfriend—each were missing. And I too have yet to experience that which they surely imagined.

We fell silent after this exchange. Not because of its vulgarity, hand movements can only be modestly coarse. I believe that they envied me for what they thought I had done. How strange that they should think me so worldly, so devilish, simply by my not answering a question.

The taller of the two then began singing a snatch of a western pop song, singing it in English.

One-way ticket, one-way ticket

Occasionally he managed to interject some other words that sounded train related; however, the detail of the song and the complexities of the English language were beyond his grasp. He quickly defaulted to repeating the tagline.

One-way ticket, one-way ticket

His friend joined in this monotonous chorus, sang it with an excitement that the recurrent words could not justify. I smiled along with this inanity. I was certain that I had heard the song before, it is of a genre that holds no interest for me. I couldn't—aided only by their half-baked rendition—recall if it was a Eurovision entry from a country that should have known better or just crummy disco music. The boys did not stop.

One-way ticket, one-way ticket

The ceaseless singing bored me but I had no wish to offend them.

One-way ticket, one-way ticket

They encouraged me to sing too. I would have preferred a better song: Templeton Ca., The Caravan Moves On. It has been in my head since seeing a camel in Fes.

One-way ticket, one-way ticket

I mouthed it, made as if to sing. It is tosh. Eventually both paused in pointing their disco forefingers and belting out that turgid chorus. Quietly the more well-spoken of the two asked me from beneath a furrowed brow, 'Hey, Johnny, what is one-way ticket?'

4.

It was soon after his plaintive question—which rendered their fifteen minutes of singing and chanting quite meaningless—that the bus pulled up in the square. With the quickest of smiles, I saw the last of those boys. Parents awaited them and they, in their rush, or perhaps for some other reason of perceived contamination, did not so much as shake my hand. Then Abdul was beside me. And the Norwegian girl alighted from whichever seat on the bus she occupied.

That was yesterday, now I am back in the square. The girl whose knock on my door never came, checked out of the hotel before I arose, and I am not a late riser. She is off to Marrakesh. I wish her and her house bricks well. Her kiss, I now infer, was compensation for the scowl I endured evening long. I have drifted back to this square because it is known to me, and I hope to eat a breakfast that will remain in my stomach for the duration of its digestion. Street food is for later in my travels, when I've got the measure of it all. Hitch-hiking again, as I surely must.

The outside seating of the Café Maghreb is all taken. The diners, men and women, wear European clothing. It is my intention to immerse myself in North Africa; however, I feel a greater confidence in the coffee and snack I might buy here. I step inside and a waiter ushers me back out. He has spotted a vacant seat on the veranda. It is at an occupied table, my co-diner an elderly lady, grey-haired. A wearer of tortoiseshell sunglasses. French, I presume, for Moroccan women do not dine alone. She shrugs acceptance of my intrusion. I do not speak to her; she is not of my generation. I bring the Herman Hesse novel I am reading out of my small carrier bag. She glances at it and lets out a short exhalation, the sound of a bicycle valve being bled. Her dismissal of my choice of reading matter only strengthens my resolve; she is not the sort with whom I choose to talk.

The same waiter who found the seat now has a coffee and croissant for me. It's very good. Of the standard I enjoyed when I was in France little more than two weeks ago. I look across the square from this elevated position; the veranda is only a couple of feet above road height but it is enough. The novel in my hand cannot compete. I see that the Moroccan day has been alive for a long time. Traders hold forth in small roadside stalls. Young men sit on the kerbside, some play dice, most simply talk. They sit in closer proximity to each other than their western counterparts would, each slapping another's leg or touching his cheek as they make a point in their lively chatter. This everyday intimacy reflects the absence of egoism here. I have worked this out. It is like the adhan which so frequently summons believers to prayer, has some running to the mosque with glee on their faces. This culture thrives on shared experience. The ritual square-off when buyer and seller dispute the price of the commodities on sale is just another part of it. The lively interaction energises these people. Not a land in which lone wolves contemplate the pack from afar. I like this about the Arabic world, cannot discern if there is a corner in it for a lad like me.

For an hour I loiter here, eat and drink very slowly, read a little, watch the town busy itself. The older lady does the same, newspaper not novel. Then I call across for my bill. The cost of this small snack is high, more French than Moroccan. I am grateful for the quality of the fare while feeling guilty for avoiding the authentic experience. I had the same sense at a harbourside bar in Marbella, Spain, about one week ago. Paying more for home comforts might be the new form of colonialism. I worry that I am lining up on the wrong side of history. Visiting only French North Africa when I really should be mixing with the Arabs. The broadness of my mind impeded by the delicacy of my stomach.

Across the square I see a familiar face. Easily done, even the man's shoulders tower above all others. Abdul—the only name he has shared with me—walks briskly towards the Café Maghreb. Stops at the cordoned off seating. I note that I am one of many who looks at him. Perhaps this is only because he is so tall. He attracts the eye by exception. It seems to be my eye contact which he seeks out. The lady beside me mutters a phrase in French which I take to be a comment about Abdul. I am unable to decipher if it is his size or his race which displeases her, or if she has a more specific objection based on direct knowledge of the man. He does not greet or attempt to greet her. He taps his left wrist as he looks directly at me. It is a sign that I am to be meeting him shortly, tapping where a wristwatch might be worn although he doesn't sport one. At least, I think that is his intent. I maintain eye contact momentarily, then look down at my book. It is disconcerting that he should assume my compliance with a meeting about which we have not spoken, and yet it is also true that he has done me no wrong. I fear my distrust of Abdul may be an inadvertent prejudice, an odious thing. He was a cordial host to Heidi and I last night, however odd it was that the visit occurred at all. I pick up my coffee cup, the empty one which I drained twenty minutes ago. I return to the paragraph I was reading; when complete, I stand. Abdul is no longer at the cordon, so I walk across the square. Before I have reached the other side, I find he is beside me.

'You are travelling into Algeria?'

'Tomorrow.'

'Money?'

I quickly realise where this conversation is bound. The prospect of securing a lucrative exchange rate is attractive but the Norwegian girl said something about the black market. A caution. 'I don't have any Algerian currency yet.'

'My friend, let the tourist office of Oujda assist.'

'I can change it in a bank. I have British travellers' cheques.'

'The bank, of course. Let me show you the best bank.'

'Can I think about it?' His clarification is reassuring. A bank and not the backroom of a private house. That is what I pictured the previous evening when the Norwegian girl told me of her conversation with Abdul's father.

'If you leave tomorrow, my friend, you must think quickly.' He and I are standing stock-still in the middle of the square. 'Come with me. See!'

* * *

I follow him only a short way before Abdul ducks through an unmarked door into a room off the square. I do the same without the need for stooping. Inside it feels cool, away from the morning sun. The room is low-ceilinged, interior walls adorned with posters of tourist destinations. Fes, Marrakesh, Casablanca. Most are in the French language, a single English flyer foretelling the wonders to be found in the tanneries of Fes.

'The tourist office,' Abdul explains.

It surprises me. I considered the explanation he gave me of his work and role to be fiction; this is his disproof of my cynicism. It resembles, in its modesty and sincerity, the sort of tourist information office one might find in Skipton or Settle. Informative and unimposing. 'Where is the bank?'

'The bank is down the street; do not worry, they will

come here to fill in the forms.'

'Does your father work in the bank?'

Abdul laughs heartily. 'He told you that?'

'No, the girl said.'

'I think my father wished to impress her. His eye is always for the ladies. His friend works in the bank, it is not my father's vocation. He works in the Sidi Maafa, the finest hotel in all Oujda. He tends the gardens, cleans the swimming pool. A good man, not a rich man.' I say nothing. Why his father sought to impress Heidi with his exchange-rate talk just another mystery. 'I am not a rich man but that may change, my friend, that may change.'

Momentarily I wonder if his words imply that he is fleecing me of money, that this will be the source of his riches. I cannot imagine how this could be the case if he is to sell me Algerian dinar for a quarter of the going rate.

He sits me down and offers me tea. I indicate that I do not wish to drink. He goes to a doorway, talks to someone in a backroom. A lady's voice. Then he says he must speak to the bank directly. Tells me to stay where I am.

After Abdul has left, the lady comes from the backroom. She is quite short, in a long grey dress that covers her completely. Head to toe. I think it is a single piece of cloth; however, there are enough folds in it that I know I may be mistaken. I cannot fathom quite how her attire unfurls. It is a young face—possibly younger than my own—which shines out from the grey circle of her headscarf.

'How're you doin'?' she asks in an improbable American accent.

I laugh. 'Are you a tourist too?'

'No. I am working.'

As she says this the American accent dissipates. I think to myself that her introductory phrase might have been lifted from a Hollywood film. An imitation. 'I'm sorry. I misunderstood.'

She tries again, back in character. 'How're you doin'?'

'I'm good. Do you work with Abdul?' She looks at me blankly. 'With the tall man?'

'Yes, yes, Mr Ramzi. He is my employer.'

'Your English is really good,' I tell her.

The girl laughs, and I see she has small teeth, the tiniest of gaps between each and every one. The pink of her mouth integral to her pleasing smile. 'That is why I am employed here.'

I think that she is looking at me with interest, as I do her. An attractive face and she holds my gaze. Her choice of attire confuses me. What does she really look like? I guess she has black hair but it is entirely beneath the scarf. Her face is thin, I cannot tell if she is generally so. Her clothing swaddles her.

'The money exchange is often done here?' I ask.

'Yes.'

'Is it...' I struggle to find the wording, have no wish to accuse the tourist board of crookery. '...above board?' The girl doesn't answer, just looks at me with her brown eyes. My phrase may be too obscure. 'Is the money good? Can I use it? Why am I getting such a favourable exchange rate?' I flood her with questions.

'Money is money,' she replies.

The street door opens and two older men follow Abdul inside. Both wear western-style suits, no ties but they look like bankers. It is their profession; the attentive giant has assured me it is so.

One of the older men takes charge. He talks in Arabic with Abdul and his colleague. The girl sits at a nearby desk but does not join in. She studies her nails, the brightest red varnish upon them. Could be an eighteen-year-old girl from anywhere the world over. She takes pride in her appearance, those parts which peep out from the shapeless sack she wears. As the men talk, I find myself drawn to her.

Watching her work, if shuffling papers is her job. I hope to do this discreetly but she glances back at me, makes frequent eye contact.

The older gentleman asks me for something. He speaks in French and I think it is my passport he wishes to see. Abdul confirms this in English. I have a small problem. I am wearing a money belt around my midriff and my documents and travellers' cheques are all in it. I don't wish to fumble beneath my sweatshirt in front of all these people. I wonder how to explain this. I stay silent, with my hands I feel the outline of the pocket in which I keep them.

'You have a money belt?' says Abdul. 'Go through to the backroom, please. Come out when you have the passport. And the money if it is in there.'

He is very perceptive and I am grateful that he has resolved my dilemma. I worry about telling anyone where my money is—that is the trust issue—Abdul seems to be on my side. Helping me to get a decent exchange rate for some Algerian dinars.

Once in the backroom, I untuck my shirt and try to twist the money belt back into position beneath it. The secretive garment that I wear is a flimsy thing apart from its leather pocket. I made it myself because the cost of buying one from a catalogue was close to four pounds. Unfortunately, the material has become snagged on the zipper of my jeans. I unbuckle them so that I can release it slowly, without tearing into the fabric of the belt. The pocket—a small leather purse that I had no use for until fashioning this odd device in advance of my trip—has twisted itself into my person. I turn it back and start to undo the small clasp. At this point the door opens and the girl walks in. She laughs. Does not get to see the fringe of a boy's Y-fronts every day, I'm sure. I like the way she takes it in her stride. Sees but doesn't stare.

'I need to work at my desk,' she says.

'Of course.'

As discreetly as I can, and with my back now turned to the girl, I rearrange myself. Pull my trousers back up fully, tuck in my T-shirt.

'Take it to Mr Ramzi,' she says, signalling for me to go back into the front room where the transaction is to take place. I do as the girl asks.

The older gentleman now instructs me in French, and Abdul clarifies the directions in English. More ritual paperwork. I again write my passport number, place and date of birth, and date of arrival in Morocco on a form while the quieter of the two bankers seems to be doing exactly the same on a different but similar form. Transcribing my details for whatever unseen authority is behind their peripatetic bank. Then they ask how much money I wish to change.

'Thirty pounds,' I say.

Abdul looks a little taken aback but translates this into French. The more talkative of the older gentleman pushes a flat palm on to his forehead. I have annoyed him.

'How long will you be in Algeria?' Abdul asks.

'A week, maybe two. I will go on to Tunisia.'

'Thirty pounds. You will also rob banks?'

I understand that this is a joke but the situation does not call for one. Abdul translates his own witticism and both older men laugh. Throaty Arabic guffaws.

'How much do you think I'll need?'

'Two hundred pounds,' fires back Abdul.

This is more than half of my money for the entire trip; I cannot spend that much on this leg of my travels. I may go on to Libya, Colonel Gaddafi permitting, or may cross to Italy and back to England through Europe, Germany if I have the money for such a detour. I will return to hitchhiking, cannot think what I would do in Algeria with such a sum. I shake my head.

We do not agree for a couple of minutes. This is the haggling from which I can take no enjoyment. When I hit upon seventy pounds, I consider the level of Abdul's disappointment tolerable. My baseless guilt recedes.

Unfortunately, I only took thirty pounds in travellers' cheques from my money belt. 'Excuse me,' I say, stepping once more into the backroom. This may be a miscalculation; I shall find out. For no reason I can readily fathom, I find myself more comfortable lifting my top and extracting money from the hidden pocket strapped around me in front of the girl than in front of the three men. She appears unsurprised by my intrusion into her room and I am careful to expose nothing of myself that would be unseemly or unnecessary in the fulfilment of my task. This time I face the girl while I move my hands under my clothing, I know that there will be no reason to unbuckle my belt or tinker with my jeans; the money belt has not shifted in the short time since I was last in this room. The girl watches me, eyes shining, the corners of her mouth upturned. There is no tension between us and I suspect I am putting on an interesting show. I smile back, think her the friendliest person I've met in Morocco.

'Men not carry the handbag,' she says.

With a nodded head, I agree. Seventy pounds in my hands, I wave, a farewell, which she smiles back at through narrowed eyes, and I return to the main office. Leave another girl in whom I feel more interest than our limited interaction can justify. And I am getting used to headscarves; through the warmth of her many facial expressions she has not hidden herself from me. I really should have asked what her name is, didn't think to when the opportunity was before me.

In the front room, I hand the travellers' cheques to Abdul as if they too need translating. He passes them on and the older men count them, the talkative one first, handing them to his colleague who then goes through an identical ritual. He transcribes the figure arrived at onto his form.

I have done my homework. Newspapers back home told me the exchange rate for my next country but not how to go about getting the cash. I called into a bank in Fes but they did not deal in Algerian dinars. The teller advised me—in slow French—that I should buy it as soon as I entered Algeria. The rate of exchange here, in Abdul's tourist information office, is barely double that given in the regular exchanges, and my reason for suggesting thirty pounds was based on the multiple of four that the Norwegian girl was told by his father. The rate of exchange that I am securing is exceptional, I should not feel disappointed but I do. The volume of dinars that the bankers count out will give me a healthy budget for the crossing of Algeria. My trek into the desert. 'Thank you,' I say as Abdul hands me the bundle of cash. 'And it's okay?'

The tall man looks momentarily puzzled by my question, then he relaxes. 'Yes, okay. Real money, Algerian money. Not pretend.' And then he translates this into Arabic and the three men laugh together.

'And okay going through customs?'

'Yes, yes,' says Abdul. 'Keep it in the bottom of the case.' I look at him blankly. 'Don't show it at customs, please. It is paper money, easy to keep out of sight.'

Bloody hell, I think. That was why the Norwegian girl had said not to touch it. Never really connected up the dots before; back home black market just means knock-off watches. My first foray into Africa, I'm learning a lot. May not be catching the drift quickly enough. I feel torn between demanding my travellers' cheques back or just boldly smuggling this shit across the border. The chance of a wealthier passage to the Sahara. Which am I: some kind of coward or that cooler guy? The sort who laughs about a cowboy currency. I would look seriously lily-livered if I changed course now. Got to hold my nerve and go with the flow. I don't make eye contact with either of the older men as I leave the office. Abdul confused me for a long time, and now I've ended up playing his game. Or he has played me. There seems to be no such mental conflict for him. He shakes my hand with enthusiasm. 'I wish you safe passage across Algeria.'

I mumble a quiet, 'Thanks.'

5.

I sleep poorly this night. My room is the same comfortable one in which I spent the previous night, and I have no false anticipation of female company to keep me astir. I expect that the girl from the tourist office is sleeping in the bosom of her family home, and I am worldly enough to know that headscarf-wearing Muslim girls do not kiss English boys' lips on hotel corridors. Moroccan ladies cannot wrestle; their clothing is a trip hazard. My thoughts have moved on to the border. It is the money that makes me nervous.

My wisest course of action may be to discard the funny money. The black-market dinars. It is only seventy pounds and I do not have the constitution of a smuggler. I could manage without it. I intend to live as frugally as possible on my travels. I believe it instructive to do just that. I hope to pick up a little work, although I have suitable qualifications for precisely nothing that I see being done around here. Not a tanner of cowhides or a turner of wood. And my limbs are all intact. Whenever I fill out the tedious forms required to take occupancy of a hotel room, I declare that I am a student. It is a lie. For a time, I earned money in a factory unloading the ingredients for industrial detergents into a large hopper. From there we decanted them back into half-hundredweight drums; the hopper was for mixing the component chemicals. Prior to that, I worked in an office that allegedly dealt with insurance—that was my first job after leaving school—I have come to think the concept of insurance inherently flawed. What happens will. I washed pots at Pinocchio's Italian restaurant, Rochdale Road, Pimhole, Bury. Cash in hand. It was an honest living but not a lucrative one. And washing up is hardly a skill that Algeria will have failed to nurture in its own populace. I wish to be a poet but even without writer's block there is no money in it. My curriculum vitae is modest and requires enrichment. When I have ticked off hitchhiking into the Sahara Desert, I shall enrol on night classes, secure the qualifications needed for a place at university. My father forbade it when I wished to go into sixth form; now I am beyond his reach. No need for make-believe in the near future. I hope to make good on the little lie which I keep writing on hotel admission forms. Turn it into the truth. This sensible course of action is still to happen and my dilemma tonight is whether to opt for a little smuggling before I put my shoulder to that other wheel. I feel no moral conflict, hesitate only because I'm fucking nervous.

    This might be the very adventure I left Bury to find. After meeting and speaking with an Australian girl in Madrid, I have come to imagine myself to be a go-with-the-flow sort of guy. If they rumble me, I should simply bribe the customs officer with my black-market riches. It's the done-thing, everyone says backhanders are a way of life down here. I know that, so far, I have struggled to be as free and easy in Morocco as I was managing in Spain. I chickened out of hitchhiking the moment I got off the boat. Those tales of Tétouan frightened the crap out of me. I tired of the cheapest—the two-pound—hotels at the same time diarrhoea first gripped my bowel. I still prefer to mingle with Moroccans than with fellow Europeans when a fair opportunity arises. The girl in the tourist office, for example. I have not lost it completely. And now this. Dare I push a small number of bank notes somewhere out of sight of the border officials? I like audacity but have still to learn if I have a little tucked away on my person. During the night I conclude that this is my final audition to be me. Wherever the money is, don't look at it, and don't studiously avoid looking there either. I'm not stupid, I can pull this off.

By morning I have determined that I should put the money in my shoe. That is very unlikely to go wrong. And it is not a different morning from the one in which I plan to hide the money in the rolled-up sleeve of my sweatshirt, ensure that I tread no awkward footsteps. Alternatively, I could chuck it in an open drain—take no chances—but I dislike both waste and cowardice. Jiminy F Cricket says I should give it to a deformed beggar; however, if I later run out of money, my regret would be entirely self-inflicted.

The shoe or the sleeve? Feels like a heady decision but it won't make a difference, will it? I shall simply walk past the customs officials humming that Templeton Ca. song while thinking about the girl in the headscarf. Not about whichever place I have hidden my little stash.

6.

At seven o'clock in the morning, I collect my passport from the hotel's night porter, sign my name on two further forms and hoist the red canvas rucksack—my travel companion— upon my shoulders. If I picture myself now, it is with my long hair discreetly tied back. The large elastic band I use is neither visible nor as effeminate as I fear a proper headband might look. I carry a full rucksack. My possessions and I are Sahara bound. I briefly imagine a spare pair of trainers tied to the outside. Dangling down. I have dreamed up this flourish to mask my shame. The only pair I have with me—

those upon my feet—have a small hole. The big toe of my left foot playing turtle. My right shoe is still in good condition, I am not a complete hobo.

I leave Oujda on the same road that Heidi and I took when she was momentarily scared by the poverty evident in the makeshift houses. I studied a road map in a shop in town, looked at it in the store, saved the cost of a purchase. It will take me an hour to arrive at the border post. Give or take; the map was not of ordinance survey standard. I choose to head off before the sun gets high, don't wish to let it cook my hatless brain. As the better housing gives way to those shanties, I smile to myself. I am powerless to improve the lot of the people living here but I will smile when I see them. I can show them that they have my trust. My limited trust, if I dwell upon it. Beneath T-shirt and sweat-shirt I wear my money belt, hidden from view.

I have rolled up the sleeves of my sweatshirt, exposing my tanned arms. It is early morning and already warm. Within thirty minutes of leaving the hotel, I pass the last dwelling on this route out of Oujda. It is just me and the scrubland for the next half hour and then I shall enter another country.

A car draws up beside me. Stops. The driver is a French girl, two others in the passenger seats. She asks where I am going. I tell her Algeria and she laughs. I try, in my early-morning French, to convince her that it is true. I like to see people laugh but my answer was not a joke, I am bound for Algeria. Her friend—or perhaps her sister—the passenger in the rear of the car, says, 'Fermé,' and I understand from her accompanying hand gesture that she believes the border to be closed.

The driver has climbed out of the car, she goes to pick up my rucksack. I rested it on the ground while talking to her. I try to stop her but she waves me away, lifts my heavy rucksack into the boot of her car. 'Come with us,' she says in strongly accented English. I am unsure. It is always tempting to go with the flow; however, my plan to enter Algeria is of long standing. I feel reluctant to change course now. The girl—the driver—laughs at me as I dither, explains in her mixture of languages that the border is open but not at the post I am walking towards. An open crossing lies thirty kilometres from here and she is happy to take me to it. 'Nous ne faisons rien d'autre,' she says: We are doing nothing else.

'And will you cross into Algeria?' I ask.

'Very boring,' says one girl, speaking for the first time, speaking in clear English. 'We went once but it is too strict.'

The other girls nod, concur with her critique of that country.

I try to argue with them, say that it is unnecessary for them to make this detour if they are not crossing over themselves.

'We take you and then goodbye,' says the driver.

Her role in life seems to be smoothing the passage of English boys from one alien land to another. Her role in my life, certainly.

* * *

The girls drop me off fewer than two hundred yards from the border post. The one on the seat beside me, the rear, points at the guards. 'Guns, guns.' She smiles as she says it, trying to frighten me as an older sister might her brother. I am grateful that these girls have kept my day on track. Once my rucksack is on my back, I wave to them through the bestirred dust. Wave at their departing tires. It was kind of the French girls to bring me so far out of their way. I should not forget them, a triumvirate of Heidi's with whom I never exchanged names.

The border post is an odd affair. Moroccan soldiers stand smoking cigarettes. One waves me through without even looking at my passport but then a different soldier calls me back. This makes me apprehensive. The soldier who has called me laughs at the length of my hair, studies my passport, and asks in French, boy or girl? I ignore this because he knows the answer. Being obnoxious because he wears a uniform offends me greatly. I find the nerve to silently hold his gaze.

An older soldier points, indicates I am to walk on, and the one who teased me passes back my passport. I consider the check to be over but on advancing to the gate, an official wearing a western-style suit emerges from a pre-fabricated cabin. He calls me in, looks also at my passport, squiggles his initials or something equally brief onto the ink of the Moroccan stamp, the franking first made when I entered the kingdom from Ceuta. Then he hands it back. 'Au revoir,' he says, gesturing that I may now leave his country.

From the Moroccan post, I walk another two hundred yards to a large double gate. Each is twelve feet tall and possible just as wide. Made of iron, crisscrossed bars so that one may see from one country into the next. On the other side, a man of about sixty years, wearing a long kaftan and a kufi cap, steps up from a small metal chair placed in the shade of a tiny hut. He nods when he sees a hand gesture from the soldiers behind me. At that signal, he opens the gate. Opens it just enough that I may walk through. I think it a funny set up. There are several Algerian soldiers in my line of vision, I know that a similar pack of Moroccans stands behind me, in the country I am leaving. They all keep clear of the gate, leave it to an old man to open and close the border. If the military presence were any closer, they might each think it a provocation. I am ignorant of their mutual politics, see only that there is no love lost.

As I pass through the gate, the man points to a building behind the Algerian soldiers, a large grey lorry parked beside it. A further two hundred yards. I walk, rucksack heavy and sweat accumulating on the small of my back, and think only how hot the sun is. The eighth of April—not even high summer—in the country containing the largest chunk of the Sahara Desert: Algeria. I have come where very few people venture. I laugh to myself at the stupidity of this Bury-centric thought and that awareness makes me smile. I am doing what I was not destined for. Bedouins and Arabs will be here a-plenty, it is Lancastrians and other Britishers who are sparse. Nowhere to be seen.

I put my head into the cabin of the Algerian customs post. A man, twenty or thirty years my senior, wearing Arabic dress, beckons me inside. I hold my passport in my hand, presume he wishes to see it. He places it on a large table, then signals for me to remove the rucksack from my back. I gesture surprise and say, 'Clothes and books.' He ignores my comment and, when I have placed it before him, undoes the elasticated string keeping the pack closed. As he is doing this he glances down at the passport and then back up at me. He stops fiddling with the rucksack in order to look closely at my photograph. The passport is only a year old, the likeness better than most. He points at my long hair then removes his small leather hat, gestures at his own shiny head, barely a millimetre's growth upon it. He smiles, my hair is funny. I relax, he is not being unpleasant. His intended joke is upon himself.

He takes a form from a drawer in the desk beside him and writes down some details. He asks in French how long I am staying. I tell him ten days. I think it a bare minimum; the Sahara could be worth a longer look. He asks to see my money. I lift my T-shirt and sweat-shirt and self-consciously remove the money belt from around my midriff. I unfasten the pocket and show him the unchanged travellers' cheques. The man writes down the amount of money I carry, then signals that I should put my garment back on. I wonder what his paperwork means. Will a man at the Tunisian border, ten days hence, expect to note that I have spent a credible amount in my passage across the country? I never considered this, that my expenditure could be tracked. I try to push the thought aside; one hurdle at a time.

Another man comes out of the neighbouring room in the cabin. He wears an official-looking uniform, brass buttons on a navy-blue jacket. His hair is permed, I'm sure of it. It is not especially long but he has a frizz in the fashion of many western pop stars and footballers. Despite his uniform, he looks carefree. Odd that he is a customs official. Then again, what was I doing working in insurance? He says something in Arabic and the man who is dealing with me gestures in reply. I don't think that there is a problem. I am the only one currently crossing the border, these two men are alleviating their own boredom.

The man in the kaftan examines my luggage once more. He puts his hand into my rucksack but as he does so, he keeps his eyes on me. I find that I cannot stop myself from reddening. He looks briefly away, pulling a book—not the Hesse but an unread Kerouac—from my rucksack. As he glances back at me, I brush sweat off my forehead with the back of my right hand. He seems to take this in. Weighs me up. 'Qu'est-ce tu as?' he asks: What have you got?

I note that I am familiar, I am tu. I think this is a good thing but feel unsettled that I am having to speak French. 'Rien,' I say. I have nothing. I hope it does not sound dismissive of his question. I say again, 'Clothes and books.' Say it in English, not thinking quickly enough of the corresponding French words. Then they come to me. 'Vêtements et livre.' That should do it. He will feel nothing else down there. A camera in the side pocket but I don't have the French to say it.

His hand remains in my rucksack as the man calls his colleague closer. I like this one more, he smiles at me; the two men exchange words in Arabic. They could be speaking about the weather for all their respective tones concede. Then the younger man speaks to me in English.

'You have the hashish?'

I shake my head.

'You have the dinar?'

I shake my head again.

He shrugs.

The older man steps across and signals that I am to raise my arms. He starts to frisk me. Conducts himself carefully, there is no roughness in his action. He watches my face all the while he performs his task. The other man speaks again.

'You have the hashish?'

'Non.'

'You have the dinar?'

'Non. Non.'

Both men look amused by me. The older man says, 'Por quoi?' I cannot answer his question but I know that he is referring to my demeanour.

The younger man, the English speaker, says, 'Which is it? This is you nervous, yes?'

I try to answer smartly but do not articulate myself well. 'I've never been searched before. I'm not used to it.'

The older man has emptied the contents of my rucksack on to the table. If he heard my earlier vêtements-et-livre comment, he must now see that I am an honest man. He waves for me to re-pack my belongings. I feel a measure of relief.

The younger man, who I am liking less now, says again, 'You have the hashish?'

I say, 'Non.'

'You smoke the hashish?'

Again, I say, 'Non.' He shakes his head, unconvinced. I could tell him, so what? In Fes, a man who looked like he could have been his granddad shared a hash-pipe with me.

This is their culture, not mine. I haven't smoked hashish in Bury apart from something that was being passed around last Christmas. At a couple of parties. Never bought any before Fes; spent only a few pennies back there. I am not so stupid as to say it.

'No hashish?'

'Non.'

When I have repacked my bag, the older man points to the door which, I believe, takes me out into Algeria proper. Before I can walk five steps, he shouts, 'Arrêtez.' I stop. He points at my training shoes; indicates with a hand gesture that I should take them off. The younger official shakes his head, and I see him smile quietly to himself.

Chapter Two

Al Aricha

1.

He sits in the backroom of the border cabin, tears in his eyes. The frizzy-haired customs official pats the English boy's hand. 'All right, boy. No change it now.' The defenceless young man looks into his comforter's eyes and the Algerian turns away. Embarrassment, perhaps.

A policeman comes into the room, exchanges words in Arabic with the young customs officer. He takes the boy's rucksack from the table on which it rests. The policeman indicates to the boy that he should follow him from the room.

In his head, the English boy wonders if he can recall how to walk. In practice it proves straightforward. He feels lost and leaden. An internal sense, with no greater manifestation than the dejection written across his face. He walks just a single pace behind the official. Out of the door, across to the rear of a waiting police van. Two more policemen are sitting in the vehicle. They wait together in silence while the first policeman re-enters the customs cabin.

The boy would like to ask questions. Where will they take him? Will they give him back his rucksack? Not of these stony-faced policemen. They are not for talking to. He imagines asking the girl in the headscarf, the one he met just a day ago, in Abdul's tourist office. She was not a swindler; it was the men who played that game. She may not know the answers to his questions—would no doubt be shocked that he has been arrested—surely smile some semblance of sympathy. He wonders for how long these imagined pleasantries will be the only comfort he can muster.

The missing policeman comes back to the van clutching a small wad of paperwork.

The van takes the boy from the border post to a police station. He does not know the name of the town in which it is situated. Only a short journey from the customs post. Six or seven minutes. He did not enter the country at the crossing closest to Oujda. The change of plan has disoriented him. He cannot visualise where upon a map he might be. Those kindly French girls may have driven him north, may have driven him south. He didn't ask. Mile after mile of dry scrubland. Algeria. That had been name enough at the time of his crossing. He knows it is the ninth largest country on Earth, read the entire article in the Encyclopaedia Britannica. To be somewhere more precise might feel less worrisome. The last-minute change of crossing point is not the sole reason for his discomposure. Not its source. Moving from van to building gives him no sense of place. He bows his head in shame for these few steps. Fails to take in the surroundings. Knows not whether he is amidst grandeur or poverty. The grey shale of the roadside and the black and white ceramic of the police station floor, that is as much as he sees. It is not changing money in Morocco that has given him this sense of contrition. While crying at the customs post, he concluded that Algerian currency is one giant slush fund. The country should feel ashamed of it. Keeping all its money to itself when even small children learn to share. His error was being caught. He is an amateur at life itself.

In the police station, those who brought him here fill out

forms. Then a policeman he has not seen before pulls him into a corner of the room. Not with force, just a roughness suggesting force might be available. He looks into the face of the policeman, the puller. It shows no emotion as the boy compliantly slides into the metal chair indicated. A wide inkpad is open before him. The policeman takes a hold of his left hand, pushes the tip of his index finger firmly onto the open tin. The black foam of ink. Fingerprinting. It is a relief to understand the ritual. And he knows that it has no wider purchase upon him. His fingerprints as unknown in Bury, Lancashire as they are here. He has seen it happen, fingerprints taken, on television. Crime dramas, policemen with accents like his father's. Ink on fingers doesn't hurt.

The English boy complies when his captor then pushes him up a corridor and into a small cell. There are two other men inside. He sits himself on the stone floor, across from a prostrate captive. The third wrongdoer sits alone on a small wooden bench.

* * *

It was back in grammar school that he first became fanatical about hitchhiking. In principle that is, dead keen before he had so much as tried it. Then he thumbed his first lift at fifteen. Morecambe and back. Proving that he could; no longer stuck in Bury. The boy had discovered the way out.

His first non-imaginary hitchhike occurred on the weekend his brother, Gary, left home to begin his stint in the Royal Navy. The younger brother was not for conforming. Hitching would not get the approval of his father. Not that he told the old sod where he went. How he got there. Avoiding his brother's send-off was crime enough on Wolseley Road. His father stopped speaking to him. Sent to Coventry for missing an event from which the family was to draw pride. Never tried to fathom the boy's reasons.

Didn't have it in him.

He and Gary had always rubbed along despite their different natures. Late evenings watching films, comedy shows, midweek football. Only if their parents were out or in bed. His father determined what came out of the television if he was in the room.

Gary told his younger brother that programmes were funnier if they watched them together. It was a compliment. The older boy's attention needed shepherding. Even football they could not enjoy equally. The younger boy laughed at the frustrations of the older. Expletives shouted when his favoured team missed their shots, leaked goals.

Gary once tried to explain how he felt about his on-off girlfriend. Sought the guidance of his brother. But the conversation quickly drifted into light-hearted grumbling. Gary could not articulate his feelings and the younger brother sensed them to be a disruptive force within. To examine was to disturb.

Bury to Morecambe, a few pennies wasted in the slot machines. Fish and chips. And then he hitchhiked back home again. All of it to avoid saying goodbye to a brother he no longer felt a connection with. Gary's vocation—off to fight whoever he was told to fight—he adjudged to be a grim one. Now, here on the continent of Africa, without a thumb raised in expectation, he makes the connection. His brother signed up for nine years. The Royal Navy. This will be his own clean break. No going back to Bury from here.

* * *

He is not frightened of his fellow cellmates. If he ought to be, the penny hasn't dropped. Neither has acknowledged his presence; they are in a police cell, must have done something wrong. Violence? It is plausible but their arguments are not with him. He will not give in to fear. Not now, not yet.

The boy from Bury looks at the man sitting on the bench. Not directly at his face. Takes in his clothing, his languorous posture. The man wears track-suit bottoms. Attire that the English boy saw upon many men in Morocco. Casual western clothes. The man's T-shirt has a large stain on the front. A black smudge; it could be oil or tar. There is no corroborative smell. A shirt washed many times, the stain now a fixture. The man isn't old but he is significantly older than the English boy. His legs move constantly while he sits on the bench. Agitated, preoccupied. Silent. The boy hopes that this is indicative of self-containment. The man is unkempt and the boy infers that he speaks no English, possibly only limited French. As he thinks it, he wonders if his powers of perception are worth a damn here. He certainly couldn't distract the customs officials. Never threw them off the scent in the way he visualised he might the night before. Everything in North Africa has a way of sliding into something unexpected. A tour of a carpet factory into the mistreatment of children.

The other cell occupant wears traditional clothing, lies on the hard stone floor. Dark-brown kaftan and sandals. As the English boy glances furtively at him, he sees that the man is sleeping. Nothing about his posture is comfortable. His back looks curved as he lies on his side. An arm that might have cushioned his head fails to do so, his right cheek intimate with the cold stone floor. But he is asleep. That, thinks the English boy, is the way to cope with a police cell. It is not the man's first time in here. Extracting what little comfort can be gleaned from the cold floor of a prison cell is surely an acquired skill.

The boy lies back on the hard stone, hoping to mirror this man's example. He has no clue how long he must stay in this barren room. He expects it to be only a short time.

This is not a proper prison. He decides that he should pretend to sleep. His glances have given him no cause to be fearful. Still, he regards interacting with either man to be folly. He closes his eyes.

2.

The boy's arm is pulled and this stirs him from unexpected sleep. A policeman is in the cell, making a demand of him which he does not understand. He would like nothing more than to brush his teeth. This unexpected desire distracts him from attending to the policeman's words. Allez is in there, it means go. Someone's going somewhere, could be him. The smell of the speaker's breath is overwhelming. He would settle for the policeman brushing his own teeth; knows better than to say it. Hasn't the French to try. The boy stands up, as he believes the man instructs him to. The policeman speaks quickly, impatiently. A few words register with him but not anything whole. Nothing tangible. The man's breath is rank. The boy fears he is missing the point. Can't get the gist of things down here. 'Tribunal.' This word he hears more than once. He hopes it is news of his imminent release. Seventy pounds is not much. Confiscate the money and release him. It's their call, it would be the right thing to do.

He stumbles along the corridor in the clutches of the policeman. Why isn't he handcuffed? They do that to all prisoners in England. He might find an opportunity to make a run for it, break out for the Sahara Desert. This idea sounds hare-brained even inside his own stupid head. In the corridor they pass another policeman. The boy is jarred by the sight of his holstered gun. He glances around at his own escort. Armed. Handcuffs may not be a mainstay in the restraint of prisoners down here. Won't be absconding this morning, that's a dead certainty.

Then the boy's mind picks over the thought. Is it still morning? He reflects on his period of sleep. It was of an unknown duration. Minutes, hours? He can discern no signposts to tell him. Knows only that sleep did not refresh him. Only his release from custody could achieve that. He hates to be penned, to feel without freedom.

When the policeman first woke him, before he even left the cell, he noticed that the man in the tracksuit bottoms was no longer present. The other—the man whose sleep he'd sought to join—had taken up occupancy of the wooden bench. The boy from Bury wonders how he managed to fall into such an absence. One prisoner left the cell, one moved across it, and he registered none of it. He might sleep through his own murder. He has no control here, can neither see nor affect what is happening in his life. Sleep is his better realm.

The policeman ushers him out into the sunshine; the light dazzles the boy. The country he hoped to look upon— obscure Algeria—is invisible behind the haze of yellow light. Blindingly bright. The English boy blinks and finds his eyes are watering. His captors will think he is crying, when he isn't. Simply floundering in the contrast between cell and sunshine. The policeman has a hold of his wrist, speaks to him. The boy guesses that the words mean no funny business, cannot be certain of it. He hopes it is Arabic that he hears spoken. If it is French, he has lost the thread completely. The man's face says no funny business, so the words should match. A contradiction in face and phrase would be most underhand. The boy elects to comply with his best guess. Fears his ignorance of the true words may unravel his intended obedience.

The policeman takes him up five steps and through the front door of a large building. As his eyes adjust to the sudden loss of sunlight, he takes in the wide entrance hall, the inlay that decorates the walls. It is a more impressive interior than any he has come across since arriving in Africa. He feels chastened by the imposing architecture. They have brought him to a place of importance—a failed hitchhiker—what is he doing here? The marble floor reminds him of the Prado Museum in Madrid. He was there less than a fortnight earlier; it felt magnificent. The paintings were memorable, as was an Australian girl he met in the youth hostel later the same day. This is not an art gallery. Little hope of an uplifting experience in the company of a policeman. It was back in Oujda that he first walked through the wrong door. The modest tourist information office. And now all choice has fallen away. He has worked that much out. It nags him like a stone in the shoe.

Once inside the building, the policeman sits on a bench to the left of the open door. He eases the English boy down beside him. The hold of his arm never loosens. It is far cooler in here than it was on the street. A gloomy light pervades the unlit interior, broken by small sunbeams that arrow in from infrequent windows. Light cannot penetrate the depth of this vast chamber. A stern-looking woman in predominantly western clothes, a long dark green skirt and white blouse, comes towards them. Sits on the bench by the policeman. They exchange a few words. The English boy pointedly tries not to listen; it does not concern him. Perhaps they are husband and wife, this a chance meeting. Coincidence that the policeman should have to bring a prisoner here. It could be a library. Very grand but the boy has yet to see a book.

The lady who is in conversation with the policeman wears a thin white headscarf across the top of her head. Grey hair protrudes; she has tied it only loosely. The woman studies some papers which she was clutching as she walked over to them. The boy notices a British passport in her hands. She studies an inner page and the boy guesses it is his own photograph she peruses. He would like to see it. The relaxed and hopeful boy who inhabits that familiar picture. Feels too intimidated by the situation to peer into her lap. She never shows him the document directly. Nor does he know how it has come into her possession. This is not a library. His mind turns it all around like a hamster on a wheel. Getting nowhere whatsoever.

Within a few minutes a shout from a neighbouring room prompts both the policeman and the woman holding the British passport to stand up from their seats. The former pulls the boy to his feet. The three go together into the room from where the shout came. It is an auditorium, a courtroom perhaps. A tribunal, thinks the boy from Bury.

The policeman pushes him onto a seat, finally releases him. No longer grips his arm; takes himself to the seat behind. The boy faces a wooden balustrade behind which sit three elderly men. Court officials, he presumes. The woman in the white headscarf, who he believes has his passport, sits next to him. 'I speak you.' He looks into her face. 'I give the English,' she reiterates.

Then a young man—another court official, the boy guesses—reads from a piece of hand-held paper. The boy from Bury knows he is hearing Arabic, cannot guess a word except a single guttural rendition of his own name. He feels frustrated that the woman has not interpreted anything for him. She told him it was her function: giving the English.

When the man finally stops speaking, the elderly judges, assuming that is what they are, confer briefly. Then one of them gives a hand signal in the direction of the woman. She turns to the boy. The judge speaks in a slow monotonous tone. As he does so, she speaks quietly to him. Interprets. There can be no other explanation.

'The state of Algeria must protect itself. Take money from the country is crime. Buying money, dinar, not from Algerian bank. Crime. Bring the money across border, it is very crime.'

Then a policeman—one who the English boy has seen before, he was in the van that brought him from the border post—stands and talks to the judges. One asks a question of the policeman. He answers enthusiastically, accompanies his reply with vigorous nodding of his head. The boy understands not a word.

When there is a pause in the talk, the woman whispers, 'You have the dinar in the foot. The policeman knows it.'

The boy from Bury wants to tell the woman it was not in his foot but in his shoe. He feels cheated out of a fair hearing. Having an interpreter who cannot differentiate these words. What else might he be missing in her mangled translation? Or is her interpretation an accurate summary of the Arabic being spoken and the court itself listening only to a travesty? A surreal take upon his alleged crime. He elects not to quibble.

One of the elderly judges speaks, quietly but audibly, and the boy realises that the young man sitting in front of the judges is writing it down. Maybe he has written every word said, the boy acquiring fame in Algeria as has never happened in the country of his birth. A criminal in a strange land. He dismissed the possibility in the ping-pong of thoughts in his hotel room just a dozen or so hours ago. His decision to cross the border—black-market notes folded into his battered training shoe—came after some consideration. Not enough, that is clear now, but he debated with himself for a long time. In Oujda, he had imagined only having his money removed. He mistakenly thought the customs officers might take it as payment for his release. He thought they would be corruptible and he would know instinctively how to execute such a ruse. He found neither of these assumptions to be true. The officials played by the book, and he never suggested it should be otherwise. He could no more bribe his way past them than he could ride a unicycle through the customs post. He is a boy without that skill. Now, in a courtroom he thinks uninterested in him, an outcome for his transgression is to be decided. He cannot recall floggings in Algeria. Recalls no news reports emanating from this country whatsoever. He would not like to be flogged but it might be for the best. A sore arse and go.

When the judge finishes talking, the woman turns to the boy. 'To prison. The British embassy we contact. The judge he say it is two years. There is right of appeal. The embassy, British embassy, contact. See how they say. It is justice.'

The boy wonders what his interpreter has failed to translate. The judge's words took many times longer to speak than this bowdlerized rendering. Two years, she has told him. Two years in prison. And the British Embassy? See how they say. What does that mean? He has no idea what influence the British Embassy might have in an Algerian town, the name of which he has still to learn.

* * *

The boy from Bury is taken from the courtroom by a man in uniform. It is not the same policeman who brought him here. A different uniform entirely. Military police, that's his best guess. The deep green of this man's clothing contrasts with the light brown of the policemen at the station. And green is not a navy colour. He doesn't think it is, not even in Algeria. The lady said prison. He is not going on a ship, not for deportation across the Mediterranean. That would be fairer to his thinking. He can understand the people over there. Europe. Wanting something a lot seldom seems to make it happen.

The green-uniformed man ushers him out of the rear of the building. A back door. A narrow flight of eight steps leads down to a gravel carpark. Red shale. Counting steps is a comforting activity. He entered through the building's pillared frontage. This building is two-faced. Nothing special about it round the back. An open-sided truck sits on a gravel parking lot. Many men already sit on the benches in the back of the truck. Some wear the same dark green as his escort, others look quite dishevelled. As his minder indicates, he climbs up two high rungs to join them.

The vehicle has come to life before he can make himself comfortable. Vibrates noisily beneath his bottom. He cannot see the driver nor guess who else maybe in the front cabin. He sits on a wooden bench on the open-sided rear. Wedged between his personal military policeman and another old Algerian. Another prisoner, his assumption. They have yet to be introduced.

The small cohort of prisoners and police leave the dusty town, move over near-empty roads. Parched terrain slips by. This is the land he intended to hitchhike across. He must be on his way to prison, one of several offenders but nothing is terribly clear to him. Nothing has convinced him today. It is not a dream, simply the stuff of them. Not a pleasing, heart-warming type of dream. This is the sort in which nothing sticks, the truth of everything slipping away. Out of his grasp.

As they clambered aboard, he saw a man throw a rucksack up on to the luggage atop the cabin. His own. He thinks it was his own, the colour matched. He would have liked to have it back. Hoist it upon his shoulders again. Two years is a long time to wait. Did those elderly judges understand it was only seventy pounds? Wouldn't a week be enough? The woman in the green dress—his interpreter—was vindictive. She took pleasure from her role in his humiliation. He thinks she judged him from the moment she saw his passport photograph. A happy boy. A lady who dislikes a smile. Two years might be her nasty misinterpretation. The woman's idea of a joke. And her English was laughable. If the judge said two weeks, she might have translated week for year. Fucked up. She or he. One of them has done it royally.

The road has many potholes. With each jolt of the truck, the boy bounces from his seat. Far more than any other passenger, he thinks. He must be the least practiced at this type of travel. These Algerians may have used such roads all their lives. The bumps are the problem. The capacity to surf them strikes him as a modest skill to acquire. The obstacle is his relentless daydreaming. He keeps putting his mind into other places. His recent stay in the youth hostel in Madrid or his brother's last home leave. He knows this reverie is itself a ploy. He has no wish to be present. His inattention causes him to be thrown around the truck—fails to prevent it—bumping carelessly into his fellow passengers. He is to share a prison with them, knocking heads an ill-chosen greeting.

Through narrowed eyes he looks across the interminable landscape. Rocky and dusty. Small thin trees line the horizon, the few close to the road are very far apart. He realises it is an optical illusion. Not a line at all, an accumulation over the sparse scrub. Few trees but the land is flat, those far away visually blend with those in front of them. The boy likes to contemplate these illusions. There is the occasional dwelling house, even an impoverished village or two. He wanted to visit—hitchhike, linger—meet the people who live in such places. Skimming past in the back of a prison-bound truck was never in the plan.

The drive seems never ending to him; his eyes struggle to stay open. Then the truck pulls up in the middle of nowhere. There is nothing here, no reason to stop. Not houses, not vegetation, not a signpost. They are in scrubland: nowhere at all. If this is a prison, it is without walls. The men are clambering down from the back of the truck and the driver has also alighted from his cabin. It flashes through the tired brain of the English boy that they are to dig their own graves. Dig away out here in the desert. He tries to push this nonsense from his mind. Sitting alone in the truck, he watches all the men who have climbed down, they appear to be adjusting their trousers. It looks coordinated. They are taking out their penises. As they start to pee along the roadside, he thinks it would be a relief to do the same. No one prevents him from scrambling down. He goes to the end of the line. Ensures he is only a pace or two from the nearest piddler. A guard must not mistakenly think he is sidling away, that could end badly. He finds that the doing of it, the micturition, is not unpleasant, despite the self-consciousness he feels among so many unknowable men. It comes to him that this piss will serve him well. He is doing as the other men do. Fitting in. Relieved, they all return to the same seats on the truck. The thin warm wind carries the stench of urine toward the re-seated boy and he feels himself gag. Then the truck rolls away and only the coarse diesel smell of the vehicle mingles with the warm, dry air. The man sitting to his left, who he assumes to be a fellow prisoner, nudges him. The boy looks up fearfully, the man only smiles. Nothing is so bad, his open face is saying. With this kind look the boy from Bury receives a little unrequested sympathy. Feels grateful to his core, returns the smile and then looks away.

* * *

Two nights before arriving in North Africa, the English boy spent time in Marbella. In Spain. Not even a full day. He hitched in, then out again the following morning. It was a far cry from the morass of worry that his North African travels have become. Still, it is a minor disturbance back there which he now dwells upon. Thinks over as the truck sweeps him into the interior of Algeria.

Marbella is a handsome place. Palm trees only yards from the shoreline. The Mediterranean Sea lapping away like a puppy at a water bowl. But the boy felt an anger, a hostility, towards the British people he saw. Feels it still. He wonders if it is an indulgence. He has not thought about the incident until now. Perhaps he is confusing those feelings he had in Spain with his tumult today. Trouble and how to react to it: never his strong suit.

Marbella sits in the south-easternmost corner of Spain. It has a Spanish interior while its picturesque harbour is rooted securely in the south east of England. One big yacht club for overdressed Brits. English, upper-class boors. Those who think that a pleated jacket bearing two vertical lines of shiny buttons is proof of their weight in the world.

At the harbourside the boy heard no Spanish spoken. Only the clipped diction of his better-off compatriots. Marbella is a colony. That's how he saw it. A colony for the modern era. In-coming money has penetrated where gunboats can no longer probe. By the steps leading to a waterfront bar, a chalkboard advertised the many wines available. Names, prices, over-wordy prose to describe the content of the expensive bottles. Every word of it written exclusively in the English language. He felt self-righteous disapproval while purchasing a glass of house red. Did so in order to sit, linger. Take in the strange culture shift he had uncovered. A rabbit hole back to England.

The outside seating was occupied by finely dressed and well-spoken people. Plus him. A wide age range and a single nationality. It excluded Welsh and Scots; the boy guessed himself to be Bury's sole representative. Possibly the only northerner. These well-heeled people were foreigners in Spain, a condition that did not enervate them. They regarded others as foreign. There is nowhere in which they would apply that designation to themselves. The boy listened in as they talked, mostly about the recently improved weather or the sailing conditions between here and Gibraltar. Old men in smartly creased trousers and matching jackets. Young men wearing white trousers and open-necked shirts. A grey-haired lady in culottes dangled a cigarette holder from her fingers. Some younger women wore shorts and T-shirts, wore them as models on a Parisian catwalk might.

He heard them talk about the Americans in Tehran, the unfortunate embassy staff who have become hostages there. The young in that revolutionary country overran the embassy months ago. Demanded President Carter return the dying Shah to stand trial; to be torn limb from limb should he ever return to his homeland. It is an impasse that America cannot resolve. The leadership in Iran—the Ayatollah Khomeini—sides with the students, whether it is openly declared it or not.

'Get them out and then bomb the place,' declared a gravelly voice. 'The situation is quite beyond the pale,' agreed another. 'The ungrateful Arabs turned on the Shah. And after he finally put Persia back on the map.'

The boy sipped his red wine while quietly despising their ignorance. Iranians are not Arabs and he felt alone in the knowing of it.

It puzzled him that these people were here at all. The old and retired he could understand if not forgive. One or two below retirement age may have been employed locally. Employed in the yacht club. The presence of so many young people was inexplicable to him. None had saved a little money from their factory jobs, packed it in, and set to hitchhiking. That is his template. He who did not belong in that place of idle leisure.

And then, quite out of the blue, these unflappable Brits had their peace disturbed. The peace they had purchased in this corner of a land that is not theirs. They did not appear prepared but, on reflection, he thinks they were. Such people are always ready and waiting. Alert to any assault upon their privileged way of life. A drunken

Spaniard staggered across the bar area, a young man. The boy now bumping uncomfortably across the arid landscape of western Algeria recalls it precisely. The drunkard's jeans were torn. His white T-shirt stained and dirty. He was shouting in Spanish. Swear words mostly. 'Cristo' and 'Mierda.' The English boy's understanding of Spanish was too limited for him to fathom what angered the young man. Watching his fellow countrymen—picking up their self-anointed sense of entitlement—made him feel a little of the same.

The English at the closest two tables arose as one. A young woman of similar age to the drunk stood up with a glass of rosé in one hand. Pointed an aggressive finger. 'What the fuck is he doing in here?' Her plummy voice sounded as a parody of Princess Margaret might. A barman stopped washing glasses, hurried to intervene. Two of the Englishmen pushed the young drunk roughly to the ground. One wore a peaked sailing cap, and the younger of the two accidently knocked a beer over in the improvised restraint. The Spaniard hit his head on a table leg and this made him swear loudly. Two more staff rushed to join the barman. Three Spanish men, in strongly accented English, apologised to the customers. Two of the staff were by now seated upon the prone drunk in place of the Englishmen who first felled him. Another staff member picked the peaked sailing cap up from the ground where it had fallen. Passed it back to the tall man on whose head it belonged. Shook his hand in apology.

In no time at all, three policemen came into the bar area. One bowed as if his role was one of subservience to those yacht owners. He appeared to be the most senior, certainly the oldest. The other two roughly manhandled the young drunk. Took him out of the elite club in which he had no right to be. The birth right of the English holding more sway than the Spanish in this surreal corner of their country. The boy now recalling the events from his own prison-bound truck never learnt to where the drunk was taken.

And as he recalls that dismal scene—the English idlers fearing it was Lucifer, come to terminate their unjustified way of life—the boy from Bury wonders whether he is now the one disturbing the peace. The good order of Algeria. He has brought currency into the country in breach of its determined regulations. He has violated the code, had no regard for the rulebook. But he doubts himself. Sees ambiguity in the connections he is haphazardly making. In Marbella, the authorities bent over backwards for the British, the English, on account of their wealth. Surely that was why. The money they brought to Marbella swung it for them. At the border post, this boy's British status counted for nothing. Perhaps the boy's lack of wealth—the pettiness of his smuggling, the squalid state of the shoes with which he sought to conceal his crime—was all that mattered. It determined everything.

* * *

The truck pulls up alongside a grey-stone building. Very large. A barren expanse extends as far as the eye can see. This is not a town but a lone fort. The evening sun is setting as soldiers and prisoners tumble out of the open-topped van. Looking around—as those in uniform permit their captives to do—the English boy sees two, three, four men in the distance. All are holding sticks, directing their skinny goats onwards. Towards better greenery perhaps, although none is evident to the boy. There is little plant life purchased on this scrub. No pasture. The goats and their custodians have drawn life's short straws.

The lonely building is just two storeys high, looks massive in its flat surroundings. The boy stares at the proud frontage, Arabic lettering in deep green across a white sign.

He can only speculate what the large curving script might say. The name of the jail written in an alphabet he does not know, cannot guess the sounds which the individual letters belie. He will be twenty-two years of age—ten percent older calculates his restless brain—before next he experiences the freedom now denied him.

A high metal fence with inward-leaning barbed wire across the top extends around the sides of the building. It reminds him of an old television series. The shenanigans of British prisoners of war during World War Two. Not that there will be any tunnelling going on, he can't picture it. No stealing of guard's uniforms while swotting up on the local language; he would make an unconvincing Algerian goatherd. Seventy pounds worth of trouble he is in, and it has bought him more, gone further, than he ever thought so little money could.

The door of the prison opens and uniformed men, wearing light blue, come out to meet the truck. Their colours contrast sharply with the olive-green fatigues of the military police, if that is the true designation of the officials who have escorted him here. Facts are elusive, he must guess and guess. The men in rival uniforms talk rapidly together. Some exchange cigarettes. The English boy notes that one of the guards shares a joke with a man he had presumed to be a prisoner. Passes him a cigarette, lights it for him. Was his guess in error? The man held his head bowed through much of the journey. It seems improbable that he is a plain-clothes policeman. Could he be a crime lord with power and influence far beyond the confines of his criminal gang? A shiver hits the spine of the English boy. He hopes for solitary confinement in this desert jail. If he cannot enjoy liberty, at least keep him free from the machinations of other banged-up criminals. And then he wonders if solitude might drive him mad. He tries to counter these thoughts, thinks of alternative explanations.

Maybe the criminal he saw take a cigarette from a man in uniform did so quite innocently. Has a brother in the armed services of Algeria as he has in the navy of his own country. There might be currency in such connections.

The boy knows he is ill-prepared for this. For prison. He is quite able to freeze his emotions, to absent his mind while remaining in a situation. He lived that way in his family home. The ordeal he now faces is of a different order. A prison is not a detergent factory. He usually allows thoughts to run amok within himself. To reach beyond his situation, let his imagination analyse or amuse. He fears, in this nameless prison, such speculation will only result in self-panic.

As the boy stands on the threshold, he sees that the light blues and the olives are exchanging paperwork. Unloading the luggage from the truck. This time the boy does not see his rucksack. Perhaps he was looking elsewhere when someone moved it; his attention flitters like a butterfly. He sees that there were just six prisoners on the truck, the other passengers were all soldiers or military police. Freemen. He wonders why this calculation was beyond him when he tried to count them during the drive here.

The light-blue uniformed prison guards shepherd the six detainees through the main door of the prison. Down a corridor. All seem to know the drill except the English boy. Last one in, lagging behind.

Then he is in a room, just him and two guards. They pass him something, a large sack made from rough cloth. Doesn't know what for. One of the guards pulls at his clothes and he realises that he must remove what he wears, don the item given. His prison uniform. He complies, unfolds the proffered garment. It is a long brown kaftan. Similar to the one the old man in Fes had worn. The hashish smoker. Lectured him on the ungodliness of alcohol.

As he takes off his overclothes a guard shouts, 'Aye!' in a

loud voice that brings two other light-blue uniformed men into the room. The boy has stopped undressing, raises his arms as if in surrender to the shouts. One of the new arrivals in the room goes to him and tugs a hand at the soft linen of the money belt which he still has tied around his person. The boy has given it no thought until now. How odd that the customs officer allowed him to retain it. The guards have it off him in double quick time.

One opens the pocket that the boy sewed onto the improvised belt back in January. They laugh when they find the money, the travellers' cheques. One of the blue-uniformed men grins up close to the boy's face, pointing at the booklet of money and then at himself. His mime suggests he is asking for a bribe; however, the English boy is sure it is a joke. His life savings are not impressive. Won't get him out of this sorry hole.

'Attendez,' says the guard, gesturing that the boy must wait. It crosses his mind that it might be of two years' duration.

That man leaves the room, returning with a form on which he begins to write, to square the circle. This is the consequence of having money on his person. He has breached a rule and a record of the irregularity must be retained.

When this refinement of his entry documentation is complete, a guard removes the money and his odd belt from the room. A remaining guard says some words in a kindly voice. The boy cannot understand, imagines the guard is advising that it is only for safekeeping. They will not appropriate it. And for no reason but lack of a better alternative, he finds that he trusts the man. The statement he didn't understand. His own imagination.

The boy has been standing in his underpants long enough. He moves to pick up the kaftan and lift it over his head. A prison guard says, 'Non, non.' The English boy stops but cannot understand the problem. 'Arrêtez,' says another guard as he goes to a cupboard at the side of the room and returns clutching a small brown oval-shaped item, an electric flex protruding from it. It takes the English boy a moment to register what he holds. When the guard plugs it into an electric socket, its whirring sound—the buzz of a fat bee—is familiar. A hairdresser's electric razor. His own mother used to take one to his and Gary's hair before they were teenagers. Became too proud to submit to parental hair-cutting. This is one heartbreak for which he has actually prepared. He anticipated losing his long blond hair during the truck ride. For a mile or two he found himself recalling a prison movie. All short hair in a Florida jailhouse. The guard, intentionally or not, is rough. The razor pulls horribly on his dirty hair. It takes no more than three or four minutes to divest him of all he had. He feels the soreness of his scalp more keenly than the loss of identity. He thinks he left that back in Morocco or Spain. Down the back of a cupboard on Wolseley Road, Bury.

After the indignity of having his head shorn while wearing only Y-fronts, a guard pulls on the elasticated waist band of his final item of clothing. The boy guesses what the gesture means: a request for their removal. He dislikes the notion. It is prison routine, he presumes; the authorities may anticipate lice-ridden arrivals. He is lice-free—pretty confident he is—knows better than to argue. Perhaps they will wash his clothes and return them to him. Or they may be burnt for the common good. The boy is indifferent to their fate. Surrenders them knowing he no longer has agency to do otherwise. As he does this, stands naked in front of two guards—the third never returned following the money belt's removal—one of them picks up the kaftan and places it on a chair out of his reach. The second man pushes him gently towards a side door. He feels threatened although the push is not rough at all. The guard opens the door and he sees what might be a small shower room. It is very bare but with tiles and a drain. Its function is clear although he sees no showerhead. The guard signals for him to stand just a metre inside the room, draws up a hosepipe from the wall. Within seconds a strong jet of cold water teases the boy. He is being washed in the manner of a pair of wellingtons on a back doorstep. The force of the water is painful on his most intimate places, unpleasant on his face. The bitter temperature takes only half of a minute to acclimatise to. This is not the Gafait Hotel but the boy copes. A wash is not an assault. Then the guard turns off the water, returns the hosepipe to its coil. Hands the boy a towel. It is large and he finds it is already damp. Other prisoners have dried themselves with it before him. He thinks this hygienic oversight makes the shower a bit of a waste of time. He will still smell of other men. Or was humiliation the primary aim of the whole ritual? Goal achieved.

* * *

When he returns to the first room, the man holding the kaftan hands it to the boy. He feels his way, then burrows his shaven head into the course material, emerges through the correct hole. It envelopes his otherwise naked body, rough against the skin. He is concerned that the touch will irritate and preoccupy him. He dislikes the absence of underwear. He wonders if this will prove to be an orderly prison. Or might it turn out to be chaotic? It is the prisoners he fears. He expects the guards to keep order as best they can. Imagines that prisoners may create subcultures. Cliques, gangs. Cannot see how a boy from Bury could fit into such a thing. Not in a prison in Algeria. As these worries worm their way through his head, he recognises that he would be similarly apprehensive if this was a prison in his own country. He is not a natural captive. A free spirit, that is how he thinks of himself. Then he pushes it a little further. What the hell are they? Free spirits: chumps who fall prey to seven-foot-tall Moroccan swindlers. Nothing more.

* * *

A guard escorts the English boy down a strip-lit corridor and then up a stone staircase. At the top the man directs the boy into the first cell. The door of this room is no more than a gate within the cell's barred frontage. He sees another prisoner already seated on one of the two low beds. He recognises him, it is a surprise and a perturbance. The man was in the truck; on arrival at the prison, he enjoyed the privilege of a cigarette. Passed to him by a prison guard. The boy tenses slightly, tries hard not to show it. The man, his cellmate, gives him a toothy smile which he can neither interpret nor reciprocate.

The guard begins to close the cell gate but another in the same light blue uniform cries out from along the corridor and then starts running. Not fast but jogging purposefully towards the boy's cell. 'Aye, aye, aye,' the boy from Bury hears the running guard call. His hands are full. It is unclear to the boy what it is that he carries.

He comes to a halt and passes a clutch of items to the guard who brought the boy to the cell. With the open gate in one hand, he takes the proffered bundle on a flat palm and passes it straight on. 'Voilà,' he says. The boy is astonished, slightly bewildered, to find himself holding The Glass Bead Game, The Vanity of Deluoz, My Life as a Man. The books he carried with him from England to Oujda. All the way to the Algerian border. He never expected to see them again. He stares at them as the guard places them on his open palms. He looks up at the retreating light blue who had jogged with these offerings for him, murmurs, 'Merci.' Then says it again, the second time his voice is clear, strong.

'Merci.' This is something to be grateful for. The first guard closes the door, the many barred gate, turns the key.

The English boy opens the Herman Hesse novel without looking up. Turns the pages to find where last he was reading. He thinks his fellow prisoner might construe his action as rude, but it gives him purpose. He stays close to the cell gate. It has grown dark outside and a strong fluorescent light illuminates the corridor. There is no light source within their cell.

The other prisoner makes a noise that the boy ignores. He makes it again and the noise begins to take on meaning. 'Come, come,' he says. English words. 'Talk with me.' The boy finds this development highly disconcerting. He thought, at the prison gate, that the cigarette cadger was a master criminal or a corrupt police officer. Never guessed him an English speaker. It crosses his mind that the man is a plant. He has seen this ruse in black-and-white films, Sunday afternoon television. A policeman or similar, sharing his cell to win his trust. Obtain evidence against him for further crimes committed. Or against Abdul and his gang of suit-wearing black marketeers. As he thinks a little further, this invention makes no sense. The other man is the mafioso, the drugs baron or politician turned bad. He cannot be a plant and the boy has committed no further crimes which he might inadvertently reveal. Abdul and the bankers ply their trade in another country. And a fake prisoner who took a cigarette from a prison guard would be an idiot. Giving the game away before it has begun. In his confusion, the boy briefly thinks that he himself may be the plant. Seventy pounds was nothing, and if this man speaks English—which the boy now hears that he does—he might say more than intended just to practice the language. The Bury boy may be able to testify against his cellmate and then walk free. This theory is a load of hairy old bollocks. More improbable than the Norwegian girl's part-time wrestling career.

'You want book?' The English boy finds that he has posed the question using broken English, as if that is as much as the other prisoner might understand.

The man shrugs but then pats his chest. 'I am Amastan,' and he points at the English boy.

Silence. The boy can think of nothing to say in reply to this proud announcement.

'What your name?'

He sees it now: the man wishes to befriend him.

'Moss. I am Moss.'

'Amastan,' says the prisoner, patting once more upon his own chest. He reaches out a hand to shake and touches his own heart after doing so. It is a ritual that Moss learnt in Morocco. He performs it again in this Algerian cell.

'You speak English well,' says Moss.

'Don't be frightened,' Amastan tells the boy.

He begins to shake his head, wants to say that he is not. The surprising warmth of this man—who he'd assumed to be some hardened old lag—gives him renewed hope.

'That is why they put in this cell,' Amastan tries to explain. 'I am speak you English. The...no say...the captain, it is good. He say, go with the English.'

Amastan's English may prove a little trying but Moss appreciates the distraction. He wants to ask why this older man is in jail. To know how everything works here, the routine. Will they get to walk outside? Play ping-pong. He never thought to find out about Algerian prison life in his pre-trip research. Mostly he just gazed at a school atlas he had stolen years before. Hasn't a clue where upon the map this jail sits. 'We go out?' he says, speculatively trying to find answers, and once more utilising broken English. Belittling the man and Moss doesn't mean to. Mimicking him unintentionally.

But Amastan laughs. 'Go out we not do. We are here.'

With his hand he gestures the turning of a key. 'Maybe someone pay?'

'Pays what?' asks Moss.

'Pay. Pay then out.' Amastan nods encouragingly.

Moss is shaking his head in answer. He understands the words but wonders if their meaning is truly shared. Is Amastan advising him to bribe an official? Did he miss a chance when the guards were getting excited about his money belt?

'Smuggling?' his cellmate asks.

Moss nods his head.

'Hashish?'

Moss shakes it.

'Money?'

He smiles apologetically, scratches his shaven head.

Amastan leans back. 'Pah! L'argent.'

Moss nods stoically. Imprisoned for smuggling a bit of money. What utter foolishness has upended him. Then he stares, tries to do so purposefully, just looking into the gaze of the older man. Moss is young, young enough to still believe that thoughts can transmit wordlessly from person to person, that through his gaze he can understand more about Amastan.

And it works, of course, reinforcing his mistaken belief. His cellmate pats his chest again, smiling. 'Me? What have I done?'

The boy nods.

'It is nothing and I hope to be gone. But it is trust that I do not. The Berber people, they beat us here. Beat the Berber people. Not with stick, with power. You know this? I have a job in the theatre.' He pronounces this final word as tea-a-tray, and in his diction, Moss hears its French counterpart.

'You're in the theatre?'

'They close down. The police close down the theatre.'

Once more the man says, tea-a-tray.

The English boy doesn't really understand a word of this. Amastan looks quite rough, he took a cigarette from a guard. He says he is an oppressed Berber who works in the theatre. Moss forgets exactly when he passed through the looking glass. Plenty of opportunity these last five or six days.

He tries to explain to the boy about the Berber people. He says that the Arabs are taking everything away. Moss is unsure what he is referring to, what has been taken from them. His theatre is a corner of resistance, that is Amastan's contention. Moss is alternately impressed and confused. This wily Berber looks like he could win a fight. Noel Coward he is not.

And then the boy goes back inside himself. It is good to be sharing a cell with a prisoner of conscience, neither violent or unpredictable, as he earlier feared. Moss feels instinctively drawn to this man's cause while knowing his own route here contains not even a hint of gallantry. A simple smuggler, too stupid to wangle seventy quid past two disinterested officials. The heroic Berber may tire of him. The privileged European, a small-time nobody who wound up in prison for no reason greater than greed. No evidence of idealism on show. And Moss hopes one day to embrace a worthy creed. He's still working it out. Hats off to Amastan. In this spartan cell, Moss alone is the convict without conviction.

* * *

The corridor lights are off and it is pitch dark. Moss stretches his legs, tries to regain circulation. He has been sitting for hours.

Amastan is not sleeping either. He asks questions of the boy. Mother? Father? Where they are now. How they have taken the news of his incarceration.

This is greater enquiry than the boy can satisfactorily answer. And the man understands only a little English. Moss offers him a few platitudes. No real insight. He wants to ask about the Berber situation, to understand exactly what has brought Amastan into prison. Does it follow a life of struggle or is oppression a new turn? The words to ask elude him. He answers the older man's questions only briefly, never shares the detail of his loveless family. He lets the Berber know of his father's working-class credentials, not of his blinkered outlook. Nor his current low opinion of his younger son. Moss's scathing assessment and determined rejection of his narrow-minded father, he also withholds. Then he lies back on the hard cell bed. Once more he tries to sleep.

He sleeps.

Moss is just a prisoner now.

3.

It is unclear to the boy whether it is through dream or conscious thought, in this fitful first night in prison, that he recalls Angoulême. It is a town in France; he was there, probably no more than fifteen nights ago. He can no longer count the days backwards. Loses himself in the detail of his many recollections. The world before his passage across the Straits of Gibraltar and the world since seem unrelated. Different epochs in a life that is no longer being lived but which mentally assaults him.

In Angoulême he checked into a youth hostel, one of about twenty young people staying that evening. Nineteen French kids and Moss. A girl and a boy approached him, asked where he was from. Was he just travelling through?

He told them, in a mixture of French and English, that he had saved up four hundred pounds. He was getting as far away from Bury as he could on two hundred and,

Rucksack Jumper

unfortunately, he would then have to turn around. Head for home. They laughed at the description of his quest as he hoped they might. They were disbelieving when he said he would reach the Sahara Desert before turning back. The English boy nodded confidently, told them that he'd worked it out. Living frugally is worth the trouble. 'Hitchhiking pays,' he said. The young French pair did not seem to understand this simple phrase, and Moss saw its internal contradiction. 'Hitchhikers don't pay,' he laughed.

Then the girl took his hand. 'Come with us to a bar.' She indicated that she would foot the bill. Moss nodded his head, shook his head. Tried to explain in his juddering French that he could pay for a beer or two. Not an out-and-out scrounger. In due course, more than a dozen from the hostel went out into the centre of town, initially supping wine at an outdoor bar. The air was very fresh—it was late March—the young people were lively. They exchanged seats frequently, talked rapidly, expansively. Many a hand gesture, faces contorted in pain and joy as they recalled events past. Moss understood little, found only one or two in the party whose English was really competent. His own French far below a standard to talk in depth. After three glasses of wine, he felt relaxed, happy, if no more connected than he had become following the initial exchange with the first girl and boy.

He learnt her name when they were setting off from the hostel—the girl who invited him—Claudine. A rather lovely name. He noticed her look at him on more than one occasion. He, keenly watching her, was unsure if the boy who first accompanied Claudine was close. A boyfriend or just a classmate. He liked how she looked. Fine features. Straight black hair across her pale skin. She looked lighter, whiter than most of her compatriots at the bar. He remembers thinking she had the skin tone of a Bury girl. Funny: that was the beginning and end of the commonality.

Claudine was a cut above, nothing Lancashire about her at all. As he sipped upon a red wine, he thought about the French girl. Watched her outline from behind. What is it that motivates this compulsion, he wondered? He would be hitching south the next day—not stopping in Angoulême—he would never see her again. Knew it from the first.

Some in the group arose from their seats, they had made a collective decision to move on, Moss never picking up the intention until now. He would do as they did. He liked to follow the path of least resistance. Would do exactly that unless it looked especially dodgy. On an evening of good cheer, this decision made itself.

The group flowed as one along the streets of Angoulême to an unmarked door about four blocks from the first bar. There were two security men on the door, whose purpose was unclear to Moss. The entire group entered without a fuss. No scowls or questions. Pleasanter all round than his foray three months earlier to Bury's only night club. The time he relented to his then-girlfriend's request. Took Sharon MacDonald dancing.

Down some steps into a basement, Moss again found himself on the periphery of the group. Music played; it was much noisier than the first bar. Moss wanted to buy a drink for Claudine. He stood close to her and pulled on her sleeve. As he tried to communicate his wish in the dark—the thumping disco beat precluded easy conversation—Claudine smiled at him and, catching the barman's eye, ordered up two bottles of beer. Before Moss could prevent it, Claudine had paid, perhaps misunderstanding his original intention.

Moss tried to guide Claudine to a seat at the rear. He wanted to talk to her. Not about anything in particular, simply to look into her face for a longer time. He imagined that this would create a more lasting connection between them on this their only plausible meeting in this life. At a table, Claudine failed to sit, even as Moss did so. Instead, she pulled him back up by the hand. Not forcefully but he followed her gentle lead. She took off her long black coat, beneath which she wore a blue dress. Moss, in his jeans and sweatshirt, felt wholly underdressed next to this chic girl. His smarter clothes were five hundred miles away, maybe closer to a thousand. Three days hitchhiking plus a night ferry.

Claudine left her coat on the seat, beer bottle on the table and pulled Moss to the dance floor. He would have resisted were she not so pretty, so enticing. Discothèques are not his scene. Others from the youth hostel were already dancing. All the girls and half the boys by the look of it. He gave in to the night. With a self-conscious laugh, he started to shuffle his feet, wave his arms, in some semblance of rhythm. Soul music is a genre he has no time for. At first, he thought the tune he heard might be an exception, a disco song he actually likes. Quickly he reorganised his thoughts. Claudine was a girl he liked—the first since Sharon—that was the extent of it. Sentimentality would not shift his dim regard for the music to which she swayed so beautifully. He realised that he did not really know her. Loved the way she had pulled him to the dance floor. A gracious gesture. Her face was pure and unwavering. The green of her eyes dominated by their black pupils, enlarged in the twilight of the club. She danced with her hips, encouraged him to dance likewise and he did his best. She grinned at his lack of coordination. Not unkindly. He had long known that his superior taste in music, his cerebral appreciation of the entire folk-rock oeuvre, has rendered his feet correspondingly slow-witted. Dancing to music is—he has worked this out—not an evolutionarily useful skill. When done spontaneously it is clearly the power of the music which pulls. The routines and moves of the discothèque, even the moves of Claudine—the watching of whom Moss found very enjoyable—are little more than an expression of vanity. The egotism of the mover. Look at me! Look at what I can do. Moss tried to push these overly cynical thoughts from his mind. Enjoy his dance with the pretty girl.

Other youngsters from the hostel were on the floor, many in close proximity to them; they exchanged words with Claudine. A very popular girl. Claudine turned to dance with a group of girls facing away from Moss. He moved himself into their group and the girls giggled at his graceless moves. He laughed along. Emboldened by drink he took Claudine by the hand. Wished to dance exclusively with her. He noted that she raised her eyebrows to a girlfriend. Did so with a smile. She might have been poking fun at him. Or maybe, thought Moss, she was as fascinated by him as he was by her. The music changed. Moss recognised it instantly while finding something strange in the offering. A disco rendition of a song he had enjoyed in its original form. The thudding beat lacked the subtlety of the sixties' version. He put a hand on the small of Claudine's back, stepped closer. Drew her into an old-fashioned dancing embrace. The girl smiled and tried to lead him in some moves that befitted this close, waltz-like pose. He was leading nothing, craved her closeness to his body without a clue about the dancing. The girl's chest just a thin fabric from his T-shirt. He is terribly inept at this dumb art; prancing has long been his term for dancing. He would have preferred snogging out the back but it didn't seem to be on offer. He placed his right hand on Claudine's bottom, her dress so thin he could feel the ridge of her underwear beneath.

Initially she seemed to allow him this and then, suddenly, she stepped back, spoke brusquely without looking at him. 'Non, monsieur! Non, monsieur!' She rebuked him at a volume which overcame the thumping music.

The boy she had been with when Moss first met her at the youth hostel came instantly to Claudine's side.

Moss stepped away. 'Je m'excuse.' He tried to say it exclusively to Claudine but she would no longer look at him. The glares in his direction confirmed that the apology was insufficient to absolve him. He went to the table, to his coat and drink. Took a swig from the beer bottle. Regretted it straight away; he is not a swaggering man. Friends gathered around Claudine. She looked fine; he had not violated her. Not much. She pulled the emergency cord before he'd done any of the things he really wasn't going to do. Moss is a caring guy. Not an animal. Thought then that he must learn to read social situations more fully. He was embarrassed, Claudine a sweet girl.

He picked up his coat, moved back to the dance floor, caught her eye to say again, 'Je m'excuse.'

She turned away. Did not acknowledge him.

* * *

Moss walked to the door and left the nightclub. A distinct chill in the air. He wandered back to the centre of Angoulême. Without trying to locate it, he found himself outside the first bar the group attended. He went inside, alone this time. House wine. He drank it more quickly than he intended. Ordered a second, drank it slowly as he wished he had the first. Truly inebriated by this time. Must have been when he touched the girl's bottom. The explanation. As he drank the wine, he worried about seeing Claudine at the hostel. She would not forgive him, that much was obvious. Never done anything like it, bloody fool that he is.

The first draft of a plan entered his head. He finished the wine and headed back to the hostel. At the reception desk, he asked the warden for the return of his youth hostel card.

'Je vais,' he told the warden. He was leaving.

'Pour quoi?' asked the warden: Why?

He tried to make up a story, pretended that his mother was ill, but he could not find the words in the language. In the end, he substituted the word morte for ill. Stated that his mother was dead. A more extreme fabrication than he initially intended. The warden returned his card promptly, a look of concern on his face.

As Moss came passed the desk a second time, carrying his rucksack, the warden said, 'Attendez.' He gave him the thirty-five francs which the night was to have cost. Moss had not expected this. There are few refunds at youth hostels. His dead mother swung it in his favour. Inwardly he felt embarrassed. Liar, molester, swindler. He went out into the night, to hitchhike. To put distance between himself and Claudine. Flee from his offence. He felt annoyed that she did not accept his apology. It was her bottom and so he probably shouldn't have touched it. If she'd done the same to him, he wouldn't have made a fuss. From here on hitchhiking would be his obsession. No getting side-tracked by girls in towns he is only a beat from leaving. Never has been that guy.

* * *

Success. A lorry took him to Bordeaux. He arrived at one-thirty, a funny time to seek a bed. He contemplated sleeping on a park bench. March, France, cold. He saw a small, affordable hotel, no lights were on, the proprietors surely asleep. Walked on. Came to a church, a most impressive building. Could this provide shelter. The Catholic faith. Is there any other in this country? He tried the circular metal door handle. He has no faith but the door opened to him. Inside the church, he put his belongings on the back pew. Stretched himself upon it, his rucksack a headrest. Was he penitent? The girl could have made things clearer when first he held her close. Moss knows a bit about religion. He's read about most of them; a couple of memoirs by those damaged by strict Catholic upbringings. He was in a place of confession. No mileage in going over the evening past. He shouldn't have touched her, not on the arse, but it was no big deal. No hands inside clothing. He wanted to confess his love for Sharon MacDonald. They each loved the other—he believes that—it fell away too quickly. She moved, left Bury. Works as a waitress in a swish Manchester hotel. Seventeen years old. It sounds like a more mundane leave of absence than his desert destiny. It was for the best, his mother had said. Moss didn't argue. His mother knows nothing. He screamed at her inside his head. On that March night in Bordeaux, he wondered if she, Sharon, still thought kindly of him. He guessed that she would. There was not a breath of anger in their parting.

And back in the youth hostel, perhaps Claudine had found a little forgiveness for him too. It's possible. She became too emotional for them to work it out together. And there was very little between them to work with. Some kind of nothing. It was unlike the depth of feeling he and Sharon have for each other. He has fled any chance he might have had to redeem himself. Done so with both. Sharon and Claudine share a penchant for disco music. It wasn't the cause of the respective rifts but it doesn't help. 'Boom, boom, boom,' he shouted in the echoey church. He hates disco. Slick, crisp, backed by a string orchestra; even the clothes are false. Can't do your living in them, nobody hitchhikes in a dazzling suit. He abhors it—corny lyrics making love sound simple—funny that the girls can't see.

4.

How he has stumbled from there to here turns out to be just a few more dollops of the same. Confusion, misunderstandings, unintended selfishness. Moss always thought of life as a succession of challenges. Only now, in an Algerian prison the name of which is unknown to him, does he fear that he cannot rise above them. He lies on the prison bed, contemplating Abdul. He failed to challenge the giant until it was too late. Knew by then that the black-market money might be toxic. Couldn't find the words to ask about its limitations until it was already in his hands. Throw it away? Yes, he certainly should have thrown it away. Given it away. The snag might be his upbringing. In the house on Wolseley Road, to throw away an old carrot was profligate, food left on plates unheard of. At a young age, he and Gary would snaffle up any penny seen on the pavement. He once saw his mother—not dead, never has been—stoop to take a ten-pence coin from the gutter. Not to return it to its rightful owner, no such higher purpose in the Croft family. Don't let it go to waste. That is the family trait. Learnt in the cradle, deployed time and again without troubling the mind. A reflex.

Is he simply shifting the blame for his predicament? Anyone but himself. He would like to take responsibility for his actions. All of them. Kierkegaard said he should. Or Immanuel Kant. One of the big guys. Moss has doubts and questions and a feeling that nothing in this life is simple. Everything has its antecedents, there are many links in every chain. Thinking about it from the prison cell, he scarcely feels responsible for being who he is. Sniffle and quibble, this is Moss's lot.

5.

Two days have passed, Moss living between fear and relief. He has talked intermittently and pleasurably with Amastan. A single meal time punctuates each day. Watery couscous and a previously unknown form of vegetable matter, eaten in a noisy canteen. A feeling of wariness pervades. Prisoners all get a little time to walk in the fenced grounds, exercise. Moss was briefly terrified when two young prisoners fought like ferrets in a sack. Did it without weapons, and still both men were bloodied from the initial swinging of fists. The fight was not stopped for an age, a seeming age. When guards finally dragged them apart, one prisoner laughed and the other spat blood at him. Unpleasant.

For a period of each day, Moss has lost himself in The Glass Bead Game. Hesse's imagined world. Amastan is a good cellmate and, thankfully, not one to intrude when Moss turns face into pillow. Cries silently.

Then, on the third day, after these unasked-for experiences, he has a visitor. Moss has anticipated no such event. When a guard tells him the man is named Mr Graham, Moss thinks it a mistake. 'Is there another English prisoner?' he asks. It cannot be his former history teacher come to see him. That would be utterly absurd.

'Non.' The guard advises him that the visitor asked for Moss Croft.

The guard takes Moss towards the prison entrance and then turns down a corridor he has not previously entered. Recently painted—he can smell it—the walls are yellow. A photograph of an oasis in the desert hangs on the wall, Moss sees it only fleetingly. Recalls how he had hoped to see an oasis, a true one deep in the Sahara. That much was in his half-baked plan.

When he enters a small side room, Moss sees a man completely unknown to him, standing beside a small table. Two chairs await them.

'Hello Mr Croft, how are you?' asks the visitor, as the guard leaves them together.

'Okay.' Moss looks down, the man's face is searching his.

'Mr Graham, from the embassy in Algiers.'

'Oh, hi,' says Moss, looking back up, taking him in. The

man wears a smartly creased charcoal-grey suit, a plain blue tie. Polished shoes with rakish pointy toes. He might be Moss's father's age, too old by far for such fashionable footwear. Or not. What does Moss really know of the world beyond Bury? Mr Graham indicates they should sit in the chairs. He has a notepad already open on the table.

'The situation is difficult,' says the visitor and Moss cannot add to this truth. 'It...it would not be disposed of this way in our courts.'

Moss shakes his head, meaning agreement by it. He too has never heard of such a thing. Two years in prison for a seventy-quid crime.

'There is an appeals process...' Moss looks keenly at him. '...but it can be very lengthy.'

'Lengthy?'

'You know? Take months and months. Mr Croft...may I call you Moss?'

'Yes.' Moss nods. Mr Croft is his father, someone else entirely.

'Moss, you are young. I've a son studying in Bristol, about your age. This could happen to anyone. Foolish, don't get me wrong, very foolish but this prison...well. Prisons here can be very brutal. Are you being treated all right?'

'Yeah.'

'They have to look after you. They could make a mistake, a miscalculation, but it'd cause a hell of a stink if a Brit came to any harm in one of their prisons. Same as in Libya. A hell of a stink. Now, you know what they want, I take it?'

Moss shakes his head.

'Square root of everything, young Moss. Money.'

'I think they took my money.'

'What? Oh, your cash; I expect you'll get that back. They want a few thousand pounds. Paying off a fine, they'll call it. The appeal court sets it but, quite frankly, we can get something agreed before then. Now, Moss, what have you told your parents?'

'I've not.'

'You didn't get a phone call? Oh, that's ridiculous!'

'I didn't...I didn't know...' Moss feels responsible for his visitor's annoyance. At no time did it cross his mind to request a phone call. He will talk to his parents when he is out of jail. Or maybe not at all. At present he favours not at all.

'You must speak to them as soon as possible.'

'What would I say?'

'I think, Moss, the first thing is to reassure them that you are all right. That is truly the case, isn't it?'

He nods again.

'But ask them about money. It might not be easy for them but it could really help.'

Moss shakes his head. 'My father expects me to stand on my own two feet. I don't want them to know I'm in prison. It'll humiliate them. My father thinks...'

'A bit late for that, I'm afraid.'

'What! Have you spoken to them?'

'Not me. The boys in the F.O.'

Moss stares blankly back at the man from the embassy.

'The Foreign Office. It's standard procedure, you see. We have an obligation to inform the next of kin. I'm not sure what's been said beyond where you are.'

Moss feels alarmed. 'If they think it was cannabis, they'll kill me. Dad will. Mum won't stop him.'

Mr Graham shakes his head. 'But it wasn't anything to do with drugs, Moss. A silly mix-up about where and when to change currency. Outrageous putting you in here really, we're simply stuck with the rules of the host country. That's the lesson, young sir. It really is. True the world over, as you know by now. We'll get it straightened out. Trouble is, I think it will take a good few thousand pounds. It's a shocking climate at present. This nonsense in Tehran has got them all thinking that we can be played.'

Moss nods. In the man's restrained words, he feels a little hope. His life is not over, provided he can raise a vast sum of money and the cause of his incarceration has not been misrepresented to his parents.

'Anything you need young man?'

Moss thinks for a moment. 'Pen and paper.' Even as he says it, he contemplates Amastan's presence in his cell. Thinks it will inhibit him from setting down a poem of any sort. And his circumstances might only inspire those self-pitying verses he so deplores.

Mr. Graham lets out a sharp exhalation of breath. 'They should have supplied that already, you know? Prisoners' rights. The problem here—in this country—is that they're mostly illiterate. In a place like this, at least. They don't so much as think to provide that kind of necessity. Few writers you see...'

'The man in my cell speaks English. He's not illiterate, I'm sure.'

Mr Graham leans forward. 'Speaks English, well, well. Do you know what he's inside for?'

'He's a Berber. Some protest thing, he told me."

'Good God! In here. Are you okay sharing with him?'

'Yes, I like him. Why? What is it?'

'Oh, the Berbers are nice enough, I'm sure. It's not our corner to fight. Frankly, I've every sympathy with them. It's all become very fractious. I thought they kept them apart from Arab prisoners. Feelings running a bit strong and what have you.'

'I've not noticed anything.' As he says the words, Moss realises that he has probably misread every cue, picked up the wrong end of all sticks extended to him, since leaving Europe. Floundering since the Straits of Gibraltar. Nothing is familiar in Africa. He hasn't a clue what really goes on.

* * *

Back in the cell, Amastan is interested to hear about the visitor. He asks him what will happen next. Moss shares his new insight: money might secure his release. Tens of thousands of dinars needed to do it. Amastan lets out a low whistle, his theatre must get by on a fraction. 'Surely this is not possible?'

Moss agrees. The Croft family has no money either. Wishes do not open doors. He tries to explain why his parents will not raise the money. They cannot and will not. 'My father will think prison is the right place for me. Right because I've broken the law.'

Amastan falls silent. Seems to contemplate the boy's sad lot. 'You have an Arab father,' he finally says.

Moss knows his cellmate intends only to be funny. Finds there is no laughter inside himself. Perhaps the Arab-Berber animosity is just more racist stupidity. He keeps the thought inside, fearful of losing his only foreseeable friend for the coming two years.

* * *

The following lunchtime a prisoner on kitchen duties ladles the rank stew into Moss's bowl. In front of him, the English boy sees a different prisoner serving Amastan. The man takes the bowl from him, sloshes a ladleful in, and then spits on the top of it. Amastan looks into his eye before taking back the bowl, does it without further incident. Moss deliberately sits at a different table to his cellmate. From afar he watches the Berber eat the contaminated meal. Does he have a choice? And why, thinks Moss, did he notice no such incident until Mr Graham's words gave him cause to observe.

Moss knows nothing of the conflict between Arab and Berber. Not its origin nor its intensity. There is no hardness within Amastan except that which is essential to get from childhood to his present age in a ruptured country. He must be the only innocent in this prison if putting on a theatre play is truly his crime. And then he has to endure the indignity of eating another man's sputum with his food. Whatever way history has sculpted this conflict, in this prison and probably the whole country, it is the Berber who is the victim. Moss decides that any anti-Arab rhetoric Amastan shares, he will respect. The man must vent his feelings.

In the exercise yard, men pace backwards and forwards. Moss notes that some barge into, or push, Amastan. Once a week there is a football game in which prisoners participate. The tackles on his cellmate can be ferocious. Before Mr Graham spoke, the boy dwelt only upon his own misfortune.

Moss tries to talk to Amastan, to ask about how others treat him. He knows the topic is sensitive, his friend a proud man. The Berber's only defence is his capacity to tolerate; prison itself is the injustice. Amastan deflects the questions which Moss poses. He talks not about himself but about 'the people.' Moss knows this refers to the Berbers. They are the only people of whom Amastan has a truly positive sense. It is their cause he champions, although he is more than civil towards Moss. Sympathy for his plight, imprisoned two-thousand kilometres from home. And the man, seemingly, has very little concern for his own fate. It could be martyrdom which Amastan seeks.

From time to time the boy from Bury manages to make lighter talk with his Berber friend. Amastan enjoys this. They joke about other prisoners, talking quietly so that no one may overhear them. There is a vicious man—fat and proud—one or two prisoners kowtow to him. Amastan says that the man is an enforcer for a major black marketeer. He has harmed people who did not pay their dues, who failed to deliver goods as agreed. Life-changing physical harm. Amastan tells Moss that the fat man is utterly stupid, a man without thoughts of his own. He simply obeys orders. He has endured time in prison before and will do so again, never tells the court the names of the wiser criminals who control him. Moss had not thought before of prisoners accepting their fate. A price paid for the lifestyle they have pursued. This thug sounds frightening but Amastan only laughs. Calls him many rude names within the confines of the cell. He tells Moss that, if bidden by his criminal superiors, the fat man would break his own fingers. Punch himself in the face. With limited English and puzzling mimes, he says the man would bugger himself. If his masters asked him to, he surely would. Amastan tells Moss that he is certain the lumbering thug is a homosexual. The stupid man could not even guess what a girl is for. Moss finds the talk funny. Up to a point. The fat man is dangerous, befitting of Amastan's vitriol. If there is narrow-mindedness implicit in his discourse, at least he loads it exclusively on this one despicable bully.

Moss makes a joke about Amastan's name. He hopes this will be funny without complications. He tells him that the English equivalent of Amastan is Stan, Stanley. Amastan shrugs but Moss tells him it is a good name. He describes the comedian, Stan Laurel, and as he talks, they find that Amastan knows who he is. He has seen him in silent films, funny films. Amastan had thought Stan Laurel to be French, quickly accepts Moss's certain knowledge that Laurel and Hardy are American. Even that the slimmer one, whose name he shares, was originally—in common with Moss—born in Lancashire. The name Stanley sticks. Amastan amuses Moss by scratching the hair on the top of his head in a way familiar to both. As Stan Laurel did in those funny movies. Moss enjoys these moments. They feel more intimate than anything else that has happened in prison. In Africa. The concern of Mr Graham was an unwelcome reminder of his disinterested family. The spirited talk of Berber dignity is not Moss's fight. Either can whisper the name Stanley to lift the spirits of the other. Roll it around the cell, invisible to guards and other prisoners. An amusement for two.

6.

At night, lying under the single blanket on the hard-slatted bed, Moss hears Amastan snore. He likes the sound of it. This man deserves some peace. The odour in the cell is unpleasant. Two unwashed bodies; their fetid piss pot. The stench is no comfort at all. A guard told him earlier in the day, when Moss asked in his most thought-through French, that all prisoners will shower tomorrow. Douche means shower. The guard said a lot more but that was the word Moss most confidently understood. He tried to ask if he would be showering alone and the guard laughed. The boy cannot tell if it is to be enjoyable or loathsome. A crocodile of naked prisoners hosed down as though putting out a fire. That is what Moss is preparing for.

It may have been this image that prompts Moss to think about his visit to Madrid, his stay in the youth hostel there. It is a recollection he has relished more than once since it occurred just thirteen or fourteen days ago. A number of days he is struggling to count precisely. It is the first time that he has deliberately brought it to mind since entering prison. Since the presence of women has completely slipped from his life. The distasteful smells in Al Aricha Prison are unremittingly male.

* * *

On arrival at the city-centre youth hostel in the early afternoon, he chatted breezily, at the hostel check-in, to an Australian girl. A woman really—definitely older than him—could have been thirty. Maybe she was younger and her outdoor lifestyle had worn her skin more hurriedly. Small and slim, youthful in all but those additional facial lines. And it was her pretty face that drew him to her. Joyous laughter lines. She looked at him through eager eyes, brown, black in the centre, and always darting across him. Up and down, then looking away. If she was older than him, she was also the more overtly youthful. Playful, elfin. In many ways he is a child, dreaming of becoming a free spirit. She—Annalise was the name shared within thirty seconds of meeting him—had arrived at that destination.

They were both at the hostel half an hour before it opened, they talked together in the porchway. Glad for the shade which gave respite from Madrid's afternoon heat. The sun was intense although it was only March. Nobody else was waiting to enter the hostel and her company is a pleasure to recall. In this prison, it feels priceless to have had that time alone with the girl. A reel of mental film to draw upon. Annalise told Moss that she was on her second trip to Europe. Slow interrail journeys, taking months and months. Doing the western parts, having travelled in Greece, Yugoslavia and Italy four years earlier. She was planning to go from Madrid to Portugal and then on to Madeira. She believed that island to be the fabled Atlantis of yore. He instinctively disbelieves such conjecture but decided she might have this one right. Annalise looked like a girl with a nose for these things.

He held her lovely tanned face in his gaze throughout their talk. And she smiled back at him, made animated gestures that Moss thought atypical of an Australian. He had little experience with which to back up this rumination. She professed love of the outdoors, and he reckoned then that this had tautened her skin. And, however hardened her flesh, she couldn't have been warmer of heart. He liked the crease lines that kept her brown eyes smiling no matter what shape her mouth drew to express the emotions her many tales provoked within.

'Your journey's all mapped out then?' he observed.

'No,' she replied, 'I just go with the flow. What happens will.'

He liked that phrase, appropriated it for himself over the following days. He would go with the flow. There could be nowhere better to venture.

Moss told Annalise that he had been in the Prado art gallery earlier in the day. 'Have you been there?' he asked.

'Loved it. The air feels cold in some galleries and then suddenly as hot as Darwin looking at the one of Adam and Eve, all of the Dürer nudes. Did you find that?'

Moss concurred but only because he loved the description. The sense that looking at paintings might make one feel hot or cold. He had not actually experienced it when he was there. Wondered if he should go back. Try again. In fact, he couldn't recall seeing the Dürer nudes, his fascination with Francisco de Goya utilising all the time he spent in the gallery. He changed the subject fearing his enthusiasm for but a single painter might expose his ignorance of the art form. 'So, you're not from Darwin, then?'

'Tasmania,' she replied, 'the cold part.'

'Tasmania, wow. But you're so tanned.'

Annalise laughed. 'That's my Italian blood. We Aussies are a mixed bunch.' Moss knows his geography, the location of the island of Tasmania; no knowledge beyond its position on the globe. He asked her if she lived in Hobart, hoping to sound more worldly than his hours spent staring at an atlas made him feel. 'No. No but you won't have heard of Launceston. My dad has a caravan park there. Good swimming but—I speak the truth—it's Australia's arsehole.'

'You're kidding. Holidays, swimming: doesn't sound so bad to me.'

'Because you've never lived there three-six-five. Childhood in the Bianchi household was just me all on my lonesome. I played with kids in the caravan park now and then, all my schoolfriends lived miles away. Six miles to the nearest. The site was round the coast, far from town. Dad spent all day everyday fixing caravans and counting his money. I left at sixteen for good and all.'

'You've not been back?'

'Oh, once or twice but not back-back.'

Moss contemplated this, while looking into Annalise's relaxed and smiling face. The girl had left her upbringing squarely behind her. Spoke of it dismissively. May have come through a more troubled childhood than her pretty face would ever let show. Was this to be his lot? He never spoke of his mixed-up feelings towards home, while worldly Annalise had dispatched her sorry past to history.

'Your mother?' he enquired with caution.

'She was there going quietly mad. When I left, it was her big chance. Divorced and upped sticks for Melbourne. I think she lives with a fella.'

Moss fell silent. He could not read how Annalise felt about this.

'Good luck to her. She was barely in my life at the best of times.' Then she looked into Moss's face. 'Don't look so worried for me, sweetie. Everyone has shit. I'm like a cat, I buried mine in Tasmania.'

'Will you be going back? To Hobart if not the Launceston place.'

'Fuck that,' she said, a grin on her cheeky face. 'I could manage Sydney. Or I might stick around. Make a life here in Europe.'

Moss loved that answer, her certainty that the break was clean.

As they continued to talk, Moss shared with her that he had fallen out with his father. He hoped to live in a place better than Bury when these travels were over. There was no future for him there.

'I'm Italian, did I say,' sparkled the girl. 'Can't speak the language but I've got the looks, don't you think? Could go and live in Rome if they'll have me.'

Moss told her that she really does have the looks. He felt himself redden slightly as he said it. He liked looking at her so much.

* * *

The pair were the first to check in. Moss had gone straight to the male dormitory, chosen a bed, and then back to the communal area where he hoped to see her again. Annalise wasn't there. He waited twenty minutes, looking at the novels on a shelf while he did so. A sign in four languages said they may be taken free of charge, replacements politely encouraged. Interesting but he wasn't fifty pages into the first of the books he travelled with. Shouldn't take if he couldn't donate. Disappointed not to see her, he returned to his dorm. Decided to shower; hoped to run into her later.

He found only a single showering room. He opened the door tentatively. There was just a sign for water on the door, a tap with a spray of dotted lines emerging from it. No indication if it was for men or women. For hombres or mujeres. Once inside he saw an array of cubicles, all behind heavily frosted glass. The nearest was open. Each had slatted wooden flooring on which to privately undress, adjacent to the plastic shower tray.

'Who's that?' enquired an Australian accent from the only occupied cubicle. Moss could see the outline of a figure; she was completely obscured by the opaque glass. He would not have known the gender without her call.

'It's Moss,' he replied. 'Annalise?'

'That's me, all right.'

'It seems like mixed showering here.' He only said it in

case she'd not noticed the set up. Thought him an intruder in the ladies' bathroom. 'Don't mind me.'

Then to his surprise, the door to her cubicle opened, her smiling face angled out. An index finger beckoned him to join her in the small cubicle.

Go with the flow, she had said that. The phrase was stuck firmly in his head. The thing to do. It was tight for two on the small square of wooden slats; Annalise's jeans and T-shirt were hanging from a peg, she had yet to remove her underwear.

'Let's shower then,' she instructed, tugging demonstratively on the belt of his jeans. 'Mixed showering is mixed showering, my friend.' He loved the way she called him friend. Rhyming it with wind in her antipodean accent.

As pleasing a prospect as this mixed shower was, he felt uneasy. Inexperienced. Talking at the check-in was hardly a date. He'd liked her instantly but nothing had prepared him for such physical closeness. An evening alone at Sharon's house flashed into his mind, not the last time he saw her, just the beginning of the end. He had told his then girlfriend that he had purchased a packet of condoms. Hoped that they could up the dial on their intimacy. Sharon shyly declined—even shed a tear—said that she was not ready. She was only seventeen, he almost three years older. He tried to accept her decision graciously. Apologised for being so forward. They managed a couple of further dates but his misstep destroyed the connection between them. And he had loved her. Thought her so clever, so funny. Sharon moved to Manchester, picked up hotel work there; he feared he had frightened her away. And now this: Moss and Annalise alone in the shower room. Not that others couldn't walk in at any time, see their two bodies through the frosted glass. He quickly learnt that the Tasmanian girl had fewer inhibitions than he. More successful previous encounters from which to draw confidence, he surmised.

More than zero. Annalise became efficiently naked and stood beneath the shower. Moss stole glance after glance of her lithe body. Loved the sight of her small breasts which stood up in the stream of water. She smiled encouragement, gestured that his jeans needed lowering. Making and breaking eye contact second to second.

He pulled off his T-shirt and as he emerged from it, the Australian girl had turned the water off. Stared at him, as rivulets traversed her nude body. Trickling from the dark hair on her head. 'What's that, Moss?'

He felt embarrassed by his odd home-made money belt. The soft linen around his midriff, with its stiff leather pocket inexpertly sewn to it. It looked to be amateurishly made, looked because it was. He told her he kept his money it.

'That's good,' she replied, 'I thought you'd patched up a war-wound. And I don't shower with veterans, I like the free and easy ones.' Moss fleetingly wondered if he was free and easy, tethering his meagre personal wealth so closely to his person. He liked her casual acceptance of him. She was again turning herself under the cleansing might of the shower head. He removed jeans and underpants and stepped over the lip of the shower. It was too small a space for two and they were virtually embracing as they washed. Moss found himself touching Annalise's breasts. No accident but he tried to look as uninvolved in the event as he could. The girl smiled and pulled him closer still, a hand to the back of his neck bent him into a momentary peck on the lips. Then his hand fumbled around her hip, strayed a little to the side before the girl pulled it back up. 'Not on our first shower,' she admonished. Smiling, almost nose to nose.

Moss felt embarrassed by his obvious excitement. Annalise quite unfazed. They enjoyed further naked embraces. She let him brush soap from her small firm breasts. He quickly learnt the correct etiquette for mixed-showering. Under the jet of water, she allowed him greater visual feast than Sharon ever had. Moss prolonged the shower like a Sunday morning lie in bed. The tiny Australian girl—woman—put her arm around the back of his head once more and pulled him into a kiss of passion. He imagined they were beneath a waterfall in distant Tasmania. Spoke not a word of his corny fantasy.

When both were clean—body and not mind in Moss's case—Annalise turned off the tap and began to shake her hair. 'Another time, Buster,' she said, lightly tapping his still-eager cock as she stepped out of the shower onto the wooden slats. And as she said it, the external door opened and someone else was in the shower room. Through the frosted glass Moss could only just make out the passage of this new person. Saw the figure walk up to the room's far end. No gender evident until a gentle clearing of a throat suggested it was a woman. Not certain, probable. The new showerer must have seen the double silhouette of Moss and Annalise through the glass. Walked past, put a few cubicles between herself and the frolickers. It only now enters Moss's head, as he contemplates the events from his prison cot, that the girl, woman—man with a high-pitched cough—would have guessed the showering couple to be two men. Homosexuals. Possibly even two women. Surely not the improbable couple that were he and Annalise. He could not credit why this should be so, knows that if he had stumbled across such a scene, he too would have given it a wide berth, sought not to hear. Not to know. Not that it would have been his business—straight or gay—but he is certain two men would have been his assumption. The most probable furtive activity in a public washhouse.

In the small prison cell, with its stench of body odour, piss even, the boy from Bury feels as if he might cry and cry for the leaving of Madrid. For never again speaking to

Annalise after so intimate an encounter. He planned to hitchhike from Madrid to Toledo the following day. A plan he stuck to. The Tasmanian girl—the enchanting free spirit who bared him her soul and her body—did not enter the hostel common room that evening. Nor did he see her at breakfast the next morning. Perhaps Annalise bathed with men as his parents' generation had done with loofas. An essential accessory. He had dared believe that the implied second shared shower which she promised his uncontrollable member would arise as unexpectedly as the first. His newfound habit of going with the flow seemed the most likely way up that sugar trail. From his current vantage point, he adduces that the likelihood has receded to an impossibility. Annalise will never enter this prison. And he realises how much he fears the proximity of these prisoners in the humdrum of eating and showering. Of exercising and sharing mutually bored time. As unpredictable as Annalise with none of the rewards. He knows, with uncomfortable clarity, what chain of events has brought him here, what he has done. His fearful focus is now upon what he must endure. He has lost the desire to be a free spirit. It has fled his confinement without him.

Chapter Three

Oran to Ghardaia

1.

That was hairy, thinks the boy. Ended well but scary hairy. Good thing he didn't use the shoe. That was his favoured spot for much of the previous night. The change of mind was pretty last minute. He walks briskly from the border post feeling buoyant and, curiously, a little closer to tears than he can explain to himself. Then he slows his pace down, does so deliberately. He feels their eyes on his back; he must show no guilt in his walk. He expects the frizzy-haired one to be watching him. Could be the other one but he seemed busier. Not so likely to be him. Moss does not turn round. Not his neck, not his torso. No cheerio wave for the two customs officials who have jiggled his innards this way and that. He squirmed like a worm, knows that he did. They did it deliberately—all that searching and questioning—hoping to catch him out.

What a swindle! That's actually the headline in his brain. Quite a scam. Not well executed, that minor failing he has to grant. A poor show but he made it through to the other side. It brings to mind his chemistry O-level: the exam was a displeasing blur. His first date with Sharon MacDonald, which occurred more than two years later, was the only time he shared his theory. The exam board muddled the papers, awarded him somebody else's good fortune. His A grade was unjustified by the rubbish which dribbled out of his pen on examination day. Today was just the same. He has evaded capture, arrest, only because the customs officials can't see an open goal. He didn't piss his pants but everything else about him said keep searching. He quivered his way passed. Nonchalant: that must be a proper smugglers demeanour. He found out he can't do it; always struggled to tell a joke without a grin climbing onto his face. Trying this palaver was stupid. The first and last time; never doing it again. He didn't cry, confess or take out the roll of dinar to offer in evidence against himself. Short of that, he was useless. He leans his head back, tries to avoid laughing although he supposes that the men at the customs post have long stopped watching by now. They might have found themselves another mouse to play with.

Both customs officials left him alone to put his shoes back on. That was their final shot and he still worried the little bundle would tumble from his sleeve while he tied the laces. The innocence they finally prescribed to him will have saved them some paperwork. That seems to be the way of things down here. North Africa. He has walked a fair way into the country now. The quickest glance over his shoulder tells him that. The customs cabin is a tiny cube as he looks back, and the border fence just a line in the dusty shale. He thinks his heartbeat is returning to normal.

Take off your shoes, the older guy, the one in Arab clothing, had gestured to him. The boy knew all along that the shoe was only the second most likely place to find his stash of cash. Frankly, they had been a lot warmer when they were prompting him to remove his money belt. That and the frisking. He feared the roll of notes might magically appear from his armpit while the flimsy linen caught on his jeans belt. They only saw his legitimate money though, the travellers' cheques. They let him put his homemade contraption back around himself; he thinks they were looking away when he adjusted his rolled-up sleeve, felt the money still lodged there. It never budged.

The customs officials were bunglers. That is why he is inside their country, not banged up like a bad 'un. He laughs. Not just to himself. The actual sound of laughter machine guns from his diaphragm. Relief is part of it, and the frizzy-haired guard was hilarious. 'Laurel and Hardy,' he says out loud, then checks himself. Laughing is one thing, talking to yourself pure madness. His lips move silently: 'I've been searched by Laurel and Hardy,' he says at no volume at all. Without stirring the dry air of Algeria.

* * *

The sun beats down, prompts him to take off his sweatshirt. It has done its job. He has walked an age from the checkpoint, more than a mile. Out of sight now. He bends forward and slowly pulls the garment over his head. Briefly, his left-hand holds the cuff of the rolled-up right sleeve and then, as it unfurls, his right-hand travels down the sleeve, catches the little bundle of dinar. He feels the squeaky texture of the rubber band that holds the notes in their tight roll as he clasps it in his sweaty palm. Money and its assigned anxiety, elation too. He pushes it into his jeans pocket then, with both hands, shoves the sweatshirt under the tightly drawn flap of his rucksack. Those two clowns were really trying to unnerve him. Asking questions about hashish. Is anyone so stupid as to say, oh yes, I've got some of that.

He can't stop thinking about it. Analysing what went wrong. What went right! It was a hell of an ordeal. Moss was acutely embarrassed by the hole. When the older man asked him to take off his shoes, his thoughts turned from the fear of them finding his illicit money to the inevitability that they would see—laugh at—the English boy with a hole in his shoe. The left trainer has a small gap. A half inch of navy-blue sock, big toe, visible to the discerning eye. He started thinking what a wretch he looked, while knowing it was the hole that attracted him when he was thinking where to hide the money. By using the right shoe, when left has a hole in it, he'd considered it possible that they wouldn't search either. The shoes looking an inadequate hiding place, somewhere contraband might fall from of its own volition. That was his initial reasoning. He only changed his mind when he was dressing in the hotel room, decided that the idea was too double edged. What if the customs officers thought exactly as he had done? Followed his mental footprints to the bounty. And he only stopped worrying about the money up his sleeve when their scrutiny of the shoes started him fretting that he looks like a pauper. This is the way to survive such a mental assault, he decides. Give off a different kind of worry than the one they're after. The smell of embarrassment masking the whiff of concealment.

What a swindle! He sweated buckets but he's got away with it. Inside the elusive Algeria with twice the spending money he originally planned. A kick in his step which his weighty rucksack cannot inhibit. He did it. Back in Bury he neither met nor heard of a single soul who has visited this place. Algeria. Moss Croft has really struck out, made his mark. Adventurer, smuggler. Everything is looking up.

Walking in Algeria feels good. Hitchhiking to the Sahara: first he dreamt it and now the finishing tape is in sight. And with a little extra cash for good measure. He got a bit close to having his hands chopped off back there, he thinks. Winces at the crudity, the inherent prejudice, he hears within his overstated rumination. There may be a hint of truth in it, of course. He hasn't the first idea about the law of this land. Moss isn't one for breaking rules, not generally. Doesn't like them, doesn't disturb them; never in trouble at school. Nothing more than a hundred lines; talking in class or tie askew, shirt untucked. Good thing he got lucky when he went big. Smuggling. He was definitely on the cusp of something nasty back at the border post. Just like the chemistry exam, he is unsure how the hell he dummied through. First the older customs official was getting excited when the younger one was acting friendly, then the younger one got a sniff of something but the older one didn't believe it. If they'd gotten their act together, Laurel and Hardy could have caught him red-handed. Clueless officials like that don't deserve success. Teasers of the long-haired and repeaters of 'You have the hashish? You have the dinar?' Abdul probably sends quite a few tourists across with money hidden upon their person. Maybe that's why they had to close the other border post. The smugglers' holding cells full to bursting. A big thank you to the French girls who brought him out here. The Laurel and Hardy crossing.

He stops in his tracks, thinks a serious thought. Annalise said she likes to go with the flow. And he does too. He doubts she lets it carry her into true danger. Police and courts, floggings or custodial sentences. Free spirits mustn't throw away their liberty. Moss has tried this smuggling malarkey but, in truth, he didn't like it. He's retiring from the game. One not out. Not much of a score, it'll do this cautious boy.

* * *

A couple of cars have passed him by without Moss so much as thinking about putting out his thumb. Absorbed by thoughts of the customs post for these fifteen or twenty minutes. He shakes his head of long hair, lets the worries fall away; searching and questioning consigned to history. Off comes his rucksack. No cars are in sight as he draws the roll of black-market money from his right-hand trouser pocket and quickly slips it under his T-shirt. Unzipping the pocket on his money belt, sliding it in. Then he tucks his T-shirt into his jeans. He hears rumbling. Turns to face the oncoming vehicle. A lorry approaches from the direction of the border post. Moss puts out a hand—a little tentatively, the lorry is travelling quickly—as it approaches it begins to slow down. He looks at the cab window, sees the driver is smiling, braking. The English boy has hitched his first ride in Africa. Effortlessly done.

* * *

Cigarette in mouth, an Arab of slight build, a small taqiyah cap over his closely shaven head, drives his lorry deeper into this new country, Moss ensconced in the passenger seat. It is not the driver's own country, he is a Moroccan. The landscape is rocky and barren. Moss says 'Merci' to the driver a few times. Cannot think what else to add. The smuggling story is not appropriate, and it's the only thing on his mind. Then the driver starts talking. Rapidly in French. Moss follows it pretty well for the most part. The driver laughs at the stupidity of the Algerian customs post—unbidden by Moss—laughs at his own all-Arab tale. Hours and hours he waited. He tells the boy about it in words while banging a hand on his steering wheel. Smiling, laughing. The border police documented a search of his lorry, 'formalités administrative.' Moss understands the term, thinks it a bit rich. The Moroccan complains about the Algerian when needless paperwork, those same formalités administrative, seem to occur in both. An obstacle to entry into a hotel room, never mind bringing a lorry into another country. The driver relates having to wait while someone more senior came to sign off his passage. 'Fou, fou,' says the Moroccan: Crazy, crazy. All along the lorry was 'vide.' Moss doesn't initially understand the word, the driver mimes it, pretends to open a box or parcel, then shrugs when he sees what is inside. Moss doesn't understand the charade but the lorry driver tries an alternate word, 'rien,' and Moss knows this one: Nothing. The driver is on his way to pick up 'viands.' He will collect meat in Algeria. The lorry has brought nothing into this country. It is empty until the pick-up. Algeria purchases little from its neighbour. Moss laughs with the driver when he grasps the point. The customs officials took forever to sign off a lorry full of bugger all.

The boy from Bury reflects silently on his own crossing. No wonder the border guards spent a long time searching him, they had only the lone hitchhiker or the empty lorry to give meaning to their work. Perhaps the lorry driver has smuggled a little something in, same as Moss. Sweet hashish or cheaply bought Dinar; the customs officer's incompetence could be common knowledge out here. Moss knows better than to ask. He guesses that nothing much goes across this border. It is not Calais, Cherbourg, nor even Ceuta. Morocco and Algeria share a substantial border: a thousand miles. Crossings may be few. The mutual suspicions of each nation were evident to him. The military presence; the border post near Oujda mysteriously closed. The French girls said that Algeria is strict, they favoured Morocco. Moss intends to remain open-minded but he is already finding it a strange place. The searchers of empty lorries and battered training shoes seem laughable, there could be more to it, of course. An enigma inside a grain of sand.

The driver comes to a halt, puts the boy down on the red and dusty roadside. A track leads to a large abattoir. Moss is on the edge of a town named Nedroma. He shakes hands with the driver, both touching their hearts after doing so. The way it's done here. Rucksack back on his shoulders, his tatty shoes advance the boy further into this unlikely country.

* * *

Two cars pass him and the third stops. Hitchhiking in Africa is child's play. He wonders if it is the company of strangers which drivers seek or if his blond hair—the stand-out westerner—is the attraction. He was never exotic in Bury. The scorching sun is the more favourable light. He can be who he pleases down here. Where the past which resonates is not his own.

The driver of his second lift in Algeria is not as chatty as the first. He glances over Moss, surveying him up and down, then turns away. Makes no eye-contact. The man must be fifty years old—forty or fifty—how skin wears in this dry heat is unknown to the boy. He wears a tailored suit with a small Arab cap, it looks funny. The suit is in poor nick: stained, a tear or two exposing frayed silk lining. Moss wants to point at his left trainer, say, Touché. His lips won't let him, senses this man is not the joking kind.

The driver addresses him in Arabic—the boy assumes that is the language—it is neither French nor Spanish and his standard in each of those is only rudimentary. Moss says, speaking in careful French, that he wants to go to Oran. Towards the large city further up the coast. As far in that direction as the man is able to take him. The driver's face never changes; no understanding appears shared. Perhaps he simply dismisses the request. He says one word repeatedly; an Arabic word, Moss assumes. The boy can only shake his head, does not know what it means. Then the man pulls the car over. He makes a sign with his hands, a crude mime depicting the curvature of a female body. Moss thinks he has grasped it, says the word, 'Femme,' in an attempt to verify, and the man nods, even appears to dribble. Moss shakes his head, to himself as much as to the driver. He worries where all this is heading. More so when the man points at the boy's privates, at his genitals. 'A-ha, a-ha,' laughs the Arab. 'A-ha, a-ha.' Then he turns back to the steering wheel, removes the handbrake. Drives on.

Moss asks the driver to stop, to let him leave the car. Still this man fails to understand, or he wilfully ignores the request. One or the other. The boy wished for a free ride and so he is getting one.

They enter a residential district where houses—each a white stone cube—line the road in symmetry, in close proximity to each other. There are bicycles next to some of the dwellings—a contraption that might be a child's wooden go-kart—but no gardens, little plant growth. The occasional window box offers a tiny splash of colour. The man is driving the car erratically. He slows down to the pace of a woman walking on the roadside. The car veers towards her, to the left-hand side of the road. The woman is wearing an unusual form of traditional dress, not something Moss ever saw in Morocco. She has covered herself comprehensively, a dull off-white robe with many folds on the massive garment; the headdress obscures her face, allows only a single eye to look out. The driver of the car has already wound down his window. He shouts at the woman, makes a hand gesture in her direction. Moss is concerned that he might be shouting obscenities although he shares no language with which to confirm this guess. The woman turns away, flaps a dismissive arm and then pulls her robe back down when it reveals the flesh of her arm. She does not engage with him beyond this rebuttal. She might be angry, being shouted at would do that. Moss cannot really tell what's going on. The woman turns her one available eye away from the driver as he crawls the car alongside her. Drives at her leaden pace. When she steps up to a house, after briefly looking into his car—an impatient flick of the hand and an Arabic word for him that Moss thinks may sit between 'go away' and 'fuck off'—the driver chuckles heartily. 'A-ha, a-ha.' He should be ashamed of the reaction he has drawn but it seems he is not. The car accelerates away as Moss again asks to be let out.

Following this awkward encounter, the man drives only a short way before drifting back onto the wrong side of the road. No other traffic is present at this hour in this neighbourhood. Another woman, this time with a small child at her side, is walking on the roadside. She also wears the one-eyed headdress and again the driver shouts at her. Moss cannot see the woman beneath the pale, off-white robes. They shield her from being known. As she walks, he observes that her clothing clings a little to her figure. Her waist is narrow, the sway of her hips visible. Moss guesses that a young mother is within the strange clothing—she holds the toddler's hand in her own—her face masked from him. The driver goes through a similar routine to the one he performed for the previous lady. Draws her attention with guttural Arabic that makes Moss wince. His shout is more penetrating than it is loud. In response, the woman gestures towards her child. Moss thinks her hand-signs mean she must feed the child; he cannot work out if she is demanding money for food, or walking on because she has her own plans for feeding this little one. Every word is outside his grasp. Hearing Arabic is like hearing music, there is tone but no meaning. The driver might be requesting sexual favours. That is Moss's sense of it but nothing is terribly certain. He may have divined it only because the man pointed at his balls before shouting at these veiled women. Why they cover their entire bodies excepting the left eye eludes him. Devout Muslims is his guess. He thinks it utter madness to shout sexualised language at them. Like doing it to a nun. Perhaps something else is occurring here. The driver might know the women although neither appeared pleased to see him. Moss even wonders if the driver is the runaway father of the toddler, perhaps it is access to the child which he seeks, not sexual favours at all. This second woman turns away from the car, discharging an angry phrase. It could be the same one with which the earlier woman signed off. The man laughs, 'A-ha, a-ha,' turns to Moss and again points at his privates. Moss signals that he wishes to leave the car but the man gives no indication that the request has been understood. Brief eye contact as one might experience with a cat or a horse. At no more than double walking pace, the car bumbles on.

The driver slows the car alongside a third woman. Another who dresses traditionally, one solitary eye looking out from her cocoon. The driver rasps a few fast words at her. Moss is surprised to hear this woman converse with him although she too sounds displeased. She speaks fluent, measured Arabic. Calm and insistent. The man struggles to get in a further word. Then, to Moss's surprise, the woman lifts the cloth from around her face, holding it on the top of her head with her right hand, she leans into the now stationary car. Her unveiled head invades the driver's window. Her features are hard, ugly even: an asymmetrical face. She is not old but life has weathered her, scarred her cheeks and chin. The man speaks rapidly when she lets him; he reaches inside his jacket and shows her his open wallet. A fat wad of notes stuffed in there. She drops her veil back over her face, covering one eye, the right, leaving only one with which to view the world, points a finger at the wallet, speaks softly now. Then the woman looks across at Moss, eyeing him through her restrictive headdress. One-eyeing him. She whispers quiet words to the driver. The tone no longer sounds to hold any complaint. Not as far as the boy can tell. The man turns off the car engine and signals that Moss should get out. As he does so, he quickly opens the rear-passenger door, pulls his rucksack from the seat behind him. The man shakes his head, indicating that he might leave his pack where it lay but the boy ignores him. The man has emerged from the driver's seat and the woman physically attaches herself to him, holding the driver's upper arm. She speaks through her veil, then lifts it once more and pushes her sullied face very close to his. The man is shaking his head and signalling for Moss to come closer to the woman. Moss ignores it, swings his rucksack on to his back and gives the man a short, definitive wave. A goodbye. The man snorts, flaps a hand, then quickly extricates himself from the veiled woman. He steps forward to Moss, shakes his hand, touches his heart. The boy mirrors his actions, does so only from politeness. There has been no warmth, no fellow feeling, in this lift. Then the man goes back to gesticulating, shouting at the woman as if to break the entente they have briefly found. As Moss turns away, the woman suddenly screeches an Arabic phrase in his direction. Moss keeps moving, believing that he can feel the three-eyed stare of man and woman upon his back.

What just happened here, he ponders? The sun is so high in the sky it must be noon. The never-again smuggler guesses that a man he doesn't know or share a language with has tried to purchase sexual favours for him from a woman he doesn't want. He worries that this might be the contrivance of his own dirty mind. No alternate explanation comes to him but that does not prove his hunch correct. The customs, this second hitch, the unusual attire of the women: very strange. It is not going to plan because there is no plan. At least he is getting the nose for when to go with the flow and when to step out of the stream for a few minutes. Let pass what he cannot embrace.

* * *

Moss walks towards what he hopes will prove to be the centre of town. Nedroma. He sees signs in Arabic lettering; many inexplicable posters bearing a photograph of a white-haired old man frowning. A strong smell of raw meat finds him through the stultifying air. A solitary market stall, only a single vendor in sight. As he moves past, he comes into the ambit of a more putrid stench, garbage piled by the roadside. Maturing in the midday sun. Moss sees a pack of dogs on the road—pauses—very unsure whether he should pass them at all. They might be feral, rabid. While he stands motionless, his hefty rucksack pulling down upon his shoulders, watching the dogs sniffing each other, fear leaves him. He alone has arrested his movement; men, women and children pass the dogs without worry. They give them a pretty wide berth and no dog approaches them. Safe passage for the townsfolk. If it were not so they would not be here, calculates Moss. Not in the long run. Algeria is strange, it is not uncivilised.

He resumes his walk; he had overthought the danger of the dogs. Then he thinks on the oddity of the women with their one-eyed veils. He spots one up the road. Only one, most women here wear headscarves. Normal ones. The round of their whole face visible to him. Not the hairline but both eyes. Moss recalls the girl in the tourist office in Oujda. Looked nice, all smiles and welcoming eyes. He is growing to enjoy the appearance of girls' faces peering from a circle of cloth. The one-eyed variety look plain weird.

* * *

In the centre of town Moss hits on an idea, the bones of a plan. At the border, entering Algeria, the older of the two officials wrote down how much money he brought into the country in travellers' cheques. The roll of dinars tucked into his sleeve—the black-market money which Abdul conned him into buying—never made its way onto the paperwork. He guesses that, when he leaves the country to cross into Tunisia, they will count his money once more. Little point doing it on entry if they don't do it on exit. And then the goons at the next customs post might put two and two together, figure out that he brought in some illegal currency if he has spent none of the travellers' cheques. He has been thinking about this as he walked across town. He could say he slept in the desert, tell the customs officials on the Tunisian border that he fasted. They would not believe him—too unlikely—and it might be an insult to the whole country. In Morocco, the state and the populace had a singular purpose: make the tourists spend. That was why young Mohammed had taken him to his father's carpet factory when he had wished only to go to his home. Shaking the shekels out of visitors is the national sport. He hasn't experienced it in Algeria yet. Expects it will come. If he arrives at the next border flush with a sum of money indicating he has spent none here, they will, at the very least, frogmarch him to the gift shop. And Moss hates spending money on rubbish.

The plan drawing itself together inside his head involves changing a sum—forty pounds should cover it—into Algerian dinars. He will keep the paperwork, have a story to tell of his modest but believable spending. The additional money, alongside the greater sum which he is hiding from officialdom, will make him a rich traveller. It could be fun. He could take public transport rather than hitchhike, not that he has any knowledge of Algerian buses and trains. Trains are great but if one goes to the Sahara, it is news to him. It might be impossible: sand dunes would blow across the tracks, bury the line for months at a time. Hitchhiking was always the plan so he should stick with it. So far, so easy. Hotels with hot water, and food that does not prompt spasms in his stomach, will be his money's target.

He finds a bank—French language signage, can't miss it—and walks through the front door. The air-conditioning feels a welcome contrast to the sweltering outdoors. The bank is empty but for two staff at the counter, both are ladies in headscarves. He walks up to them, talks to them in his best French. They say they will change his money. Happy to do so.

'Attendez,' he says, stepping away from the counter and out of their line of sight. He lifts up his T-shirt and fiddles quickly with his money belt in order to extract the paper folder of travellers' cheques.

'Monsieur,' says a throaty voice and he realises that one of the ladies from the counter has walked around to see what he is doing.

'Je m'excuse,' says Moss, trying to tuck himself back in. 'L'argent.' The woman is young, she is chuckling. Perhaps she feared a heist but found only an English boy undressing. It is funny, the joke on him. He waves the travellers cheques at her. 'Pour changer,' he announces.

'Ici,' the woman says, wagging a finger for him to return to the counter. Then she unleashes a delicious laugh. He goes where she points and the other lady holds a hand out for the cheques. She is much older, doesn't seem as amused as her colleague. Both wear white headscarves around their faces, a little black hair protrudes from the scarf of the younger one. Moss keeps glancing back at her dark eyes; the older, sterner woman conducts the transaction. She keeps her head bowed. On his instruction, she tears two twenty-pound travellers' cheques from the perforated booklet. The woman asks for his passport, gives him a form to complete. He sets to work on the task. There are more questions than he anticipated. Occupation, date of departure from the country. It is as tedious as checking into a hotel room. The younger bank teller comes back around the counter, offers to help him. He realises he is sweating a little. His stash of black-market dinars was in the money belt. He can't imagine she saw it while he was tinkering away down there. Can't have. She tries to explain a question to him, one that he has left blank. It asks where he is staying. 'Je vais aller à Oran,' he tells her: I will go to Oran.

133

She takes the pen from his hand and writes something in the space. The meaning of her contribution is unclear to him: Arabic, all curves and dots. 'Tout est bon,' she says: Everything is good. Although he enjoys the timbre of her voice, her dark eyes, Moss decides that he wants away. The copious paperwork is tiresome. It comes at him thick and fast in North Africa. He imagines the stern-looking lady copying his signature, attaching it to a concocted confession. I am a dastardly smuggler, it might say. Nonsense but he can't get it off his mind. The older lady is counting out money for him, passes it across the counter, and he says, 'Merci.' With a single heave, he hoists his rucksack onto his back. Two paces towards the door, he turns back, a smile of thanks for the younger girl. For her rich voice and beautiful eyes.

As he leaves, the girl calls him back. Moss ignores the cry; he has the money, done here. Stepping into the sunlight, he looks left and right, up and down the street to orient himself. Decide where next to go. Two steps forward and he feels a hand on his upper arm. Flesh on flesh. He turns and the younger bank teller is looking into his eyes from just a few inches distance. 'Votre passeport,' she says, handing him the essential document.

He feels like a fool. Why run from her? A girl who wants to help. 'Merci.' He would like to hear that laugh again; can't tell a joke in French, nor know what a girl like her might consider amusing. 'Merci,' he repeats and the girl nods, retraces her steps into the cool interior of the bank.

Moss contemplates what it is that makes him feel—with every form filled—that he is cheating in an exam. Again, he wrote student in the box marked occupation. What difference does it make? He could write poet laureate or rat catcher to the Queen. The forms are pointless, no one reads them. Not in a million years. Deep in the Sahara lives Saladin, a paper-eating monster to whom every last shred of the tedious forms is fed with a pitchfork. The more time spent writing the answers the more nutritious the meal. The creature—a Sphinx of enormous proportion, stomach expanding as the papier mâché inside grows and grows—thanks all the pasty Europeans for their time and effort. It kept their delicate skin from the oppressive sun for the duration of the form filling. Gobble, gobble, gobble. Then Saladin shits it back out as sand. Moss has figured out why the Sahara's expanding, figured it within a couple of hours of arriving in-country.

* * *

He feels hungry, hasn't eaten since Morocco. Moss walks across the road to a small café. A cold sandwich is prepared before him. It is odd, not like any he has eaten before. Flat bread, no visible grains. He is game for what comes. Nods at his slim stomach, it must prepare itself. The café owner—or employee, he cannot discern which role the man fulfils—is friendly. Indicates to the boy that he might like some sauce drizzled on to the meat filling. Moss nods again. Why not?

He takes his sandwich to eat in the town square. Two bites in and the chilli sauce makes his eyes water. Got suckered into that one again. He is hungry, averse to waste. Soldiers on, eating and sweating.

Two boys come across the dusty street to speak to him. Ten or twelve years of age, judging by the size of them. They seem to be laughing at him, may have noticed his struggle with the chilli sauce. Or it could be his European ethnicity that amuses them. He has heard English people laugh at foreigners many times, it's their turn.

'École?' asks Moss. They should be in school.

'Finis,' says the smallest of the Algerian boys. Finished for the day or finished for good, Moss would like to know. Cannot think how to ask without implying either that they are lying or their country is backwards. Before he can form a question, the older-looking boy asks him where he is from. 'D'où viens tu?'

This strikes Moss as a cheeky question. The boy's use of the informal tu suggesting a familiarity which they do not have. The boy is skinny, wears a thin smock with buttons down the front. He has seen circus clowns wear similar. Like a housecoat but of firm fabric. And it is covered in red dust, must have been rolling on the ground. The other boy wears western clothes: jeans cut away at the knee; a T-shirt advertising Coca-Cola. The same red dust on his clothing. The impertinence, the over-confidence of the boys, is a quality Moss lacked when he was their age. A good show in a kid, he thinks, smiling conspiratorially at them. 'Manchester,' he says. Bury is too insignificant to register in Nedroma, Algeria. 'Je viens de Manchester.'

'Manchester United,' they say in unison.

Moss smiles, nods. 'Oui.' He makes kicking and heading motions. Tells the boys in his piecemeal French that he plays football for Manchester United. They laugh and shake their heads while beckoning him to come with them. He puts on his rucksack and follows them across town. Periodically biting chunks from the eye-watering sandwich.

The boys lead him a short way. They move easily, light steps, while the English boy sweats beneath sun and rucksack. Through a ten-minute walk they exchange names and the boys make incomprehensible jokes. Then Coca-Cola points at a large wooden structure ahead, a sports stadium. The boys lead Moss to an entrance; they stop a few yards from it. A turnstile restricts entry, a man to the side of it looking at Moss and the boys.

The boy in the housecoat shouts, 'Manchester United,' points at their new friend. The man on the gate calls out in Arabic to Moss, beckons him to come forward.

'Football? Le ballon?' Moss asks, wondering if he will

have to demonstrate his overstated prowess.

'Ici,' says the man, ushering him through the turnstile. Moss thinks he ought to pay something to pass into the stadium but the man—beard, kaftan and a taqiyah cap upon his head—requires no money. His status as a Manchester United player has swung it. He wonders what team might play inside this small stadium. At pitch side he sees just a few hundred people watching a game of football. They play on a shale surface, something that the boy deems more suitable for tennis than soccer. Then he checks himself, he should be going with the flow. The pitches constitution suits the town, the climate. He has yet to see a blade of grass in Algeria. Or feel a drop of rain.

He finds the game to be competitive, fast, though not of an especially high standard. Before he has fully taken it in, the referee blows his whistle. Full-time, Moss thinks, it explains his free entry. However, the players stroll into the centre of the pitch, huddle in two groups according to their strip. This is half-time, managers or captains are verbally inspiring their teams for the battle ahead. Round two. A few people close to him try to attract Moss's attention; they point at his rucksack. An odd thing to carry to a football match. He would like to talk with them but finds the heat exhausting. Moss places the rucksack on the bench beside him. Other spectators give him space. He wonders which is the home team. In England he is wary of shouting for one side unless he is confident it is that team's supporters he is among. Here he is neutral. Couldn't be more so: neither team's name is known to him.

The second half commences. Moss wonders if the soccer players are professional. Guesses they are not. As the game unfolds, he finds himself mesmerised, as he can be watching Bury FC or the Wednesday night football highlights which he and Gary used to watch on television. He notes the flair players, their imaginative passing and bold runs stirring the crowd while also enjoying the more predictable, the ebb and flow of the commonplace. In his languid stupor, Moss is surprised and shocked to see, following a challenge of no great intensity, two players throwing punches at each other. Other players pull them apart but, as the referee whistles for play to restart, the same two men resume swinging at each other. This time the shrill whistle blows for longer. It seems only to presage greater mayhem; other players join the fighting. Moss guesses this may be about some underlying team or town rivalry. The innocuous tackle on the field could not have been the sole precursor to such anarchy. The crowd on the opposite side of the pitch are shoving into each other. Moss sees a small swathe of them fall over in unison. Before he can fathom the scale of the unrest, police are on the field. They hold batons in their hands. One blows loudly on a whistle as if to supplant the referee. Some spectators, older ones, seated on benches, stand as one, and the boy wonders if they are leaving or joining the fray. They seem to be conflicted by the choice while Moss feels instant certainty. Leaving his chosen option. His earlier close shave with authority—at the border post—was sufficient for one day, no wish to become embroiled in whatever ruckus this is. He tries to be inconspicuous as he departs. Blond hair, giant rucksack. Fat chance. And as he moves through the thin crowd, Moss notes how the throng parts for him. He has a certain status. He cannot name it or understand its parameters. He is clearly not to be mistreated; men angered with each other pause to smile at him as he walks by.

And he did like the cheeky boys, their easy acceptance of a man from faraway England. They secured him free entry to a football match. Weren't to know it was a ticket to a riot.

* * *

From the stadium, Moss quickly makes his way to the main highway. The town of Oran is on the signposts. It is over a hundred miles away. Many more kilometres. He senses that dusk is nearing but wishes to leave this inexplicable town. Not for him fighting and one-eyed prostitutes.

He arrives at the entry to the fast road, the main route east. He comes across a long line of hitchhikers—eight or nine individuals or pairs of youths—all thumbing lifts. He must wait in line. He recalls a similar experience in the Alps the previous summer. Two hours wasted, compliant with hitchhiking etiquette, as those who got there before him attracted lifts. Today he is feeling lucky, rules are for the unimaginative. He stands in place at the back of the queue. Will not overtly annoy these fellow practitioners of his art.

In France, it had been girls, single or in pairs—foolish to be trying, some might say—for whom the cars always stopped. Picked up first every time. The order of arrival made little difference if a good-looking girl showed up. Here in Nedroma—the whole of Algeria, he supposes—female hitchhikers are not in the game.

At the back of the straggly queue, with a trick or two in mind, Moss balances his rucksack on the roadside. Its metal frame does half the job and the boy also wedges two small stones under the right-hand corner. With that, it stands upright: an imperious rucksack. In his head, he hums a tune, a song by Templeton Ca., the thinking man's light-rockers.

Our horses eat on the open pastures

He only mouths it, barely a sound. It's the first line of a favourite. Slowly, he starts to dance to the music inside his head. It is not a good or an elegant dance but it is unexpected, extroverted. Expresses the joy he is feeling. A free spirit hitching a lift in Algeria. He starts to let the words out of his mouth. He's not got a great voice but he's sung along to the record many times in his bedroom in Bury.

> *Come the morning you'll not even see us*
> *We will have gone to where the wind is born*

This might set him apart from other hitchhikers. All are trying to leave Nedroma on this late April afternoon. Only Moss dances. He gives the chorus a bit of volume. They might know it around here. Might not. A young Arab hitchhiker a few yards up the road stares open-mouthed.

> *The caravan moves on and on*
> *Just the way it's always done*
> *Today it's here, tomorrow gone*
> *The caravan moves on*

With this fitting song—and on the word, caravan—the boy jumps across his rucksack. A funny and slightly athletic move, it draws attention to the unlikely balancing act that his belongings perform. The word comes around again and so he repeats his splay-legged jump. The caravan is moving on. As he begins to sing verse two a car slows down, those inside looking at him as they pass. It comes to a halt at the front of the queue. Moss saw four adults inside. The passenger door opens and a woman emerges. She wears western clothes, amusement writ on her elegant Arabian face. Pick a hitchhiker, any hitchhiker. She points down the line to the boy at the back. 'Tu, tu,' she says. He can lipread it, see that her finger is directed at him. It is Moss Croft, the boy from Bury, who this car has stopped to pick up. The handsome woman will take no other.

* * *

The lady wears jeans, a yellow blouse with navy-blue embroidering and a small scarf around her neck. It is not across or covering her jet-black hair. He thinks this means something. That she is not so religious seems about the size of it. And nor is he; Moss has no time for superstition

Oran to Ghardaia

whatsoever. She ushers him to the rear of the car. Her attire is casual—a pair of jeans—and still she might be the most elegant person he has ever stood next to. A face both alive and calm, he feels befriended before she has spoken more than the simple 'tu' which picked him out of the line-up. Gave him reason to believe his good fortune is multiplying. She takes the rucksack from the boy and starts to lift it into the already-full car boot. Moss tries to assist; thinks her too refined for such physical labour. The Algerian lady is gently assertive, lifts it despite him. She might be his own mother's age. Forty-something. Slim and rather tall. She speaks to him in the clearest French, asks where he is from. 'Angleterre,' he replies, and she begins to speak in his language. Not fluent but better than his own French.

A man, her husband Moss presumes, sits in the driver's seat. He smiles warmly when—boot closed nonchalantly by his capable wife—the pair come around to enter the car. The lady opens the rear passenger door and a girl, who he thinks may be his own age, certainly no younger than Sharon MacDonald, wearing jeans and a black sweatshirt bearing the emblem of a single silver palm tree, emerges.

'S'il vous plait,' she says, inviting Moss to sit in the middle of the back seat.

He realises that her clothing is similar to his own. Far cleaner, casual, no headscarf in sight. A young man—the girl's brother he presumes—sits against the far door. He turns to shake Moss's hand and then touches his heart. The girl gets back inside the car to sit beside him. The three young people are packed in closely and Moss feels nothing but acceptance emanating from them. The Templeton Ca. song worked a treat.

'Where are you going?' the family members ask him in two languages.

'Oran.'

'We also. We live in Oran. Nous habitons à Oran.'

They are so pleased to have him in their car, to talk with him, to drive him along the coast to their hometown. And the feeling is mutual. Moss relaxes for the first time in Algeria.

* * *

They drive towards distant Oran. The young adults in the car—Soufiane and Asia, the names they have shared—insist on talking English with Moss. A long day gets easier. The pair are remarkably fluent. Moss learns that this family have holidayed in Paris, Rome and London. Enjoyed a visit to Moscow three years ago. It's the first time this hitchhiker has met anyone who's been there. The father, Mustapha Lellouche, says when asked that he 'works for the post office.' Moss guesses he does more than deliver letters. He might manage the regional postal service for Oran, for all Algeria. These are the first North Africans he has met who know Europe.

This company is more cultured than any he mixes with in Lancashire. All four are exceptionally polite. They defer to his knowledge of the west, of British and American lifestyles, while their many insights evidence that it is quite unjustified.

Soufiane is a well-spoken young man. A tendency to mild sycophancy in his conversation. When Moss explains where Bury sits on the map, the young man says, 'A cooler climate than London then, which I recall was oppressively hot.' He studies geology at the University of Oran and seems to regard Moss's arrival in his family car as manna from heaven.

Asia tells Moss that she is not yet at university; she is to attend at the beginning of the next school year. She tells him that she looks forward to everything about university life except parting from her best friend, Samira. The English boy hears great weight in her voice as she speaks of this.

The parting will be a wrench, the price of her education.

He suspects Soufie—as the sister calls the brother—of playing his first joke on Moss while Asia is telling him about her best friend. The sister speaks of shared interests, even shared and borrowed clothing. Soufiane says, 'She will be your girlfriend.'

Moss does not initially respond to the comment. When Soufiane presses him, he confirms that he does not have a girlfriend. There is such a vacancy. Moss tells him that he is travelling through Algeria, plans to be in a different country before the month is out. Without saying as much, he wishes to imply that this is not a good basis on which to form a relationship with a friend of his sister.

'Samira would like to travel,' says Soufiane.

Oran is far along the coast of this vast country. The young people talk as Mustapha drives: life in Europe, in North Africa; pop music; student life, which Soufiane enjoys and Moss has fabricated a version of for himself. The boy seldom confesses his unemployed status. Annalise alone has drawn it from him on this trip. When there is a lull in the conversation, he finds himself picturing the girl named Samira. Why he should do so is a puzzle even to Moss. Asia—who sits beside him—is very attractive, of a similar build to the Australian he was briefly close to in Madrid. He thinks she might be a fraction taller, a fresher, darker complexion. She wears her black hair long and loose. Asia is off-limits. He senses it, cannot put a finger upon how he knows. She shows him genuine warmth but he thinks it an extension of the family's welcome. Moss is still to fathom this culture. He doubts if Islamic girls meet boys or date them the way they do in Bury. Moss imagines that Samira might look like Asia. The offer of her as a girlfriend suggests that she is more available. An Arabian free spirit. Or it could be that Samira weighs twenty stone and has no front teeth, that the very suggestion was dredged up from a wicked streak hidden deep within Soufiane.

The English boy enjoys the speculation, expects even time will not reveal an explanation. When they reach Oran, he will head for a hotel, never to see these good people again. He likes them, it is his best lift by a distance. Soufie's joke about the impossible girlfriend is a riddle.

* * *

When Soufiane and Moss hit upon a common enjoyment of music, there ensues a long talk about American and British pop stars. One likes them all, the other is more choosey.

'Johnson Ronson really rocks,' says Soufie.

Moss finds something comical in his use of the slang. And he was praising the corny music of Ronnie Prousch just a moment before. 'He's good. Do you like Templeton Ca.?'

'Moss, Moss,' says Asia, voice rising, 'we purchased their record last week. Their latest.'

'I bought it,' says Soufiane proudly, pointing a finger at his own chest. The man with the same taste as their guest. 'Not the record. I have the cassette tape recording.' He dips down to his feet where he has a small holdall. From it he fishes out his latest musical possession. 'Baba, Baba...' he starts to say.

'Yes Soufiane,' says Mustapha, 'must we all endure your music now?' He plays a role, his tone of voice holds no complaint.

As the small spool is handed across, Moss sees the cover. We Are All Here. Not their latest album at all, released in nineteen-seventy-eight. Moss loves it. 'Side two,' he whispers to the boy.

'Put on side two, Baba,' says Soufiane.

Within moments the car is full of sound: The Caravan Moves On. Moss wants to tell them he was dancing to this song when they picked him up. Cannot, it would sound too foolish. No song played on the roadside but his own coarse singing. No dancing either, not in a manner likely to catch on. Jumping over a rucksack is not the Charleston.

> ***We build the bridges that bring you together***
> ***Lay down the roads and the railways too***
> ***Connect town to country to commerce***
> ***Shovelling, hammering, all that we do***
> ***The world turns with our shoulders to it***
> ***Heave-ho, we're making it spin***
> ***Turning the soil and hauling the water***
> ***Together, we can do everything***

'This is a very nice song, boys,' says the refined lady. Moss relishes her approval, hears it as he might were she praising a poem from his own pen.

* * *

Later, during this long car journey to Oran, the boy from Bury enquires if Mustapha and Khadidja—the latter is the name the siblings' mother has insisted he call her—have any knowledge of reasonably priced hotels in their home city. This elicits an alternative offer from Khadidja. 'You are a student, Moss. There is not much money for students, even in Angleterre.' He is not a student but has misled these people into thinking he is. On the money front, he doubts if this family will see merit in his smuggling story. He may never tell it another soul; Sharon McDonald would appreciate it should he come across her again. Called him a lucky sod for getting his inflated chemistry O-level. 'You would like to put your head down with us, Moss? In our home.'

He loves their company. Moss agrees without reflection. The whole family are delightful. The prospect of a hot shower sounds terrific too. He doesn't think to object, to imply it is too kind of them. As they drive along, he finds it a gift that they speak his language. This family superior to his own, he feels he belongs with them and not in Bury. Khadidja picked him out because of his amusing rucksack dance while his own father denigrates hitchhiking start to finish. There's no contest.

When they—the Lellouche family—comment how great it is that Britain has a woman as its prime minister, Moss hears only how forward thinking they are. Khadidja says it first and Mustapha backs her up. Then he queries if she— Britain's ground-breaking premiere—is not also a bit too right wing. 'We like the lady more than the iron,' he says.

Moss feels himself in total agreement. Strongly dislikes Margaret Thatcher while seeing that a woman in charge is progress in its own right. When Mustapha takes up the theme, says a little more, that her plans may create problems for the British people, Asia laughs out loud. 'Baba, Algeria is about twenty times worse.'

Moss is able to join in when he hears the whole family laughing. He likes dissenters.

They are driving through darkness by this time; Moss thinks about his own family so far away to the north. His father has gained nothing from Thatcher's reforms—there is less work for self-employed plasterers—but he adores her for reasons that make no sense to Moss. That she has pulled the rug from under the unions, made a lot of working people poorer. His mother votes the same way as Ronald, never contradicts him. And then Gary too. 'It couldn't go on how it was,' he told Moss when confirming that he also voted for the hectoring woman. Moss alone could read the runes, saw the middle-class warrior for what she is.

Reflecting on it here, he thinks how wonderful it is to be among the broadminded. Being in a country with dubious politics of its own, makes it doubly surprising. Moss feels inordinately lucky to be in this car, heading to Oran. A night in the home of a like-minded family. The first of his life.

2.

Sunlight angles through the drawn blinds, slices of brightness cutting into the edges of the lounge floor. Moss grunts from under a blanket, from the firm leather sofa. The lounge of the Lellouche family home. Only as he stirs, as Khadidja calls out, 'Good morning, Mister Moss,' does he truly awake. Recall where it is that he sleeps. She comes to him and places a hot beaker of tea in his hands. Beneath the bedclothes, Moss wears a pair of Soufiane's western-style pyjamas. Khadidja is still in her night attire. An unfastened towelling robe around her, thick flannel black-and-red-checked pyjamas cover her where the robe falls open. 'It is the Earl Grey, English tea.' The leaf is unknown to the common boy from Bury. 'Qu'est-ce que c'est?' she asks, and he sees her point at his crudely handcrafted money belt which lies on the floor beside the sofa.

He feels flustered. Knows what an odd and irregular garment he has fashioned for himself. 'Pour mon argent,' he explains: It is for my money.

The kindly lady furrows her brow. 'Sois prudent avec l'argent ici,' she tells him: Be careful with money here. There can be nothing to fear in this family home, she might be saying something darker than he has heard before about Algeria. Or it could be typical motherly advice, he's not had much of that. Not any he paid attention to.

The boy's clothing—the content of his rucksack minus books and camera—is in the family's washing machine. The party only arrived in the house at ten o'clock and all were ready for bed. A strict rota of showering occurred beforehand. Moss insisted he should not be first although Khadidja offered it. He thinks himself overly spoiled by these generous people. Felt guilty, the smuggler among saints. He insisted Asia showered before him, then, putting her head round the lounge door in her towelling robe, she said, 'Moss, Moss, go to the water.' He had smiled gratefully at her. This house is an oasis to him, their ways familiar and superior to any life he has so far known. Khadidja leaves him to drink his tea having advised that he should dress and come to breakfast. His clothes are elsewhere and he missed the chance to say so. To remind her.

Moss contemplates what he knows of them, the Lellouche family, and it amounts to only a little. Their house must be in a residential area of Oran. It was too dark on arrival to glean what type of neighbourhood he is in. He thinks it detached, his guess based on the holiday destinations they spoke about, not visual confirmation. Mustapha, the father, is well-educated, authoritative and kind. Moss heard him speak tenderly to each of the family members and even with appreciation for Moss's contribution to the conversation. A man of standing who listens attentively to an unemployed boy from Bury, although Moss remains coy about his employment status. Khadidja is so obliging. Her warmth is motherly, never ingenuine. She loves her children, extends that freely to their new friend. He recalls how she insisted on putting his clothing into the family washing machine at ten-thirty at night. 'It will help you along,' she said. He cannot imagine his own mother being so thoughtful. Not to him, not to Gary. And strangers don't get across the threshold at eighty-two Wolseley Road.

Soufiane is endearing, probably the same age as Moss, give or take. He is in his second year of university, has a generous nature. Pressed Moss for details about Johnson Ronson and the British band, The Browns. Moss had been so keen not to disappoint that, for a short time during the car journey, he even sang along with Night Shift. Never told Soufie that he thinks it maudlin, The Browns' very worst song. Both the Lellouche kids called it their best. And when Moss reflects on his male friends back home, they are coarser by comparison. Not rough boys—although Bury has plenty of them—but none would state their views nobly, expound upon their tastes with such evident commitment. Soufiane has class.

And Asia? In the night Moss found himself thinking of her; attracted to her, as he had told himself not to be. She has an easy relationship with her brother. Less passionate about music, more so about politics. She did not hold herself aloof and yet Moss felt there was something reserved about her in comparison to girls he'd known in Bury. Compared to Sharon or more so Annalise in the hostel in Madrid. And he is intrigued, tries to dismiss it but cannot, that she, Asia, followed Soufiane's lead in lining up her friend, Samira. His next girlfriend: what a promise. 'She will make a nice amour,' Asia told him quietly when the conversation lulled during the long drive here.

* * *

Fearing the family might consider it rude if he stays away, Moss walks self-consciously into the kitchen. All the family except Mustapha have gathered together. Soufiane immediately runs from the room and up the staircase. He returns clutching a navy-blue dressing gown which he passes to Moss. Khadidja and Asia are both in dressing gowns and pyjama's and he is pleased to be no longer underdressed. Soufiane wears jeans and a T-shirt bearing a facsimile of the cover of Corn Belt, the best-selling Johnson Ronson album.

'Where is Mustapha?' the English boy asks.

'Working,' says Khadidja, 'always working. He did not wish to wake you. It is important the children sleep.' And he did sleep, thinks Moss. Slept like a baby in their welcoming home. When requested, he sits down at the kitchen table, eats a little bread and cheese, drinks coffee, the constituent parts of the Lellouche family breakfast.

Soufiane tells his mother that their guest should stay another day and night. Turning to Moss, he says, 'We will show you Oran. And we did not eat properly together yesterday.'

He nods enthusiastically, then looks at Khadidja. 'Ça va aller?' he politely asks: Will that be okay.

Khadidja pulls a serious face; Moss guesses that she has other plans, that it is inconvenient for him to remain. He regrets accepting Soufie's offer before asking. Then the mother puts her right hand above her breast and breaks into a smile. 'The children so happy you here,' she says. 'Of course you stay another day.' Her contemplative face was a tease; she is not a mother to deny her son his wish.

'Merci,' says Moss. Repeats the word, 'Merci, merci.' The mother reaches both arms out and pulls Asia and the English boy gently towards her before just as quickly releasing them. Feeling an astonishing warmth in that fleeting embrace, Moss wonders if his presence is concurrently doing some unknown good for this family. He cannot think why else they would draw him—a long-haired boy with little more in this world than the modest stash in his crummy money belt—to their collective bosom.

* * *

At Khadidja's request, Moss takes a pile of freshly laundered clothing from her. With it he returns to the lounge that doubles up as his bedroom. He quickly folds away his bedding and places it discreetly at the side of the room. He chooses fresh clothes from his limited range, puts his money belt on first and then jeans and a T-shirt. Assembles the rest of his clothing into the main chamber of his rucksack. There is a knock on the door and he calls out, 'Come in.' Asia tells him that they will go and see the biggest mosque in Oran, the boy smiles back at her keenly. It is the company and not the destination which motivates him. She adds that she has a surprise for him, before turning for the door. Leaves without telling him what it is. He has an inkling, a firm idea, but not of how he should react if he is correct.

The three young people put their shoes on in the porch. Moss feels self-conscious about the deteriorating state of his left trainer; no other seems to notice. They set off from the house. Looking back, the boy from Bury sees Khadidja smiling from beneath her luscious hair. She patted his head kindly as she saw them off, a quick Arabic expression spoken to Asia at which her daughter laughed. Moss imagined only that she encouraged a good day. It feels to him like she is his mother: a surrogate he is too old to seek but grateful to have found if only for this two-night stay in Oran.

It is eleven o'clock on an April morning and already the sun burns.

* * *

Together the two siblings and Moss stroll through the neighbourhood in which the Lellouche family live. It lives up to the boy's expectations: a cleaner and better maintained district than any he saw in Nedroma. Soufiane speaks of life at university. He says that the students have diverging opinions, then he uses a phrase new to Moss. 'There are those of us who have forgiven France and there are those who have not.' Moss senses a sombre warning: he is with friends but the people of Algeria are not all like Soufiane and Asia. Moss hates colonialism—it is the left-wing position—his hair colour and the pigmentation of his skin may lead many in this land to assume he bats for the other side.

Soufiane declares that university suits him and then

posits that this is equally true for Moss. The boy simply nods. He does not enjoy lying but, having already spun the yarn that he is a student, he cannot contradict it. Does not wish to declare himself a liar alongside the unemployment he might correspondingly confess.

As they walk, he hears Asia, behind him, talking in Arabic. When he turns his head, he sees another girl of a similar age to Asia, walking arm in arm with her. This girl is, with her free hand, removing the headscarf that she wears. The new girl lowers her eyes but Asia smiles, mouths the name, 'Samira.' Moss is awestruck, she is the most beautiful girl. An inch taller than Asia, long black hair falls around her narrow face. She is carefully but casually groomed. The headscarf's removal leaves her in tight jeans above which a simple white T-shirt clings to her slim body. Her exposed arms are delicate, richly tanned, all shades of bronze in the intense sunlight. The boy realises he must speak. Cannot just stare, pleasing as the prospect is.

'Bonjour,' says Moss, to which Samira giggles quietly. Soufie has stalled their conversation and Moss falls in step with Samira, with Asia at her other side. The siblings talk of a girlfriend has prompted it. He has no clue as to Samira's thoughts on the match. And the words he has inside himself—the wish to learn who she is, to understand their unlikely prediction—remain a silence of unasked questions. He glances frequently at Samira's face, beguiled by her quiet nobility. The depth he senses behind her dark brown eyes.

'Les cheveux sont longs,' says Samira: The hair is long.

Well, thinks Moss, if that is a problem, it can be rectified. Khadidja must have a pair of scissors back in the house. He would sound a fool to say such a thing out loud. And maybe he is exactly that. Crossing Algeria, dipping into the desert. Just one more night in the company of this inviting family. Soufiane's promise of a girlfriend in Samira was surely a joke. Asia might be showing him off to her best friend: amusing to relate. Her family—generous spirits that they are—have picked up a boy who danced by the roadside. The Rucksack Jumper. He is a curiosity, not Cleopatra's suitor. He guessed overnight that this intrigue would have a sting in its tail but finds the only flaw is the sheer impossibility. He does not live in Oran. He feels attracted to Samira and it isn't even half the story. Like the headscarf-wearing girls of Fes or those strange one-eyed women of Nedroma—as the English boy thinks of them, behind their discomforting veils—Samira is beyond his comprehension. This takes time to shape in the boy's mind. Asia and Samira, Soufie too, look and talk like students might in Manchester, London, or Paris. They enjoy similar music, wear the same clothes. It crosses Moss's mind that Soufiane's contemporary Arabic music collection, and Samira's headscarf—which she has tucked away in her sizeable handbag—are the deviations. East not west. Interesting to him but obstacles to many westerners, to those ex-colonialists who seek no forgiveness. Believe their country can do no wrong. He pictures Samira again in the small item of traditional clothing which she was removing when first he saw her. If it expresses her culture, he is pleased for her. Provided he can see both eyes; please, Allah, don't give the poor girl a squint. Minor divergences should not be cause for division between people. Fingers crossed. Moss has read a bit about Islam, can't make head nor tail of it.

And North African girls—Moroccan and Algerian—are never quite western. Covered. Not always the faces. Legs certainly. Whether it is those great potato sacks they wrap around themselves or the nicely cut jeans of the two he accompanies today. The knee is forever unseen. He has the good sense—the reserve—not to question this incessant genicular obscuration. The social mores are different here, and it is for him to accept, absorb, not try to change that which is none of his business. It is the interaction, the shy smiles and friendly irrelevancies of their words, between he and the few girls he has come across in North Africa, that has been strangest for him. They behave like twelve-year olds, shy in male company. It prompts in him a hitherto unknown need to do likewise. Asia has been different; he infers that her interest in him is purely an engagement of intellect. She is an attractive girl; however, she has spoken to Moss as a boy might. Not without femininity but without giving it directly to him. Samira, he thinks, is as firmly wrapped and indecipherable, as Annalise had been loosely wrapped, quickly unwrapped. One closed and one open book. He finds her mystery intensely desirable. Soufie's prediction that she would be his girlfriend was prophetic, whatever the joke and however impossible that it might come to pass. Her face will be lodged in his mind on his dying day.

* * *

They stop to sit in the shade beneath a spreading tree. Only then does Moss recognize that they are in a public park, his attention diverted since the girl joined them.

Samira asks—her English less precise than her friends—'What subject you study at university?' Before Moss can answer she adds, 'You go Oxford or Cambridge?'

This is awkward for Moss, requiring him to lie a little more. He wonders again if he has been foolish to embellish his life story. When first he joined the car, coming from Nedroma to Oran, he doubted that the Lellouches would have been so welcoming of an unemployed factory worker. Thought the parents may not have wished such a person to sleep under the same roof as their daughter. He sees now that they are of a broader mindset than he thought likely upon meeting the elegant Khadidja. They are themselves while Moss is stuck inside a work of fiction.

'I'm at Manchester,' he tells her.
'Manchester United?'
'No, the University of Manchester.'

Through her scatter of questions Moss sees that Samira is not as worldly—as Europe-aware—as Asia and Soufiane. This delights him. He cherishes hearing from someone who lives a life alien to his own. But what should he ask of her? She is not an exhibit. The siblings' portrayal of her as in need of a western boyfriend may even be unkind to Samira. A joke upon her. He cannot guess the punchline and a girl so fetching cannot want for suitors.

When pressed he tells her, as Asia and Soufie listen in, that he is studying English literature. He hopes it is not a subject they are able to grill him knowledgably about.

'I study geology,' says Soufiane. 'I think it a practical subject. It will help me secure a job more easily than literature might. Algeria has work in oil exploration and mining and I might also choose to work abroad. America, for example, which I think more difficult to enter just for reading books. For the study of literature.'

'I will study psychology at Tlemcen,' says Asia, taking up Soufiane's topic and not as its champion. 'We were visiting the university yesterday. Driving home from there when we collected you.' Moss enjoys hearing those words, learning that he was collected. 'I could study criminals but, truthfully, I like to understand more about all kinds of people. Not only evil-doers. What it is that makes some of us think one way and some another? I will not be studying with any job in mind, doing it foremostly so that I expand my understanding.'

'Yes, Asia,' says Soufiane, 'it is a good course for you. It is quite different for boys. You will never have the responsibility of being the head of a household.'

Moss sees the logic in the young man's words while thinking they belong to another age. Back in Lancashire, men head most of the households, excepting those who have made themselves scarce. Buggered off like Sharon MacDonald's father. It is patriarchal nonsense and having a woman as prime minister proves it. Time's up, it cannot go on for another generation. The vista must look different here in Oran, Algeria. Even in the Lellouche household. 'What will you study?' he asks Samira.

She looks a little crestfallen by his question. 'Je ne vais as étudier,' she replies: I will not study.

Soufie adds excitedly that her parents plan for her to marry. They are at an early stage, a suitable boy neither found nor agreed upon. As he annunciates these facts, he gives Moss a knowing wink. 'She must marry before she is twenty.'

Moss is shocked, he glances from Soufiane to Samira. She has lowered her eyes, so different from the steady gaze she gave him when naively asking about his studies. He wants to query whether she is fighting back. Presumes from the first that Samira does not wish to comply with her parent's wish. What has it got to do with them? Setting a date, a deadline, without a suitor in sight, incenses the boy. How can they? It is hardly a trivial detail.

He turns to Asia, not wishing to embarrass Samira with ill-thought-through questions. 'Would you marry if you were not in love?'

She thinks a little before answering. 'I hope Samira is in love when she marries. Or perhaps a little later. Weeks, maybe months. Love comes to people who dedicate their lives to being together.'

This answer surprises Moss. He had presumed that his host family share the western values with which they seem so familiar. Now he starts to see them as a bridge, rooted in Algeria, in the Arab world, visiting Paris and London with truly open minds. He wonders if he has failed in his travels to date. No idea how to be so acceptive of contrasting outlooks. He falls back on the conclusions he would have drawn had he never come here. Asia's words about marriage are alien to him but perhaps she is wise and he ignorant. Asia was raised by Khadidja, by Mustapha. A steadier hand than Ronald Croft.

'Will you have an arranged marriage?' Moss directs at Asia.

The prospective psychology student narrows her eyes before answering. 'There is a boy,' she says. 'His family are like my family. We are waiting and thinking; we expect to marry but nothing is...' She pauses, takes her time to find the words '...set in the rocks, I think you say.'

'But you are in love?' he asks, slightly bewildered now. Asia betrothed? He never expected this; his contrary assumption based primarily on her youth.

She grins at his question. 'Not yet,' she says, 'but I like him, his family. He is a clear-thinking man.'

They walk on in silence, eventually broken by Soufiane. 'I have nothing arranged and will keep it this way while I am at the university.' Moss does not respond, a most obvious thought lodging itself in his head. Soufiane continues. 'I have not decided whether to make my life in Algeria or in Paris. Even America. My father thinks I might be able to do my masters in the Massachusetts Technological Institute, or perhaps at the University of Cambridge, in England. And you could go there too, Moss. I could also join an exploratory programme in south-west Africa. It is exciting—scientists live like kings in Angola and Zaire, those places—my studies have excellent prospects. I must decide which path I am to go down before choosing who to marry, for she will have to accept the choice I inflict upon her.' He laughs at his own pronouncement.

Moss still cannot speak; he finds this situation ridiculous. He wants to hold Samira in his arms. Wants to be with her forever, finds just enough insight to work out it is infatuation driven. Her face he could look into for a lifetime. He also sees that she is unobtainable. All they have in common is in this moment: two young people mutually attracted. Or more probably only one young person with that sense, the pretty girl may share none of the desire he feels. None of it amounts to something they could carry through time. Forever strangers. Soufie, on the other hand, seems to have an easy relationship with Samira. Her parents want her to marry. If Moss were in Soufiane's shoes, he knows that he could and would wish to marry her more dearly than work in Angola. Should he tell him? Or does Soufie not see it that way. Perhaps Samira has a hidden defect? Her rudimentary English a disappointment to the high-achieving geologist.

Moss turns to Samira. 'What happens if you don't?'

Asia explains the question to her.

Samira looks directly at the English boy, speaks in two languages, 'Il faut que je trouve un homme. I think it is right I let the parent say a man, mari.'

'Her parents will suggest a husband,' Asia clarifies.

'I don't think she really wants to do this yet,' says Soufiane. 'She is young like Asia and I. Like you, Moss.'

'Non. Si l'homme est gentil avec moi...' And there Samira stops mid-sentence.

Moss looks at Asia. 'If he is kind to her, she will be happy,' the friend translates, adding a conclusion which Samira failed to express.

Moss nods at this, signals that he understands the words. He does not agree with the sentiment. He thinks marriage is about love although he has seen little evidence of any emotion stronger than loyalty between his own parents. Recalls Sharon MacDonald—the one person who fleetingly reciprocated his love—pointing out that even that basic requisite was beyond her own parents' emotional grasp. He thinks he is a romantic in the face of contrary evidence, has no wish to shift his view. 'I hope you find him,' he tells Samira, and she again glances her eyes downwards. He might be wounding her with goodwill.

* * *

The four young people saunter towards the centre of Oran. Aimless chatter, less intense than discussing Samira's need to marry, occupies them. Soufiane asks Moss questions about Ronnie Prousch, the pianist from Birmingham. Moss disliked his sentimental tunes back when they were in the UK charts—cannot fathom this young man's tastes— answers politely. He even wonders if his dismissal of his friend's preferred musical choices constitutes a prejudice he has yet to overcome. However, the more questions Soufie asks, the more Moss recalls how dreadful Prousch's songs really are.

'Did you go to a girl's school?' he enquires of Samira and Asia. Pop music exhausted.

'Yes, I am a girl,' Samira replies, smiling coyly at Moss as she says it.

'So you've had few opportunities to meet boys.'

'Peu-être. But is not meeting. I see boys...dans la rue, boys, they not make mari.'

'The boys in the street are not husbands, not future husbands,' Asia interprets for Moss.

'Thank you, but not worry for me, please?' Samira seems a little agitated that Moss has raised this topic again. He tries to apologise, becomes flustered. Fears he may have offended her. Soufiane, for the first time in Moss's presence, speaks Arabic to Samira, something that makes her giggle. She puts a hand to her mouth and steps back a pace. Then she nudges her shoulder into Moss's, he feels the contact acutely. It is a physical spontaneity that only Khadidja earlier today, and now this bewitching girl, have shared with him since Spain. 'You want me? To marry. You have the dowry? Not much. Young girl just need house.'

Moss thinks she is teasing him. Doesn't know what he should say. 'Oui. Sure. Tu habites en Angleterre avec moi.'

Samira squeals and jumps in the air, looks delighted with his offer to take her to live in England. Live together. In this moment she looks no more than thirteen years old. Innocence and joy written on her laughing face. She looks at Asia and says, 'Mari,' the word which Moss, a few moments earlier, learnt to mean husband. She touches Moss's recently washed fair hair. A sign of affection he doesn't dare to interpret. 'To England, I go! To meet the Queen and the Manchester United.'

Soufiane takes Moss's right hand and shakes it, does not touch his heart at its conclusion. Moss appreciates this change, the European-styled formality. 'Now you must meet the father-in-law,' he declares.

'Papa,' Samira squeals again. She is cavorting with laughter, it is hilarious. Moss is unsure exactly where the humour lies. It is a joke but his wife-to-be finds it funnier than the words merit. Uncontrollable mirth.

Asia seems to sense his discomfort. She shakes her head, a broad smile upon it. 'Moss, Moss, you like Samira?'

He nods tentatively. He likes her a hell of a lot but he's a Rucksack Jumper, just a wave of the thumb from leaving town. Pretends he's a student just so the lovely Lellouche family put him up for a couple of nights. Hopes to gather up a thimbleful of Saharan sand while he is here, not a wife. Samira is the prettiest girl he's ever seen, not really grasped her character yet. They are like kids with each other—that's the boy-girl thing in this confusing land—and Moss has never thought himself a dowry-payer. Anything over seventy pounds would be out of the question. She would make the most enticing bride. On this Earth, he thinks to himself.

For no evident reason Samira starts to cry. Moss is

shocked. She pulls on his arm, pulls him a little closer to her. They are looking into each other's faces and the English boy is not sure what he is looking for. Wants to undo whatever has drawn these tears. Not a clue what might do it. Has he answered her question incorrectly? Upset her.

'You a nice man,' she says. 'Not nice joke me.' He doesn't understand, simply nods his head. 'I not wife you but is not you.' He holds her eye. 'The father, he...' Samira lets out a hiss from the side of her mouth. A sharp Arabic word.

'He's not very nice,' says Soufiane.

'The word she used meant bastard,' advises Asia.

Then Samira cries bitterly. 'He hate you. He hate you only because not Arab. He hate Asia because she like Paris. I think he hate me for I like Asia and she like Paris. That is how much the father is hate. He hate sans raison.'

Moss gently puts an arm around Samira's shoulder, rocks her as she cries. Tries to keep it to a gesture of comfort although he is very unsure what is acceptable here. Then he whispers to her, 'My dad too,' quickly translating it for clarity. 'Mon père aussi.'

The pretty girl—tears streaking kohl across her cheeks—starts to laugh a little. A short and bitter chortle, one which spits a tear or two out with it. 'Vraiment?' she asks: Really?

Moss nods. 'He's a proper bastard.' Soufiane looks surprised but Moss hears him say an Arabic word to Samira. It might be the one she used a moment before.

She pulls Moss a little closer. 'Bastard,' she says with a slight lisp, trying the English word.

Moss laughs at this. 'Soufie,' he says, 'can you translate, narrow-minded bigoted bastard.'

Soufiane laughs and says something in Arabic to Samira. Those words. She holds him closer and he feels her shaking. With tears or with laughter. She clutches him so closely that he cannot distinguish which it is. 'The fathers no good,' she says as she pulls away, again looking directly into Moss's face. Tears no longer flow and, with the heel of her right hand, she quickly cleans her cheeks. Her face is again proud, grace restored. 'The fathers no good,' she repeats with a confirmatory shake of her head.

'Mine is the bane of my life,' Moss tells her. Neither Soufiane nor Asia can interpret bane. They do not know the word. He tries 'messed with my head' but neither sibling can mould this phrase into satisfactory French or Arabic. Samira looks bemused by their attempted translations. 'I will never be like my father,' he tells Samira, speaking slowly, wanting her to understand that the rift is final. 'I am nothing like him.' He starts to wonder if this is a precursor to a proposal of marriage which was not his intention when first he opened his mouth. 'I don't hate anyone,' he continues, stuck in a diatribe he cannot complete. He doesn't say, everyone should love everyone else, because, if it was that simple, it would have already happened. Nor will he tell these people that he loves them, let himself sound so saccharin. It would only emphasise the cold, unloved feelings with which he has spent too much of his life. He hasn't come to Africa looking for pity, he really hasn't.

Samira puts her arm loosely around his waist; she tugs on it. 'Thank you,' she says, then lets him go. He wonders if that is it; has he passed and failed the audition all in one take. It is probably the best outcome he could have hoped for. Then she touches his hair again, his freshly washed long fair hair. 'Beaux cheveux,' she says, 'j'aime cela.'

'She loves your hair,' Asia interjects. Ensures he does not misinterpret the extent of Samira's love for him.

Again, she takes a hold of his hand. 'I am your wife in another life,' says Samira slowly.

Moss puts his hand behind her head and pulls her forward so that their foreheads are touching. He dismisses the impulse to kiss her. Won't do anything so rash that it might sully her memory of him. Of their only day in each other's company. Then he lets her go. He nods as they retain eye contact. 'Another life,' says Moss.

Samira is laughing again. Moss notices that Asia and Soufiane are both putting two fingers into their wide-open mouths. The international gesture that this is making them sick. He laughs along with them; he has been stupid, sentimental, let a childish infatuation show. He will never forget this beautiful lost girl, Samira of Oran. That is as much as he knows.

* * *

As they continue to walk across the city, Moss feels closer to these three young people than he has been to anyone since Sharon left Bury in January. He savours their company.

The North African sun overheats him, penetrates the very top of his head. Asia advises that they will enter the Demaeght Museum. 'Cool and interesting,' she says.

Inside it is air-conditioned, the kind of cool this hot day requires. Restorative of good brain functioning. Moss and Asia are keen to explore the display about the war of independence. The girl helps Moss to read the more complex passages of French which accompany several exhibits. Soufiane seems agitated by these offerings. 'We should let the past go to sleep,' he says. Moss doesn't argue but thinks Soufie terribly naïve. Loves the West too much to understand why many of his fellow students hate it. Soufiane advises that there is an exhibition upstairs showing artefacts from the region's ancient history. 'From before we were Arabs.'

Moss enjoys hearing these cryptic words, pulls on Soufie's arm pointing at him and back at himself. 'When we were cavemen.' And we all were, he thinks. Forget the

French, the Arabs, and the despicable crusaders; once upon a time we were all just cavemen.

Samira accompanies them as they pass the many displays, seems to look only half-heartedly, never stops to read the explanatory texts. Moss fears she has fled to that other life in which he has no part. She cannot walk away from her father as he—the western boy—has done. Can't jump over a rucksack, bring forth a life and fate a world away from that already allotted to her.

* * *

They drink coffees and mint teas at a café near the Pasha Mosque. At an adjacent gift shop, Soufiane buys Moss a bar of chocolate in a wrapper depicting the iconic building. Moss shares it, eats a piece or two. He does not comment on its displeasing aftertaste. His friends do not appear to share his aversion. They exude real pleasure in its eating. It really is odd chocolate. He tries not to wince when eating, not to reveal his stunted appreciation for the gift.

Moss comments on the many posters on walls and lampposts—political, he thinks—showing the same serious face of an elderly gentleman beneath Arabic script. All indecipherable to him.

'They are pictures of President Bendjedid,' says Soufiane.

'It is propaganda,' says Asia. 'The man has all the power, the people have none.'

Moss nods, he has no grasp of the political system here.

'One party, not a contest. One political party is all that is allowed,' continues Asia.

Soufiane and Samira show no interest in the topic.

The posters proliferate across Oran, street after street. Moss recalls seeing them staring out from lampposts in Nedroma. He thinks it Orwellian, seeing the president's face at every turn in town. His name, President Bendjedid, is difficult for a boy from Bury to remember. In his mind, he attributes the name Battypapa to the face. President Battypapa, keeping all his funny money in the confines of the country. His all-seeing posters checking that the women in Nedroma cover their right eye, that all the chocolate makers piss on their fermenting cocoa beans. He wants to tell his friends about the parody president while fearing there may be insult in his satire. The belittling of their country. Keeps it to himself. And he hits upon Battymamma, the crazy woman running his own country. Moss is broadly even-handed.

* * *

Before they return to the Lellouche family home, towards the end of the afternoon, Samira starts to wrestle something from within the cumbersome handbag she carries. Moss is momentarily curious, then recognises the garment she withdraws. Returning her headscarf to its rightful place, obscuring her jet-black hair. Becoming a girl other than the one she appeared to be in the company kept on this day. The face now peering from the headscarf is the same girl, the same perfect symmetry. Alluring in both renditions. The scarf is a piece of shell. He likes her rampant hair. Moss thinks—but elects not to ask—that her mother, surely her stern father, expect her to wear it outside her home. This is why she puts it back just as she is set to return. A pretence. Compared to many in this country, the well-cut jeans and short-sleeved top which her parents permit are a surprising westernisation. But the scarf remains. As he thinks these thoughts she glances away from his gaze, seems suddenly less confident in catching his eye. The boy from Bury finds himself shaking hands—an excessive formality—with his wife from another life. The girl whose face he may picture forever and whose future he hopes never to learn.

* * *

Khadidja welcomes Moss back into her home as she might a visiting nephew. She smiles asides at her own children while asking him alone if they have treated him properly. Did they let him choose how to spend the day? When she learns that Samira was in their company, she simply says, 'Poor girl.' Moss doesn't like to hear it while harbouring similar thoughts. And the perspective of this progressive family may be the unusual one around here.

Khadidja advises that she has mended two pairs of the boy's socks. When she took them out of the washing machine, she found them beset with holes. Asia laughs at her mother. Speaks sharply to her but with good humour. He didn't follow the French but understands something on the lines of 'boys can darn socks' to be the core of her discourse.

Moss says a simple, 'Thank you,' and a 'Merci' for clarity. Feels quite overwhelmed by her kindness. And Khadidja—not Asia—knows of his limited sewing skills. Has seen his hapless money belt.

'We shall eat when Father comes home,' says Soufiane. Moss recalls how, on Wolseley Road in Bury, his family frequently took meals without his own father present. Ronald Croft's work was unpredictable in its finishing times and a meal more peaceable for his absence.

* * *

As darkness falls, Mustapha comes into the home and the family meal commences. It is a lavish affair, many courses. Moss compliments the food, does not comment on the absence of meat. Feels a little virtuous, it is a first for him at a dining table, egg and chips aside. What it signifies he does not know. He doubts if the Lellouche family are vegetarian through religion. There are no visible signs of piety in the home. Meat is not in short supply in this country. It was abundant in the market which the young people walked through earlier in the day. Live chickens and the darker meat of the already departed. Goats, Asia advised him. Perhaps the family is not as wealthy as they appear—Soufiane has said they are off to Paris in July which suggests otherwise—the food preparation is spectacular. Perhaps they just like chickpeas, and Khadidja has spiced them ever so nicely.

Later in the evening Mustapha speaks to Moss alone. He asks about his literature degree, what his intentions are on completion of the course. Does it justify the time Moss must invest in it? This seems the core of the matter, and it is a testing conversation for the boy although the older man is being both practical and supportive. The principal difficulty is that Moss has made up the entire story: he likes reading books, doesn't study literature in the conventional sense. They mean what they mean to him. Hasn't written an essay about them in four years. The time during which he has worked in a menial office job—insurance—and then as a packer in a detergent factory. His father did not permit him to study and he is not the type to follow his brother into the navy. Orders are for ignoring: if Confucius didn't say it, then the old guy missed a trick. The sage will not have said, lie about how you spend your time, particularly if it embarrasses you. That is Moss's very own pearl and he thinks it has worn thin.

He reflects on the conversation when again he lies beneath a blanket on the family's sofa. Night time. It was odd. Mustapha talked paternally while laying no claim to Moss and knowing that he would take his leave of this family on the following day. Moss suspects that Soufiane told his father some of the words he exchanged with Samira, the bigotry of their respective fathers. That was kids' stuff in Moss's mind, not really for the ears of their parents. Samira has not shared a word of it with her obnoxious old man, he couldn't be more certain. He thinks himself quite able to stand on his own two feet, with or without a fictitious literature degree. Moss wonders what words Soufiane might have used in place of bigot and bastard, or perhaps he shared these with his father. Why not? He sees that the Lellouche family trust each other across the generational divide. That is weird, and it makes him feel very happy for the two siblings, his two friends. Alone, on the sofa-bed in a suburb of Oran he cannot name, a chill comes over him as he pictures the girl. Samira cannot flee as he has done, nor will her elders offer wise counsel.

3.

At ten-thirty the following morning, Moss is back hitchhiking. Khadidja packed him a sandwich, a water bottle, gave him a lovely hug. Soufiane shook his hand after they'd exchanged addresses and agreed to write to each other. Earnestly so in Moss's mind. And Asia surprised him, planted a kiss on his left cheek. He unwittingly moved his head as she did it. Their lips brushed but she was still smiling when their eyes met. Must have sensed it was not deliberate. The boy pictures the over-formal handshake he shared when parting from Samira, it comes to mind while contemplating the other girl's kiss.

On the roadside he ponders whether he should dance and leap across his standing rucksack. There are no other hitchhikers in sight, no one to out-hitch. His previous roadside conjuring rustled up so warm a family, a day of joy. A wife waiting in another life. He decides he shouldn't jinx it, must not exhaust his good fortune.

When a car pulls up beside the thumb-waving boy, he sees a lone man at the wheel. An Arab wearing a western suit without a tie. He beckons the hitchhiker into his tired Renault. Moss lies his rucksack across the backseat and then sits next to the driver. As they begin to talk, it is quickly evident that the man is not especially conversant in French. He speaks in the language but his accent is difficult for the English boy to follow. The Algerian seems equally bewildered by Moss's snatched sentences. The man is travelling all the way to Algiers, Moss gathers that much. He is unable to pinpoint, for the driver, where he wishes to be set down. Tries to express in French his wish to turn for the desert at the most direct road. One which goes due south. He might as well be asking for a rocket to the moon judging by the puzzled look that the gentleman returns him. He has remembered the names of towns on his route, will watch out for signposts.

When Moss points at the car radio, wondering whether a little music might entertain them, the driver shakes his head. He repeatedly says a word that Moss doesn't understand. Then the man presses the buttons on the radio a few times, eliciting no reaction from the contraption. It is broken; if the man has already told him so, he has done it in Arabic. He smiles, neither embarrassed by the shoddy state of his car, nor especially disappointed by the radio's loss of function.

To compensate for the absence of a radio, perhaps, the man begins to sing. For a split-second Moss feels terrified by the strange wailing that he emits. Then he grasps the pleasure it gives the singer and his ear picks up the hint of a tune. A pretty strangulated melody to Moss's way of thinking, still there is sufficient repetition and musicality in it to draw enjoyment from. Moss puts his head back and laughs. The man grins widely at this, sings a couple more lines in his high-pitched Arabic, then points at Moss saying another word which Moss does not know. He assumes it means, Sing! Moss is a little self-conscious, he is inside a car, not on the roadside jumping over his rucksack. Then by verse two he is belting it out like a diva. The Caravan Moves On is his song.

You find us strange, our clothing unusual
Speaking a language which you can't understand
We might be why you lock your doors at night
When we pass on the street, you take your child in hand

He could be describing the driver, or the driver's perception of Moss. It is an apt song and he is pleased not to have to explain it. A compassionate song—in Moss's view—but it might be between the lines.

The caravan moves on and on
Just the way it's always done
Today it's here, tomorrow gone
The caravan moves on

As he finishes, he points back at the driver, then quickly withdraws the accusatory finger for fear of offending. The man is quite relaxed in his company, takes the hint. Sings in Arabic once more.

On this long journey there are many silences but the singing in particular seems to have thawed the early frostiness, and there is no tension or displeasure in their inability to fully comprehend each other. In a town called Chlef, the driver parks up by some shops and gestures for Moss to accompany him. They sit at a café, eat a small meal, Moss takes out money to pay. He has plenty having crossed the border with the illicit bundle. The man will have none of it. For the first time his driver looks cross: he is paying for his guest and that is that.

When they drive on, the boy reflects on the exchange at the café. He fears that his status as a hitchhiker might, in Algeria, mirror that of a beggar. He likes the company of strangers which hitchhiking provides, has no intention of milking it. To take what his driver can barely afford. Moss is a citizen of the first world; there is an inordinate amount of good luck in that chance occurrence. He feels powerless to explain this; everyone he meets has their own understanding of who he is. For the Lellouche family he was the student friend of their children, and to this man, he is a traveller in need of charity. He is all these things, he surmises, experiencing life from the centre of a kaleidoscope comprising the subjective experiences of others.

Some way further down the road, Moss is able to indicate that he wishes to head for Aïn Oussera, a town he circled in his atlas back on Wolseley Road, Bury, and which he now sees on the signposts. A gateway to the Sahara. The man shakes his hand as he is leaving, touching his heart immediately after doing so, his face showing the sincerity that this denotes. The boy from Bury feels moved that this man has paid him such kindly attention, bought him a meal, and all to hear a couple of pop songs sung. If they failed to understand each other they did not let it harbour ill-feeling. Another two hundred miles of the arid scrubland are behind him.

* * *

Moss stands by the side of the dusty road, pondering the falling arc of the sun. He decides, despite the hour, to press on for Aïn Oussera. He worries that he could be left in the cold desert night if a ride is not going all the way; however, Algeria is his lucky country, the thumbing a great success. Pleased to have got so far so quickly. He balances up his rucksack, his need for a lift requiring serious application. The song plays once more inside his head. He moves with the steady drum beat only he can hear.

> *It is my grave that your house is built upon*
> *You might be me if you could just look inside*

When the chorus comes around, he jumps once more over his upright rucksack, stops only to show that purposeful thumb. Then on the repeat of the word caravan he does it again. A baby gazelle. Several cars pass, no more than several, and then one which passed him at quite a speed, just as suddenly comes to a stop a hundred and fifty yards up the road. The driver climbs out and waves back at him, beckoning him to come to the car. The rucksack dance is pure hypnotism. Up to the car he trots, the driver already standing by the boot. As he takes the rucksack, he shakes Moss by the hand. The driver's wife—traditionally dressed, black headscarf obscuring her mouth—vacates the front seat of the car for him. Moves into the back with her three children, one now travelling on her lap. The driver seems initially to have assumed that the hitchhiker is French, adapts quickly to the reality, slowing his speech down to ask Moss many questions about Margaret Thatcher and Manchester United. The back of the car is silent except for the smallest child who whines periodically. Earning himself the occasional 'tsch-tsch' from his mother. The driver, who has said his name is Muhammed, conducts all his conversation in French, his commentary understood well by Moss. His diction clear. At one point the English boy turns around to the man's wife and asks—in his best O-level French—what her name is. The lady lowers her eyes and one of the children buries his head in her clothing. Moss turns back, a little embarrassed, unsure if she even speaks French. The driver is shaking his head but then smiles at him. He seems to see that Moss meant no disrespect however much his direct approach confused Muhammed's wife.

They drive on in silence until Muhammed resumes questioning Moss. Where will he stay in Aïn Oussera. The boy confirms he is to source a hotel and Muhammed queries if he would like to spend the night in their home. It feels the oddest request to Moss; not that there is any animosity between them but, unlike Khadidja in Oran, he cannot converse with the lady in the car. It is prohibited. He sees only kindness in the man's request while feeling uncomfortable about the prospect. And he really needs to shift a few Dinars. Moss declines, says he is meeting a friend. It is a poor story: he cannot name the hotel they are to stay at. Doesn't think Muhammed buys it. Whatever he makes of the story, he shakes Moss's hand warmly, touching his heart, when dropping him off in the centre of town.

Night has fallen, the streets dark with only a smattering of street lights. He knows he let the driver down by failing to visit, grant approval, to his family home. But what would it have been worth? Muhammed has got this far in life without it; the blessing of a Rucksack Jumper is the most double-edged of the lot. They lie and they lie and they lie.

With money in his belt, he seeks a place to stay. A hot shower essential, accompanying restaurant favoured.

* * *

At the Elwatania Hotel, Moss believes he has found what he is looking for. When the young man on the reception desk sees his passport, he uses it as an opportunity to practice his English. He praises the tenacity of the two Scottish players who Manchester United bought a year or two back, asks if Prince Charles will ever marry. Moss finds it bizarre to be talking such nonsense on the edge of the Sahara Desert. He asks about the restaurant.

The other young hotel clerk says, 'Fermé.' Moss understands that it has closed for the evening.

The Anglo-enthusiast cuts across his colleague. 'Couscous for you. I will tell the chef we have an English guest.' He leaves for the kitchen, returns before Moss has finished the tedious form filling, insists on carrying the rucksack to his room. Moss asks again about the food, once more the man tells him that he will have a meal.

He unpacks a book to read later, a change of socks for the morning, decides not to shower because the restaurant is soon to close. On arriving downstairs, the same young man who assisted so much at reception shows Moss into the dining room. It is very dark within, and a middle-aged couple in western dress—Moss guesses they are French—drink coffee. A group of four young men in Arab clothing occupy a table on the far side of the room.

'Am I too late?' he asks.

'No, no. For you we are prepared.'

Moss sits for about twenty minutes, wishing he'd brought the novel he is currently reading down from his room although the dim light would have made reading it a challenge. The French couple—if that is what they are—leave. The English boy receives frequent glances from the table of young men. He would like some bread but feels it would be too great a nuisance to ask. Then he thinks water might suffice, wonders if asking will embarrass the staff. Doubtless they should have served it already, have forgotten to do so. No staff enter the dining room and it is not appropriate to ask it of other paying guests. The glances from the young Arab men are not unfriendly but when they confer among themselves, he has the impression that it is him they talk about. European, hair over his shoulders as he has seen no North African wear it. On balance, he wishes he had brought his book.

In time the English-speaking hotel clerk brings a plate of food: couscous, vegetables and lamb. 'For you! The Hotel Elwatania is proud to have another English guest.' Moss can only speculate how long it is since the last of his countrymen was here. Before this man has left his table, the other clerk from the reception desk brings bread, a carafe of water and a glass. Moss smiles at the belated telepathy.

As he tucks in, the group of young Arabs look and speak in his direction. The English-speaking hotel clerk goes to them, exchanges a word or two and in unison they begin to shout, in strongly accented English, 'It is good. It is good.' They act as cheerleaders for their country's food and they tell a simple truth. The food is good.

After a time, the chef comes from the kitchen. Moss tries to thank him for the food, for working a little longer this evening to prepare it for him, but the cook himself repeats the word 'Merci' many times. It is as if the eating of it is the task deserving the thanks. The chef disappears back into his kitchen. Within a couple of minutes he returns, an elaborate plate of ice cream in his hands. Moss gratefully eats it as soon as he has finished the couscous.

He is tired. This day began amid the warmth of the Lellouche family, and now he is on the cusp of the Sahara Desert. He desires just a shower before sleep. Tomorrow he will go into the dunes. He always imagined it but few in Bury believed he could. Certainly not Ronald Croft, his discouraging father. He told him he would never get this far. Told him so at volume. The moment he stands to leave, the young men from the neighbouring table come and shake his hand. The restaurant is otherwise empty, so he goes to the reception desk where both young men who had checked him in sit behind the counter. Moss takes out his wallet to offload the first of his smuggled dinar. The English-speaker shakes his head.

'The restaurant is closed,' he says, 'but we treat English good.'

Moss wonders how this establishment makes money. His nationality may make so infrequent a show that the minor loss of income barely registers. He has a hundred and ten quid to spend before Tunisia. May need to start flushing dinar down the toilet if he is to get rid of the darned things. Three days he has been in Algeria and a cheap sandwich in

Nedroma is as much as he has paid for.

4.

The following day, the English boy successfully hitches a ride in a small truck otherwise carrying live chickens to the town of Aïn Maabed. As he travels this short distance, in the bright sunlight he sees—as he could not during the final lift of the evening before—that he is travelling across desert. He has arrived.

It is a vast plain of red and grey stone that stretches before him. Small pockets of windblown sand nestle in the lee of the larger stones. On the horizon, in every direction he looks, the sun dazzles against a yellow hue. He imagines that this is the effect of further sand. Over the horizon will be rolling dunes and sand blizzards. Bedouins.

His lift drops him off in the centre of town before eleven in the morning. It feels completely different from Oran; in the architecture of this desert town there is no obvious sign of a European past. Moss guesses that it has no such past to report. The market place where he sits drinking coffee is a babble of talk. A man walks a camel past the coffee kiosk. Men wear turbans and women—without exception—cover themselves in traditional dress. From his many posters, President Battypapa watches Aïn Maabed.

After his coffee, Moss decides to seek a hotel. He will stay here, it is intriguing, unfamiliar. Smaller than Fes but just as ancient in appearance, and likewise thriving in its street life. In Aïn Maabed, he sees none of the hustlers of that earlier Moroccan town. The boy guesses that tourists are too few for it to be a viable profession. The socialism of this land does not create great prosperity, still the people have a certain pride. Neither beggar nor hustler has approached him in Algeria. The desert air is dry and Moss feels great clarity to his thoughts. He checks himself, occasionally wise. 'Mirages,' he mutters. Says the word out loud for the remembering. Repeats it slowly. 'Mirages.'

* * *

He finds a hotel, nimbly fills in the voluminous paperwork. Once in his room, he takes a short nap.

Arising in the early afternoon, Moss leaves the hotel, walks up the main street and out of the desert town. Initially he is on a main road, and when a dirt road appears tracking left, he chooses to follow it. He is seeking out the Sahara Desert. Doing what he has planned, if only to turn back at first sighting. A flash of insight tugs at him: it could be unwise. He knows nothing of what he may come across when straying from the major roads. He has been lucky so far. And he thinks his good fortune should continue so long as his intentions remain worthy. If it is not true, what else could be the point of this life?

When his watch tells him that he has walked for ninety minutes—and he is beginning to curse himself for not bringing a drink on his trek beneath the African sun—he sees one or two buildings ahead. And palm trees. Back in the town a little greenery had been evident, since heading out he has seen only red and yellow stone, a thin dusting of sand and the grey ribbon of road. If there is greenery then this small settlement must surely have water. He focusses on the palm trees thriving ahead. There are many palm trees. He walks towards them but the settlement gets closer only slowly. For twenty minutes of further walking, the white of the box-like buildings blinks at him in the penetrating light. Each step is heavy in the intense heat, each minute a little longer than its Bury counterpart. Moss is certainly parched.

On arrival he sees that it is a tiny oasis, an outcrop of palm trees more than of civilization. It smells fresher than the desert. The palms of an oasis. He cannot see it yet but

Moss feels the presence of water upon his skin. It is carried by the air. He is a water diviner. The pores of his skin seeking out the universal elixir. There are no people in sight, two or three tiny dwelling houses, some outbuildings. He can hear the bleating of goats. They are nibbling what little nourishment there is, the greenery to be had.

A jolt of surprise comes into his throat when he notices him. Moss's no-people-in-sight assumption is a falsehood. An old man stands next to the gate of a small goat enclosure. He does not wear camouflage but the boy did not initially spot him. The old man's pale-yellow robes failing to register their difference in the thin wash of colour. The man is not overtly speaking but his lips are moving, no sound is coming out, or certainly none that carries to Moss. Twenty yards away. He speaks incessantly—old-man words—for himself alone. There is not a breath of wind.

'Bonne après-midi,' the English boy says, directing it clearly towards the only visible person—surely the only other person—in this spot of sweet-smelling calm. Moss cannot imagine that there are others hidden within the landscape as this old man had first appeared to be. 'Bonne après-midi,' he repeats.

The old man does not respond. He watches his animals, looks upon them intently while mumbling his goat-related incantation. He appears timeless, biblical in his own way. A man—hermit—in a small desert dwelling place, speaking only to goats. Less than two hours walk away a vibrant town exists. And it will hold no interest for this man, not in this boy's estimation. Its uniquely Arab hubbub is of a modern preoccupation, it could add nothing to his contented subsistence. And a boy from the West? Moss is invisible to the old goatherd. The man could not perceive the meaning to the thoughts in Moss's head, and this has reified into an inability to so much as register his presence.

'Bonne après-midi.' Nothing. 'Bonne après-midi.' Moss

stops, he feels oddly relieved that the old man has won. Bury and its sons have no place in the Old Testament. He can see this oasis and the old man who lives here, and still his youth and his British nationality—his otherness—prevent him from breaking through. From truly entering the place. He wonders what the name of this little outpost might be. He had hoped to ask the old man but decides, on reflection, that it should remain his secret.

Bonne après-midi, Moss thinks to himself, and realising it might upset the strained and strange balance of the world were he to take so much as water from this timeless oasis, he turns his back and saunters again in the direction of Aïn Maabed. A long walk ahead but all he has seen, smelt, the feel of the warm wind caressing his face, has given him succour.

* * *

Walking back, the boy's thoughts tumble this way and that. In the library in Bury he used to read the many magazines. Stole a copy of Time at the turn of the year. The American news magazine. Ayatollah Khomeini was their Man of the Year. A controversial choice, a role in the incarceration of American hostages in the Tehran embassy. Moss is bright. He understands that the award is for the scale of the man's impact on world events. It is not a sign of approval. Hitler and Stalin each received the accolade in their time. Didn't leave the world a better place, sure as hell stirred it up. Moss has never seen those copies.

The magazine's reporter managed to secure an interview with the great, or the terrible, man. A journalistic coup. Khomeini had a certain perspective—nothing Moss felt any kinship towards—clearly not a stupid man. However, in his essay following the meeting, the journalist wrote that it was unnerving to see the narrowness of the Ayatollah's outlook. He uncovered that Khomeini had never heard of William

Shakespeare, of Wolfgang Mozart. This was the source of his concern.

'Bollocks,' thinks Moss as he brings it to mind on his slow hike back to Aïn Maabed. There are a bunch of famous Persian poets. He can't name one and he hopes to publish the stuff himself one day. The reporter got it wrong, thinks the world begins and ends with his own knowledge. The old goatherd had a point. Bonne après-midi means nothing. It is only ever afternoon in one small quarter of the world at a time, morning, evening and night enveloping the rest. Our perspectives are shrouded, not by differing cultures and experiences, but by the sheer egoism that makes us think others should think as we do. He'll write a poem about that one day. The more obscure its wording, the truer shall it be.

The town is coming back into view.

5.

The next morning Moss is back on the hitchhiking road. A short lift from town brought him out to the main highway only to discover that the lorry was Algiers-bound. He waits again by a dusty roadside, pointing south towards Ghardaia. It was a must in his pre-trip planning. A desert town, a picture of which took up fully half a page of his encyclopaedia. He wonders how much further south to go. He loves being in the Sahara but it will not talk to him.

As he watches the cars pass him by, he thinks it's time to start jumping over his rucksack—dancing like a dervish—cheating the rules of the road.

The previous evening in Aïn Maabed was a quiet one; he successfully paid for his own dinner. The hotel room was comfortable; six pounds a night and no complaints from Moss. He recognises that he is outside the tourists' ambit, adjudges that it has been the case since he entered Algeria.

People stare at him but no one tries to sell him anything. If he initiates interactions then they occur—except at that small oasis—if he does not prompt it, they leave him to be other. Ten solid hours of sleep he gobbled up in that comfortable bed, an open window encouraging movement to the dry air which surrounds him. He is becoming accustomed to his status. Superman when he hitchhikes, the unassuming Clark Kent when he does not. A car is coming so he begins to swing his hips, maybe he will dance this one to a halt. He breathes the words of the song.

> *The caravan moves on and on*
> *Just the way it's always done*
> *Today it's here, tomorrow gone*
> *The caravan moves on*

Hippy lyrics, he always thought, Bedouin down here. A dog whistle to the drivers. The car flashes its headlights, slows. Stops some thirty yards ahead of the boy.

As he approaches, he sees the capital F on the rear bumper. France, a French car. The driver many years his senior—possibly the same age as Mustapha Lellouche—with a girl, Moss's age or younger, sitting in the passenger seat. They exchange greetings. They are going to Ghardaia. Moss is grateful for the ride. He sits in the back, his rucksack beside him. The pair must have a boot full of their own luggage.

'Je m'appelle Moss.'

'Bonne, je suis Guillaume, et ma fille s'appelle Véronique.'

The father and daughter prove to be decent company. Véronique a touch monosyllabic. Guillaume tells Moss that he is divorced and currently living in Algiers; he also maintains a flat or house—Moss is unsure which—near Marseille. His daughter lives with her mother in a town called Nîmes. Moss is disappointed that he does not know where it sits on a map. He has spent so many hours looking through his stolen school atlas, it is unusual for a place name to stump him. She says that she has left school and will study art in Paris in September. This year is, in Véronique's words, 'pour moi.'

Guillaume sounds sceptical of how she has spent the year thus far. At one point he says that his daughter is 'perdu.' Declares her lost. The tension is visible in Véronique when her father shares this assessment. He is clearly pleased to be showing his daughter the sights of Algeria, giving structure and meaning to the pause in her education. Moss thinks she is no more lost than he, less so with a Parisian art course upon her horizon. And her tour with her father is surely more conducive to a successful holiday than the independent travel the Norwegian girl—Heidi, back in Oujda—embarked upon. Véronique's father must be the antivenom to unwanted male attention. She is monosyllabic simply because she is a teenager. Her prolonged absence from Guillaume—living on a different continent—makes the father over-think it. Moss does not share his insight: they are spending time, might work it out for themselves.

* * *

Coming into a town called Laghouat, Guillaume explains to Moss that, being French, he requires a break in the drive, must utilise this time of day for the eating of a fine lunch. Moss laughs at the words used. The longer he speaks French, the more proficient he becomes. Moss starts to thank him for the lift but Guillaume talks over him. Reaffirms that he will be driving to Ghardaia. He invites Moss to join them for the meal. The boy is a little taken aback by this generosity. Guillaume told of how he has waited for a town large enough to have a decent restaurant. In Moss's view they have passed several; Guillaume must have a more refined culinary sensibility than Lancashire has instilled in this Rucksack Jumper. He is unsure if Véronique is so keen on retaining his presence. She is never uncivil but directs all her conversation towards her father, even when discussing topics that Moss has raised. He tries to object, suggests that Guillaume and Véronique may wish to dine alone. His driver dismisses it as unnecessary politeness. He will eat.

* * *

They sit on a terrace which overlooks a garden kept green by the diligence of a small, carefully constructed, irrigation stream. Spring flowers bloom, the colours match the floral table cloth. Moss thinks this comfort—class—indication that it is really a French restaurant, however far south of that country it sits. It is a more sumptuous establishment than any Moss has entered in Africa. In his whole life. Guillaume orders food in conversation with a waiter. No menu is seen, no price discussed. Moss thinks he could offload a few smuggled dinars here should he pick up the tab. The suggestion might be as rude as the Arab with the broken car radio deemed a similar offer two days ago.

A waitress in a mid-length western skirt, crimson and wearing tights beneath it despite the Saharan heat, puts plates of green in front of each of the three diners. To Moss the food is a puzzle, he has never before seen or eaten the like.

Véronique senses his dilemma. 'Les artichauts. Ils sont bons,' she tells him.

Moss hears that she is telling him they are good, asks for a repetition of the keyword before understanding he has artichoke leaves in front of him. He tries to watch the father and daughter eat without making his ignorance too obvious. They simply put the fattest end of each leaf in their mouths one at a time and then draw them out again. He does not see them eat any part before discarding it. Is this food or simply a good luck ritual? The boy from Bury puts a leaf in his mouth, sucks a little—tastes nothing whatsoever—puts it to the back of his plate. Tries another which, unsurprisingly, is no better. His fellow diners' actions are as pointless as his. Artichokes must be the emperor's new food.

Véronique, who is at his side, nudges him with a smile on her face. 'Mordre avec les dents,' she says: Bite it with your teeth.

With this insight Moss now sees that both have scraped a little white flesh from beneath the skin at one end of the leaves as they drew them through their clenched teeth. He—relaxed and unclenching—has no more than sucked off the water in which the leaves have been boiled.

After the exchange, he gets to grips with the artichoke but both father and daughter are laughing at him a little. Not cruelly. Guillaume asks about his hometown—about where, even how, he was raised—as if this will explain his vegetative ignorance. 'What is your father's profession?' he asks in French.

Moss smiles to himself. Plastering is not a profession at all, not a blood-relative of accountancy or optometry. It is but a trade, a simple if deft skill at which Ronald Croft must labour repetitively.

Moss answers truthfully for once. The artichoke trap has caught him. Embarrassed but not ashamed. His shame in his father is far more personal than that: an intense dislike of the man's pride in his own ignorance. His crude racism. Plastering was never the problem. Moss chooses not to share these ancillary thoughts with Guillaume. Veronique may wish to compare notes on the strengths and shortcomings of their respective fathers, not that it will be happening today. And, of course, both father and daughter believe him to study literature. They must be impressed with his academic prowess now they have learnt of his modest start in life.

The second course is a beef dish. Tender, mouth-watering, it includes another vegetable which Moss cannot identify. Aubergine, he learns from Veronique. He eats this one without incident, the mechanics of doing so no more challenging than hoovering up fish and chips. The boy recognises this to be food of distinction while knowing it is an area of ignorance for him. The tastes are subtle, herby aromas with which he is unfamiliar. He does not dare to comment; in his life to date, faggots and dumplings have been among his favourites. He no more belongs in this lavish eatery than he did at the oasis with the goatherder the day before.

After eating Guillaume lights up a cigar and Véronique a cigarette. Both offer one to Moss and he takes the latter. He never buys cigarettes, seldom smokes at all but does not wish to spurn their effortless geniality. He is going with the flow.

Then they drive on to Ghardaia. Moss thanks both father and daughter for their hospitality, their company. It is approaching dusk as, once more, he seeks a hotel.

* * *

Moss utilises his new-found aptitude for completing the paperwork required to stay under a roof in Algeria. The clerk takes his passport, places it in the hotel's safe for the duration of his stay. He parts company with just a small measure of the money he carries secreted on his person. The clerk leads Moss to his hotel room. This one is situated across a courtyard behind the reception area of the building. A small terrace of rooms, each with its own external door, form a square around the small garden. A couple of palm trees and a stagnant pond.

The room is warm as he enters. A bricked off corner

might almost be an en-suite. It contains a cemented sealed square of brick in which cold water stands. The hotel clerk explains that this water is for washing. Shaving should he choose to. With a simple mime and a hand on the bucket beside the water pool, he shows Moss how to flush the adjacent handle-less toilet. The English boy smiles wryly at the novelty of this. A few nights here will be instructive, he thinks. And the absence of rain makes it inevitable that they must economise on the wet stuff.

* * *

That evening the boy from Bury walks into the main square in Ghardaia. Warm air embraces him contrary to his expectation of cool—even cold—air down here at night. The streets throng with men, not a woman in sight. They look tall, many must reach six-foot-six. The tallest men all wear blue. Blue robes with white headdresses atop. Abdul's cousins, thinks Moss.

He stands and takes in the square, turning right around. Three hundred and sixty degrees. Looking at the people who surround him. It is only a minority who wear the distinctive blue robes of the Tuareg. And those who do gather together. Those who don't—the browns and greys that Moss also saw in Aïn Maabed—are apart from them. Each huddle in their own clothing-affixed tribe. In the words of the detergent-box, these colours do not mix. Moss tries to spot people in jeans or western jackets. People like himself. There are none. Not in Ghardaia. Nor are there any restaurants or other indoor gathering places. Not any apparent to Moss. On the street the crowds gather around market traders, still selling their wares at this late hour. One or two serve food but not anything which entices Moss. He is still quite satiated from the earlier fare. The beef more than the artichoke. He sees a man with some kind of fryer, an electric cable running into the property closest to his stall. He serves chicken to the brown-clad men gathered around him. Food for the browns, served up on grease-proof paper. Moss sees no sign of spice or even salt, maybe he is missing something. The men talk and laugh as they eat, small goblets of chicken skin showing on their bared teeth.

And then all eyes turn to an unexpected sight, every man looks on as a veil-less woman strides out from a nearby building. She wears voluminous blue robes, layers of clothing gathered around her, obscuring her shape entirely. A well-groomed mane of black hair crowns her. An unseen band keeps it from falling across her deep-brown face. Moss wears one too; his is a plain elastic band. Her hair is longer than his; spilling over the shoulders of her blue dress. Dress or robe? The swaddling mass of clothing, black hair lying across the rich blue fabric. To Moss, she looks a most confident woman. Not old but certainly older than he is. Traditionally dressed except for the absence of headscarf, face out in the open. The only woman on the streets of Ghardaia tonight. Lioness.

A man says something loudly, sharply. The English boy is unsure if he directs it at the woman or if his cry is simply about her. Arabic remains impenetrable to him. The woman shakes a dismissive hand, she continues to walk by. Then a different man—a young man probably of no more than Moss's own twenty years—jumps up, rushes in front of her and obstructs the woman's passage. Stands in her path. He is thin, wiry. His demonstrative arms move like the sails of a windmill. He shouts directly into her face. The confrontation makes Moss feel uneasy. The woman is gesticulating back at the boy. She does not like him; he is preventing her from walking where she chooses to go. The boy touches her hair as he spits out more Arabic words. Whatever he is saying Moss cannot understand it. An alien language. It crosses the English boy's mind that he is telling her to wear a headscarf. It's just a guess; he could even be propositioning her in the manner of the car driver in Nedroma. If that is his game, she will have said no. The lady is treading her own path. The young Arab—brown clothing not blue—is repulsive to Moss. He is not treating her as he should. This is clear even without knowledge of the customs of the town. Moss wonders if a lone female is, through custom or ordinance, prohibited down here in the Sahara. He feels innately drawn to her. Moss is on the side of the blue-clad lioness, cannot think how he might express it. As it was at the tiny oasis outside Aïn Maabed, the perspective of a Lancashire lad is of no relevance here.

The woman changes her approach. She stays her arms, no longer waving in mimicry of the angry man. Speaks clearly and directly at him; she is seeking eye contact while he glances up, down, away and across the square. Men and women looking into each other's faces is a rare thing down here. Muhammed's wife wouldn't do it when he turned to her in the back of the car two days ago. Still in Arabic and beyond Moss's comprehension, the handsome woman is telling the man some simple home truths. That is what Moss thinks. A second man has come across and now the two men are listening to the woman's discourse. The second man is laughing, Moss thinks it unkind laughter. He even pats the wiry young man as if in solidarity. And then Moss realises that a number of the men in blue robes, five or six—many of them look to be old, sixty or seventy years—are now standing close to the taunting men. The wiry young man takes hold of the woman's wrist. A man in a blue robe instantly brings a stick down on his knuckles, forces the release of his grip. The swipe of the improvised weapon seems also to have caught the woman's arm, to have hurt her quite badly. She let out a cry and now she winces, holding her hand, her wrist, clasping it to her body. Swaddling it in the excess of her blue robes as if nursing an infant. Moss believes—based upon the timing of the swipe—that the blue-robed man's intention was to protect. But the woman is cross with him, with the old one whose colour of clothing she shares. She speaks to him. Shouts. Moss hears in her voice that she is on the verge of tears. In physical pain. The blue-robed man puts a hand to his heart; Moss thinks it a gesture of apology. Other young men have stepped forward, responding, it seems, to the injuring of the young brown-clad man, even though that was retaliation for the aggression shown towards the innocent woman. Voices are raised. The woman recovers something of the lioness, again speaks levelly to the many men who surround her, while caressing her damaged arm. Her face—the only woman's face on these bustling moonlit streets—looks positively animated. A coil of hair has come loose, it bounces defiantly in front of her eyes, as she speaks to the blue-robed man whose precipitous action has injured her. She continually cossets her wrist. Then she turns on the assembled men in brown. Voice up a notch, a harangue for the lot of them. Moss sees that there is more difference between these people than simply their clothing: the older blue-robed men are taller and darker skinned than those in brown.

The police arrive, bringing to Moss's mind the football match he left early on his first day in this cloven country. Four policemen place themselves between the assembled groups. Battypapa's militia, summonsed by the watching posters. One policeman speaks brusquely to the woman, points for her to leave the square. Can they do this? Her presence seems to have been the cause of the disturbance but not her actions. She has been the most composed of the lot. At least until she was injured. Moss thinks she may be arguing with the president's goons, worries it is unwise. Then she turns her back upon them and begins to walk.

Moss watches the police, they remonstrate with the

crowd of men, both blue-clad and brown. The man whose knuckles were hit by the stick shows his hand to a policeman, who in turn shrugs. Not interested in an injury so minor. The blue-robed men begin to disperse.

Moss decides to leave this tense crowd, as he had that football match which went awry several days earlier. He lifts his head and sees that the woman is walking from the square to the alleyway, where his hotel is situated. He walks briskly in her direction, hopes that she does not misinterpret the urgency with which he follows her. Moss notes that the woman enters his own hotel. She is only a few steps in front of him by this time. He catches her up at the desk. She speaks in Arabic but only to name a room number. The receptionist passes her a key with its wooden attachment bearing the inscription fourteen.

'Quinze,' says Moss and collects his key as she steps away from the desk. He follows the woman out into the courtyard, their rooms are adjacent.

'Je m'excuse,' says the boy from Bury.

The woman turns and looks into his face. Her own is quite calm despite the heady confrontation she has been through. Her eyes are black in the middle—intense—a film of kohl sitting thickly upon her lashes. He sees that several strands of her hair are straying from their formation, angling across her dark, intelligent face. She has a tiny scar beside her right eye, a blemish, a small patch of paler skin on her left cheekbone. Her skin is weathered, tautened by wind and sun. Moss thinks she looks magnificent.

'Ça va?' he asks, feeling as he says it that his question is ill-put. How are you? Far too informal, imprecise; he wants to understand what has happened and whether she is distraught. Were the events that preceded her quickstep to the hotel a typical occurrence for her or something exceptional? And why is she alone on the street when no other women are there at this time? Every woman for five hundred miles might be wearing a headscarf.

'Les choses vont bien, mon garçon,' she tells him: Things are going well, my boy.

Moss feels sarcasm, unsure if she intends it or not. His face burns red. 'Les hommes, mal,' he says, his French indistinct, his point vague.

'Tout, tout,' she says. 'Bonne nuit.' She smiles at him as she enters her room. The hint of a smile, she closes the door behind her. Takes no more questions from the over-curious English boy.

All men are bad, this Tuareg feminist has told him. He has had greater acknowledgement from her than he received at the tiny oasis the day before, and still his understanding, his admittance to the life of this country, remains in abeyance. Everything he sees fascinates, bewilders and excludes. Tonight, he has seen a man harassing a woman, who in turn was poorly advocated for by an old man with a stick. Disinterested police sought order, not justice, and a resigned, headscarf-free protagonist, told him that men are rubbish. He has arrived where he intended—reached the Sahara Desert—yet struggles to understand what is occurring right in front of his eyes. There are few Western faces here and he has not found further Algerians to match the sophistication or the simple goodness of the Lellouches. The family he stayed with in Oran. Who collected him, as Asia so sweetly coined it, when first he jumped over his rucksack. He determines that he will rest in this town, stay in Ghardaia for a few days. It is in the Sahara Desert, he is here. Made it. Then he will head back towards the coast, Tunisia, then straight to Italy. He had thought of going further, deeper into the desert—Tamanrasset his map had boasted—but that must be the journey of another boy in a parallel life. He has seen an oasis and it was a pleasing sight. Its nourishment did not flow towards him. Moss is ready to turn.

Rucksack Jumper

Chapter Four

Trip to Bury

1.

As I awake, I am momentarily confused by the size and softness of my bed. This is a pleasant feeling, barely dissipated by the certain knowledge that the redoubtable Sir Norman is in the next room along. He could be sleeping, maybe dressing, and still more likely working. Reading briefing notes or drawling a slew of letters into a Dictaphone. No sound comes from beyond the wall but I believe it to be his habit. Early rising, working all hours.

He was only moderately fearsome company on the train coming here yesterday afternoon. When he told me that he would take a light evening meal in his room, in order to look through some papers—which he advised were unrelated to our purpose up here—the realisation that I would not have to endure a shared evening meal with him was a relief. That tells you how diffident a civil servant I am: happy to forego the opportunity to promote my profile in the department. My standing with the gaffer, as the northern footie players say.

The Midland Hotel, Oxford Street, Manchester: truthfully, it is the finest place in which I've ever slept the night. I hope my work will soon enable me to stay in hotels of similar class further afield, even exotic in their location. Manchester is anything but that. I enjoy having a double bed to myself, although I must arise from it very soon. The last time I slept in such a large one—and I am not sure that it was quite this size—was in the rented place in Fulham, with Christine. That didn't last. 'Still hope,' says my father, referring to the fact that we are not yet divorced. I have no hope at all and the divorce cannot come quickly enough. Until then, I fear I will be one of very few officials to accompany Sir Norman on a mission—a grand title, I know, but that is how he refers to all excursions outside the city of Westminster—who still lives with his parents. I considered lying about it when he gave me the personal grilling on the train; however, speaking such falsehoods is quite simply not done. Not if one hopes, in time, to become a senior civil servant. Of course, one may dissemble, obscure, fail to answer or tell an ad hoc truth of no apparent relevance to the question asked. That all goes with the territory but, as Sir Norman has said—and not directly to me, to a room full of us hopefuls at the last departmental conference—lying is strictly the domain of elected politicians.

'You are married, aren't you, Winterbotham?' You will spot the inherent assumption within the wording of the question which Sir Norman put to me on the train. We were sitting opposite each other. There were only a couple of people, aside from he and I, in first-class, both of whom were reading The Correspondent. I expect that they were actually eavesdropping given the dullness of that paper's recent fare. And with that small and disinterested audience to bear witness to the honesty of my reply, he asked me the socially laden question, you are married, aren't you?

Well, I must admit, I took a moment before I confessed. 'Separated, Sir.'

He pulled a bit of a face, then muttered, 'These days.'

His utterance seemed to imply that it is a consequence of us bumping over into the nineteen-eighties. That nudging of the number seven to the eight on the decade

Trip to Bury

counter has led to all of this flummery, the divorcing and remarrying that he surely sees as a harbinger to societal breakdown. Christine and I actually separated last July, hardly the good old days but still the nineteen-seventies when we last called ourselves a couple. And when he, at that same departmental talk in which he so elegantly warned us off blatantly lying, and which also took place around last July if memory serves, advised us of the intricacies and complications of living overseas—embassy life, consular life—Sir Norman touched on the need to be flexible. 'Not all marriages can stand the strain,' he said. I suppose he thinks that sacrificing your marriage for the good of the diplomatic service is one thing, while breaking up less than two years in, and Christine and I never getting ourselves out of West London, is a very poor show.

I felt a need to make my position clearer. 'I think we neither really thought enough about what marriage entailed before embarking on it, Sir,' I said yesterday. 'We're still in touch, working on it. Might get back together.' I was only giving him my father's line. They are of the same generation and I imagine they value the same hokum.

'Marriage guidance, are you having that? The counselling.'

I personally dislike the whole experience of sharing personal information even with my reflection in the mirror, so having this grilling from Sir Norman while my marriage awaits its coroner's report was beyond mortifying. Still, it is not a matter that I thought worth flinging myself from the carriage to avoid. 'Just trying to work it out for ourselves,' I replied. Dissembled really.

The next thing he said was a relief to me. 'We are not opium, four letters?' Solving my personal dilemma was on the back burner and he re-immersed himself in the crossword he hadn't touched for thirty minutes. I'm not one for all that cryptic stuff, so I just shrugged and picked up the novel I'd been reading. A hefty tomb about colonial India, I'd thought it would impress when I selected it; subsequently found Sir Norman pays no attention to anything I do unless it relates to an instruction of his. I was finding the damned thing hard work.

* * *

It crosses my mind that my ill-advised marital status and inability to solve crossword puzzles may have contributed to Sir Norman's decision to dine alone last night. For my part it was a chance to explore Manchester. A bit of a hole compared to the capital; however, I enjoyed a decent meal in the north of England's very own Chinatown. So that was an experience. And I sank a couple of pints—cheap northern pints—in a pub with a television playing. The sound was on low but two screens flickered away. T.V. in the pub, no one in there watching it. Not that I could see. I think it is only there to make a night out feel like a night in. Northern folk are funny. It might have been there to replace conversation, and on the evidence of my night in the White Horse, it is a failure. I found Mancunians to be as friendly as our folklore declares them. For the most part, there are exceptions.

It was an old fellow—my father's age, not yet decrepit—who first started talking to me. He asked if I'd come straight from work, did so, I believe, on account of my ironed shirt and pressed trousers. I realised I had overdressed the moment I entered the pub. My second-best suit is the only alternative clothing that I have brought with me, my best was awaiting its use this morning. For the mission. Anyhow, I like to think I smartened the pub up a little with my presence. It was a pleasant enough building, mid-Victorian, late-Victorian. Christine knows that stuff, it passes me by. The carpet looked pre-war to me and not

Trip to Bury

terribly clean. Stained and plenty of them.

I told him—the old chap who asked—'Yes, I have come from work.' A train journey from London in the company of Sir Norman counts as such, it really does. Obviously, I would not be telling the old fella why I was up north or the nature of my work. Foreign Office manoeuvres, very hush-hush. In this instance it is only for the protection of personal information, at other times it can be state secrets we must keep mum about. It's instilled in us from the off, never blab a word. He suggested I was an accountant and I nodded, as I might have done had he hit upon my true vocation, when blind guesses like that have little chance of ever being finding the mark. Far too many options, countless. I didn't lie, you will note. I nodded my head and the gentleman became confused by the incidental timing of it. He seemed pleased with himself after saying it, never realised he'd barked up the wrong tree.

'Up from London, are you?' he asked. My accent is not—in my view—a giveaway. It is a ubiquitous accent, the Queen's English, spoken as it should be. I suppose that is another type of giveaway. 'Odd that they need a London accountant up here, is there a company in trouble? You're not closing someone down, are you?'

Having believed he had guessed my occupation at his first attempt, he continued to barrage me with further speculation. Quite amusing. This northern Sherlock Holmes could not see how inept his deductive skills were. Unaware even that he was in a maze. 'Not at liberty to say,' I replied which, given the falseness of his assumptions and my wish not to disabuse him thereof, was quite true. I can't answer a question based on balderdash but I was able to let this fellow believe whatever he liked. And he liked to think he had figured me out. 'How about you?' I asked, flipping the subject around in order to arrest his futile inquiry. 'Have you been at work today?'

I saw him smirk to himself. I knew what he was thinking. Truly. Was I really asking if he was unemployed? His face said it all, and that had not been my intention. I'd seen him buy his table a round before he wandered back to the bar and started chatting to me. He didn't look hard-up in its truest sense. 'Aye,' was all he said, until I enquired further. He wanted me to drag it out of him. You know the type. Hoping to prove that I, a clueless London accountant, had no insight into northern jobs. And I don't profess any particular knowledge of the broad economic variety. In my role I generally undertake a bit of research, commit it to report and then move on. I don't collect facts. I'm in it to resolve a situation—not to win quizzes—and the areas I look into are often obscure. Algerian law, lately. Law and prisons, how they function in that country.

'Lathe operator,' I got out of him after a suitable quota of polite enquiry.

I smiled. Was he trying to prove a class distinction between us? I don't put on airs and didn't really like him implying that I do. It struck me that lathe operating is a good outcome from a secondary modern education. It sits in the category, best of the rest. A skill involved, I wouldn't doubt, and still it cannot be a truly satisfying job. Much too repetitive. Then again, accountancy might be a shocker for all I really know. I wasn't looking to get into a debate about it. 'Is that your son with you?' As I asked the question, I glanced towards the table he'd arisen from. There was a young man sitting at it plus two others who looked to be in the same age bracket as my lathe operator.

'You're a perceptive bugger,' he remarked, which I do not believe to be a statement of fact. My guess—the sole intention of which was to change the subject—clearly hit the nail on the head. And—if you want to follow my reasoning—the young fellow I pointed at was surely the son of one of the three oldies. My chances were not as remote as his haphazard conjecture about accountancy. Northern fool. 'He's a funny one,' the man continued. 'Won't work as far as I can tell. His mother says it's socialising. We were told...' The man lowered his voice considerably at this point. The pub was busy, I could not imagine his son picking up a word. '...last year of school, mind, he's autistic. Last year of school before they drop that one on us. Took their bloody time those teachers.' I nodded; made the sympathetic face I've practiced. Expect to deploy it on Mrs Croft later this morning. 'I'm still not sure I believe it,' he added.

That struck me as an odd thing to say. And even talking to a lathe operator in a pub is a bit of a departure for me. My job is very factual, it's not really about psychology at all. I don't think so. I've never knowingly come across these kinds of people. Mentally handicapped, the strange ones. My mother works as a teaching assistant, and she has talked about an autistic child once or twice. I am like my father, I'm afraid: we do not pay Mother's ramblings too much attention, it only encourages them. I do recall her telling us, on one occasion, that this particular child would become anxious about the silliest of things. She gave an example: his behaviour when they put up a new classroom clock, one without a second hand. The autistic boy began to watch it all day because he feared if he took his eyes off it, he wouldn't know if it was moving at all. Is that anxiety or just plain madness? I don't know. Perhaps we have a range of different words for the same thing. Watching clocks is certainly not a rational way to spend one's time.

'Will he be anxious if I talk to him?' I only asked this to extend a bit of friendship towards the man who had chosen to share something which I considered rather personal with me.

'Let's try,' he replied.

* * *

I followed the man to the table at which his friends and son were seated.

'Keith, this posh chap would like to talk to you,' he announced.

It struck me that he could have said something along similar lines far more casually than he managed. I suppose his clumsy formulation is simply the lathe operator's way. And I am not posh, I secured a grammar school education by dint of my own endeavours. 'Hi Keith, I'm Dave,' I said, reaching out a hand. Seeking to shake his.

'Sorry, I'm Derek,' muttered the lathe operator, his father, and he leant across and shook my hand rather firmly. Keith, meanwhile, said nothing at all. Held his own hand close to his stomach. Hunched himself nervously over the rim of his pint glass.

'Nout to worry over,' said one of the older men who was sitting with Keith. 'It's nice to talk to people of your own age.'

I puzzled over how stilted these men's interactions with Keith were. It must have been embarrassing for him, down the pub with his father and two of his father's friends—assuming that is who they were—and then getting a lecture about the merits of mixing with the young. The icing on a cake of no pleasure.

'I think the pool table is free,' I told Keith. 'Do you play?' He still didn't speak but arose from his chair. I guessed he was game for hitting a few balls, less so for a spot of chin wagging.

At the table, I put the twenty pence in the slot, Keith didn't offer or seem to note my generosity. He may have regarded it as a furtherance of the benefits system on which I presume he relies. 'Off you go,' I said to him, once I had removed the triangle from the pack.

Keith struck the ball well, his shot certainly spread the colours.

Trip to Bury

'I'll try for spots,' I told him and aimed at a ball. I hit it square on but the blighter rattled the jaws of the pocket. Came back out.

'Useless.' That was the first word Keith had spoken to me. I wondered if it was fighting talk; hindsight tells me it was unwitting rudeness. He then aimed at the same ball—a much tighter angle than I'd had a go at—and sunk it well. Dashed good shot, can't take it away from him. After that, he potted two more before he missed one. It's possible he did that deliberately. He certainly left the white in an awkward position. Snookered me.

I duly missed hitting a ball altogether and Keith spoke again. 'Two shots.' This referred to the extra shot awarded to him on account of my error. He used his first to set himself up and then potted three more balls. He was streets ahead.

'You're a good player, Keith,' I told him. I'm not churlish about this, getting a hiding from someone intellectually inferior. Pool is only pool and one should always take such things on the chin.

'Yes.'

I managed to pot one and only one before he sunk his last spot and then said, 'We name a bag in this pub.' I'm not from up north but I was able to interpret this as the local rule of choosing a pocket for the final winning ball. Bag, pocket: funny. He pointed at a corner and duly potted the black in it.

'Well played.' I offered him my hand again. Keith didn't take it but nor did he turn away. 'Where did you learn?' I tried.

'Crappy table at home. It's easy on this. It's decent.'
'Who do you play at home?'
'Right-hand plays left-hand. Sister doesn't play.'

I noticed that Keith's glass was empty and offered to buy him another which drew a nod. When I'd fetched two more pints of cheap northern bitter, we sat away from the older men and I tried to tell him about living in Twickenham. Told Keith that I still lived with my parents, mentioning that for a couple of years I lived away in Fulham. He only grunted in reply; his timing suggested he was listening. I was keen not to talk about work, having led his father to believe that I'm a chartered accountant, and—as I have said—I do not like to lie.

'I was married for a time.'

Keith looked up into my face.

'I am still but we no longer live together.'

He looked back down.

'It didn't work out.'

Keith grunted which may have meant my observation was obvious.

'Not everything does, Keith but I find if you keep trying—give everything your best shot—some of it goes okay.' This was me at my most philosophical which, frankly, is also me babbling.

'Where did you meet?' Keith was finally curious.

I began saying the syllables of the Young Conservatives but cleverly rescued myself, turning it into the Young Conservationists. In the nick of time. It came to me while speaking that I was sitting in a working-class pub in the heart of a city where they would elect a house brick to parliament if it wore a Labour Party rosette. Keith again looked directly into my face; I think he bought it. 'In London,' I improvised, 'there is no countryside to speak of, so we try and look after gardens, public spaces. The Young Conservationists help to keep them in shape. Keep them natural for the wildlife.'

Keith looked sceptical. 'There's no wildlife in London.'

'Foxes and squirrels and all the garden birds. Herons too.' I was quick to defend the worth of my imaginary pastime.

'Foxes?' queried Keith. 'You're weird.' He stood up, three-quarters of a pint in his hand, and started to saunter back to his old-man table. 'And shit at pool,' he said over his shoulder. Maybe that's autism, or maybe he guessed that I'm a Conservative after all. In my defence, I had tried gamely to do my good deed for the day.

Derek wandered across the pub to where I stood. 'All right, son?' he asked.

How could I not be? It was his son whose conduct was hopelessly awry. I'm two or three rungs up on what may yet be a glittering career. Definitely all right. I nodded, then lowering my voice said, 'He's a useful pool player, doesn't have terribly good manners.'

Derek laughed. 'David, David, do you think I haven't spotted that? It's a good day when he sits in the pub with his mouth shut. Last week he called the barmaid a whore for no reason but a decent skirt she was wearing. Nice pins too. He's a fucking nightmare, pardon my French.'

'How old is he?' I asked.

'Can you guess?'

'Twenty, maybe twenty-two,' I ventured.

'How old are you?'

'I'm twenty-nine.'

'Then maybe you share a date of birth. What can you do with 'em, eh? Good for you, David, with accounts, accounting. Keith would have had the head for it. Numbers, he's good with numbers. The trouble is he couldn't sit an exam to save his life. Thanks for playing a game with him, he'll tell his mother about it all of next week. And the one after, I expect.'

2.

That was last night in Manchester, my only ever night in the north. Except a three-day trip to Edinburgh which

Christine and I took when we were courting. It cost an arm and a leg, separate rooms and what have you. And now, as I dress, I mentally prepare for the day ahead. I will drive Sir Norman to Bury, where we must advise the parents of a wayward young man exactly how they may spring him from an Algerian prison. I've read all the relevant papers—made calls—and Sir Norman advised, on the train coming here, that he would like me to lead the discussion. Office colleagues have told me that the boss is the world's worst delegator, so he must have seen something in me.

I showered before I went out last night but do so again. I am determined to be odour free in the car taking Sir Norman to this Bury place. The fug of cigarette smoke in the pub—none of it mine, I hasten to add—permeated everything. My hair needs two plastic sachets of shampoo; needs a cut, I infer from it. Once I have scrubbed away the White Horse, I put on my very best suit. No tie. Not for breakfast, it can come later. A casual pose, I figure Sir Norman needs to see how relaxed I am about it all. It's only Bury.

The corridors in this hotel are wide and carpeted. The laundry trolley is outside Sir Norman's room. His door is open and I presume that he vacated it before the cleaners moved in. Through the open doorway, I can see the rear end of a black-skirted chambermaid as she makes up the bed. I don't stare for long but she's young and slim. And bending over. Perhaps I only imagine that she is young. Never see her face. I step back into my own room and quickly pack my bag. I fear that I am behind Sir Norman in my timing although I have planned the trip, I know that I'm on schedule. I leave my case in my room, step back out to the lift.

The aroma of coffee leads me to the dining room and, on entering, I see Sir Norman's side profile. He holds a coffee cup in his left hand and a newspaper in his right. I give my room number to the uniformed lady standing by the door and go to him.

Before I arrive, and quite loudly, Sir Norman says, 'You forgot to order The Correspondent.' He has a grade-three thunderous look on his face. More tomato than beetroot. It won't get me the sack but he is displeased. In the office we laugh about the pompous crotchet when we witness these little outbursts. Those on the receiving end take longer to see the funny side. 'This is dreadful,' he adds, making a sweeping gesture at yesterday's Evening Clarion. I presume it to be the only gratis paper available in this hotel.

'I'm sorry, Sir,' I grovel. 'Mrs Winstanley didn't put it on the list.' This refers to his secretary's instructions for me. I am not shouldering responsibility for this mishap alone.

'Are you late?'

'No, we've plenty of time. The car won't be dropped off for another hour.'

Mrs Winstanley instructed me to ensure her charge is able to enjoy a leisurely breakfast. I've managed the timetable to accommodate this. It seems the old bugger isn't in on the plan.

'Yes, but we really want to get this over with, don't we, Winterbotham?'

'Yes, Sir. However, Mrs Winstanley made the appointment for ten-thirty and it wouldn't do to arrive early. Or not so early that the Crofts feel unprepared. They would still be vacuuming or whatever their sort does when they have important officials making house-calls.'

He nods, concurs with my reasoning. Likes the adjective I attribute to him, I expect. 'Get you some breakfast then,' he commands. I notice saliva collecting in the corner of his mouth as he says this. He can get away with it—sixty and knighted—but it looks slightly disgusting. I don't tell him, hand him a napkin, or any of that. I would if it was my dad; Sir Norman is trickier to handle.

The fare in this select hotel is rather good. Filter coffee, fresh fruit and muesli. I try to enjoy it while giving Sir Norman the right impression. Making up for last night, his dining alone stunt.

'Did you go out on the town then, Winterbotham?' he asks.

'Not really. Well, a little. Just to eat.' This is a garbled answer; I don't care to tell Sir Norman about losing a game of pool to a subnormal chappie in The White Horse. 'I had a light meal in Chinatown.'

'Ah, yes, Manchester's hidden minority. Of course, they're all Honkers you know. Well, not the true Honkers—not colonials—but Hong Kong Chinese to a man. The real Honkers—our lot—will stay out there until the red army roles in. It could be like Saigon come the end, mind you. Those fellows who served you, the Chinese Honkers, the restaurant business is only a side-line. Banking's their big game, you probably know.'

I didn't know this and ponder whether to question his certainty. In the restaurant the previous evening I ate a Pekinese dish, and I know Beijing—its new name or, more precisely, the better rendition of its ancient name—is a long way from Hong Kong. In the event I let it go; sometimes the best course of action can be inaction. Sir Norman is the font of all knowledge in our department; that's how we play it, whether he's being truly wise or a bottle of claret beyond its far shore. We agree to whatever he says. It's his ship at the end of the day.

'Can't stand the stuff myself,' he continues. 'Too greasy by far.'

Sir Norman goes back to the local newspaper and I eat my muesli. A waitress comes across. She is dark skinned, not black but not white either, might be mixed race. So young she should be in school. A shy face. She asks, in a strong Mancunian accent, if I would like some toast. I say,

Trip to Bury

'Yes, please,' and she asks the same of Sir Norman.

'The other lady is serving me.'

'It's all right. We wait on all the tables. What would you like?'

'I'd like the other lady, please?' He says it rather firmly and the little waitress looks down. Then when she puts her head back, I think for a moment that she is going to speak back to him—argue—but she just nods and turns away.

Sir Norman goes back to his newspaper and in time an older lady walks across and places toast in front of me. 'Would you like toast, sir?' She asks it with a brusqueness to her tone. Not the right way for a waitress to speak to him, but I understand the point she makes.

'No thank you,' says Sir Norman.

Well, we all know what that was about.

* * *

After breakfast I ask Sir Norman if he is happy to wait in the foyer. There are thirty minutes to kill before the hire car is due to arrive.

'Where will you be, Winterbotham?'

'I have to collect my bag from my room. I was going to listen to the news before the car is delivered.'

'Yes, do. I'll see if reception can get me a proper paper. Something's afoot in that damned embassy. The yanks in Tehran. Not that I've any inside knowledge, you understand? I have a hunch. There's a logjam to break their all right. It makes our mission look like child's play, eh, Winterbotham? Only one lad stuck and that with a reason of sorts. A prisoner not a hostage.'

'Yes, Sir. It should be child's play.'

In my room, the only news report I catch—I missed the headlines listening to Sir Norman's assessment of the new Iranian regime; 'Can't last' being its central tenet—is a long-winded account of the funeral of Jean Paul Satre. Tens of thousands of Parisians turned out to follow the cortege on Saturday last. The reporter speculated upon this in the light of Satre's certain atheism. The existentialist no longer exists.

The French are an unpredictable lot, I really think so. Fancy that many people—ordinary people, surely, if it was tens of thousands—turning out to pay their respects for the passing of a man of such impenetrable and depressing philosophy. I could ask Sir Norman what he makes of it all but I imagine he will be dismissive. That seems to be his mood today.

I return to the foyer and confirm to Sir Norman that I have learnt of no new developments in Tehran. I give it a go and say, 'Long World Service report on the funeral of Satre at the weekend.'

'Who?'

'Satre. Jean Paul Satre.'

'That bloody devil, eh? A giant of something or other, no use to us. Marxist, wasn't he? The all-talk variety. Most of them are, young Winterbotham. The Communist Party is on the decline in France, by the way. Not before time, and definitely on the decline.'

I'm never really sure how to take Sir Norman's observations and insights. He's a stick-in-the-mud but a sharp one. He will have learnt all about French communists at a senior level briefing sure as night follows daylight saving.

* * *

A young northern lad delivers our car to the hotel's front door; I sign the requisite paperwork and then carry Sir Norman's bag to the boot. I watch on as the doorman picks up my own.

'They would have done that,' says Sir Norman. A most petty admonishment; I was alleviating his burden, carrying his bag.

The car is top of the range. A Ford Capri. I see from Sir Norman's face that he is less impressed than I. He opens the rear door. 'Not much leg room.' Initially I think his comment pointless, only two of us are travelling so what does it matter. Then I wonder if it was his intention to sit in the back, review paperwork or do The Correspondent crossword. I couldn't have stomached trying to do either in the back of a car constantly stopping and starting across ten miles of urban traffic. Sir Norman is different. His comforts and discomforts fit only the mould around him. He occupies the seat next to me as I'd always, if incorrectly, imagined he would. Talking to me for half an hour should not be beyond him. And we still haven't a strategy for this meeting; he hasn't said a word about my briefing paper.

I have not been driving much lately. I let Christine keep the car when she and I separated. It was not a financial concession at all, I was deliberately freeing myself of that encumbrance. I'm currently paying half her rent, which galls me a little. My father says it reserves me the right to move back in. Heaven forbid. Today, I am entrusted with Sir Norman's safe passage to some God-forsaken house on Wolseley Road, Bury. I've studied the maps, confident of getting the directions right. I worry that I may crunch the gears a couple of times. I have a terribly off-putting passenger.

'You do know how to drive these contraptions?' The old boy's questions don't make it any easier.

'I'm competent.' I say it primarily to convince myself of what truth there is in the statement.

* * *

The Capri starts up easily enough. The city centre is predictably congested. I have taken this into account in my journey planning. I'm nothing if not thorough. Early in the drive, I recognise that I've missed a turning—keep it to myself—my preparation, scrutiny and memorisation of the city's layout, enables me to make a small adjustment. We keep to the right trajectory although my diversion passes us in front of Strangeways Prison.

'Well, we could offer to house the lad here, I suppose?'

I laugh when Sir Norman says it. He has quite the sense of humour. It is a rum affair, no question about it: this young lad from Bury has earned himself a prison sentence for exchanging a hundred and forty pounds or so on the wrong side of the Algerian border. A fool but hardly a threat to the state. I have gathered that Algeria thinks its currency sovereign property, not for trifling with. The poor lad didn't get our briefing paper, and it wasn't enough money to buy a camel. Now it's up to us, diplomats—all the king's horses and all the king's men—to rectify his indiscretion. To leave no discernible stain between our respective nations. In truth, I'm disappointed not to be speaking to the parents alone. Sir Norman coming on this one is disproportionate. I believe I could have handled it perfectly well. Algeria is the irregularity for us. Not young men in foreign prisons, they are ten a penny. And it is I, not my haughty manager, who has done all the spadework. Spoken to the French, their lot in Algiers. It's his decision to make, I suppose. Maybe he just fancied a trip to Bury. See how the other half live.

'Was the restaurant busy last night, Winterbotham?'

Conversation seems to be the order of the day. 'Reasonably, Sir. Quite a few customers. Yes.'

'Did you chat with them? The northerners. Folks from oop north?' Sir Norman feigns an accent only for the one word, and I duly laugh. I expect his disdain for northerners extends to anyone who has not spent at least a couple of afternoons at a royal garden party. His snobbery is a disappointing trait. To me at least, grammar school boy that I am, the son of a plumber. My father's done well, runs a firm of nine plumbers these days. The word in the office is that when Sir Norman has to meet bereaved relatives, mothers and fathers of murder victims, in Rio or Rome—victims of terrorism occasionally—his compassion is genuine, heartfelt and appreciated. So strange that this able thinker should invest so much energy in remaining aloof.

'Quite a few of the customers were Chinese.'

'Hmmm.'

'There were some English though,' I add, realising that I need to make an effort. Speak about what interests him.

'You talked to them?'

'Yes.'

'And how are things oop north?'

I think it would be sycophantic to laugh at the same joke twice, so I do not. 'There was a man with an autistic son. He was frustrated. His son is my age but doesn't work. Not incapable but he has a kind of phobia against a lot of things. He barely said a word, the son.'

'Were just the two of them dining together?'

'Yes,' I allow across my lips because I do not wish to tell Sir Norman about The White Horse or my playing of the bar game, pool. I do not know how he is disposed towards beer. I fear he would misinterpret the time I spent with the working classes.

'No mother—wife—enjoying the meal out with them?'

'I understood that she was at home, Sir.'

'He takes the son to a Chinese restaurant without her. Funny business, don't you think? Are you sure they're not divorced? I don't say it to embarrass you, Winterbotham, it just seems more likely. He takes the son to a restaurant because he can't go around to the house. Wants to do his bit which is creditable. Did you catch his job?'

'Lathe operator, Sir.'

'Then I'm correct. On their meagre wages, no lathe

operator would go to a fancy Chinese restaurant without his wife. Well, wife or lover, bit on the side, as I'm told you young ones call it. Ha-hey! Not without a dashed good reason. Which brings us back to your fellow last night having no choice. Lives in a bedsit or some such.'

'I expect you're right, Sir.' He is always right, even when he's wrong. What a strange world Sir Norman must live in, never given the opportunity to learn from his mistakes.

'Poor choice, wouldn't you say?' He continues to pontificate on the scene he has imagined. 'An autistic kiddie, phobia's you said. That sort of boy is hardly likely to eat chow mein and what have you. Potatoes and a pork chop, that's the ticket for those kiddies.'

'He wasn't really a kiddie, Sir. He was my age.'

'Yes, but not of your breeding, Winterbotham. Lathe operator, parents divorced, oop north. Ha. Can't begrudge them a night out though, can we?'

I used to hear a lot of this nonsense in the Young Conservatives. Frankly, I found it distasteful, as I do when I hear Sir Norman at his most patronising. I know I'll forgive him if he praises my work today; however, these are modern times and Sir Norman of all people should understand that. Maggie Thatcher's Tories are a much better mix. Anyone who works hard can make it now. She's putting all the old fuddy-duddies out to grass. The House of Lords. 'No, Sir. Even the boy had a good time.'

'And what of our boy out in Algeria?'

'Good question, Sir. We have to bring him back...'

'Not we, Winterbotham. He has to come back, and do so quickly before the papers pick it up. But we wish to remain the indirect link, don't we?'

'Yes, Sir. I understand your point. I expressed myself poorly.'

'Hmmm.'

'I am not sure that the parents really understand their

son's predicament.'

Sir Norman nods his head at this.

'Justice in Algeria is not good even for the common citizens, certainly not if they're prisoners of conscience...'

'No, Winterbotham. That is true but not relevant to our case. This lad from Bury is not a prisoner of that sort of tomfoolery. Not by any stretch of the imagination. Smuggler, isn't he?'

'Yes, Sir, but...'

'So, we will not be giving his parents a false impression that he has been wrongly incarcerated. Unnecessarily but not wrongly.'

'Understood, Sir.'

'Look, you've only done a couple of public-facing meetings so far, you need to get a feel for them before you go out to a consulate. That's your plan, is it not, Winterbotham?'

'Yes, Sir. Very much so. Or an embassy, Sir.'

'And have we lined you one up?'

'No, Sir. Not yet. I've applied for Stockholm.'

'Very nice. Then this will be good experience, Winterbotham. You lead off but don't stray from the brief. Your knowledge of Algeria can be tip-top, that only helps us behind the scenes. Anyhow, I'll chip in if I have to. To keep it all on track. Graham, our fellow out there in Algiers, he seemed to think they'd prove rather tricky.'

'Yes, Sir, I wrote up my telephone call. Mr Croft was not really amenable to any deal at all but, as I said in the briefing paper, I do not think he understands the situation fully. I gathered from the start that he's not his own son's biggest fan.'

'Ha, eh? Well, you're not a parent yet, Winterbotham, and you've a bit of, shall we say, rapprochement to work through—maybe a bit of humble pie to eat, for all I know—before you can become one. Sometimes one's own children don't turn out as hoped. No one wants a smuggler for a son, wouldn't you guess?'

'Yes, Sir, but this boy's father seemed disinterested. Derek, the fellow last night with the autistic son, he was disappointed but he hadn't given up.'

'No, and nor will this fellow, Ronald Croft. He just needs the right pep talk. You can do that, eh, Winterbotham?'

I nod. Pep talking is new to me and I can't take Croft Senior down to his local for a game of pool. It's just not the way we do it in the FO.

3.

We arrive at Wolseley Road and it is the depressing row of identical red-bricked terraced houses I expected. The Croft's house sits directly opposite an old mill. One that's still in operation by all indications. I expect the spinning of cotton has long ceased. It's probably used as a warehouse these days. There is no parking space near the house, so I turn up the first side street I come to. Cars are parked bumper to bumper on this one too, then as I edge up the street, I see a space. Show Sir Norman my prowess at parallel parking. Swing it in first try, suspect it passes him by.

Sir Norman takes his brief case out from the rear of the hire car. I have just a small notebook which I keep in my jacket pocket. It isn't my intention to intimidate the boy's parents; to win over is not to browbeat. My training is the more contemporary. In front of the house by our parked car, a woman in a housecoat is vigorously brushing the front step. She pauses briefly to watch my esteemed colleague rummage in the boot. He's the only knight she'll be seeing today. She with the rollers in her hair.

We walk past a string of terraced houses, turn back onto Wolseley Road. I see the number seventy-four on a door

Trip to Bury

and count along. Number eighty-two—the house we seek—also has its digits displayed on the front door. Many houses do not. I don't look at Sir Norman as I press my finger to the bell. He likes to see confidence, so I'll display all I can.

A woman wearing a grey skirt, an off-white blouse, answers the door. 'Mrs Croft, I presume?' Goodness me, I think to myself, I sound like Henry Stanley.

'Yes, is it...' She turns her head to Sir Norman. '...Sir Kinsley?'

'Norman Kinsley, Sir Norman,' the great man answers with a smile.

'Do come in. Both of you.' I don't think she gave me a second glance.

She ushers us into the hallway and, as Mrs Croft closes the door behind us, I feel like a caged animal. A little gerbil. I'm in a tiny narrow hallway. A red and black carpet runs under our feet and up a staircase onto the landing above. Two people couldn't pass going up and down. A tiny house, neither elbow room, nor breathing space.

'Ronald,' Mrs Croft calls out, 'our visitors are here.'

The first door opens and a stocky little man with tortoiseshell glasses peers at us. His face looks about as miserable as sin. 'You'd better come in here,' he says.

I wave Sir Norman in front, hoping that this is the polite thing to do, and Mrs Croft and I each wait to be the last to enter. I let her win the contest; it is her house.

As she follows me into the room—a dark and cluttered lounge—she says, 'Would you like a cup of tea, Sir Kinsley?'

'Sir Norman. That is very kind,' he answers.

'Will it really take that long?' says miserable face.

'I'm Dave.' I reach out a hand to be shaken. 'Dave Winterbotham, from the Foreign Office. Sir Norman Kinsley, my manager, also wished to meet with you to discuss this delicate matter.' I note that the old

215

curmudgeon has a copy of The Compendium on his side table. It's my newspaper of choice too, solid Tory fare. So far, so good.

'Tea's all round,' says Mrs Croft as next I shake her hand, and Sir Norman is pumping the arm of old misery guts. I feel more confident than I anticipated. Mr Croft is the obstacle but not one whom his wife fears.

'It's very good to meet you both,' I say when Mrs Croft is finally sitting down, and all of us except Ronald Croft has a drink in our hands. 'I know you are both most concerned about the welfare of Moss.' Mrs Croft stares at me. Imploring me to continue, I think. Ronald sits poker-faced and it strikes me that he is as uncomfortable in this situation as young Keith was in the pub last night. 'Our man out there has been to see Moss in the prison, it's just outside the town of Al Aricha, quite a way from Algiers...'

'We're sorry for his inconvenience...' Mr Croft has interrupted me before I have made my actual point. '...but we didn't ask him to go, to meet Moss.'

'No, quite.' I have to agree with his narrow point. Mr Graham did not visit at his parents' request. 'We regard it as a duty to monitor the welfare of any British citizen who has been detained abroad, and it's particularly true within...' I search for the phrase before settling on the most apt. '...lesser legal systems. The circumstances of his arrest may have been a bewilderment to the poor lad. Most currencies can be changed almost anywhere in the world but he chose to go to Algeria...'

'He did.'

'...and that has brought him to this unfortunate juncture. Our embassy has tried to contact their government at a senior level...'

'We've not asked for this.' Mr Croft sounds quite determined that the diplomatic service should forgo its duty towards his son. Give it a miss. I have to say, this is a novel parental angle from my limited experience.

'No, I am aware of that but...' I pause here to collect my thoughts, hone my wording. '...I do not imagine you would wish your son to suffer if it is easily and legally avoidable.'

'How do you mean?'

At this point Sir Norman—whose knighthood has, in Mrs Croft's eyes, merited a china teacup, while she and I drink from silver jubilee commemorative mugs—decides he can manage better than me. I thought the early exchanges were going satisfactorily given the resistance. I'm building as much rapport with Misery-Face as he will allow.

'The Algerians have applied excessive punishment—not like the Saudis if you have been worrying about the boy having his hands chopped off, nothing like that in Algeria, I'm pleased to say—his imprisonment is disproportionate. They've done this for only one reason. They have certain crimes that they are determined to stamp out. Political protest mostly. The currency issue—the matter your boy has transgressed—is more a matter of national pride than criminality. Do you follow me?'

'Go on?' This is Mrs Croft speaking, she is clearly starstruck by the man's elevation to a knighthood. His words cover the same ground that I was going to. Except for the political point which I wouldn't have raised. Certainly not after he advised me against it.

'Their currency is a bit of a basket case,' he drawls slowly. 'Put simply, they wouldn't get two beans for it if they sold it on the open market, and for this reason, they don't allow it out of the country. By doing this, they can set their own exchange rate, name a price, make a bit of foreign currency by charging a far higher figure for it than it's worth in real terms. It makes only a small difference. When they sell produce, some mineral or metal which they mine in the desert, it goes for dollars, fetches the market value, you see?

Tourists are the principal target of their currency manipulation. That's fair enough, I suppose. It's their country, so they can set whatever rules they like. The problem, of course, is that Algeria has ten thousand miles of border. Is it that much, Winterbotham? It's thousands...' He continues without pausing to hear my best guess and that would have been considerably lower. '...I haven't measured it but it's a giant of a country. Mostly sand of course, hence nothing much to turn into currency. And with that great long border they can't really stop money drifting out from time to time. And ordinary citizens may be very pleased to get their hands on some foreign reserves even if it is at rates far lower than the state-run banks will permit. They don't change their own citizen's money like that you see. That would defeat the object, use up all the foreign currency reserves. So, in Morocco and Tunisia—France too—there is something of a black market for Algerian dinar. Moss told our man out there that he was tricked; frankly, we're not sure how that worked. In the eyes of the law, of Algerian law, he did wrong. Do you know this story?'

'Could you tell us, please, Sir Kinsley?' says Mrs Croft.

'At the border he was caught with a small quantity of dinar in his shoe. That he'd placed it there does incriminate him, nothing for us to quibble about on that point. But it was only a hundred-and-forty-pounds worth at their inflated reckoning. I presume he paid a lot less than that.' Sir Norman pauses but neither Croft speaks. A little sip from his china tea-cup and a smile at the fawning Mrs Croft. 'And he is paying considerably more now. I know you will have dwelt upon that already.'

'Then he wasn't tricked, was he?' observes Mr Croft.

I decide to show Sir Norman my own worth. 'He was certainly aware that he should not show it to customs. How he came by it, and whether he understood the consequences of being caught, is another matter. Many westerners mistakenly believe that they can bribe officials in these countries, that you can smooth over all difficulties with a little back-pocket money. To your son's credit, we have no reports that he tried any of that. It can backfire, truly it can. And we do have sympathy for his plight; your son is only a month or two out of his teens. He didn't understand what he was getting himself into by changing money in Morocco. We think that is where he bought it. It's what he told our man out there.'

'Shouldn't have gone then, should he?' Mr Croft remains singular in his line of argument.

'No, you are quite correct to say that the young lad has made a poor choice or two. But...' Sir Norman, who has tagged back into the tussle, allows his voice to arrive at its gravelliest. '...Her Majesty's Government cannot endorse foreign governments detaining our citizens for reasons that are predominantly spurious. When Algeria's own citizens commit such crimes—smuggling—they will be punished for it. The small amount your son carried across the border, however, would attract no more than a twenty-eight-day or possibly a fifty-six-day punishment. Those are the typical sentences for Arab smugglers. Her Majesty's Government abhors inflated sentencing of its citizens, while not in any sense endorsing the misdemeanours which understandably offend the foreign power. The...' Sir Norman is suddenly stuck for words and most of those he has said came from the briefing paper which I wrote. He turns and addresses me. '...Winterbotham has some information about Algerian prisons.'

'Yes, Sir. The prison in which Moss is currently being housed has been operative since nineteen-sixty-five. We understand that there have been fifty-six deaths of prisoners in the jail during this time. This is high and we believe it includes no more than eight suicides. There have been nine cases which have been assessed—not by the foreign office but by international campaign groups—as possible sub-judicial killings. The government of Algeria disputes this. They deny human rights abuses like a reflex. We do not trust their word, think the analyses of the campaign group are plausible. Not that we have been able to verify them. There are other jails in that country where such events—illegal executions—are, sadly, beyond dispute. And the bulk of the deaths at Al Aricha have been prisoner-on-prisoner attacks; we believe that these can occur primarily because of the very poor levels of supervision in this jail. Within custodial provision across the whole of Algeria for that matter. We have no reports—no direct reason to believe—that your son is subject to any mistreatment. We strongly suspect he is finding the experience traumatic. The likelihood is that guards are keeping a watchful eye on him as best they can. They don't want a diplomatic stink, not for failing to protect a UK citizen. The sparse numbers of ill-trained prison staff remain a concern to us. We cannot be certain if he has been accepted by his fellow prisoners or if he is being—and please do not be alarmed, simply keep this in mind—targeted, possibly mistreated, by them.' I look directly at Mrs Croft, knowing that my words must worry her. Give her cause for concern. She blinks her eyes. I don't see any tears but if they come it will be no bad thing. 'Mr and Mrs Croft, the system of fines that Algeria operates is both a face-saving way for that country to turn around its petty injustices—its overly punitive sentencing—while also ensuring British citizens, or other first world visitors, do not suffer unduly for their minor indiscretions. Algeria is not a country into which many British citizens venture, so we have been talking with the French for whom this scenario is a more common occurrence. Crucially, we have asked them—the French—to contact the ministry of justice in

Algeria on our behalf. This is where you will be able to help Moss.'

'Help Moss?' Ronald Croft's voice has risen up an octave. 'I didn't ask him to go. What's the help? I don't understand your point, young man. Do you want me to bake him a cake with a file in it?'

To my surprise, Mrs Croft laughs out loud at this crass joke. It feels quite wrong to me. Surprising and unpleasant. She had been listening closely until now. To my impassioned and fact-based summary; I thought she sympathised.

'Mr and Mrs Croft,' says Sir Norman, 'your son has been sentenced to two years in this...well, it's probably a hell hole. Spartan was all our man said. And he also said that Moss looked pretty washed out by the experience. Unhappy. We believe that a payment of around four thousand pounds will secure his release. This would happen at the appeal stage but the courts there are happy to rush these things through if we've made it clear we will comply. It is a delicate matter. The fine would be set by a court: none of that bribery nonsense. It would secure his immediate release. Release within days. It is not the British Government's policy to fund alternatives to custody, however, we will coordinate the legal support should you wish it. And we advise that you do wish it, and we also recognise that this is a large sum of money. You may wish to talk to us about that. About how it might be secured should that be the primary obstacle.'

Mr Croft has a glazed look across his face as he replies. 'Talk to him about it, to Moss. He should have smuggled in four thousand pounds shouldn't he. I'm not the one in an Arab prison.'

Sir Norman looks a little ruffled. He might have been rash to talk about raising the fine before we had won them over. 'I understand you have another son, Mr Croft, Mrs

Croft?' he says.

'Our Gary is in the navy.' Mrs Croft draws her knees together as she says it. Places both her hands upon them.

'Good lad,' says Sir Norman approvingly. Then he looks Ronald Croft in the eye. 'I don't expect he can rustle up a gun boat. The problem is, you will be feeling very let down by young Moss. His tomfoolery at the Algerian customs. Very unwise of him, so it makes sense that you feel this way. I think, primarily, he has let himself down. He's going to find he's put a small scar on his future. Spending time in a prison like that. Now, we would not wish that small, but important, misdemeanour to ruin the whole of his life. As young Winterbotham said, life in those prisons is unpredictable. He might be having a shocking experience. I'm also wondering if the money needed is more than you could easily muster. The last thing we want is people losing their homes...'

'That boy,' interrupts Mrs Croft, 'hasn't so much as sent us a postcard. He hitchhiked out of our lives, Mr Kinsley, and we don't require him to hitchhike back into them.' Her voice is a grim monotone. 'It was shocking to learn his whereabouts from our own government. From the department you are the minister for. Phones and letters that boy doesn't use, and it's not that we haven't taught him how. It is us that he's not interested in. We put a roof over his head but he wanted the stars. Well...' She turns her head, looks out of the window and into the road. '...he's made his bed.'

The room is silent, unpleasantly so.

'I see,' intones Sir Norman, 'I see.' He glances at me and I begin to speak but no words emerge from within me. We are checkmated. In the end I simply mouth his words, I see, when actually I do not.

'It's not the money, Mr Kinsley,' says Mr Croft. 'I always pay what's due. It isn't me that owes it, is it?'

Trip to Bury

'Thank you for your tea, Mrs Croft, a delightful cup,' says Sir Norman. 'Come on, Winterbotham, London awaits us.' He stands and I do the same. 'Give Mrs Croft your card, please?' he asks of me.

I do as he asks; we shake hands limply, then Sir Norman and I take to the front door, advance the four or five steps from lounge to exit of this miniscule house in godforsaken Bury. All the gloom of driving into Wolseley Road comes back to me. Is it just the Crofts or is it the water they drink here, the air that they breathe, which makes them so damned cantankerous?

As we step outside it feels chillier than it did earlier in the morning, Sir Norman's face is redder than I've ever seen it. He has turned a shade of Ronald Croft. Only his unruly hair tells me I am walking away with the right man.

* * *

We pass the same tiny houses until we arrive at the car. Once inside he simply says, 'Which one was worse?' I contemplate the question, cannot answer it.

As I drive back to Manchester—the car is to be collected from Piccadilly Railway Station—I ask my passenger, 'What now, Sir?'

'Hmmm, we get our man out there to send the ruddy peasants a postcard. Can't do any harm, eh?'

I fail to laugh at this. Their conduct perplexed me enormously, that of the mother and the father. What parents cannot forgive a silly stunt like taking money across a border. It wasn't marijuana, it certainly wasn't heroin. The quantity was minimal, holiday money. Pathetic. In our department we are familiar with helping families whose offspring have become embroiled in far darker conduct than anything Moss Croft has done. There is, quite frankly, little chance of releasing heroin smugglers. Most others— particularly if the sentencing has been excessive—we can help. Navigate a face-saving way forward. What country really wants our wayward youth filling their jails? 'Does the department not have the money,' I ask?

'Yes, yes, we have to make it look otherwise but we will be able...well I hope the next generation of the Crofts is not as crackpot as that pair. Perhaps he'd rather stay in prison and take his punishment like a lunatic. What do you reckon?'

'Well...' I think I must engage with Sir Norman, banter with him in the hope that it will lighten his mood. '...I can't blame the boy for wanting to get as far away from that house as he could. Wolseley Road, Bury or prison in Algeria? Perhaps he made the right choice, Sir.'

'Ha! Now that's funny.'

* * *

On the train journey back to Euston we again sit together in first class. Sir Norman has a sausage sandwich courtesy of the dining car and I have elected to try British Rail's tomato soup. We are neither of us enjoying the culinary experience.

'Waste of a day really', he says. 'We weren't to know, of course. Usually, these chaps come around. Your speech about the sorry state of the prisons over there moved me, Winterbotham. You will note, I have a heart, whatever you hear said in the office. Dashed good work, so you really mustn't be discouraged by the outcome.'

'Thank you, Sir.'

'Could you get back on to the French when you're at your desk, please? See how quickly they can—you know—line it up. I'll stump up the money. By hook or by crook. But this one has to be kept utterly confidential, my lad. It is not standard policy to work it this way around. In fact, it is so far from the policy we'll have to pretend it didn't happen. Inside and outside the department,' if you follow me. Thanks

Trip to Bury

for all your work on the case. Bloody inedible sandwich.'

Chapter Five

City of Bridges

1.

Moss climbs down from the lorry's cab onto the roadside. He is at the edge of Constantine. The signpost says he is already there but the city has yet to show itself. The lorry driver speaks only broken French, he laughs repeatedly. Moves his arms like a windmill to show what has amused him, and it is the English boy. For Moss, the whole roadside dance has become double-edged. It stops the cars, serves a purpose. It has also turned him into an exhibit: the Rucksack Jumper. He no longer enjoys being a curiosity, a thing which people are surprised to have come across. A boy—young man—with long fair hair, speaking no Arabic at all and not proficient enough in French to make more than superficial conversation. He longs to share a bottle of wine with an Algerian as thoughtful as Asia Lellouche and discuss the similarities and divergence of Christian and Islamic culture. He finds instead that he boasts about watching Manchester United play in their famous stadium and confirms that his country's prime minister is indeed a woman. Wine is pretty much out of the question. His best guess posits that Soufiane and Asia never touch a drop.

From the lorry, Moss walks in the direction that the driver has pointed. The road into Constantine. He sets out, believing from the exchange that he can comfortably complete the journey on foot. Then, after rounding a corner, he is astonished by the awe-inspiring sight he stumbles across. A bridge. He is on the edge of a huge ravine. The road on which he walks sits on the plateau above it. The route into the city crosses a spectacular suspension bridge. It reminds him of the famous one in Bristol. Isambard Kingdom Brunel. Not so famous around here, he guesses. Why would it be? Algeria's is tonnes better. The landscape is dry, rocky. All hues from yellow to dark green pricking the red and grey rock face. The vegetation here suggests rain is an occasional friend, that it may come. This boy has seen none of it. The bridge is breath-taking, an impossible crossing made good through the application of bold geometry. Beautiful. Moss takes in the vast expanse of rock-strewn country, peering at the deep gorge sloping away in front of him. Crossing the high bridge is the only way to reach the looming citadel of Constantine. He makes his way towards it, rucksack securely on his shoulders. Mesmerised by the sight, the thin strips of metal that form the elegant structure across the mighty chasm. There are a multitude of buildings beyond, still small in his vision. A city beckons, once he crosses the high bridge. Walks across the sky. The sun is hot, penetratingly so. And a twisty wind lends him an occasional cool gust to enjoy. Traffic passes, grunting, coughing noisy traffic for the most part. This astonishing city is one to walk into. An impregnable fortress sitting proudly within its geographical defences.

As he reaches the lip of the bridge, the boy looks down. The sides are steep, falling away, a little vegetation below, barely any greenery. Thin brush amongst the rock. He sees something down there, a goat perhaps. It is far below him, he cannot see its outline, notices only its movement. A living thing in the deep pocket below the plain on which he walks. The depth of the ravine pleases Moss. He imagines another world down at the bottom. A world which he cannot, from his current vantage point, see how to reach. As he turns back to look along the roadside path and resume his march into the garrison across the water, a car slows, the passenger window wound down. Two men are gesturing, two young Algerian men offering him a lift. This is crazy, he has not so much as stuck a thumb out. He has certainly not danced, not jumped over his rucksack. Without asking, they offer him a ride. Sniff out the Rucksack Jumper even as he tries to move amongst them incognito. He waves them away, hopes his gesture does not appear rude. It is unsuccessful. His hand signals have no meaning here. The car stops completely and the young man in the passenger seat emerges onto the roadside. He shakes Moss by the hand, touching his heart after doing so.

'Farouk,' he says, to the English boy.

Moss introduces himself but also explains in his best French that he intends to walk across the bridge. To see the view up and down the ravine and survey the river below.

Farouk leans into the open car window and speaks quickly to the driver, his friend. The driver laughs and nods, then shouts something which Moss cannot understand. The car pulls away leaving Moss and Farouk together on the roadside.

Farouk advises Moss that the other man has introduced himself, that his name is Djamel. Farouk—speaking slow French which Moss grasps well—tells him that Djamel will wait for them on the far side of the bridge. Moss is slightly bemused that he has so little choice in the events to come. He knows that he only refused the lift because the bridge demanded further attention from him. This young man seems to have instinctively appreciated his need to look down, take in, walk slowly across a bridge this fine. That is a plus. On his travels, he seldom comes across Arabs so attuned to his personal idiosyncrasies.

As they make their way over the ravine, in step, Farouk

tells Moss one or two things about himself. He is a student at the University of Constantine. He wishes Moss to visit the university. 'Nous faisons un échange,' he suggests knowingly to Moss: We do an exchange. The Algerian laughs as he says it. Moss does too, laughs more manically because he would be exchanging university tuition in this North African city for unemployment in Bury. Farouk is a poorer barterer than he can guess. The English boy fails to share this insight with his newfound friend.

As they walk along the bridge, reaching the midpoint, Moss stops, removes his rucksack and leans over the railing. He is astonished to see that this is not the only bridge. This high bridge spans the top of the ravine but deep below amid white rock and hovering over a little thread of river—not a river worthy of this massive ravine or monumental bridge, but a river nonetheless—sits a second bridge. It looks tiny from this height, this far above it. Moss is fascinated. The river is nothing—a tiny trickle—this is a bridge over a bridge.

Ahead of him, he can see the amassed buildings of Constantine. Farouk tells him that the city's name is derived from the Roman Emperor. It was a part of that empire many hundreds of years ago. Moss thinks it improbable that those ancient people should have come to this arid spot, unlikely yet true. History is a blur to him and the longer ago it occurred the more unfathomable. There is no reason in history, he thinks, one thing leads to another only because the alternatives have slipped away. No logic belies any particular unfolding.

Moss feels compelled to tell Farouk something about himself. The problem is that the longer he travels, the more he finds he is losing touch with who he is. Wandering alone in this land that will not authenticate him, the Moss Croft he knew is disappearing from his own sightline. Being proficient in no language spoken here; from an alien culture; unable to explain himself beyond living so close to the famous Manchester United football ground that many of the young Arabs think him a mythical person. These are more than barriers to intimacy, they make him feel invisible. How tiresome being mythical turns out to be. 'I am not French, I am English,' he tells Farouk in French. Farouk nods. Moss thinks he looks relieved. He has met no other English in this country. If Farouk guessed him French, he will have thought his talk stumbling, inchoate. 'I live near Manchester,' he adds. After a silent pause which gives Moss hope that Farouk is not going to ask him about the football, he continues. 'I have come a long way in the cars of hospitable strangers.'

Farouk stares at Moss, clearly not certain of the sanity of what he has just said. Moss hopes something was lost in translation and that it is not his intended phrase which causes Farouk's look of consternation. He cannot be certain: Rucksack Jumpers are few and far between and the general population may consider them to be as crazy as shamans. Moss has spotted this more than once during his time in this country. The two men continue to walk over the giant structure. Moss never stops looking down, taking in the enormity of the ravine. Pondering the significance of bridges.

* * *

After crossing the impressive bridge, Moss enters the waiting car without hesitation. The slow amble confirmed for him that Farouk is a friendly presence. He hopes to find Djamel of a similar disposition. Moss tells the boys that he needs to find a hotel.

'Ten minutes,' says Farouk.

'Twenty minutes,' says Djamel.

As the car pulls away Moss sits silently on the rear seat. Recalls for himself alone the strange encounter earlier on this day. His first lift of the morning as he left Biskra, the town in which he rested his head the previous night.

The ride found him quickly. As often happened, the Templeton Ca. tune which he hummed inside his head attracted it without recourse to leaping and dancing. He will make the effort if needed but his hitchhiking powers just get stronger and stronger. On climbing inside the car, he thought the driver looked European. When Moss began to jabber something in his rudimentary French, the man said, 'English?'

Moss nodded: it is his nationality. The accent of the driver was strong, neither French nor a native English speaker. Les Français are the only other Europeans he has come across in this remote country. The man was a balding fifty-year old to Moss's inexpert eye. The type of flattened out red-veined nose that once inspired his ex-girlfriend, Sharon MacDonald—back in Bury, when pointing out men similarly endowed—to coin the phrase, sclerosis of the snout. This man pointed at himself and said, 'Deutsch.' A German, Moss learnt.

'Je m'excuse,' said Moss, beginning to explain that he had no German language to share. Mid-sentence he stopped and laughed at his own stupidity. 'You speak English?' he asked, changing tack.

'Ja,' said the man.

Moss shared his name and thanked the driver, choosing simple words to do so.

'Ich Heiβe Hermann. No, this is not right. I am called Hermann,' the man replied.

As Moss slowly told Hermann about himself, that he is hitchhiking across the country, that he has been into the Sahara, likes the Algerian people but often struggles to understand them, Hermann's face broadened from its rather severe first impression to a bemused smile. 'How do you like Algeria?' Moss asked his driver.

Hermann shrugged.

'But you are on holiday. What have you seen?'

'See! See! I have seen much, Moss. Holiday, no. I work in this country. I work just for the present. I was in Nigeria but it is worse. Much worse. Here, in Algeria, I like my job. The country, I do not like. Crazy politics.'

Moss thought he understood the meaning of the man's words. Or maybe not. Even English is starting to meld into the uncertainty that his own musings have become during his prolonged time down here. He no longer trusts himself to attend the words of others. Not with the diligence needed to gather their intentions. He fears that he subverts their commentary to his own end. 'What work do you do?' he asked.

The German gesticulated, pointed down the road. 'I go to work today,' he told the boy. 'You will see.' Then, as they drove further in the arid landscape, Hermann asked Moss a question which caught him off guard. 'Do you watch the moon landings? When you are a child, do you watch these?'

Moss confirmed that he'd seen all of them on television. Smiled to himself as he said it. It was a fascination he had shared with his father, knowing that men had travelled so far. That they had put their feet upon the surface of the moon. Then Hermann seemed to be saying something to the effect that he works for the space programme. Surely this is impossible, thought Moss. Algeria needs no moon rockets: its landscape lends credence to the notion that one has already landed there. He quickly realised that Hermann was struggling with the past tense, did not know how to conjugate verbs within it when speaking in the English language. Moss asked him if he used to work for NASA.

Hermann nodded. 'Rocket science,' he announced, patting a flat hand across his own chest, impressing the boy enormously. Hermann, volunteer chauffeur of Moss Croft, was a man of note—the boffins' boffin—a real-life rocket scientist. 'Florida. I am working in Florida.'

They talked about it as best they could but Hermann's English was not precise. The English boy wondered if he really worked in Florida for so long—four years he told Moss—without picking up a better grasp of the language. However, in the long silences Moss simply recalled his own father's fascination with those missions. The conversations they shared. Moss was still in primary school when Apollo Thirteen was out in space, crippled, a watching world fearing the worst. His father—now the despised Ronald but not so ten years earlier—was almost tender with his young son during those worrying days.

'Will they get back here?' asked Moss. 'Back home.'

'We hope so,' his father replied. 'They are brave men, son, they knew what they were getting into. We must be prepared for the possibility of them just losing contact.' Moss stared at his father, unblinking. 'The places mankind is going to nowadays, it's staggering. Maybe we aren't really meant to be in space at all. Those men are pioneers. It's what they do, risks they are prepared to take.'

Moss would ask questions about travelling to Mars or to other stars. Ronald was not one to speculate beyond his bland, 'You never know, son,' or, 'Maybe in your life-time,' answers.

Moss recalled listening intently to President Nixon's speech after the crew of the Apollo Thirteen mission had safely returned to Earth. The young Moss understood that they made it through the diligence of the hard-working scientists on the ground, and in this morning's magically conjured ride he realised that, seated right next to him, was one of those unsung heroes: Hermann. Both Moss and his father had contemplated the valour of the three astronauts who had endured—for several days—the shockingly high likelihood of meeting the loneliest and most remote of all possible deaths. Only the younger Croft had, like Nixon, recognised the contribution of the men working in the backroom, making the calculations. Giving the stranded astronauts essential and life-saving advice. His father had called them hangers-on, shown interest only in the astronauts. Moss smiled inwardly as he reflected upon it in the German scientist's car. They could have been on their way to the moon on bicycles as far as his dumb father understood the science. In Ronald Croft's world it is every man for himself.

Momentarily, the boy from Bury imagined that Ghardaia has been his moon, around which he has done the necessary slingshot to make his way back. Hermann is again on the backroom staff of this meticulous project, re-entry to come in a few days' time. Palermo, Sicily. The oxygen of Europe awaits him just a few lucky rides and a big ship away. This is just another daft thought of mine, Moss told himself, while hoping his prolonged silence did not appear rude to the rocket scientist kindly taking him a small step homewards.

* * *

After travelling on the main highway for half an hour, Hermann pulled the car off the main road. The minor road quickly turned to gravel, a ribbon of red grit laid out on the light grey desert. A bridleway for camels. A proliferation of signposts indicated some importance to this hurriedly laid thoroughfare. The boy even saw Battypapa on a couple of posters. Very strange. Not so much as a goat out here in whom that paper president might instil his authoritarian fear. Then, ten minutes down the rough track, they arrived at a checkpoint. Two men carrying guns came out of the small hut and greeted Hermann as they might an old friend. The boy inferred that their guns were part of the uniform, worn but not raised. Hermann climbed out of the car to talk to them. Many gestures, few words. The German pointed in the direction of Moss, and the two men looked at him through narrowed eyes. Hermann laughed—audible to the English boy inside the car—and he guessed that his driver was offering the men an explanation for the hitchhiker's presence at this place. A military facility of some kind. 'Garçon,' he heard Hermann say: Moss is a boy, insignificant. He was passing through, taking neither notes nor photographs. Moss still thought the men with guns might be cleverer than the scientist on this narrow point. Rucksack Jumpers are not welcome at army bases the world over. Don't even wish to be.

Despite Hermann's protestations, the two men came to the car window and knocked upon it. Moss wound the window down. It flashed into his thoughts that they were customs officials belatedly putting the world to rights, but this didn't quite fit the facts. Hermann was a rocket scientist, not a petty-smuggler rounder-upper.

'Passeport,' said one of the men.

Moss signalled that he needed a moment. He put his hands under his shirt and fiddled deftly with his money belt, quickly bringing out the document. He left the other contents of his hidden pocket unaired. The two men studied it together, first his photograph and then spending twenty or thirty seconds scrutinising the stamp from his crossing near Oujda. The older man spoke quietly to the younger and, in response, the apparent underling wrote something in a small pocket notebook, his rifle flapping on its sling as he did so. The boy's documentation proved him to be in the country legitimately whatever code Hermann had broken by bringing him to this well-guarded facility. They were not impolite, still Moss felt sweat dribbling down the back of his neck.

Hermann got back in the car and the men waved him through the check point. 'They are assholes,' he told Moss, the apt Americanism making a timely return to his active vocabulary. 'I boss the programme, then they want stop me bring visitor. Pah!'

'Will we be here long?' asked Moss, thinking how much he would rather be on the move than around soldiers with guns. He didn't say it out loud but the boy could not hide his discomfort. Not when he was answering their questions, showing the soldiers his passport. It may have infected the German, Hermann seeming more agitated than he had been at any earlier point.

'I give them papers,' he told Moss. 'My workplace but today I not work. I just give the papers.'

As he drove over the gravel track, Moss saw a large collection of prefabricated buildings, a small village worth of them, and in the distance, a quarry was glimmering brightly in the early morning sunshine. The rock face had an intensely white surface, almost silvery as it sparkled beneath the hot sun. Moss speculated that this place could be a mine for diamonds or silver. Possibly just classroom chalk. 'What is made here?' he enquired of Hermann.

The German made two or three small plosive sounds within his jowly cheeks, opening and closing his right hand in time with the strange noises. 'Bomba, pooosh,' he said. 'Bomba, bomba. Pooosh, pooosh.'

* * *

The car arrives at a hotel in the middle of Constantine. Moss reads the name, Pension Ahmed Bey. It looks modest and he has no wish to imply he is affluent to Farouk or Djamel.

As he gets out, Farouk asks Moss if they could meet again at eleven the following morning. He thanks the driver for the lift and Djamel returns his smile. There is no reason to refuse this request. Farouk was surprisingly easy company on the bridge. The English boy likes to make friends with Algerians of his own age. 'Tomorrow,' he says, 'eleven.' He is going with the flow; it was the mantra of the Australian girl in Madrid and it has served him well. He harbours a small fear that something concomitant may be flowing out of him. If the flow gives, does it take in return? An immutable law of nature.

* * *

Moss rests on his bed in the hotel room. Falls into a fitful sleep. When he awakes, to his surprise, it is well after seven in the evening. He has missed a few hours, his unconscious-self needed elsewhere for that stolen time.

And where was he when he was sleeping? For a second it comes to him that he was in Ghardaia, that he was in the room of the woman from the square on the first evening. The woman who wore no headscarf, stayed in the letting room adjacent to his in the courtyard hotel. Lioness. This must have been a dream. He never saw her again, however much he'd hoped he might. And as he tries to recover the dream, he finds he is losing it. He thinks his father was also there but the only memory he can find is of a real conversation when his father advised that he should leave Sharon MacDonald alone. This was not in his dream, the imagery has gate-crashed his conscious mind, infiltrated his initial reflection upon the feisty Tuareg lady. In some way he knows that he loved Sharon. Still thinks her a better person than he is. And his father said only unfounded platitudes. Insults at bottom. 'I expect a lot of boys have gone out with her once or twice,' and, 'She's not had the steadying hand of a father.' Even, 'They're not really like us, you know.' The last comment sickened Moss. He feels all the usual frustration no matter how far away he is from the constricting home he contemplates. Why is it that his gormless father always imagines the worst? He is incapable of appreciation. Ignorant criticism, the sum total of his thought.

The boy pulls on a fresh sweatshirt, grey and inconspicuous, over the T-shirt that he is wearing for the third hot day in a row. Into the evening gloom he ventures. His usual quest is for something to eat. After this unplanned rest he walks into the night with a hunger for stimulation. No need for food at all.

On the street, he sees another poster of President Battypapa. Remembers Asia Lellouche's stark assessment. That man has all the power, the people have none. He stares out from his posters, indifference written on his cruel face. Moss wonders if this visual propaganda can do more than get up the noses of Algerians. He doesn't feel close to an answer. When Algerians speak with him of politics, it is exclusively to ask about his own country. Laugh that a woman is holding the reins. Asia Lellouche aside, he has found Algerian politics to be taboo. Not a word in the presence of an outsider.

No more than a couple of hundred yards from his hotel, the boy from Bury passes an open door. He hears that the encased room is alive, awash with noise, the sounds of many animated people. A party perhaps. He sees no sign to indicate what is within, whether it is a private or a public gathering, and so he starts to walk on. A man standing close by directs some words towards him. He guesses that the man spoke French but Moss was paying insufficient attention to gather the meaning. As he turns back and faces him, he notices the beer bottle held discreetly by the Algerian's side. He is a sharp dresser, this street-corner man. A navy-blue jacket, white shirt with wide collar. His appearance reminds Moss of the Brits he saw back in Marbella, Spain but the attire does not fool the boy. This well-dressed man looks too pleased with himself. He is on a street in Constantine, Algeria. With a beer in hand, he might be pretending to be in Paris. Those British yacht owners in Marbella were convinced that they were at Cowes

Week. Not a scintilla of doubt in their minds.

The man wears a smug little smile. Clearly sees where Moss's eyes have come to rest, then he brings the beer bottle in front of his own face and points at it. 'En voudrais tu?' he asks.

'Oui,' replies Moss. He would like some.

The man takes him through the mysterious door and to his surprise he is inside a bar. It looks as it might were it in Cherbourg or Angoulême although no signage or outdoor seating announces its presence from the exterior. The smartly dressed man makes a signal to the bar tender who quickly brings Moss a slim bottle of beer. This is not a Lancashire pub however familiar it feels to the boy. Moss guesses that he will have to pay at the end of the evening, not before the consumption of each drink, as he likes to. The custom here follows that of the country's old colonial power. At least this aberration is less unsettling than the haggling of Morocco. Relaxation is really all he seeks; he has the dinar for a few beers. He feels pleased with the random assembly of his life, stumbling across a pub in Constantine. The flow delivers.

Within two pulls on his bottle, Moss finds himself surrounded by young Algerian men—not excessively young, his own age or slightly older—they are friendly, they wish to talk. Moss wants to ask about the bridges but cannot think how to phrase such a question. He says, in French, 'The river is small.' This would have been a curious opening gambit in a conversation anywhere—self-absorbed rambling—it is what he has become. He finds his patience growing thin and his need for meaning both honest and obscure. In his mind he visualises the tiny stream below the high bridge. What he hopes to glean from these young drinkers is a mystery even to himself. One shot, he thinks to himself, he's got only one shot in Constantine. Why go on about Manchester fucking United?

City of Bridges

A young man places a forefinger and thumb gently on his upper arm and guides Moss to a nearby table. 'I am Yacine,' he tells Moss, speaking in clear English. 'How are you?'

'Fine.' A speaker of his own language is a godsend to Moss, fatigued as he feels. 'A little tired but fine. How about you?'

'Me?' replies Yacine, 'I am a medical student, it can be very hard work. Tonight is not for any of that, I am drinking a beer with you!'

'Is this a regular bar?' asks Moss. Yacine does not answer straight away. 'I've not seen bars in Algeria. Is it allowed?'

'Yes, yes. The bars may be few; however, we drink alcohol in Constantine, in Algeria. Bars close at eight o'clock, all bars.'

'Phew,' whistles the English boy. 'It closes in a few minutes. Do you think I can get another before they do?' He nods at his beer bottle as he speaks. Yacine shakes his head slowly from side to side, lips upturned in a smile. Moss thinks he is not saying no, just bemused by Moss's thirst. 'It's only my second,' he says defensively. Yacine waves a hand toward the bar and catches the barman's eye. Two further beers arrive promptly at the table. 'I will pay,' says Moss.

The medical student waves a nonchalant hand. Payment need not be debated. 'Are you a fisherman?' Yacine asks Moss.

Is he a fisherman? This doctor sounds barmier than his own wayward tongue. 'No, I don't fish.'

'I understood that you were looking for a river.'

'I found a river,' says Moss. 'Below the high bridge, deep in the gorge. On the edge of town, that one. The river is so, so small. I laughed at how grand the bridge is, the engineering needed, just to cross a tiny little stream. Very, very small river, a tiny river and such a fantastic bridge.'

Yacine furrows his brow. 'I think a man might wade across this river,' he states, 'but that gorge, that great ravine, to get across that any bridge must be an impressive one, do you not think?'

Moss is quiet for a moment. 'You are right, Yacine,' he states as he reaches out a hand to shake. After they shake, Yacine, whose bemused smile is back, touches his heart but Moss fails to do so. Then as they have settled back in to their seats Moss quickly remembers and belatedly places his hand upon his heart. 'Je m'excuse,' he implores. He hates having broken the custom. It is never his intention to be disrespectful, it was just an oversight as he contemplated Yacine's wise words about the ravine. The bridge is not just crossing the river. It is spanning the great expanse which the endless flow of water has torn out of the hillside over geological time.

* * *

A little after ten o'clock and Moss is drunk. Not so seriously drunk that he is ill, nor a degree of drunkenness with which he is unfamiliar. Never got like this so far from home before. His state is compounded by physical fatigue and the disorientation he feels simply from spending time in an Arabic-Roman city. Drunk and exhausted. That sort of gone. The strain of understanding new words and customs has caught up with him. Overtaken him. Rendered him drunk before the drink and now he has that to contend with also. Did Hannibal come from Constantine? He doesn't think so but surely someone famous did. Someone long ago. Cleopatra? Monk Elba, perhaps? The irritating acoustic guitarist whose self-pitying songs made it into the charts a few years back. It was him, the miserable Monk. Moss grimaces. History always flings trite connections into his mind. The melodrama of Cleopatra bathing in donkey milk; Elba's sentimental tunes. Not a chasm needing a sizeable bridge. Moss is not the first Lancashire lad to find himself drunk in the upstairs room of a pub. If he is the first in this specific bar it is a testament to his determined travel. His flow-going. He has retained enough insight to know that he has turned boor—never really made it as a wandering poet—and he has drunk too much to step away.

Yacine told him just after eight o'clock, when many drinkers had already left the bar, 'We will go upstairs.'

When the words were spoken, Moss felt momentarily wary. He had trusted Yacine following his thoughtful words about the grand-bridge-tiny-river conundrum, surely this was not a sexual proposition? He has heard those leanings are rife in these parts, however deftly hidden. 'The bar will serve drinks,' added the medical student. 'There are blinds on the windows upstairs.'

'A lock-in,' laughed Moss. Yacine needed this term explaining to him. He was surprised to learn that in Britain, with its liberal laws covering alcohol sales, the same after-hours practice might occur. A little further along in the evening, the only difference.

No more than fifteen people are in the upstairs room, and Moss is supplementing a fortnight's worth of bewilderment with his sixth or seventh beer. He is beyond counting. All but Yacine in this private function room are now studiously avoiding the inebriated English boy. His coherence in French has plummeted far below its modest norm. There is no music in the room and Moss thinks the sound of the drinkers' collective talk akin to that of a barn full of farm animals. Grunted Arabic accompanied by neighing laughter. The same barman who served in the room below is again in control, organising and pouring the drinks. It is a regular event, Moss presumes. Bottles of beer from the downstairs room now sit on a tiny table, and three or four spirit bottles stand upright on the floor next to the seated barman. He appears at ease, the host of a flawless party. Wryly, the boy from Bury giggles to himself. His thoughts run free. This must be the fag-end of the prohibition era, he decides. Battypapa's posters are everywhere but the man is old. A paper tiger in every sense.

'Come and meet Denise,' says Yacine.

The English boy stands and follows the medical student up a small flight of stairs arriving at an attic level, stooping beneath the sloping ceiling. A girl in a pub in Algeria? Moss is experiencing one novelty after another. Yacine knocks at a door, it has a number upon it. A little brass-gold curl protruding from the plain dark wood. Six.

'Entrée,' says a lady's voice.

Yacine turns the handle and both men go inside. Moss sees a lady sitting on a small couch. A generation older than he, she is quite plump, stockinged legs beneath her short black skirt. Two young Arab men occupy chairs close to her. She has a lot of make up on her face and Moss—cogs turning rather slowly in his brain—appraises that neither dress nor face are Arabic. He also sees the single bed beneath the blinded window, made up with a light blue counterpane. He is in her bedroom. What an extraordinary place to find himself.

In his stupor, Moss asks her if she is English. 'Français,' comes the sharp rebuke. Moss nods but thinks he need not apologise, he asked it politely, didn't wave a flag in her face. The lady, Denise, appears to go through a similar thought process. In a softer tone she says, 'J'aime l'Anglais.'

'J'aime les Français,' Moss tells her like an echo. Can manage that much of her language despite his many beers. 'J'aime l'Algeriens,' he adds for fear of offending his hosts.

But the men shake their heads, one says something that makes the others laugh. Moss thinks it was, we all love the French, and he cannot see why it is so funny, or even very probable, in a room full of young Algerians. Then, as if on cue, all the men start to leave. Moss laughs. 'This is fou,' he mutters to himself, mixing up languages. They are leaving him alone with a dollied-up woman of his mother's age.

When the other young men have left, Denise addresses him. 'Tu as l'argent? she asks: You have the money?

Moss struggles to find the words, giggling as he tries. 'Can we talk?' he asks using her language. 'Who are you?' This question sounds foolish even to the intoxicated boy. Denise just stares at him. 'How did you get to...' Moss pauses, momentarily struggling to recall the name of the town whose bridges mesmerise him so. '...Constantine?'

'You are young,' says the woman. 'The boys told me they have a traveller.'

'Voyager,' says Moss, repeating her French word for his sort, liking this word's application to him. In his mind he is no longer Moss Croft but someone more worldly, more exotic. A man of derring-do, freshly arrived in this Constantine bar from his thousand-mile camel ride across the desert. When he was down there, he rescued twenty Tuareg damsels from a nomadic harem in which they were being held against their will. Wonders if this lady is free to leave or needs him to spring her, as his newfound character is apt to do. 'Je m'appelle Vim,' he tells Denise, 'Vim Voyager. Bonsoir et comment puis-je vous aider?'

He laughs more and more while Denise pointedly does not. Ignores his offer of assistance whether or not she accepts his newly minted name. 'Tu as l'argent?' she repeats. This makes Moss giggle uncontrollably. He puts a hand under his shirt and dextrously pulls a large Algerian bank note from his floppy money belt. Then he spreads both hands, as if he is performing a magic trick. The note simply falls to the floor. Moss has developed the hiccoughs; laughter and beer the genesis of his spasms.

'Qu'est-ce que tu as?' Denise asks: What do you have? She is curious to see the garment he wears around his midriff.

'Not for you,' he says in English. 'Cette.' Moss points at the note he has dropped: that is all that she may have.

Denise scoops up the money. 'Merci,' she says.

She stands and puts the handsome note into a saucer which sits on the top of a low chest of drawers. Then as she is standing, she slides both of her hands under the hem of her dress and quickly unclasps the elaborate garter belt which holds up her stockings. Moss is fascinated while thinking that now is the decorous moment to depart. This is not his thing. Using a prostitute is not going with the flow, it is adding to the poor woman's degradation. As drunk as he is, he understands this much. Denise is not Sharon or Annalise. She is a world away from Samira. Not a woman he could make love to while feeling a meaningful connection with her. So he won't do it. He finds that his cock has ideas of its own. Hopes that the French woman does not detect its rising interest. Moss feels disappointed that mind and body cannot retain a united front.

'Viens au lit,' she says: Come to bed.

Denise is now sitting on the edge of the light blue counterpane. She rises briefly to remove her knickers from beneath the black skirt, her blouse is open and Moss watches her pendulous breasts swing as she is stooping.

'You could measure the minutes with them,' he says, in English.

The cruelty in his words do not appear to register with the French woman. 'Quoi?' she asks.

'Je m'excuse,' says the English boy, standing and walking towards the door.

'Non,' she says, jumping up. 'Tu es bourré.'

Moss thinks she is offering him butter. He does not know that her word means drunk. His laughter and hiccoughs resume as he pictures butter's involvement in sex with a woman of his mother's age. She has again risen from the bed and her hands are upon him. She pulls him into an embrace which makes an unwilling arm feel the warmth of her naked breast. He is very concerned that his penis might get its way. His brain is against it. He must act quickly. Vim Voyager must come to his own rescue; do it now. He mumbles some confused words, mostly in French but not entirely. 'No. Keep the money. I don't wish to offend. I didn't ask. It isn't you. Enjoy the butter.'

Denise tries to remove his clothes but his insistence makes her stop. He moves away from her, out into the corridor before he looks back. From the doorway she laughs at him. 'Tu es bourré,' she repeats, patting down the skirt beneath which Moss has seen but not touched.

2.

Late on his first morning in Constantine—wristwatch by the bedside, telling Moss he has wasted the better part of it—he remains under the covers. Awake but feeling much the worse for his many beers of the night before. A light knock on the door of his hotel room; a strongly accented shout. 'Bonjour, Monsieur.' It is a woman's voice. The boy is naked, rises from his bed and quickly pulls on the underpants he wore the day before. His clothing is strewn across the floor. He got in a bit of a state last night. He opens the door just the tiniest crack. A young woman, wearing a dark green headscarf which melds into her long dress of the same colour, stands outside his room. 'Les hommes,' she tells him. 'Les hommes sont ici.' Moss is momentarily paralysed. Which men are here? She has told him they have come, but to whom does she refer? Denise's henchmen; the dastardly customs officials. Through the crack between door and frame he can see that the girl is appraising the condition of her fingernails. Then she repeats her assertion. 'Les hommes pour toi.'

He is conscious of his state of undress, and Moss always

imagines girls wearing headscarves to be religious. Muslim nuns. He knows they aren't quite that but it must mean something or other. A little bit religious or they wouldn't bother to cover themselves up so meticulously. Samira took hers off when her parents were out of sight. This girl smiles at him. She can see only the narrowest slice of him through the crack of the door. Being careful to keep his near-naked body out of her line of sight, he pokes his head around, puts his long unwashed hair into the corridor. 'Who,' he asks in English. 'Qui?' he corrects himself.

'Les étudiants pour toi.'

Now it is all coming back to him. 'Merci,' he says. 'Je m'excuse. Moment.' He closes the door and dresses quickly, throwing on clothes from the day before. He would like to brush his teeth but the water is down the corridor. In the shower room. It would be impolite to leave Farouk and the other one waiting. What was his name? As he is leaving the room, heading for the stairs down, he notices a red wine stain on one side of his T-shirt. He cannot recall where this occurred. He bumped into a table or two in the upstairs room. The evening has become a blur.

In the hotel foyer, he sees Farouk, the young man who walked with him across the high bridge the day before. There are three further men accompanying him. One must be Djamel, the driver; the name has come to him, it sounds like James. Moss cannot be certain which one he is. Didn't take in his face when he sat behind him in the car. They all come to shake hands, touch hearts. Moss feels self-conscious, he hasn't showered nor put a comb to his straggly long hair. They laugh and he is unsure at what. Moss apologises for being ill-prepared, asks if they are happy to wait ten minutes before leaving the hotel. Farouk shrugs. They grant him the delay. He had completely forgotten this pre-arranged engagement until the girl in green said the word students.

Moss returns to his room. The task in hand draws his attention away from the hangover. He runs along the corridor to the shower room, washes quickly. Disappointed to find that the water is not warm at all. He forces himself to remain beneath its stinging flow while soaping his arms and legs savagely.

He recalls the Shrödinger's-cat discussion from little more than twenty-four hours earlier, his inability to catch a thread of sense in the cauldron that is modern physics. Yesterday morning, when he was travelling in Hermann's car, after the strange and stilted visit to the bomb factory—driving across further arid terrain, red rock amongst the yellow and grey—Moss asked the rocket scientist to explain it to him. How can the cat in the famous conundrum be simultaneously alive and dead? It was not his intention to catch out his clever driver, the boy was simply curious. Meeting a bona fide physicist seemed like the opportunity to find out all about it.

Hermann seemed to know the answer, very happy to have the question put to him. He chuckled a little which contrasted nicely with the existential irritation he otherwise exuded. He talked quickly, possibly knowledgeably, Moss couldn't tell. His English was beyond hope. Moss gleaned nothing from it at all. Hermann strung together sentences of unlikely words but seemed to be substituting German phrases for all the more complex concepts. Quantum cats don't make choices, they do the lot. That was Moss's interpretation but he couldn't write a paper on it. Not one that might convince another that there is a grain of truth in quantum theory.

The boy now under the cold stream of water in the Pension Ahmed Bey decides to trust it. The German words meant it stacks up. Must have done or Hermann wouldn't have been smiling. Moss—beneath a cold stream of water—wishes to be simultaneously beneath a hot shower; he would like to pull a quantum lever that gave access to such a parallel universe. One should be close at hand; Hermann would agree. Einstein and the guys worked out the laws of physics, super-smart, what happens will. Battypapa's rules are daft, he only makes them because he can. The laws of physics don't stop beer being sold after eight o'clock. That's just this old killjoy's nonsense. Moss reckons no paperwork is required for entry into the better hotel in that other place. Plenty of hot water and the overblown bureaucracy done away with. Things are going okay here but a quantum lever would be an improvement. Not too much to change but definitely get a hot shower. And maybe wipe out his simple-minded antics in the upstairs room with Denise. Knock a couple of beers off last night's slate. Reverse the hangover, please, Mr Shrödinger. In fact, quitting drinking at eight is a decent shout provided it's done voluntarily. Coercion is the aberration. Moss thinks that his absence of comprehension, inability to grasp whatever Hermann explained, is the biggest factor preventing him from slipping between parallel states, and then he realises he might already slip between them. How could he recognise the differences in alternative universes from the perspective of the single one in which his consciousness sits? He starts to think himself as clever as the German, figuring it all out without a single equation. Then he checks the thought, should not get ahead of himself. For all he can prove, he is only here.

In the small bathroom, he hastily brushes his teeth and then with a towel around his waist he emerges into the corridor, sees the girl in the headscarf again; she has her back to him as he hotfoots it to his room. He pulls the door behind him not knowing whether she turned or not. He was decent enough, indecorous but not obscene. And the girl looks his own age, not old like Denise who was all for getting him undressed the night before. He pulls a few clothes out from within his rucksack. He needs to source a laundrette soon. Khadidja washed everything in the rucksack but he has spent a sweaty day in each item once or more since then. Mostly more.

* * *

He returns to the hotel lobby where the four young men wait for him. They shake hands yet again, and Moss realises he has instigated this. Needed or not. He did not catch the names, first time around, of the two men who were not there yesterday. Nassim and Aziz, he learns on second telling. He tries to remember the names of the four. Aziz is the only stout one. Djamel is the tallest. Nassim is the other one. It should work.

'Come with us.' Once again Farouk is the leader, the organiser. He enunciates his French clearly, speaks in easily understood phrases. Moss appreciates the attention the young man has invested in him. The hotel is a good one— or will be when the boy locates the quantum switch, gets the shower sorted—and it was Farouk's thoughtful judgement which brought him here. They shared meditative time on the high bridge, Moss enjoyed that immensely. And now he has returned, an appointment which had slipped the English boy's mind largely because he feared his own behaviour might appear aimless to others. He is surprised that Farouk and Djamel have retained interest.

They go to the car. It is parked just outside the hotel and once again Djamel is to drive. 'The university,' Farouk tells Moss. 'You will see it. Where we study.'

Moss grins and says, 'Exchange.' This is a private joke inside his own head. He cannot tell these kind men that he has only unemployment in a dour Lancashire town to exchange for a glimpse of their place of higher learning. Their university in its remote and unworldly setting. The former Roman citadel.

They drive away from the old town. Moss looks keenly as they pass over a different high bridge. It is not as spectacular as that seen yesterday but quite a sight, nevertheless. Farouk says something to Djamel and, on the bridge, he brings the car to a halt. Farouk and Moss get out to look down once more at the narrow ribbon of river below. Is it the same river, Moss speculates to himself. It is certainly no larger. He looks at the sloping sides of the ravine. The incline, he adjudges to be a little less steep at this crossing than the one yesterday, and this bridge sits slightly closer to the bottom of the gorge. There is no further bridge below.

When their car first came to a stop there was no other traffic; now, after fully two minutes parked up, cars have built up behind them, and a barrier in the centre of the road prevents any from overtaking, moving along. A driver toots his horn. Farouk smiles, waves to the driver, and puts a brotherly arm around Moss. 'Anglais,' he shouts. Moss puzzles over whether this explanation will really mollify the impatient driver. To his surprise, he sees the man tilt his head and smile at him. He even mouths something with a facial expression which the boy guesses to constitute a welcome. Moss no longer needs to hear words to fathom what is happening. The powers of the Rucksack Jumper are multifarious. He and Farouk climb back inside the car and Djamel drives on.

* * *

At the University of Constantine, the man called Aziz is keenest to show Moss around. Demonstrate for him what a fabulous place of learning they have on this arid plateau. Aziz has no English but—like Farouk—he speaks in clear French. 'I am studying chemistry,' he tells the English boy. As he says the word, 'chimie,' he mimes the filling of one test-tube from another. Moss instantly understands the discipline referred to. The other men leave them and Aziz takes the unemployed boy from Bury into a large modern building, dedicated to the pursuit of science. They enter a laboratory. Moss turns his head this way and that as strong odours rear up at him. Sulphur and something acrid, like vinegar but staler. Aziz laughs at Moss's wrinkled nose. The room fizzes with experimentation. A string of cluttered benches at which many young men and one or two women in headscarves are working. This is not a lecture or a structured class as far as Moss can make out. They each seek the answers to their own personal quests.

Aziz introduces the English boy to several of his fellow students. They shake hands in the traditional way but Moss does not try to remember their names. Once more he feels like an exhibit. The boy last sat in a classroom in nineteen-seventy-six. He fears they expect him to have some knowledge of their subject. He has none. He could tell them of his visit to a bomb factory three or four hours up the road, but that tale might backfire. Battypapa does not advertise his weaponry. Surely not. The men with the guns would get as funny with Algerians coming to take a look as they were with him. Moss decides that he must explain to Aziz that he studies literature: a lie but one to which he has long reconciled himself. Aziz appears to listen, does not engage him on the subject. He simply introduces Moss to further male students. More budding scientists.

At one bench a boy calls out to Aziz, and he indicates to the English boy that they will go over to the caller. Another boy hands him a pair of protective glasses. The instant they are upon his face, a massive flash of white light flares up before them. Something—magnesium, Moss thinks, but it is only a guess—burns up in an instant. Moss starts to turn away. The boy who called them across shouts, 'Regardez!' Turning back, Moss sees green-tinted yellow froth climb out of the test-tube and across the bench. Its growth in volume is rapid, astonishing. In five seconds, there is sufficient to fill half a dozen buckets, all from the tiny quantity of liquid within the narrow glass tube. Moss smiles, two or three more goes should bring a cat back from the dead. He keeps his hypothesis under wraps; they cannot read his expression here.

* * *

Aziz takes Moss to the University refectory where the other three young men sit together, food upon plates. Moss accompanies the chemist to the serving hatch where a bearded man serves each a bowl of food. A tagine of some sort. Meat, Moss is unsure from which animal. He asks about payment but Aziz shakes his head.

While the young men eat, Farouk and the fourth man, Nassim, ask Moss many questions. They speak quickly, use a few French words with which the boy is not familiar. Mostly he understands, guesses the gaps.

Moss confirms for his new friends that he is neither married nor betrothed. They seem to think this a happy state. Moss furrows his brow for a second, wonders to himself if these men might frequent Denise's chamber; it is impolitic to ask and they don't seem the sort. He asks the four young men before him if they are married and all shake their heads.

Nassim declares, 'You have had a girlfriend,' and Moss replies with ambiguity, enjoys the status which his affected nonchalance on the matter brings him. It seems as though they want to ask more but Farouk in particular has turned shy. Then Aziz repeats the word for girlfriend: 'Copine.' He laughs, nudges the English boy. Moss feels that they are expecting confession or entertainment through description of what he—a western boy—may have done with such a creature. If they ask it directly, he will definitely send them to Denise. The discussion, however trivial, brings Sharon MacDonald to his mind. Moss has no anecdote to share, nothing from so personal a coming together which he can give these nosy fledglings.

Nassim then asks him about the hostages, the hundred plus stuck in the American embassy in Tehran. Moss is out of touch with the news and turns the question around, seeks information from the young men. 'Are they still being held?' They tell him that nothing has changed in weeks. Moss shakes his head. 'It is a bad situation.'

They all agree upon this. 'It is difficult,' says Farouk.

Moss tries to lighten the mood. Enquires about the town's nightlife but they do not give answers that make an impression on him. He asks directly if they ever drink alcohol.

'No,' they declare. Djamel shakes his head as though the question is an affront. The portly Aziz makes a joke about the matter. 'Ha-ha, les Anglais.' He mimes drinking beer, being tipsy. The other men laugh along, it is all very good-humoured. Moss detects a hint of envy at its kernel. He momentarily thinks Aziz might have recognised that he is hungover but dismisses the notion. These four nice young Arabs have no true conception of drink, no experience of it. He supposes they have no knowledge of the unmarked bar which he stumbled across so close to the hotel to which Farouk and Djamel brought him.

Moss asks the four boys where they live, whether they are in student halls or still with their families. For all four it is the latter.

Farouk wishes to tell the English boy about his family. His father he describes as 'un commerçant.' Moss contemplates this unknown word, makes the connection to commerce, to trade. When he tests these English words, Farouk nods enthusiastically but it is hope, not knowledge. Farouk goes on to tell him that his father owns four

255

donkeys. Moss thinks the man could ply his trade on Blackpool beach.

Farouk has two sisters and a brother. He is the youngest and both sisters are already married. They also live in Constantine. Farouk is an uncle to two boys by his eldest sister, a girl from the younger. Moss notes the pride with which Farouk tells him this. He knows that his own lack of family feeling is a rarity. The product of unusually fraught relationships. Or probably just the single sour relationship with his father, although he feels disconnected from his mother and even Gary now that he has joined the navy. He tells Farouk that he has a brother in the Royal Navy, simply to share something personal and to finally be truthful with these well-meaning students. Farouk repeats this to his three friends and all look a little concerned. Moss can't think why. He doubts that they share his aversion for all things military. That would not square easily with their evident conformity. He decides to contemplate the matter later, work it out. To keep the conversation lively he tells them that his older sister, Suzanne—an older sister that he neither has nor so much as imagined having before opening his mouth—fronts a rock band. They have secured a recording contract. The contract concept seems difficult for the boys to understand. Moss is sure that the word, contract, is not the issue. Why a singer might need one is their stumbling block. They are far more interested in Suzanne than they were in Gary. Genuinely impressed. Nassim asks him what she wears when she is singing. On the stage. Go to Denise, thinks Moss, as he says some guff about tight leather trousers. 'Cardboard House is the name of the group,' he tells them, and they all say they will listen out for this band.

After the meal, some of the students have classes to attend but Djamel does not. He says he will drive the English boy back to his hotel. Moss protests. Says that he can walk, the others insist he should not. Moss knows that from the hotel he will most probably walk around the town for as long or longer than it would take him to walk there from here. He enjoys the stimulation of seeing, hearing and smelling each town and city his journey lays out before him. He does not wish to offend these young people to whom he feels gratitude for their openness while puzzling over the paucity of rebellion within them. As Moss and Djamel are leaving they all agree to meet the next day. Farouk insists they will come to his hotel again, do so at one o'clock because this will accommodate their university commitments. Moss wonders if they have politely set a later time because he was not ready at eleven this morning. Their given reason could be truthful, of course. They do not come across as complicated people.

* * *

Driving back to the centre of Constantine, Djamel is silent but Moss infers from his demeanour that he has something to say. Something ominous if his facial expression means anything. Moss speaks as they cross a bridge over the ravine. He says it looks different and Djamel tells him that this is not the same bridge. They are returning on a different road. Moss thinks it a meandering route—it takes longer—and he wonders why the young man chose it. His drawn face suggests driving is a chore. In time they pull up at the hotel and Moss tries to be as jovial in saying goodbye as he was earlier with the more easy-going Farouk.

Djamel says, 'Wait. Talk for a little time.'

Moss concurs but finds only that they endure another awkward silence. Moss does not try to fill it. He has nothing to say, nor does he wish to deprive Djamel of the opportunity to air his worry. Finally, to break the impasse, the boy from Bury states that he is tired. He feels this from the previous night's drinking. Hasn't talked about it with

Djamel or the others, they would only disapprove. Djamel waves away the comment. 'It is so early,' he says. Then he puts on a face in which Moss detects serious intent. 'Will Suzanne come to Algeria?' he asks.

This is a simple question for Moss to answer. His rockstar sister, Suzanne, is fictitious and this carefree state permits her to do absolutely anything under the sun. It simply requires Moss to say it, prescribe for her a course of action. He is the puppet-master; there are no limits. 'Yeah,' he replies casually. 'Cardboard House have a little tour planned but not to Constantine. Only Algiers. They will be playing Casablanca and Cairo while they're in North Africa. Three nights in Cairo, I think.'

Djamel nods, eyes enlarged and grateful for the information. 'When?'

'Autumn,' says Moss. He is confident that the word, l'automne, is true French but Djamel seems unfamiliar. 'Novembre,' he substitutes and Djamel nods, understands.

Djamel repeats the name of the month with evident satisfaction. 'I will go to Algiers. I like leather.'

'I'll be there too,' says Moss. Djamel's eyes glisten when he hears this. 'I will be in Algiers, setting up the sound system. The speakers and microphones. Cardboard House put on a great show.'

Djamel steps out of the car as Moss is leaving, comes around to shake his hand again. He says the name 'Suzanne', a quietly repeated name, as if only to himself.

The Lancashire liar feels inwardly conflicted. This is hilarious. He can fool anyone about anything. Award himself degrees, a sister who fronts a rock band, and even smuggle currency if push comes to shove. Conversely, he thinks himself a hypocrite, quite a departure for the left-wing Bury boy. He is Vim Voyager, the world's biggest gobshite. He should not use the powers of the Rucksack Jumper to make fun of the good people who befriend him. 'Merci,' he repeats again, this time to Djamel's back as he returns to the driver's seat. 'Merci, he says to the car as it moves away from the kerb on which he stands. He knows he must recover himself, get back to who he was at that border crossing. The idealist who came to Algeria with love and peace in mind, not this other boy. The one for whom rash mockery of those who treat him well seems the only road his mouth will take.

* * *

Moss sleeps for a few hours in the afternoon. Catches up. It is again dusk when he rises. Early evening. He thinks he should avoid alcohol. Last night was an embarrassment. Nor has he any hunger; the plate of food he ate at the university was substantial. He picks up the novel he is reading, The Vanity of Deluoz. A good book but a frustrating one. He experiences its rambling narrative as he feels drift in his own life. The book slips from his grasp to the floor as he contemplates his situation.

He has pretended to be a student. And not simply to these naïve boys in Constantine but in almost every lift he has taken through France, Spain and Algeria. It was a lie he told Asia, Samira, and that funny French girl travelling with her father into the desert. He even pretended it in the company of the Norwegian girl, and her wrestler schtick was far the funnier. Back in Bury, one or two of his old friends, class mates from school, are university students now. He keeps up with them, Moss has an enquiring mind. He was not the one who failed to get into university but the one whose father would not countenance it. Ronald Croft told him that studying sociology or literature—the subjects that Moss wished to take in Sixth Form—would not lead to work. Far better to get a job and have an income, that was the plasterer's reasoning. Moss recalls Mustapha Lellouche, the kindly father in Oran, talking to him about the same matter. He queried what Moss could really do with a literature degree. Never resorted to his father's tub-thumping, it was a pleasant enough chat. And even Soufiane—Mustapha's son—had suggested that his own practical degree was superior. Alone in his hotel room Moss starts to laugh to himself. Geology is the solution. If he had only told his father he was going to work as an engineer in the copper mines of southern Africa, not hitchhike to the Sahara, that would have won his approval hands down. Just a couple of notches short of being an astronaut. That boat left port without him; no matter, from now on he could tell the drivers and their kinfolk that he studies geology. He would receive still greater approval from these practically minded North Africans. 'Degrees are easy come by when you award them to yourself,' he says out loud.

Thinking it over has brought the Lellouche family to Moss's mind. Their easy hospitality. Tears are tracking down his cheeks as he remembers them. He cannot understand why he cries, recalls well that they were a loving family. Khadidja was special: so good to him, never judging. He wonders what she saw in him or if she is simply that nice to everyone. To the world. What a marvellous way to be. No cynical lying about rockstar sisters from her. He tries to picture Asia, Khadidja's clever daughter but only the higher-cheek-boned visage of gentle Samira comes into his mental view. The friend of Asia's whose father must be the photographic negative of Ronald Croft. His father and hers share the same offensive outline but with all the colours inverted. Xenophobes from different lands.

When he told his parents that he had given notice on his job—his factory-hand of a job—that he was going to hitchhike to the Sahara Desert, his mother simply left the room. Perhaps she admired his adventurousness, could be that she didn't. She certainly wasn't for pre-emptively contradicting whatever slant his father was about to put on it.

'You can't do it,' said Ronald. 'Go and try, but just think about it. You haven't the gumption to hold a job down, so if you imagine yourself Lawrence of Arabia, you really are a lunatic.'

'I've planned...' Moss had started to tell him but before he could shape a rebuttal, his father interrupted.

'You can't do it!' Shouted the words at a volume that sent the cat scurrying from the lounge.

'I bloody will,' Moss retorted at a similar volume, immediately regretting the unnecessary use of the swear word his father had again driven him to. As he thinks of the meaningless scene, the boy who fulfilled that prophecy, made it into the desert, reaches down to the floor from the bed he lies upon. He moves his hand around, grasps a hold of the fallen novel. As he thinks about his father—the man declared hitchhiking to be sponging, implied some moral defect to the Rucksack Jumper's art—he hurls the book angrily across the room. To his dismay it slams into a mirror hanging precariously from a hook on the dado rail. Dislodges it. The mirror slips and shatters, shards of glass upon the wooden floor. 'Oh, not that!' says Moss. He feels deeply ashamed of what he has done. Breaking up a hotel room like a stupid rock drummer.

* * *

In the evening, back on the street, Moss twice passes by the door of the bar. It is after eight, the lights already out. He could knock, look for a back entrance, give another large Algerian banknote to Denise. For greater return should he choose to do with her what he would rather do with someone other. Simultaneously, he tells himself that this is not who he is. Not with a prostitute. Not this Moss Croft. He keeps on walking. Searching hard for nothing in particular.

Rucksack Jumper

His thoughts turn from Denise to the young woman in the headscarf who was at the reception desk when he reported the broken mirror. Moss anticipated a fine, a reprimand. A form to complete with explanation and apology for Battypapa. His vandalism deserved nothing less. Turned out nothing like that. She was gentle with him, and he found himself revising his view of her. Contemplating if he dared ask her out for supper. When she came to tell him that Farouk and his friends were in reception, he had considered her an obstacle. Now he sees that this was a reflection upon his guilt for speaking to a traditionally dressed woman while virtually unclothed. She probably didn't even look through the door—open only a crack—Muslim girls don't bother with men. Rules are rules. He noticed this morning that she might be only a little older than him. The same age even. Why think negatively of one who came up the stairs to fetch him, a diligent receptionist. He had not been himself this morning, he thinks, then laughs at the very notion. If he is not himself then who on Earth can he possibly be?

He should have owned up to breaking the mirror, instead he told the girl only that it was broken. Not how. She was apologetic. The same girl as this morning, her lovely face clear to him. It shone from the circle of her deep green headscarf. Her smile beguiling. In the morning he had imagined her aloof. Above looking upon a boy in his underpants, most likely. Tonight, she told him, in slow clear French, that she was sorry if the hotel staff had failed to fix the mirror properly to the wall. At the time, Moss was pleased; he did not want to be in conflict with this young lady, and there they were, not arguing. In the evening air, Moss reflects upon his failure to advise her that he threw a book across the room which hit and dislodged the mirror. Without doubt the cause of the breakage. He never owned up to his pivotal role in the whole misadventure. He let the kindly girl think that substandard hotel fittings were to blame, not his own deranged outburst. He realises that he is not only capable of this duplicity but, more specifically, nobody notices. Everyone treats him like a simple soul. They see their own best qualities reflected in him. Even the curly haired customs officer did it back at the border. Moss wonders if he has become a mirror for the optimism of others: it's a natural enough transmogrification for a dancing hitchhiker. And these powers have brought him far but he fears some kind of karmic reprisal. It could all catch up with him sooner or later. Then he laughs at his own baseless fear. 'God can't see me,' he says out loud to the Algerian night. Moss is an atheist. A very, very poor one but it still counts. Rucksack Jumpers know the whole show is daft. Silver balls within a cosmic pinball machine. What happens will.

He had gone down to the reception desk in two minds about whether to own up or not. He could have paid for the breakage—money is not the object—but did not wish her to think him a vandal. The lady in the green headscarf saw the bloodied handkerchief that Moss had wrapped around the base of his left-hand thumb. She queried if he was all right. Real concern. He explained to her that he had tried to clear up the broken glass from the mirror and one shard had cut him.

'Je suis vraiment désolé,' she said: I am so sorry. She never queried if it was his fault. Désolé might mean more than sorry, thinks Moss. Desolated. Buying her dinner, sharing some kindly words—some precious time—might compensate for the desolation he inadvertently wrought within her. He really should have asked.

After seeing and understanding the nature of the injury, the lady in the headscarf beckoned Moss to accompany her into a small utility room. Once there she washed his wound, attended to him as a nurse might. He enjoyed feeling her smooth hands tending to his. She fetched a small bandage from a first aid box, a container Moss did not recognise until she opened it up. The green colouring and Arabic script upon it having no meaning for him. She kept looking into his face. Assessing if he was faint, or in need of a transfusion, perhaps. Or just enjoying the eye contact as he did too, it is a rare thing in this land. Between a girl and boy. She repaired him expertly and sent him back into the trenches of the Constantine night, where once more he finds himself walking past the closed door of the unadvertised bar. If he knocked, if someone let him inside, the stairs could take him up to Denise. Again, he takes no such action. Knocks not upon the door. It is the absence of the young lady from the hotel he is ruing. Voulez-vous dînez avec moi? He could have said it. Dînez isn't couchez. Her refusal would not have maimed him. Her acceptance would surely have cured whatever this melancholy is which he cannot shake. It might have flipped the quantum switch. Given him a hot shower; released the hostages in Tehran; undone the dreadful crusades of long ago. Christian and Muslim should never fight. It seems they do but Moss will have no part in it. He would like to make that clear to the girl on the desk. She fixed his hand. Must see it the same way. Perhaps it's not that simple. Still, he thinks, the ill which we do and the good which we do must echo through history long after we are gone. He would like to leave a positive legacy. Walking along the street to the centre of Constantine, Moss wonders if he is Confucius or a lunatic. 'It's a very close call,' he mutters quietly to himself.

* * *

An ice cream vendor continues to trade at this late hour. A small kiosk with a few metal chairs on the pavement beside it. Moss sees a girl and a boy of his own age eating cones. The girl wears jeans, a sweatshirt. She looks Arabic but could as easily be French. Moss buys an ice cream and sits at a neighbouring table.

'Bon soir,' he tries.

The young man talks with him, seems friendly enough, asks where he is from. The English boy tries to catch the girl's eye. As he does so he thinks his own actions foolish. She is with a boyfriend but Moss feels starved of female company. As he thinks it, he wonders if he is kidding himself. He is not a young man who has enjoyed as much of it as he would like to have done. It's simply that—here in North Africa—females appear further from view than ever felt to be so in Lancashire. In France or Spain. The young man asks him if he likes Constantine.

'Oui, oui,' he replies. Moss remarks once more upon the fine bridges that span the ravine. His fellow ice-cream eater furrows his brow, probably takes the spectacle for granted. Moss guesses that he has always lived in this city of bridges, fine structures that bring the roads from coast and desert across the ravines which surround it.

The girl speaks, not in French but in Arabic, and it is Moss's turn to furrow his brow. 'Ma soeur aimes tes chevaux,' says the young man: My sister likes your hair.

'I haven't even got a horse,' says Moss loudly in English. He grins smugly at them, at his playfulness with the French language. His pun is a hilarious thing. Neither Algerian so much as smiles—they don't get it—and the English boy rises from his folding chair, feeling suddenly ashamed of his effrontery. Moss walks away. He likes the bridges but otherwise he has lost the thread completely. It seems he is not himself after all.

3.

Moss sleeps only poorly. He feels remorse for the stupid non-joke he tried to make at the ice-cream kiosk. Two fine young people may go through their lives knowing his rudeness as their only interaction with an Englishman. Behaved as a drunken holidaymaker might in Blackpool or Benidorm, not one who has mastered the art of hitchhiking, trod a path to the Sahara Desert. He regrets that he did not try and befriend the girl from reception. Rolls the feeling of it around in his mind like he is reducing a boiled sweet. Might asking her out have been offensive to her? That is the one that worries him. He wonders, when he returns to England, if he should find himself a place in Manchester. A job, any job. Track down Sharon MacDonald who found work as a waitress there. He isn't really sure why they stopped going out together but they did. He wants the despondency of this sleepless night to end so dearly that he climbs out of his bed at an earlier hour than he has ever done on this continent. An hour unseen by him since he gave up his paper round. He starts to read the novel by Philip Roth, only to find he is not in a reading-about-others frame of mind. He hurriedly scribbles a few lines on paper. A poem about a face seen through a door which is only narrowly ajar. He cannot decide if it has real meaning. Sometimes a glimpse is all we see.

Moss leaves the hotel at six-thirty in the morning. He has not seen the sun this low in the east since the day he left Morocco. The morning air smells fresher to him than it does in the heat of daytime. His sleeplessness determined this course of action; he is pleased to be outdoors.

Moss has it in mind to walk again to the largest of the magnificent bridges and this time—pocket camera in his hand—he will secure the view for posterity.

He notices many men gathered around a newsstand talking rapidly, excitedly. Not something he expected to see at this early hour. They are older men, not the sort of people who take an interest in him. Many of the papers are in Arabic. He sees a photograph of a crashed military helicopter on the front page. Cannot discern what the story is about. In a French language paper, the word 'Téhéran' gives him pause to purchase a copy but he does not. His spartan vocabulary will not suffice. Hasn't the proficiency to read a broadsheet. Something has prompted excitement—even a degree of agitation—in these men. He can only speculate what it might be. They are more demonstrative with one another than he has seen before. Perhaps it is their way at this hour, before work commences. Moss grins at this possibility, his inevitable ignorance of the true sound and demeanour of the working Arabs this early in the morning.

He walks quickly. At a street vendor he purchases a strong black coffee. Its bitter taste is welcome. Breathes life into him. Coffee is better than beer, he decides, although he has effortlessly avoided that vice in North Africa. One embarrassing blip two nights ago.

* * *

His trek to the edge of the city is a straight line. It takes him under an hour to reach the high bridge he had hoped to find. The one he walked across with Farouk on his arrival here. He steps out on to the sturdy structure. It is the shape which he admires more than the engineering. He considers this, his bias. If he were a practical man, like Soufiane the geologist, or Aziz the chemist, it is likely that he would value the conception of this structure. Dwell on the importance of each component within its grand assembly. How cleverly it has been tied into the rock face on each side of the ravine; the finely calibrated geometry of the high towers from which the cables suspend the bridge aloft. But for Moss it is being here that matters. He looks down upon the feeble river. He takes photographs looking to the city, looking to the road back to the west. Looking at the other bridge far below. He likes to think about the narrow river down there which has miraculously orchestrated this whole affair. Standing in the centre of the bridge, he imagines that he has achieved stationary flight. The bridge is incidental. He is in mid-air. Between places. On no side of the divide.

* * *

He returns from the centre of the bridge to the town side of the ravine. He passed a path before he stepped on to the bridge itself. If path it was. He goes off the road and—between two enormous rocks—steps on to a red stone trail. It could be a footpath down. It is dusty, his training shoes slide it is so steep. Moss is agile. His camera is an impediment in his hand. He stuffs it up the sleeve of his thin sweatshirt. Puts it in the very place where he had the illicit money which he smuggled across the border. Money he is only slowly disposing of, despite his best efforts. This crazy country is too generous, he thinks, expelling a laugh from his gut. The path down the ravine is even steeper than he expected. Barely a path at all. He jogs and slides, must slow himself down to avoid toppling over. Tries going down onto his haunches. Uses his lowered centre of gravity to prevent himself from slipping. He realises how old and worn the grip on his training shoes has become. Bugger it, he thinks to himself, he can do anything. He sees a flat rock sticking out a little below and pushes off to jump on to it. Success. Looking back, he sees that he is a quarter of the way down the steep gorge already. This is easy, he thinks. His pulse is racing. The sweat on his brow trickles into his wide-open eyes. Stings. He goes back down onto his haunches, slides a few yards at a time. It is really just steep stony hillside that he plummets down. No path is discernible. He is simply going around the scant vegetation; he has little purchase on the loose red stone. He correctly imagines it is discolouring his jeans as he slides his bottom upon it. His arse is his brake; Moss laughs about it. What biological engineering! He decides he can go faster, brake less, preserve his jeans. He is like an Olympic bobsleigh competitor. An unlikely toboggan run beneath the high desert sun. He is good at this. Faster, faster; too much; he brakes a little with the arse; ouch; faster. His left foot hits a fixed rock, ouch, he rolls over, spread-eagles himself on the sloping red ground. Brings himself to an uncomfortable halt. He screws up his face concentrating on the foot. Damn! It really hurts. He overdid it, skiing in worn out training shoes. Now he is unsure what damage he might have done. Sitting himself up, he takes off his shoe. Rubs and rubs the foot in his hand. It is very sore, tender, but he can move it. Not broken. The world still turns. He notices blood seeping through the bandage on his left hand. He has reopened the wound he inflicted on himself last night, not shards of broken mirror this time, but from spreading his hand upon the red shale. He looks up. The bridge appears as magnificent as ever. Then looks down. He is three quarters of the way to the bottom; the low bridge is really quite close to him. He can do anything, he thinks. Common sense is certainly not a barrier. Onwards and downwards.

The path, he has now decided, is not a path at all but a chance accumulation of scree tumbling down the steep side of the ravine. He sees that a short way below he will reach the low road. The minor road that crosses the river directly below the high bridge. The non-path will get him there. Tentatively he steps and slides the last short distance. His ankle is okay, twisted, lightly sprained. These are doctor's words. Buggered hits the spot just as accurately. Not an amputation job. Moss grins to himself. He has done worse and got home from football.

Arriving at the bottom, Moss decides he must walk across the low bridge—the companion piece to his entry into the city—if only to turn around and come straight back. In all the time he was heading down he saw no cars on the lower bridge while the high one seemed forever busy. Occasionally even congested. Down here is a quieter world. He walks gingerly on his turned ankle. The English boy at the bottom of a gorge in Algeria wonders where the river goes. It moves surprisingly fast, although it is only a narrow tape of water wending across the hard rock face. He sees the minimal greenery clinging to the water's edge. There is little soil to speak of down here. Not much for life to purchase itself upon and yet a few bits of vegetation thrive. A small bird flitters passed him. He sees thin trees ahead, not many, just the occasional one. Few of the tree roots are truly below ground, most sit out from the rock face, dangle themselves in the water. He scrambles to the river's edge and does likewise with his throbbing ankle.

* * *

Ghardaia, how long is it since he left? Five nights, six nights, no more than that. After the confusion of his first night there—the fracas on the street involving the lady in the room adjacent to his—he took it upon himself to champion the Tuareg cause. Look out for the blues: it became his mantra. He understood—or possibly imagined, the distinction has become a fine line for him in Africa—that those in blue robes were Tuareg people. As the water cools his swollen ankle, he tries to ransack his memory, his book knowledge, his reasoning skills. Wants to know if those people—the Tuareg—are endangered. As he thinks about it, he concludes they are not. Only animals can be endangered, not people. People are dangerous, that's the sum of it. A people, a tribe or ethnic type, they might be mistreated—injustices to put right—but if they believe themselves endangered, they are mistaken. Missing the point completely. It is the division into separated humanity that is the problem. Deep down, we are all the same, this is Moss's firm conviction. Endangered is an odd term to ascribe to any mortal. Today will always become yesterday. It is not indicative of the endangerment of days. He recalls how the Tuareg seemed like second-class citizens. Segregated from the main Arab population, their dress was the obvious divide, and something subtler was in the mix. They conducted themselves in a different manner. It may have been only the one lady who truly gave him this impression. Hers alone is the remembered face. She was not typical Tuareg. She spoke French and—inexplicably—wore no headscarf. No religion, he guesses. Approves the choice.

In the town square on his second night in Ghardaia, Moss looked upon the barely mingling masses. Stalls with blue-robed sellers, sold to blue. Brown-robed sellers sold to brown. He alone—the boy in jeans and sweatshirt—crossed tribes, could not conform with the local apartheid. At a blue-robed food vendor, the boy from Bury joined the queue. All were tall and he quite small by comparison. In this he found a determination. To know these people. An old man—white headdress atop his blue robes—waiting in front of him, turned and looked down at Moss. Took his eyes directly.

'Bon soir,' said the English boy. He knows his own face to be a friendly one. No misinterpretation could possibly arise.

The man shrugged.

Moss asked—in French—if the food was good. 'La nourriture est-elle bonne?'

The man gave no reply but turned back to the vendor, partook for himself of the hot food. A little meat in a broth.

Moss's turn came. He asked questions. What the food was called, what it contained. The vendor was not aloof as the customer in front of him had been. He spoke words to Moss, Arabic words he couldn't comprehend. Tuareg words, perhaps. Moss is unsure if they have a language of their own. Tuaregese. He imagines they do. He realised then that his chosen team—the blues—did not speak French whether it was Tuareg or Arabic that the man directed towards him. The lady the previous evening was the exception, she spoke a little of it to him. Was she mistreated because of that knowledge? The absence of a veil. One of her own team hit her with a stick. By smelling and then pointing, Moss chose a meaty broth at the stall. He could not discern the flavour with certainty. Goats were the only animals he had seen in five hundred miles. He took the broth but was able to share nothing more with his non-conversant multi-cultural brothers.

This is the top and bottom of it. He's a Bury lad, no place inside any big tent. He is not a Cambridge-educated anthropologist who can ably cram in pre-field-work language lessons. He cannot bridge the divide between the knowledge-thirsty present and the misunderstood past. He is not a chameleon who can quickly adopt the mores of an unknown tribe. Become Tuareg; become Arab. He will never truly be Samira's husband, not in this life. He can be a literature student from Manchester, a sham one, in truth. He can slide down a ravine on his bottom, turn his ankle and laugh about it. These skills, if such they are, do not make him any wiser. He recalls it was after that encounter with the Tuareg woman in Ghardaia that he decided it was time to turn around. Head for Sicily, for Europe. Perhaps his travels do make him wiser, he thinks, learning where he does and does not fit in. He struggles to accept it. Dislikes the compartmentalisation of people when he knows we are all the same. Fleetingly, he contemplates Samira, and recognises that the other world—the one in which she truly is his wife—would provide him with greater comfort than this sorry offering. The life he is condemned to lead.

* * *

He wonders where the road goes but no longer has the stomach for adventure. His ankle throbs. Not totally unbearable, even when he puts weight upon it, just a long way from fun. Having crossed the low bridge—performed the ritual—he crosses slowly back again to the Constantine side. This low bridge is far shorter than the one above, simply bridging the narrow stream and some of the low, uneven rock, not the whole vast airspace which the ravine has cloven from the plateau. He then glances at the path he slid down. Pretty much fell down, truth be told. He cannot imagine climbing back up that wall of loose stone, not with his turned ankle. He walks a little along the road, hoping to see a sign or possibly a gently inclining road back to town. Out of the silence he hears a truck approaching and instinctively sticks out his thumb. This is his calling. The truck passes and then draws immediately to a halt. Not thirty yards ahead of him. Two men have their heads out of the windows and they both wave him forward. He glances down at the state of himself. Jeans and sweatshirt covered in copper-red dust, his left hand and arm crusted with blood. The flow from the reopened wound on his hand stopped some while ago. He realises that if he were to hitch a ride like this in France or Spain, the driver might take him straight to the hospital. Or, failing that, the nut-house. Algeria is a different land.

The men grin at him. Smiles showing yellowed teeth, a fair few missing altogether. The passenger alights, stands beside him on the roadside, indicates that he is welcome to ride with them. Moss enters the truck. It is intimate, three men including the driver sit upon a single bench seat. English in the middle. They initially exclude him from their conversation—he thinks it an oversight, unintended—then they change language into simple French while their ancient vehicle rattles along in Arabic. Moss establishes that the men are not going to Constantine but to a village a little way outside. He has not figured out how the roads work. Never seen a map of Constantine. This one is so far below the high bridge, its route to town is not in his mental picture. The men are amenable to helping him. They will divert their journey, take him into town. Moss feels moved. They are not wealthy, poor men indeed. Working men in stained trousers, and they interrupt the requirements of their day to accommodate the fool who fell down a ravine. He wants to thank them but does not know how. The driver is a madman at the wheel. Moss has hitched enough rides in this country to recognise the normality of it.

The truck enters a square familiar to the boy. Moss indicates that he would like to get out here. He wishes to trouble them no longer.

The vehicle comes to a halt. The other passenger gets out first and then Moss follows. Clumsily he bashes his arm on the side of the truck. It doesn't hurt but he worries that he has broken the camera carried within his rolled-up sleeve. Not to worry, he thinks, tapping a finger to his head. He can remember everything.

As the passenger is sliding himself back into the truck, Moss scrabbles into his money belt, then he leans into the open window and offers the driver a large Algerian banknote. 'Non,' shrieks the driver. The boy's attempted recompense has insulted him. The passenger even puts his head out of the window and spits on the ground. A lift was offered and it cannot be refused—downgraded to a taxi-ride—after the event. Moss begins to say sorry, repeats it, tries to shake hands but the men will not do as he bids them. The truck shifts into gear, froths away erratically along the road.

* * *

Moss feels the stares of the people on the street as he walks back to his hotel. He must look a sorry state. His clothing reddened by dust; blood streaked on his left arm. He thinks about those two men who treated him so well. Wishes he had not offended them. Never intended it. They seemed quite indifferent to his appearance or injury, never spoke of it. On reflection, Moss considers it is the reason they picked him up. They saw a boy in distress. There is a certain type of man who will always assist another in such circumstance. Not to draw attention to the person's difficulty or their role in its amelioration. Simply because it is the right and selfless thing to do. A reflection not of that man's personality but of the social code he keeps. Those scruffy Algerians have their counterparts in pit villages and on rugby league pitches across Northern England.

* * *

Back inside the hotel, Moss sees the girl in the headscarf. Not a green one today but it is the same girl. She wears an orange headscarf, her dress—the large all-body robe—is blue. He tries to imagine how she really looks; he preferred the green. Too short to be Tuareg and the shade of blue too dark for those other people. Would she be able to remove it if they shared dinner? Just the headscarf, she should keep the rest on. Moss is only thinking first date. Her hair is probably very nice; a shame she hides it. A shame for him, he'd like to see it in full. Her black hair might even look like that of the Tuareg lady, and this girl has the sweeter face. He sees no anger in it at all. He'd be interested to learn what she thinks about all that. If she prefers to keep the scarf on, that will be okay. Moss isn't the sort to insist. She greets him but there is shock on her face. The blood and the dirt, he must look like the victim of a mugging although the true explanation is pretty funny. Clambering down a path that no one but Moss knew was there. She says something to him in Arabic, quickly adjusts this. Into French. 'What has happened?' He is sure that is her question.

He wants to reassure her. To take her on a date unless Battypapa has prohibited it. The sharing of a meal between a Muslim and so lapsed a Christian should offend no one. He hasn't brought a dowry with him but a date is not a marriage. 'Je suis allé faire une promenade,' he says: I went for a walk. He sounds like an idiot, and the girl looks troubled by his pronouncement. 'Comment vous appelez-vous?' he asks. He needs to know her name, then he can ask the date question properly. Call her by it.

'Je m'appelle Samira,' she answers, reaching out to take his bloodstained hand. Moss withdraws it. She is lying. Samira is the other girl. More beautiful, frankly. But life is not a beauty contest. This girl was kind to him yesterday. The bandage. He fears she is taunting him, pretending this name is hers. He has no idea how she knows what has gone before, his association with the prettier girl who truly bears that name. This one is not called Samira; she is ridiculing him.

The girl in the headscarf talks to him. He thinks she is asking if she may wash his hand as she did yesterday evening. The cut opened up again but it is dry now. Red dust upon it. Moss shakes his head. He is not married to Samira but they have some sort of engagement lined up, all set for that other life. Just a quantum button away. This girl is taking the piss, not allowing him proper recall of that other time. Oran. This would-be Samira has stepped ahead of him, beckons him into her medical room. Or whatever she calls the little cupboard with the first aid box. 'Non,' he says. Continues to shake his head. 'Mon clef,' he says, asking for his room key.

Fake-Samira looks perturbed. It comes to Moss that it really could be her name. He doesn't know much in this country. It might be the Algerian equivalent of Susan or Jane. A Samira behind every other veil. He'll try and work it out. Sitting and thinking can do that on a good day. He'll not go into the little room with her. Not now he has already said no. That would look stupid.

The girl reaches over the narrow counter, passes him his hefty room key while standing next to him. He could have picked it from the hook himself, didn't think it was the right thing to do. She being the receptionist. As the girl puts it in his hand it slips from him. He'd put forward his wounded hand. The musical note of a deadened triangle sounds as key hits floor. They both stoop to gather it from down there and their heads collide. He makes a short yelp, not of pain but of anguish that he may have hurt her. She has arisen, key once more in hand. He apologises. 'Je m'excuse.' She rubs her head, the top of her orange headscarf, and still she smiles for him. He wonders again about asking her on a date; the headbutt seems like a contrary indicator. 'C'était un accident,' he says. She places his key in his right hand. The uninjured hand. Moss thanks her like a broken record, twice says sorry for knocking heads, and then he goes to his room.

* * *

When Moss has showered and put on some unstained clothing he feels better. Thinks clearer. He decides that Samira really is the name of the girl on the desk. She told him it was so, why should he doubt her. He's been a bit infatuated with the other one—because of how she looks and having a shit dad just like him—he doesn't expect to see her again. Not if he thinks about it rationally. He used to do more of that. The notion that the girl on the desk knows anything about the one in Oran is nonsensical. His brain must have been overheating. Climbing down a ravine in the African sunshine will have done that.

It's almost one o'clock by the time he has assembled himself. Cleaned and dressed more smartly than he has in quite a while. Moss takes himself down to reception where he expects Farouk, and probably his three friends, will soon arrive. If they are not here, he could speak to the new Samira. The trouble is he doesn't trust himself to say the right thing. He even thinks he should speak to her father first. Clear the date-thing with him. Or with Battypapa. And he's not doing that, Moss doesn't grovel to dictators, full stop. It's not the way of the Rucksack Jumper. They have secret resources; jumping over a rucksack is the closest we have yet to a quantum button. The doing of it turns a sponger into a distributor of joy.

As she is looking up from her paperwork, Moss torn between another apology and embarking upon a passionate kiss, the door opens. Farouk, Djamel and the other one, have arrived. Not the fat one, he hasn't come. There will be no kiss with Samira. Disappointing—he was readying himself—but it might even be illegal. He isn't sure. The president's posters must be keeping their eye on something.

* * *

Farouk speaks to him, barely attended words. Moss is still pondering the girl to whom he flashed the quickest smile before stepping out of the hotel. He hears the name Aziz, presumes Farouk is explaining the young man's absence. He waves it aside. Djamel tells him they will not use the car. 'Today we will buy you dinner.'

'I will pay,' says Moss. He would like shot of his excess money. Can't smuggle it out of the country, utterly pointless. The three boys all laugh. They walk only a short way down the street, past the newsstand that Moss saw earlier this morning, and then they enter a large café. Just behind its counter are the ovens and gas rings where meals are cooked. Three men in white—three chefs—are plying their trade. Farouk calls something in Arabic and the chubbiest chef turns around and grins at them. It is Aziz.

The chemistry student turns out to be a jack of all trades.

Aziz cannot join them for food because he is working. He promises Moss a fine meal. This—couscous and goatmeat—is the cause of excitement for the boys. Moss is back in Oran in his mind. It is the first Samira he should have asked on a date. She was on his wavelength, not as standoffish as the students.

They sit at a table waiting to be served, Moss answering yes and no, oui and non, to a range of questions while thinking of other things. Of two girls who share a name. Then Aziz comes across carrying a heavily laden tray. Places an assortment of good food upon their table. It looks terrific, he must grant them that. The three Algerian boys insist that they can eat nothing until Moss first tries each dish, each sauce.

* * *

As the English boy eats the assorted vegetables and fried meat, he remembers the newsstand. 'What happened in Tehran?' he asks. He hopes the American hostages have finally been released, it could drive a person mad being kept prisoner in a country where they don't belong.

The boys look excited, Nassim smiles broadly, bared teeth. 'God intervened,' says Djamel. Moss does not believe this. God jumping onto the front page of the news sounds highly improbable.

Farouk takes over, equally animated. 'The Americans sent helicopters to get the hostages,' he tells Moss. 'They send them to kill the Iranians, to fetch the Americans. God did not like this plan.' He glances at his friends, as if seeking assurance that this story should be told in full. 'They crashed into each other. The Iranians did nothing; the Americans crashed their helicopters together. This is what God can do. All the soldiers in the helicopters are dead; the hostages have to stay until America does as they have been asked.'

Moss wants to object; this is all wrong. God killing American soldiers isn't really a fair fight, and the newspapers shouldn't even report it. Not what God does, they're only guessing. The hostages are innocent people, Moss is pretty sure they are. Unless they worked for the Shah's secret police before all this. Before the revolution that ousted him. That would complicate matters. A U.S. military rescue sounds a bit hare-brained to Moss. And helicopters aren't designed to fly from America to the Middle East; even he knows that and he hates all things military. These Algerian students supporting the hostage takers is a surprise. He knows that the Iranians are Muslims too—it might stand for something—but what about the rule of law. He can't say as much or he'll only start sounding like his father.

'What will happen?' asks Moss.

'America will stop thinking it can rule the world,' says Nassim. The one who has been most silent, most thoughtful. Moss thinks this might be a good point but fears the mobs in Tehran may be a poorer force for good than the American military. The sort that put every woman in one-eyed veils. In this café in Constantine, he cannot give his thoughts voice. They would surely sound provocative to these young men who have invited him to dinner. He wonders to himself if this reluctance to debate the issue makes him more mouse than man. Also, he cannot quite believe what has happened. Wants to read it in the British or American papers. Carter sending in the military is the last thing Moss expected. Never thought the President who pardoned the draft-dodgers would go reaching for the gun cupboard. The circumstances in which the helicopters have crashed remain unknown to him. He reckons God had no part. The boys insist it was Him. It's scary to Moss. Boys who study science attaching themselves to this improbable notion on the basis of no worthwhile evidence. Helicopters crash: if God is behind this one, He should own up to the lot. A deity with a screw loose if you think about it for just a moment.

'I am leaving Constantine tomorrow,' the English boy tells these friends he can no longer trust.

All three sigh, saddened that he is going. 'Back to the University of Manchester,' says Farouk, and Moss nods.

They ask questions about the university, about the term times. Moss tells them that all universities in Britain take two months off at Easter because that festival is so important to Christians. They nod, happy to have learnt something of his culture.

'It is sad,' Nassim tells Moss, 'Easter is sad; Jesus is killed.' Moss agrees but feels more glee in his nonsensical lie, his fabricated explanation for his long sojourn in North Africa, than any sadness he can muster for the Saviour.

'Djamel has told me that you will come back with Suzanne,' Farouk reminds the boy.

'We want tickets,' Djamel tells him. 'Can you send some to us?'

'Give me an address to send the tickets to,' Moss instructs them. Immediately, Djamel is writing upon a napkin.

After they have eaten Aziz comes over to the table. Moss thanks him for the food, tells him that it was very nice. In truth, he is feeling sick. He imagines the cause to be unconnected to the meal, to the fine food. It might stem from his inner angst about a deterioration in the political situation. The excitement here over a couple of downed American helicopters. He wants to get to Italy. He hates the idea of Muslims and Christians fighting each other, can see no role for him if it all kicks off. Nothing better than hostage. Moss tells the friends, as he once designated them, that he will walk himself back to the hotel. He needs the air.

As they make their farewells, the three boys stand and wave from outside the restaurant. They raise a small chant: 'Cardboard House, Cardboard House.'

Chapter Six

Nuoro, Sardinia

1.

This boyfriend of mine is a funny one but I think it is going to work out. If it doesn't, I will kill myself. Or perhaps I won't. It is something that I say to myself and to my friend, Sperancia. I tell her that life is pretty stupid and we would all be better off dead. Me in particular. She doesn't like me saying it—not a bit—she says our lives are God's gift. I used to laugh about all that. Silly God dishing out the misery, then insisting His minions must stay the course. And now this boy really does make me happy. Not God you will note, just a nice young man. Having him in my life makes me feel that tomorrow will be better than today. Have I gone soft? If the answer is yes, then it is a better state than I expected. And when I talk about happiness, I don't mean the giggly affair that many girls in school partake in. I am a more serious person than that. Truly. I am pleased to be in a proper relationship, one of heart and mind. It brings me new insights about myself. I feel enriched, being with him makes me a deeper person.

My boyfriend—his name is Moss—hates me talking about killing myself. I have stopped doing it in his presence. I think that the life and death dichotomy is different for him; he has never been a Catholic. I am uncertain what it is that he has against death in principle. In practice it might be very messy and I do find him a little squeamish.

Catholics must not take their own lives. Some pope or other decreed it and that has cast the matter in stone. Others, those never under the sway of this religion shouldn't care two hoots. However, I have thought about it only as a lapsed Catholic whilst my boyfriend is a lapsed Baptist. This may sound a paltry thing, his religion young and frivolous in comparison to the ancient and daunting one from whose grasp I have unshackled myself. However, the feelings which his religion may stir—particularly the ones that linger deep within him where he might mistakenly believe they have lost their hold—they are unknowable to me. I am learning not to be dismissive of something just because it sounds stupid. I have appraised that Moss is a boy with very strong feelings and, of course, I like this quality. He has nice blue eyes too.

He stays in my uncle's house. I must clarify this point: Moss is not living with my uncle, simply renting a room from him. Uncle Patrizio owns the house but does not reside within it. It is the house which my grandparents spent their lives within. My mother and two uncles also lived there, long ago when they were children. Patrizio is the elder, the inheritor. My Uncle Andrea is the youngest, he lives far away in Sicily. Uncle Patrizio already had a house, and so he has begun to let out the rooms in this second property. It provides him with an additional source of income. As a consequence of this good fortune, he intends to help my mother financially. When he told me this at the turn of the year—while still renovating the old house—I was pleased. Now I worry that Moss's rent will pay for the food on my plate. It should not be so; I do not wish to be beholden to him. He and I are equals. That is how becoming a couple must work. The only way.

It was precisely ten days ago when Uncle Patrizio told me that an English boy was to be living in the house. He said it only as a matter of fact. Wanted my mother and I to know he had filled the fourth of his letting rooms. When I heard it, I decided to contrive a meeting with this visitor from afar. One reason for doing so was to practice speaking English. In addition, I had an inkling that he might have qualities more interesting than simply his native tongue. Since I have introduced myself to him, he and I spend more time together than I do with anyone except my friend Sperancia. She is in many classes with me at college. I like her but it is circumstances which force us to spend most of those hours together. With Moss it is by my own choice that I am by his side.

I think it will work out between Moss and I because he is a lost soul, and he says that finding me has helped him to find himself. I cannot guess what he means exactly but these are good words. Finding is good and being lost is a sadness, not a crime. I should add that I am more flexible than most about crime. It is necessary that I think this way because Moss has told me he was recently in prison. In fact, I think a little bit of why I love him is actually this terrible fact. He is not somebody who you would easily take for a jailbird. He is gentle and maybe a little frightened. Do you think that spending time in jail may have done this to him? He was imprisoned in Algeria. Imagine!

I wonder if this boyfriend of mine has helped me to find myself? I did not think of myself as lost, simply that life is horrible and killing myself might improve it a little. No, that is not an accurate representation of my thoughts upon the matter. It is the door marked exit. Bringing the whole sorry affair to a close can sound like a good thing on some days of the week. The days before Moss came into my life. To say it is for the better is absurd. If I killed myself, I would be no more. Nobody to compare this with that. No more me. I once told a priest that I felt I might do this. End it all. It was quite stupid of me to speak about it with such a man. I had already stopped going to church, so popping into the confessional to ask a self-deluded henchman of our bitterly anti-communist pope if He—the non-existent God who lives only in a book—would mind if I tried to get into His imaginary heaven earlier than planned was self-indulgent silliness. I used to be quite immature before I met Moss.

I have stated already that my friend, Sperancia, is in many of the same classes as I. However, she studies English as her optional and I am taking politics. I, too, learnt English in previous years but have not kept it up. She is the more fluent. It is easier for Sperancia, her family took a holiday in London last year. I was jealous even then although I had still to meet Moss. Could not guess that I would soon acquire an English boyfriend. Do you know that the only time I have left Sardinia—this island of endless tedium—was a family trip to Sicily? That is where my mother's younger brother, my Uncle Andrea, now lives. Isn't that ludicrous? For a little short of eighteen years, I have been on this Earth and the limit of what I have seen and where I have been is this irrelevant Mediterranean island. A brief stay on an equally unimportant one, better known only because of its mafioso. I think it pitiful: Nuoro, Sardinia, is all I know. Being born amongst simpletons has been my misfortune. I believe that having an international boyfriend will help me overcome the stigma. My peasanthood. Moss has travelled extensively but doesn't boast about it. Nor does he believe it to have been an exceptional learning experience. When I said that prison must have been exciting, he shook his head. Told me it was actually shit. I think my impatience to be somewhere else might have made me mis-think all that he has been through.

I do fear that my boyfriend will soon tire of this backwater. I cannot leave the island tomorrow or even the day after. School is my prison. I simply hope that Moss will stay. Wait until I have completed my sentence. For the time being, he has a nice room in my uncle's house. He has me. One day I intend to be a woman of the world, not a schoolgirl in Nuoro. I even think he and I could one day move in the intellectual circles of London or Paris. Do so together, the poet and the polemicist. Or Stockholm which is smaller and there are no Catholics, a quality which I consider very favourably.

Sperancia, who is the finest student of English in my school, can talk to Moss much more easily than I. She does not do so. Not often. She understands that he is my boyfriend. She has interpreted conversations between he and I once or twice. That has been very helpful. Mostly, I love to talk to Moss alone. The absence of a well-understood common language—my boyfriend cannot string a sentence together in Italian—is not a barrier to our communication. It is a state that propels us to a greater intensity of connection. Perhaps I would love him less if he spoke Italian. And as for Sard—the provincial language of my peasant stock—if he so much as uttered a word of that coarse tongue, I would dump him. I have told him this and Moss only laughed. I think it means he will not cross the line.

* * *

Moss pays for the room which he is renting from my Uncle Patrizio by working in the town bakery. The price of the room is high—in my honest opinion—but I have not told Moss of my appraisal. He would want me to ask my uncle to reduce it, for we are family. Unfortunately, I have no influence with him. My uncle treats me as he always has: quite nicely but like a child. And for my part, I do not get on with capitalists. That is the nub of the problem.

It amuses me to think of my boyfriend spending his mornings kneading bread. He comes out of the bakery looking like a ghost. Flour in his short hair, upon his face and clothing. I have asked him—Sperancia helped with this conversation—what he hopes to do for a job after this. I am certain he has greater ambition than being a bun-maker. He laughed and said, 'Poet. Or maybe a novelist.' I did not consider his reply to be funny at all, it is a fine occupation and certainly one befitting my boyfriend. Moss followed this up by saying, 'I need better things to happen to me than just being tricked into an Algerian prison. Not much to write about there.' I think his tale might be very instructive. He is too sad to tell it yet, and may have still to learn what the moral is.

I have asked Moss if he will take me to England when my education is complete. I do hope that, when I made the request, I phrased it better than I just have. I should like to have him as my companion on a journey to his home country. I am his girlfriend, not his luggage. And maybe in that faraway place we can finally live like a modern couple, sharing a flat and a bed. I do not expect my boyfriend to look after me; I am an independent girl regardless of the commitment he and I have made to each other. I will never be his burden: if it were drifting that way, I should go straight for the noose.

Later today, when my boyfriend has finished work in the bakery, we will meet. Moss and I spend every available hour together although we never see each other in my mother's house. She has told me I should find a local boy, not one from far away. She is worried that, because I love a foreigner, I will leave Sardinia. I tell her to stop worrying about what she cannot change. It will happen. Nuoro is nowhere and I simply have to leave.

When my brother has finished his own job for the day, he will drive Moss and I to meet my father in Oristano. This will be the first time that these two have met. I think my mother's only objection to Moss is that he will not stay on this tiny island. My father can raise no such grievance about the matter, he didn't even stay in Nuoro with my mother, my brothers and I.

* * *

I worried, the first time I went to see Moss, that I might appear licentious. I had heard of him while knowing it impossible that he had heard of me. I don't throw myself at boys. Not often. Why would I do that when I live on an island full of only the most stupid of them?

I am happy to report that he proved easy company. Moss had only just taken the room in my uncle's house. Uncle Patrizio told me of the English boy on the day he moved in. The following day I called upon him.

Sperancia—who remains a dedicated Catholic and for which I only reluctantly forgive her—told me about the English boy. She learnt of him, met him indeed, through her beloved church. The priest who presides over The Sanctuary of Our Lady of Grace—what puffed up names these churches bear—let the English boy sleep in the church hall for the first couple of nights he was in town. Father Domingo asked her to speak to him because she is so fluent in the English language. She will do anything a priest asks of her. In their clutches like a well-heeled sheep dog.

Sperancia told me that the boy is incredible. He had hitchhiked from Cagliari, having arrived on our island from Africa, from Tunis. She said he is very modest. He spoke about his circuitous journey from England to our town as a good idea gone wrong, not as the adventure she and I both agreed it sounded to be. Sperancia said to me—and it is a phrase I keep repeating to myself—'He has acquired his worldliness so young.' Do you know, her description impressed me so much that, before I'd even set eyes on the English boy, I asked Sperancia if she was in love with him?

'Not in love,' she replied, 'I admire him.'

Rucksack Jumper

When my uncle told me about letting the room, I knew straight away that it must be the same person. Nuoro is too inconsequential a town to receive two English visitors in the same month. And if Sperancia could practice her fine English with one from that country who came here via Africa, it seemed only fair that he should spare a little time to improve my more elementary knowledge of the same.

Uncle Patrizio does not know that I have a key to his house. My father—who lives in Oristano, but until a little over a year ago resided with my mother, two brothers and I, here in Nuoro—acquired it when my grandfather was still alive. Still living in the house where Moss now sleeps. My father passed the key to me some months ago, saying I should give it to my mother but I did not. Nowhere is it written that a daughter must be a go-between for her rancorous parents. Before visiting Moss, I had used the key just twice and both of those times were before Uncle Patrizio began letting out rooms in the house. He started to do this only last month. One of the occasions was to sleep off drinking a substantial volume of wine. Two bottles. I have sworn never to drink so much again. I was experimenting and did not wish my mother to hear me vomit. The other occasion I shall not tell you about. Not for the time being.

* * *

When I went to the house, and this was only nine days ago, I let myself in. I could have rung the bell. There is no obvious reason why I did not. My thinking at the time was that by using my key I would gain the upper hand. I expected that the English boy would feel obliged to talk to me. He might think he had a duty to do so because he rented his room from the Cossu family. Looking back, this was a sign of my then-immaturity. An affliction my boyfriend is rapidly curing. I do not want to have any hold

Nuoro, Sardinia

over him at all. It is my firm prediction that we will remain together, a true couple, voluntarily sharing our lives, without coercion or obligation.

I realised on entering that I had given no thought to the other men in the house. My Uncle Patrizio has told me he also lets rooms to another bakery worker and two young men who work for the municipality, something to do with construction. The first of these moved in five weeks ago. I do not give Sardinian boys a moment's thought, so certain am I that my destiny lies outside this island. On arriving at the house and letting myself through the door, I imagined meeting only the handsome English boy who Sperancia admired so much. When I walked into the kitchen, a naked and hairy monster surprised me. An ugly man with nothing but a towel wrapped around his person.

'Chi boles?' he asked, demanding of me what I was doing there although it is my uncle's house and not his. Indeed, there were times in my childhood when I visited daily: my Grandparents were better company than my mother and father. I shrieked, for he really did look like a monster, and to my horror, he lent forward and removed the towel from his waist and started drying his hair with it.

I am not a stupid girl. I knew straight away that he was not English. He spoke to me in horrible Sard. I had simply entered a house let exclusively to young men, and this big oaf had earlier taken a shower. I know that he did not plan my intrusion. His compulsion to show me his manhood—which did not impress but disgusted me—is indication that he is a certain future rapist. For my part, I should not be afraid to kick him in the place which would compromise that calling. If he were to try such malignancy with me, then I would do it. Kick away the fencepost. He continued to dry his hair, so I did not kick but shrieked a second time. I was not unduly scared; he was towelling himself, nothing more; however, it was the only protest I could think to make. You see, I believe a girl should be able to choose when to, and when not to, look at a boy's willy. They are not for the taunting of girls. Straight after my second scream the lounge door opened and a boy with very short fair hair emerged. Even as the door was opening, the naked man put the towel back around himself. My second squeal was really not as silly as it must have sounded. It brought out the boy I sought and covered up the one I did not. Screaming is not my preferred form of communication, and I intend to keep it in reserve only for very particular situations.

'Hello,' I said to the English boy, ignoring the oaf as best I could.

'Hello,' he replied.

'I am Joanna, Patrizio's niece.'

'Who is Patrizio?'

I realised that this boy was not yet on first-name terms with my uncle. 'Mr Cossu,' I modified.

The almost-naked man said something further to me in Sard. I paid him no mind. As I listened to the English boy, who asked me if I had come to collect money on my uncle's behalf—at least, he offered me money, his words were incomprehensible to me—I became aware that the horrible oaf, once more wrapped in a towel, was apologising. I do not think he was sincere. I expect he felt no shame for that which he had previously done. He will have heard me invoke the name of my uncle, recognised that I am in some way close to the man on whom his residence is reliant. Feared that I might have him evicted. Would that I should ever wield such power. The English boy stopped talking because of the man's rant. Being an integral part of the low-life scum who make up the majority of this town and island, the oaf spoke only in the Sard language. The English boy did not understand a word—I could read that on his astonished face—nor did he wish to compete with the oaf. Moss is very polite. In every way he is superior to any

Sardinian boy.

I brushed the apology aside. The towel-wearing man said he thought I was an intruder, so wished to scare me away. He spoke an obvious untruth. His private anatomy is quite pitiful, if it could scare a nun, I should be most surprised. His apology gave me a little satisfaction. 'I am only fourteen,' I told him, 'I should report you to the authorities.'

'No lu podes impreare,' said the dumb oaf, imploring me not to, and looking incredibly scared as he disappeared into his room.

I smiled to myself. I am actually seventeen years old but quite short of stature. And his is not the first penis that I have seen. I glanced at the English boy; I do not think he was listening to the Sard. It meant nothing to him, I was certain. And I hoped he did not hear or understand my lie, telling the oaf that I was fourteen. I feared that understanding it would diminish any interest that the English boy might have or later acquire in me. The wish for the company of a girl aged similarly to himself, that is.

I asked the English boy if we might go into the lounge but I could not recall the correct word for this room in his language, so I just pointed at the door.

He nodded and we stepped into it together. I was quite surprised by what I saw. The room was not as I expected. A large unmade bed dominated it and I was surprised to see a washbasin in one corner. It was my turn to apologise. I had not meant to enter the boy's bedroom which I now saw to be the function of the old lounge. I did not know that my uncle had plumbed in the basin and changed the lighting. The curtains were drawn together although there was still daylight outside, and it had a single light bulb, not the small chandelier of my grandfather's time.

The English boy did not seem embarrassed and I am broadminded. I quickly decided that, in principle, being in a bedroom with this handsome boy could be a lot of fun. I am not, however, the sort to jump into a boy's arms before learning a little more about him. I did not know if the English boy was even thinking about the two of us taking to his bed, the many adventures we might enjoy within it. I rather suspect he was still of the view that Mr Cossu—my uncle—had sent me only to check that all was as it should be. Nothing broken or stolen.

We returned to the kitchen and I sat down at the table, patted the chair next to my own. He sat upon it and I told him that I wished to learn English. To speak that language to a proficient standard. He seemed pleased; however, he emphasised that he is not a teacher. 'I'd like to talk to you,' he added.

I said again that my name was Joanna and put out a hand for him to shake. He took it and then, as he let it go, he touched his heart. I thought it a lovely gesture.

'Moss,' he said. 'My name is Moss Croft.'

'Joanna Marras,' I said, repeating myself. I have learnt many English words but they seldom come to the fore in my Italian brain. I should have been doing better than this, saying my own name over and over as if it is yet worthy of shouting from the rooftops. I said, 'Joanna Marras,' once more, pointing a finger at my breastbone.

Moss laughed, not outwardly, I saw a smile pass briefly across his face. He mimed something which I took to be playing upon a keyboard. An electronic synthesizer perhaps, for that is a form of music which I like to hear. 'Your name,' he said, 'Joanna. It means piano, in London.' He repeated this strange lie, tried to justify it. 'Apples and pears,' he said, and some more Joanna-piano nonsense.

I do not understand English very well but feared Sperancia had got it wrong, that this boy might be one of the crazy ones. And if he had talked such gibberish to her, then Sperancia's elegant looks might explain such an occurrence. I know some boys become flustered—get jellied brains—in the company of beautiful girls. Sperancia is taller than I, shapely legs, all the attributes that might bring about that affliction. I am plainer but not ugly. I hope not. Boys pay me only a modicum of attention, and the explanation for his mumbo jumbo lay outside my grasp. I recalled my friend telling me that this itinerant English boy had acquired worldliness while still young. His youth was evident, an unlined face. I thought I must drag the wisdom out as best I could. If none was forthcoming, I had a home to go to. He remained of interest to me but it would dwindle to nothing if he continued to talk this silliness. A piano-playing mime while repeating my name.

'Sometimes I feel that I want to kill myself,' I said. That seemed a good basis for a serious talk, although it might not have been first choice in a less troubled mind than my own. I had actually practiced saying the phrase in English some months before. I'd even imagined speaking it aloud to an English visitor and that was to have been Ronnie Prousch, the gifted songwriter. It was the frivolous imagining of my younger self; to the best of my knowledge, he has yet to step upon these shores.

Moss looked a little shocked after I said those words. 'No,' was as much as he spoke. I could see that he was thinking about what I had said. And I might have been stretching a point. I have sometimes felt that despondent; however, it was far from true on that particular late afternoon. Not while I was at the kitchen table with a handsome new English friend. That would be the poorest timing.

I nodded my head, there could be no going back once I'd made this statement about my outlook, the dissatisfaction I have always felt with my life.

'Why?' he asked after the longest time.

'Nothing here is good,' I replied. 'My friends are all

Catholics; they cannot see what I can see. That this God they worship is a fraud. I don't like to think myself better than my friends. I dislike vanity but I happen to be right about this. Every priest is just pretending, every last one of them. They offer up bogus prayers to a make-believe God, and deep down they all know it. This upsets me, and I cannot undo what I know.' I said all this in broken English and a lot of Italian. I didn't speak any Sard to this boy and still choose never to do so. He has no need to learn the parochial language of the small-minded islanders. I am not certain that he understood a scrap of it. He continued to look at me with a worried expression on his face. Concerned, perhaps, that he might have to administer a life-saving procedure to my unresponsive corpse. 'I will not kill myself with you,' I said in clear English. I hoped that this reassured him, only to recognise after saying it that he might construe my words as a wish for him to look after me, that it would be the only certain prevention. I was pleased that I had arrested his silly apples-and-pears talk but feared he might think me a hopeless case. 'I will show you where we play pinball,' I told him next. I took hold of the boy's hand, hoping he did not think me forward. I needed to lead him because I did not have the words to explain exactly where we were going. I suspect he was clueless as to my intentions but he trusted me. My face is not beautiful, simply an honest one. I liked, very much, looking into his. 'You know pinball?' I asked in English. 'We go and play it.'

He smiled and said, 'Yes.'

We left my uncle's house and I let go of his hand. I enjoyed feeling his in mine but we were not yet intimate and this is a small town. If a girl holds a boy's hand the local newspaper will not report it only because there is no need. Word always gets around. And at this point we were two young people, one English and one Sardinian. I was showing him my hometown, not yet my heart.

'Moss,' I said, trying his name and pointing.

'Joanna,' he replied. This sounded very nice to me, the way he articulated my name. Very different to how these stupid islanders say it. His unusual diction made me sound like the one from far away.

'We can play pinball and drink beer,' I told him. The boy smiled back at me and I thought to myself how well I had judged him, intuitively guessed that these were activities he would enjoy.

* * *

As we passed Via Liguria an idea came to me. It was both the cleverest and the stupidest idea I could have had. Quite a lot of both. Again, I pulled Moss by the hand and we walked up a side street. I let him stand on the pavement while I went up four steps and rapped upon the door of the house in which Sperancia lives. I knew that she would be able to speak with the English boy more freely than I. Her grasp of his language is excellent. I thought she could translate for me all the things I had failed to say. Even as I waited for her door to open, I also feared that Moss might find my pretty friend better company than he did me.

Sperancia's mother answered the door. She called her daughter, who quickly put her shoes on and came down on to the street. I felt cross with her for looking so nice—so feminine—that day. She was still wearing her school clothes and she has lately taken to wearing her skirt shorter than she ever used to. Copying me, I must add, although I do not have long tanned legs as she does. And I had changed into my old jeans and a light-green sweatshirt to visit the boy. I wear such unisex clothing most of the time. It is casual, as am I. And the short skirt I wear to school is simply to demonstrate my disinterest in the claptrap which priests and nuns tell us. I am surprised Sperancia has taken to it; I think her favourite priest, Father Domingo, would advise her to lower the hem. Wear it trailing along the ground as he does his cassock.

When Sperancia saw the English boy, she immediately spoke to him in his language. The two had met before, of course, and I worried that she had a rapport with him greater than any I had yet established. I spoke to her in Sard. I hate this language but did not want Moss to understand the words I directed at my friend. 'You told me that you are not in love and I think I am a little bit.' That is what I said. I know it sounds absurd, and perhaps I am the craziest girl in Nuoro. If he was going to rant about pianos and apples again, I would have to call it off—Sperancia could have him—but I feared she might win him over while I still had first claim. I am not a jealous person; my friend was simply behind me in the queue.

Moss spoke rapidly, in English, to her. She turned to me and said, 'He is worried that your uncle sent you because he has done something wrong in the house. He has not paid the rent but understands it is not due until Monday.' I started to tell Sperancia that she could reassure him my visit was not to do with the rent, she simply cut me off. 'He says you have everything to live for, Joanna. You are young and life may turn out nicely in the years ahead. I do not understand why he says this.'

I ignored the last part and just said to Moss, 'No money. Nothing wrong in the house.' He still looked puzzled so I explained to Sperancia why I had gone around there, my wish to meet the English boy. Curious about a boy from so far away.

She translated this and Moss smiled, gave me a thumbs up sign. In my finest English, I said, 'I never leave Sardinia. No, once only. I go to Sicily.'

He smiled at me, then said something about all going where we wish. I heard him say the word kill in the mix. I didn't follow it exactly but Sperancia started talking over him. Speaking in Sard. 'Have you told him you want to kill yourself? Idiot! Why should he love someone who doesn't plan on sticking around?'

I thought this comment worthy of an ignorant priest. I love Vincent Van Gogh and Cesare Pavese, and I have concluded that it is their suicides that make them so attractive. They take this stupid life more seriously than all the duplicitous priests, all the boys who flop their willies out because a girl is in the room, or even Sperancia, riding two horses with her short skirts six days a week and lighting candles on the seventh. I didn't say this. I could also see her point. I was grateful that Sperancia attacked me only in Sard.

'I don't think I explained myself well to Moss,' I told her in Italian.

My friend made a hand gesture, laying out a flat palm—meaning now was my chance—and what I said next, she translated to Moss, faithfully, I am sure. Sperancia has always stood by me, did so when others at school used to tease me. She was cross about the killing-myself thing only because she had no intention of taking Moss from me. A true friend.

'I did not mean to alarm you,' I said. 'I am not planning to kill myself but I do sometimes feel this way. I am not like you. Not yet. I am not free to journey anywhere I choose. I am trapped in school...' As I said that last word, I held my hand up to Sperancia and said 'college.' This sounds better than school and it is true. I am at the technical institute and some of my contemporaries are working. One even has a baby—ha-ha—it is wise that I ensure Moss doesn't think me a schoolgirl, and correspondingly accurate. 'Many in Nuoro,' I continued, 'are trapped by family and by their miserable circumstances. Especially those who cannot see it.' Then I said a phrase—in Italian of course—one I had not previously recognised about myself: 'I am a free spirit who is not yet free.' I believe Sperancia translated this well because the English boy again looked directly into my face, locking me in the gaze of his fine blue eyes. It was then that he took and squeezed my left hand. I felt a connection with him that was more substantial than any before. Despite her help, I started to regret asking Sperancia along with us. I think I might have kissed the boy but for her inhibiting presence.

We had arrived at the Piazza Veneto where we all sat on a bench. I took the middle. Moss started to talk slowly, much of which I understood and my friend helped if I prodded her, or she recognised that a particular word was beyond my grasp.

'I am not such a free spirit,' he said. 'I thought that I might be. I have hitchhiked from my home town...' Then he said its name, which Sperancia also asked him to spell. It is called Bury. When first he said it, Sperancia thought it was a word meaning nut or seed, but when he spelt out the letters, we realised the place is one big graveyard. The name made me shudder. I think he may have spent his childhood underground. Bury could be even worse than Nuoro. He has been very wise to get out of there, I am sure he has.

'I travelled from Bury to the Straits of Gibraltar using only the goodwill of others. Thumbing lifts. French people were nice, friendly, although people in my home town had said it would not be so. In Spain the people were proud to talk about their country. I saw Madrid, I went in the art gallery and loved the paintings of Goya, even though they were scary to look at. Fascism is over in Spain. I think it was over long, long ago but the people could not bear to fight again, so instead they waited for the old sod to die.'

Those were Moss's words for the Generalissimo. Old sod. I thought then that he even thinks like me—this English boy—that he might be a little bit communist.

'And then I saw the English in southern Spain.' A frown

Nuoro, Sardinia

clouded his face. 'I hated them. The stupid tourists in Alicante didn't care for Spain, just for the sunshine. They were pointless people. I was only disappointed in them. What I hated most was the behaviour of the rich ones. Yacht owners, wealthy people, those who are clever enough to learn to speak the country's language but choose not to on principle. They lord it over the Spanish as if they are a servant class. They do that to people from Bury too; it seems to me far worse to be doing it in a country that was never theirs in the first place.'

I only half understood this but Sperancia is a true scholar, she explained it all well. We even started to jabber between us, she and I, and Sperancia explained to Moss what we were saying and he kept squeezing my hand. In Italy it is the Milanese and the Torinese—probably the Genovese but, of course, I have never been to these cities—who lord it over the Sardinians and Neapolitans and the Calabrese. The rest of us. Lord it: I love this English phrase and—as Moss also taught me to say—I hate the fuckers that do it. Sperancia was not so keen on the second phrase. All words that refer to sex frighten Catholics.

The boy continued talking, he told us about Africa. He crossed in a boat from a place called Algeciras—neither Sperancia nor I had heard the name before—going from there to Ceuta, a Spanish enclave on Africa. I know a little about that one: they should give it back. He said that the crossing was rough and many people seasick. He recalled that the Moroccans were not self-conscious about this at all, and the consequence of it horrible. They were simply sick on the floor or on their clothes. This struck me as very odd. Surely a turbulent sea churns the stomachs of everyone regardless of their nationality?

He said something confusing about spending time in Morocco. That it was very difficult to understand the people, that one of them tricked him terribly. I asked many questions. 'What was the consequence of being tricked?' and 'Did they rob you?' Moss seemed to go into himself, to be less willing to talk about the experience. At one point he turned to Sperancia and asked if she hoped to go to England once more. I cut her off before she replied. It was nice of her to translate his words for me but that did not permit her to strike up an independent conversation. Never forget the queue. And she is really very pretty—taller than I am— this could appeal to a boy like Moss. I think she blew her chance back when he was sleeping in the church hall and Father Domingo as good as set her up on a date. Life is unforgiving, that is a lesson I can teach her even if her priest will not. Moss lives in my uncle's house now. His church-hall days long behind him.

'I am fearful that I sound prejudiced,' he said, 'and I do not want to imply that it is the fault of those people.' Sperancia tried to verify who Moss was talking about when he spoke these words. We think it was the Moroccans, or Arabs generally, but what he actually meant by it remained vague to me. 'I could never understand them like I can understand you.'

These words warmed my heart. It was plain to see he had felt the same connection to me as I did to him. I felt sad on his behalf that he had not found any warmth in Africa. I also hoped his words did not imply he felt a similar connection to Sperancia. If he liked her a little that would not disturb me, I do too.

'Look into my face,' said Moss. 'When we smile at each other, we both know what it means. If we lie, smile falsely, we will surely catch each other out. When you speak to me, I might misunderstand your words but your intention becomes quickly clear. You said some crazy stuff—well not really crazy but scary—about wanting to kill yourself. It was sincere—don't do it, anything like that—but do you see? We can share thoughts and ideas.' He paused here while

Nuoro, Sardinia

Sperancia ensured I'd understood what he said. I liked the concern he was showing for me. 'In Morocco,' he continued, 'I could speak French with people. It is easier for me than Italian which I have never studied, still there was an invisible barrier. The people made presumptions about me. A western man with long hair and a rucksack on my back. Presumptions that never left them, no matter what I said.'

I stopped him at this point. 'Where is your long hair?'

He laughed, shrugged. Said only the word, 'Gone.' That struck me as not an explanation at all. I even thought that an African might have tricked him into cutting it. He could have been hypnotised and then the spell-maker cut off the long hair. 'I wondered if I might have made similar presumptions about them, the Arabs whom I met. I suspect that I did. But they were not clear thoughts that I could extract and analyse. In fact, I could not unpick them because I didn't know for sure if I was doing it. I think that these thoughts were not in my brain but in my blood. They are like a venom. I do not like to say this but my experience has made me think it. Perhaps I shall forget it all in time and recognise that a couple of people took advantage of my naivety. Nothing more. I am still trying to make sense of it all.'

I felt electricity go through me as Sperancia interpreted each word Moss spoke. I put my arm around his shoulders. I hope he did not think me forward, it was apparent to me that he needed comforting. I thought that the people who have tricked him must have done so nastily. There was not the semblance of a smile upon his handsome face throughout this interesting and intellectual talk. It was the first time it had been so—his smile wiped—since first I entered my uncle's house, met him. I felt heartened to learn that he is, deep down, a long-haired boy, even though I like to look at him with short hair. Moss has a very expressive face, it is occasionally doleful but whenever I take his eye, he smiles. This inner misery must help him to understand me and my periodic feelings of helpless anger. Life does it to the best of us.

* * *

On the day on which I met Moss, we drank Coca-Cola in the Café Bramante but left the pinball machines to the stupid boys of Nuoro. Many of them hang around those machines all day and all night. One of them was Zirominu. I did not recognise him at first but he came across to shake Moss's hand who, in turn, introduced him by name to Sperancia and I. Zirominu is the boy—man really, when asked he admitted he is twenty-two years of age—who had shown me his little penis when first I arrived at my uncle's house. I did not tell Moss about that incident. He knew that I'd seen him wearing a towel, not that the oaf had deliberately removed it. I was worried that Moss might feel a need to fight him, given the sexual aggression Zirominu had shown towards me, and Moss is the smaller of the two. I can imagine it is very nice to have a man fight with another about you, it just seemed a lot to ask when the transgression came before I had even introduced myself.

When we parted, having all walked back to my uncle's house, I asked Moss—in my English which began to improve the longer I was in his company—if he would like to meet me again. His face lit up. 'Friday?' he said.

That was probably the second-best answer he could have given. This happened on a Wednesday and, I think, Thursday would have been quite in order. He could, of course, have held me tightly to his chest, maybe brushed my lips with his own and sworn never to let me go, but that is the sentimental fare within magazines for stupid teenage girls. Moss and I are not silly romantics, I even think we are both verists. Not the sort to chase fairy stories. Whatever we have together, it is a choice we make. The best love is not a blind magnet but the result of being true to one's better thoughts and feelings.

2.

My boyfriend works in the bakery, as I have told you. When we met on the Friday, I took the liberty of being on hand as he came out of his workplace. I laughed when I saw his hair, which is fair anyway but whatever he was doing in there had given him a dusting of flour. I told him it looked like he had been sugared. He smiled but I wonder if he thought I was saying he looked effeminate which he actually does not. You can trust me on this, honestly.

At the beginning of our second meeting, it was too early to call him my boyfriend. I already felt strongly that I wished to spend time with him. I could say no more than that. By the end of this rendezvous, we were a couple. Truly. This is how compatible we each are, one with the other. Moss and I are soulmates, I am certain of it.

We went from the bakery back to my uncle's house and Moss told me that he needed to shower. He looked away as he said it. I think he is rather shy, nothing like the oaf, Zirominu. I stayed in the kitchen while the boy showered himself. I could sit in that room knowing that Moss, unlike the oaf, was not a boy to parade around naked. Of course, if he were to do so, I can imagine I would like to take a look. Such goings-on are for later in our friendship. And not so very much later, I hope.

In the fridge I found a carton of apple juice. Moss had written his name—Moss Croft—across the top of the carton. I had never heard the name Croft before I met Moss, I liked it as soon as I read it. Later that evening, with the help of a dictionary I have owned for four years, I learnt that it is a Scottish word. A sort of house. I decided to try some of the juice because it is not a flavour of drink that my mother purchases and I am always keen to experience new things. When the boy entered the kitchen, he was wearing jeans and a T-shirt. He had no socks on and his short hair looked very funny. Still wet and nibbling up in every direction it could go. My own hair may be straggly after a shower but I would not come to meet Moss until I had dried it and shaped it. I think I am actually vainer than he is. My boyfriend is naturalistic, he takes everything as it comes.

I asked him if anybody else was in the house.

'Not as far as I know,' he answered.

It would shock my mother, and even Sperancia, to know that I—a girl of seventeen—was alone in a property with a young man. And neither of them knows that I had been alone in this very house with a boy before this day. Eugenio. He went to my school but had left it by the time I invited him to the house. Working in the building trade. A boy with good muscles except the one inside the head. This was when the house was empty of occupants and I used the key which my father had given me, asked that I pass to my mother. Eugenio was never really my boyfriend. He asked me out once or twice, more than a year earlier, but I turned him down. Then a month or so before our secret meeting, I learnt—if rumours teach us anything—that he had made love to a girl from the school year below my own. The girl around whom this gossip attached is called Vittoria Piroddi. I like her, she is an outsider—as am I—a girl whose mother and father no longer share the same roof. I never asked Vittoria if it was true, if she did indeed have sex with Eugenio. Such questions can sour even mildly cordial relations. I was a little envious though, she being younger than me and having already experienced those special feelings of arousal. If only with a boy as witless as Eugenio.

I am unsure if it was jealousy or curiosity which prompted me to ask him—Eugenio—to meet me at the house. I didn't tell him precisely why I wanted him to come; I expected that he might have the brains to figure it out for himself. Why would a girl ask a famous lover-boy into an empty house? He came as asked and then seemed surprised, even a little nervous, when I told him what I wanted him to do. It made me think him not the Giacomo Casanova of town gossip. I insisted he do his best and I am a girl who generally gets what she wants. He undressed and came into the bed but the silly boy had no contraception. We were only able to make love a little; I insisted on a certain caution. Two days after this occurrence, Eugenio left for Cagliari where he had already secured a job at the port. I was aware that this would occur before making the request of him. I simply wished to experience sex. I would never keep a Sardinian dockhand for a boyfriend.

I am pretty sure that I am no longer a virgin. We did enough but it was not exceptional. I have decided that I should never tell Moss about it. I did not tell Sperancia and, discounting Moss, she is my best friend. Some things are very, very personal, to be shared with nobody but one's journal. At times I can feel a little regret for doing those naked things with one as limited in intelligence as Eugenio. And at other times I am glad that I have not waited forever or been Roman Catholic about sex. That would contradict my most profound sense of self. I have not really decided either way whether I should or shouldn't have. I know that I asked him to do it to me, I take responsibility. And I did not become pregnant. I am curious, not stupid.

After Eugenio and I did what we did, for a short time I lost all interest in our physical bodies. It is more than eleven weeks since the event took place. This new boy has prompted me to consider all things sensual once more. To contemplate what we can do to each other with our hands, our mouths. The touch of flesh on flesh. I must admit that being in the house alone with Moss made me want to ask him to do a little something of that order. I did not say it, fearing that is not the way boys and girls become acquainted in England. Certainly not in the graveyards of his terrible Bury.

* * *

Moss poured himself a glass of apple juice from the carton bearing his name, then he asked me if I wished to eat a sandwich. We were neither hungry. Moss suggested that we walk out of Nuoro and take ourselves up into the hills. He said that he enjoys the wilds of nature and this confirmed what I already thought about him. That he reaches into his experiences, a boy with depth. At the front door, before we had opened it to the world, I stopped him and, looking directly into his face, I got up on to my toes and kissed him on the lips. He returned my kiss—looked at me for another second—then put his hand around the back of my head and kissed me again. I had noted the smile on his face between these two kisses. There was no misjudgement of the situation on my part, he welcomed my advance. In the second kiss, I felt his tongue inside my mouth.

We left the house and as we walked Moss asked me my age. I thought this odd because I had told him what it is two days earlier. I said once again, 'I will be eighteen in three months.' My English is improving so much in his company that I was able to be very precise about it. Say exactly what I would have told him were we speaking together in Italian.

* * *

It was on this date—I am happy to name that Friday spent together as our first date, having quickly established that kissing is something we like to do together—that my boyfriend told me the terrible thing about being in prison. Well, not so terrible. Quite unique and special, I think, but he made it very clear to me that he did not enjoy the experience. When he was telling me about it, there were moments when I wished Sperancia had been present to interpret his English words. Even without her I grasped most of it. Gathered in his tale.

In a town with a funny name in Morocco, a giant of a man befriended Moss. And the giant was a sneaky one. He changed Moss's money into Algerian currency at a very nice exchange rate; however, what he gave him was really illegal black-market money. The giant wanted Moss to smuggle it over the border. I asked if he had to take it to someone in Algeria—they must have Mafia there too—but my boyfriend could not understand my question no matter which language I tried to pose it in. At the border the Algerian custom's police searched him and searched him. I think he found it humiliating. A boy in school told me that customs men put their fingers up your bum-hole if they think you might have drugs wrapped up in condoms squirreled away in there. They found the illegal money in my boyfriend's shoe, and then they marched him off to prison. I didn't have the English language to ask, only hoped that the customs officer tried the shoes first.

In prison, Moss shared a cell with a much older man. He was initially frightened by him and then they became friends. Moss did not say it, but prison camaraderie must work this way. If two murderers share a cell, they would be wise to get along. I think the man sharing with Moss—his name was Stanley, which does not sound Algerian to my ear—was a political prisoner and not a murderer. I know nothing about Algerian politics, he might have been a revolutionary or simply scared of conscription. Moss did not make this clear. I wondered if they could have been put together because Moss was really another political prisoner and the smuggled money planted upon him as an excuse. A set up. I tried asking Moss if it was communism for which he had been locked up. That strikes me as a far more likely reason than money in a shoe. I think my English may have been poor. He only shrugged.

All the while we were talking, we climbed a steep path into the forest. I told Moss that wild pigs and sheep live in these woods. He momentarily looked worried as if such animals might be dangerous. He said they have neither in the countryside around Bury. At this point I once more kissed him, I think it aided his relaxation. I assured him that the wild boar would not trample us to death. And if they had done so while this handsome young man held me in his arms, I cannot think of a more romantic exit from this mediocre life.

Moss told me that he is not at all sure how come he is out of prison. The court sent him there for two years but he was only inside for three weeks. He understood from an embassy official that his parents could bribe the court. Algeria sounds to me to be very, very similar to Italy. Moss told me that his parents have no money and his father doesn't like him which I expect makes him sad. He didn't know what really happened next. Before his release, he took a phone call in the prison office. This was from someone he knows called Mr Graham but I could not understand how he fits into the story. He is not family. Mr Graham told him that a fine had been paid on his behalf. He said it was—and I remember the English words because Moss went over them twice to explain what they meant—'paid through another channel.' It means Moss doesn't know who paid to get him out of jail. I wonder if Moss has a secret admirer who is rich; he laughed at me when I told him my theory. Moss thinks he cannot return to England unless he earns the many millions of lire needed to pay back the unknown benefactor. He will not save up such riches while working in the bakery. He is too clever for such a job but cannot do better work here because it is true that he sounds like a moron when he talks in Italian.

I still find it strange to recall that first date in the countryside above our town. As we walked, we were mostly in the shade of the trees, their branches thickening with the spring foliage. Moss was very sad when he was telling me about prison, he even feared that I would reject him because he had briefly resided there. Nothing could be further from my mind. There are periodic clearings in the forest and the sunlight can be intense. Alongside the gloom that came over him in telling his tale—explaining the short hair—we did an awful lot of kissing. I think that will have helped him and, personally, I liked both. Prison must have been squalid and miserable but I love a man who spits in the face of authority. Feeling his arms around me—his hands briefly felt the skin beneath my sweatshirt—was a pure pleasure.

3.

My boyfriend worked throughout the day on Saturday. When he had finished and once more showered, he said that he wished to go to the bar where there was to be football showing on the television. I agreed; however, I do not care to watch football myself. It is oafs kicking oafs, watched by lazy oafs. Perhaps Moss is an exception and they play the game more nicely in Bury, Lancashire. I have learnt the name Lancashire and like it better than Bury-in-the-Grave. Moss has no wish to return to either.

On our way to his chosen bar, I insisted that we call on Sperancia. I wished to talk with her if my boyfriend wanted only to drink beer and cheer the Napoli team. I have told him not to support the northern team, Milan. He laughed at this, saying he is a northerner. When we discussed the matter, we agreed that he is more a southerner in Italy. The south is poor and the north arrogant whilst apparently the opposite is true in England. Sardinia, of course, is neither north or south. Sperancia tells me that it is a beautiful island. She consorts excessively with priests and this has given her rose-tinted spectacles which mistakenly see the hand of God within nature. I understand our island to be nothing more than a penal colony for the stupid. Animals devour other animals; plants compete for the best soil. Thrive or wither. A few nice sights but they are here by chance alone. I have explained to her more than once that even if the bible is not the fairy story it all sounds—and I really think it is—everything in it took place two thousand years ago, not a word since. God has conked out, snuffed it. We are on our own.

Moss drank quite a lot of beer while he watched the stupid football but Sperancia was good company. She told me that Father Domingo gets as excited as a schoolboy when he talks about Sister Alfonsa. It is funny, and only a dumb priest could ignore beautiful Sperancia and develop a crush on an overdressed nun. I told her that the lot of them should pass over the stupid celibacy, take off their vestments and habits, and do whatever comes naturally. Sperancia got cross, giving me one of her sterner looks; these always make me laugh. She will agree with me when she finally has her own boyfriend. Or passes a naked hour with a dockhand.

Once Moss had finished watching—Napoli lost but I only minded who he cheered for, not who won the silly game—the three of us went to a café which serves hot dogs. I hate America but love their funny sausages.

In the café, I said to Moss that he should tell Sperancia about going to prison. I wished I had not said this because he blushed sharply. Seeing this, I guessed that he did not wish my friend to know about prison because he secretly loved her. He will have gathered that she is not at all keen on sin. I was very confused by his reaction. Just the evening before, Moss had kissed me with his tongue.

Nuoro, Sardinia

He didn't answer my question—changed the subject actually—said that he had been in Tunis. I was feeling like a Bolshevik because his coyness with Sperancia hurt me so much. 'Did you go there from prison?' I asked.

He put a hand on top of mine, I think he saw that I was upset. 'I did,' he replied. 'I told you about prison because you are my close friend. I am ashamed of having been there and I have no wish to tell everyone about it. Sperancia knows now and you may have wished to tell her anyway. She is a good friend of yours.'

When he said this, I realised that he had confided in me because he loves me. My concern that he might love Sperancia was a mistake, and it had led me to embarrass him. I told him not to feel ashamed, stupid money is not a good enough reason to go to prison. 'The Algerians were racist to you,' I said. He ignored my comment, and when I thought about it later, I realised it was only Moss I cared about. I do not, generally, have any objection to the incarceration of greedy bastards.

'In Tunis,' said my English jail-bird to Sperancia and I, 'Three Jewish girls talked with me.' He had a story to tell which I scarcely wished to hear. If I am naïve, so be it. I would like to be the only girl from his travels who Moss recalls. This is the problem with having a boyfriend: no matter how much happiness it brings, a similar volume of insecurity settles in for the ride. The fear of losing him keeps me awake at night. 'I did not know they were Jewish. Jews and Arabs all look alike.' Moss gave a little grin. 'Am I allowed to say that? Well, I have, did so because it's true! I went into a bar in Tunis city centre—it was the day before I was to sail here—I was sailing at six o'clock the next evening. I had a ticket for the night boat to Sicily.'

I interrupted at this point. 'You didn't say you have been to Sicily? I have also been to that island.'

Moss shook his head, 'I stayed on the boat, came straight

on to Cagliari. Hitchhiked from there to Nuoro.' I smiled to myself at his recollection. He was coming straight from Tunis to Joanna Marras. I wanted to tell him this but did not. I sometimes laugh at Sperancia with her talk of the Baby Jesus and the Beloved Virgin. I cannot let her see a gramme of sentimentality seep from Joanna Marras.

My boyfriend continued his story about the Jewish girls oblivious to my discomfort. 'I went into a bar to drink coffee and eat a sandwich. I had only come to Tunis on a bus from Algiers that morning. I'd arrived in Algiers the day before, on an open-topped truck from the prison in the desert. There they housed me in a police station for one final night in their country. In Algiers. Unpleasant but at least I had the cell to myself. The Algerian authorities had been paid to release me and they were taking no chances. When they put me on the bus the next morning, I think there might have been someone watching, following. Making sure that I left the country. Someone on the bus like a kind of escort, just not one who ever made themselves known. I had the feeling there was, cannot be certain. Anyhow, I was glad to get out of there. I shouldn't hate Algeria—might have enjoyed it if I'd got to hitchhike across it like I planned— and yet I do. The customs officials threw me straight across the border, no search, no questions. Somebody wrote down my passport number but they were through with me. Kicking me out, never to return. Money had changed hands and that was all they wanted. In return I was to be set free. God alone knows who paid. I wanted to thank the person who did it, but I also felt soiled by the whole sorry business.'

This word, soiled, took some working out. At first Sperancia thought it meant that Moss had defecated himself. She was very embarrassed telling me that this had happened, and then it turned out to be her translation error. Feeling soiled just means feeling dirty, you could even say that my boyfriend felt shitty. No physical shitting took place. As Sperancia explained once she'd talked it over with him, 'Moss felt the soiling in his head and not in his trousers.'

'In the bar I ordered a sandwich,' said Moss. 'In Tunis the food was normal. I'd had weeks of bloody awful prison food. I bought a toasted sandwich with some kind of cheese in it. Coffee too. Sitting alone on a table, I started humming the words of a song. An obscure album track by Templeton Ca. that I like.

'Which song?' I asked.

'To Paradise.'

'I know the band but not the song,' I told him. I found myself thinking about another of theirs, The Sea at Night Time. It's a fast number and the lyric is poetic. I should like it to be playing on the radio when Moss and I first make love. I did not tell him this, Sperancia was present and the music I choose for Moss to seduce me to is none of her business. And in any case, he has not said directly that he will. He seems like a normal boy, so it should happen sooner or later. He has a nice room and the bed is large.

'On the next table there were three girls, they looked about my own age. I quickly realised that they were laughing at me. I thought that they were Arabs. They wore westernised clothing, jeans, sweatshirts, although one had a kind of headscarf. It was black and she let strands of her hair slip out of the bunch around her face. It looked good on her.'

I wanted to stop him, ask, how good. I was jealous. Here he was, telling me that a Jewish girl he hadn't seen for a week or more looked good. Perhaps I should buy myself a similar headscarf, I couldn't form the words. Moss talked over my gurgling for air and Sperancia kept whispering to me what the difficult words meant.

'I went across to them. "Je m'excuse," I said. I asked why they were laughing. One of the girls guessed I was English.

Rucksack Jumper

Not immediately but after I'd spoken a little in my tentative French. The girl who wore the nice headscarf said, "Why do you talk to yourself?" I told her I was singing a song I like, doing it too quietly to be heard. The girl asked me which song. When I said it was To Paradise, she told me she liked it too, even asked me to sing it to them. I declined. I love Templeton Ca. but my singing voice isn't so great. After this funny introduction, I joined their table. They probably thought I was lonely. Couldn't have known I'd just come out of jail and I wasn't going to tell them that. I asked about them—what they did—and they told me that they were studying at the university of Tunis. Then one said quietly, "We are Jews." I was surprised to hear it. "You're Jewish!" I thought all the Jews lived in Israel. Or America and some in England. Probably Italy too but mostly Israel. I didn't know that any lived in Arab countries. I think I exclaimed it too loudly because all three girls signalled that I should hush. I didn't think they were really frightened; they were all studying there. I asked about their families. One girl came from a city to the south that I had never heard of, the other two had family right there in Tunis. I learnt from them that there are Jews living in every country across North Africa and in the middle east. "There are Jews in Iran," one of the girls said, as if to prove the extent and success of their diaspora. I only tell you this because it gives me an inner hope. Jews living among Arabs. None of the fighting we're always hearing about. I asked the girls how the local population treated them and they said, "Quite well." One girl, whose English was no better than my French, said something to the effect that they keep their heads down. That's a shame. I think everyone should be proud of who they are. Yet it fascinated me that they could live openly in Tunis, these Jewish girls and their families.'

He had no more to say about them but I remained worried that he thought the Jewish girls attractive.

Nuoro, Sardinia

Particularly the one wearing the headscarf. Why else would he talk about those girls when he has Sperancia and I? Well, actually, he only has me because I don't share, but we were—all three—sitting together. No need for him to be thinking about Jewish girls.

I told him then, and without needing my friend to translate, 'It is worse for me in Nuoro than for those funny girls in Tunis. The Jewish girls may feel apart from the Arabs. Maybe they do not dress the same and this makes them stand out. But they have each other and quite a lot of other Jewish families by the sound of it. If all else fails they can go to Israel. A long way to go but it is open twenty-four hours a day to all those of Jewish descent, I understand. I am stuck in a stupid Catholic country, teeming with stupid Catholic believers; the Communist Party here is a sell out; and I do not want to go to Russia because First Secretary Brezhnev likes missiles more than he likes his own people. I am the only true communist in a messed-up world, and there is no God and still everybody in Nuoro dutifully goes to church. Except for a few stinking alcoholics and they are really not my kind.'

Sperancia looked a little shocked, probably because she is one of the stupid Catholics, but I have told her all this before. I deliberately let Moss know that I am a Communist. If he had turned out to be one of those who hate us, I would have sent him straight back to Bury. My uncle should not let his house to a heartbreaker. At that moment I felt like a solitary believer, a communist without a commune. Moss was laughing at me—which I thought rude—he actually looks nice when he smiles or laughs. I think it was only looking into his unblinking eyes which stopped me from crying.

'You're feeling sorry for yourself,' he said, and it is a pointless phrase my father started to use after he separated from my mother. I wanted to hit him—hit my boyfriend—

not hard, just to feel his muscles and see if he would hold on to me to try to stop it. I could not do this in front of Sperancia. She is scared of sexual feelings. Saves hers up for confession with Father Domingo which is far more perverse, don't you think? 'Lots of us want a better, more equal society, if that's what you mean by communism. And it isn't hard to see that the politicians who try to do it—like you say, in the Soviet Union, and in China too from what I've read—have missed the mark completely.' It pleased me to learn that he agrees with me about communism. 'You are not so alone but it feels lonely realising that there are no easy answers.' I thought when he said these words that I was finally hearing the worldliness that Sperancia first saw in him. I liked this, knowing that I was able to appreciate his intellect and sometimes feel his tongue upon my own. 'The plight of the Jews is something else, Joanna. I don't think it pays to compare your situation to something like that.'

I couldn't help myself, I leaned into him and kissed him on the lips. Sperancia could confess that to the priest, or maybe confess her jealousy, which she might have been feeling. I had not, at this point, told her that Moss was truly my boyfriend. And she had said from the start that she admired him.

He responded to my kiss a little; I found him quite shy in front of my friend, far more than he had been on our date the evening before. When we were alone in the countryside, he held me very closely in his arms. Squashed our chests together in a manner I enjoyed. I hoped his reticence was not because of any feelings he might have for Sperancia. She is taller than me and her hair is very nice but she is much more inhibited. I cannot imagine Moss would like that. I don't think she has ever kissed a boy and—I have thought about this—his having been in prison will deter her every bit as much as it spurs me on. Sperancia is very clever, she receives better marks than me for her schoolwork. I made a mental note that next time we are alone, I should remind Moss that she is quite boring.

* * *

Our hotdogs were long gone but I used some money that I had found in my mother's purse to buy three coffees. It allowed us to sit and talk a little longer. I think his talk of Jews had made us all say something about religion. Sperancia speaking only twaddle, of course. Moss told us both that he went to a crazy church called the Baptists when he was small. Not any longer, thankfully. His mother took him, not his conscience. He said that he had never been to a Roman Catholic church. He also said that half the people in Bury are Catholics. I wondered if the dividing line there is a strict as for the Arabs and the Jews but I didn't raise it. I feared Moss would only laugh at me again. In Sardinia, there is scarcely a divide: it's the Catholics versus me. I was trying to explain this point, how make-believe God has a monopoly around here when Moss turned to Sperancia.

'Will you take me with you to church tomorrow?'

Now I wanted to hit the boy without feeling anything sexual at all. Just violence for Moss after that. I thought to myself, why is he asking her on a date when he has just kissed me?

'Everybody is welcome,' began Sperancia, and then she went on to say that Moss must not eat the host because that would offend God.

Now it was my turn to laugh: it is hard to offend made-up people, in my humble opinion. And if God doesn't want Baptists to eat the silly wafer, he should send a big bolt of lightning and kill the fuckers. I thought I should say this. A bolt of fucking lightning is coming for you, Moss. I thought he was chasing Sperancia and that was not a course of action I could stand by and watch. If I was God, I might have sizzled him there and then. But my boyfriend—almost ex-boyfriend at that moment—turned to me and said, 'You'll come too, Joanna, won't you?' So, it was not a date with Sperancia that he was setting up. It was to be a little look-and-see into the religion I have rejected. The madness of Catholicism. I felt a bit better learning that it was for this purpose and not to spend time alone with Sperancia, that he wished to go to church. But not much better frankly. I did not understand why he wouldn't take it from me that the Roman church is shit. After all, I had deferred to his view that the Jewish girls were having a hard time. 'You'll come too?' he asked again, as I stared at them both.

I had no wish to sit in church with my mother and brothers. None. All of my family still delude themselves that prayers and beads can save them from damnation. I think it is more probable that our Nuoro-on-the-hillside is the hell they hope to avoid. 'You go with Sperancia,' I told him. I knew that I should not appear jealous, it might be off-putting to a boy. I have learnt as much from the stupid teenagers' magazines which I only bother with because reading Karl Marx is actually very tedious. 'I will wait outside and meet you after you've knelt and prayed and felt something or nothing. Sperancia stays behind to help with the young Catholics, so it will just be you and I once you are done with big, fat, pretend God.' I thought to myself that we could go back to my uncle's house, perhaps into the room that used to be a lounge and now accommodates Moss's bed. A roll upon it might get the religious hogwash out of his head. I hoped that he would like to see me, or better still to feel me, without clothes on, as I should him.

'No,' Moss implored. 'Come with us to the church service. It can't hurt.'

I glanced at Sperancia who translated his last phrase: I had understood it correctly. I was so cross by this time. I

Nuoro, Sardinia

began to think this English boy from Buried-Deep in Lancashire to be a very stupid one. 'I do not go to church. I do not pretend that I believe in God when I do not. I do not let the Catholics think, oh, we were right all along. Joanna has seen this now. I do not eat this Corpo di Cristo as if it is a true thing. A wafer passing through me and making me one with that dumb dead ox who died on a cross so that we might all crucify ourselves for the following two thousand years. It can hurt me. It does hurt me. I think it makes me mentally crazy watching everyone succumb to the beckoning of the sinister priests, demanding that we all live like the long-dead people of the violent and plague-ridden biblical times. As if such stupidity might earn them a berth in heaven. Which will be like Nuoro without the pinball machine.'

While I was saying these angry words, Moss came close and held me. Hugged me in his arms more tightly than he had ever done before. It came to me that he is not such a stupid boy. I wanted the embrace and he knew this through intuition. Maybe through love. 'I'll take that as a no,' he said. I think Sperancia even smiled because this might have been funnily said. At my expense, I do believe, but I found myself no longer cross with him. Hugs can do that. For what he said, the funny phrase, maybe I should have still hit him. What he did, how he held me close, proved that he truly loves me. I knew he did not wish to prompt the hurt I was feeling when we talked about the stupid church. I am a strong girl but I cried because of that hug. And maybe because I usually do cry if I think about how God and Jesus came and went—here and gone, nearly two thousand years, eighty generations past—high time we all let it go. We are alone and I am the only one who faces up to the bitter truth of it. Moss looked to Sperancia and said, 'Sorry, I'm not coming to church after all. I'll stick with Joanna.'

Again, I became confused by his words. Misunderstood

for a time. Sticking with me is good, I now know. At the time, I asked Sperancia the meaning of this word, and when she told me, I was initially upset. I did not wish Moss to be stuck with me, I wanted him to choose me. I tried to explain this, and Sperancia will have put my Italian into faultless English but he just hugged me again. 'See! Stuck!' he said. When I did not smile, he kissed me until I did. I began to realise this word, stick, meant something else. It can mean wanting to be stuck. Moss chooses to be stuck with me, as I do with him. We are adhered.

* * *

Sperancia left us and I think this was because of all the kissing we did. I knew that she would pray for my forgiveness at church on the following day. Stupid Catholic drivel. There is no part of loving another person which requires forgiveness.

Moss and I walked out of the café and up the main street. 'Can we go somewhere quiet?' he asked. Of course, this made me think he was hoping to get more sexual than just a bit of kissing. I did not want to appear overly prurient by asking him about it directly. I just took him to a place I know. It is around the back of one of the churches. Not Sperancia's church but run by the same nonsense firm. The big bad Catholics. I had kissed boys in this quiet place before; Eugenio had placed his hands within my clothing long before it became rumoured that he did what he did to Vittoria, and then—for sure—did something very sexual with me. I find it funny that the priests hear their pitiful confessions just twenty paces from where I have shamelessly ignored their edicts.

We sat down on the ground. Moss seemed not to be self-conscious at all although I knew that the grass would make my buttocks damp, and might stain that part of my jeans that he affectionately calls my bum. I decided it would be worth it. I embraced the dampness.

I looked at Moss and was surprised to see a pained look on his face. He started talking but seemed very distant as he did this.

'In Tunis, in the café where I met those Jewish girls, I also met two Tunisian boys. This was after the girls had left, gone back to study. The Tunisians were friendly to me and I liked this. They joked about Tunisian politics. I could not understand all their humour but I thought of them as dissidents. Not ones who plot against whatever ogre runs their country, just the young and cheeky sort.'

When Moss said this, I gave him the thumbs up and said the Italian word, 'Dissidente.' He liked this and now we both say it—dissidente—when we are feeling subversive. I thought then, and continue to believe, that we are kindred spirits, although he doesn't seem as impressed as I hoped he would be by my communism. At heart, I know that he and I are both dissidents.

'The two young men invited me to eat an evening meal with them. I agreed because it was to be my last night in Tunisia. In Africa. After the horrible experience of going to prison, I did not expect to go back so soon. Never, most likely. To spend my last night there with friendly people seemed a nice way to end a difficult relationship.'

These were Moss's words. I asked him to explain them. His relationship with Africa was the one he was referring to. And the idea that if you have a love-hate relationship, you should end it so that you remember the love, struck me as a wonderful thing. When Eugenio first went to Cagliari, I remembered only to hate him. Perhaps Moss is improving my disposition, removing the bitterness, although I have not had a chance to try his system yet. And I do not believe it would work at all if he were to leave me. The loss I might feel would be too great. I expect I would kill myself. Give that a go.

'When I went to the restaurant which they had told me to come to, the two young men met me but we joined a table with many others. They sat me down next to an older man. Not very old, maybe thirty. After we had eaten the food, I noticed that the two men who had invited me were no longer in the restaurant. They barely talked to me that evening. This frustrated me because I did not enjoy the company which replaced them. It was mostly just typical of my brief experience in North Africa. The men wanted to talk about Manchester United because that city is near Bury. They laughed that England has a woman as prime minister. I don't laugh at that. Women can run countries every bit as well as men do. Margaret Thatcher is the disappointment. The man beside me, the older man, was very nosy. He asked personal questions that I did not like to answer. He told me that he was a homosexual and that he liked young boys. I did not like this conversation. I never heard any other Arabs say this kind of thing. I know it goes on everywhere but I thought the social code in those countries pushed it into the shadows. It surprised me to hear it spoken of in a brightly lit restaurant. I tried to show that I did not judge although what he said about boys sounded wrong. Quite wrong.' At this point Moss paused and said something that annoyed me. He said, 'I know you are still a girl, Joanna, and I have kissed you but I am determined not to take advantage of you.'

I had to make him explain this phrase, and when he did, I said, 'What if I want to make love?'

'You are a young girl and I am patient.'

I punched him on his arm, quite hard, and said, 'I am eighteen, eighteen in three months.'

He took me in his arms and kissed me before resuming his story. 'When it came time to pay, the older man indicated that he would settle the bill. I tried to object but he insisted. Then he said some rubbish about not having

Nuoro, Sardinia

the right money. Could I pay with Tunisian currency? he asked. He would give me a one-hundred-dollar bill which I could change in the morning and then give him back the balance. I did not wish to do it but he was a forceful man. Not easy to argue with and I had plenty of time in the morning to go to the bank. It was hard to refuse. We walked out of the restaurant as a large group. I became a little disoriented in the city centre. Before I could work out the way to my hotel the older man was pushing me into an alley way. All the others—his friends—seemed to have melted away. This man—he was much bigger than I am—began trying to kiss me. On the lips. I hated it. I don't have anything against homosexuals, it is simply not what I am. He even tried touching me. Down my trousers. I pushed him away. It should have been easier for me than it proved. The man had a beer bottle in one hand, still taking the occasional swallow. I think he might have been a bit drunk but not very. Not out of his mind. And he was a hard man, had a hard stare. Crazy-nasty. When I pushed him away, he smacked me forcefully across the face. I was shaken, dazed by the power of his hand, with which he immediately hit me again. I lost my hearing for a moment. He again tried to kiss me but I hunched my arms around my head. He punched me and shouted, "Money." I could think of no better way to get out of the situation. I gave him his hundred-dollar bill. Money is a burden not a salvation, Joanna. We might all be better off without it. Then I said "Goodbye" but this bastard just grabbed hold of me again. I waited and as he tried to put a hand down my trousers, I rammed my head—the top of it—as hard as I could into his face. He cried out, and I saw instantly that I had drawn blood. The bottle he was holding dropped to the ground, I heard it smash as I ran away. Ran like it was an Olympic race. And I had not floored him; I heard him start to come after me but once I was out of the alley and on to a properly lit city street, he gave up. My fear might have helped me to run faster than I ordinarily can. He mugged me, I suppose, but frankly it was only half a mugging. I gave him only the money he'd given me. The taste of his mouth on mine made me spit frequently but the man had got nothing of what he wanted. I wasn't raped. I wasn't hurt except a bruise on my left cheek. To tell the truth, the top of my head hurt even more, and that had been my weapon in retaliating against the bastard. I hoped I'd broken his nose. I really did. I remember that when I had run down a couple of streets, got away, and then figured which direction led back to my hotel—the heavens opened.' I did not understand this phrase but Moss carried on talking and his subsequent words explained its meaning. 'The rain that fell was heavy, so heavy it hurt the top of my head where I had struck it into the man's face. It had barely been raining for a moment and the streets were like rivers. I could see the water running into the drains but they couldn't cope. Not with the downpour frothing the city. My clothing was wringing wet. I might have been in a bath, so drenched was I. My training shoes sodden from walking in an inch or two...sorry...in several centimetres of water. It was flowing down the road; the night sky had opened up. A cloud had burst and all the water that the sky could hold dropped upon Tunis. I have never known rain like it. When I finally entered my hotel—I say finally, probably no more than fifteen minutes of walking in that torrent—I brought in my own water supply. I stood at the reception desk waiting for my key. It was not yet eleven o'clock but the whole city seemed to have come to a standstill. My clothing heavy with water, I stood in a large puddle which I had fetched inside the hotel. And Joanna, what upsets me now is that I cannot think about Tunis, or Tunisians, without bringing the mental image of that bullying homosexual to mind. I don't know what hold he had on the two boys who took me to meet him, or how many other tourists he's tried to rape. I can think to myself that all the other Tunisians are nothing like him, that all the other homosexuals are nothing like him but when I think of either of these groups of people, his is the image in my mind. I worry that it is driving me a little crazy. On my mind when I should forget it. Like I say, I avoided the worst. I got lucky although I feel horrible recalling the event.'

I was most unsure what to say to my boyfriend. Before he told me this terrible story, I'd hit him for not wanting to be more sexual with me. I found myself guessing that his terrible ordeal had put him off sex altogether. I wondered how I might heal him of his affliction; I like the old Monk Elba song, 'I Can Show You How,' which explains it in a very subtle way. The problem was, I had already learnt that Moss isn't a fan of his, so singing a few lines could have proved futile. I said nothing.

'I just wanted you to know.' Moss looked immensely sad when he said these words. 'I have not told any-one else. I don't even think I will. I just wanted you to know.'

I hugged him then. Moss held my eye and I his, tears were tippling down my face. I was mostly sad that the awful man attacked my boyfriend out there in Africa, while also feeling loved that he confided in me. The shocking tale. I think he also felt a need to explain why he is reticent about all things sexual. It is possible that he also fears impregnating me but that can be prevented. I might need to tell him how to go about it and will do so when the time is right.

He walked me home and we did not kiss on my doorstep for fear that my mother, or one of my brothers, would be watching. I have never felt so closely at one with another person in my whole life. As long as I have Moss, I know with certainty that I shall not kill myself.

4.

When I meet my boyfriend today outside the bakery, we walk back to my uncle's house together. Moss always calls it his house but he is only renting a room. It is more mine than his, I like to think. This could even mean that I own him a little—not in too possessive a way, I hope—just so that I have a say if he stays or when he goes. In my mind the latter must only occur when I am able to travel with him. To London, England or one of those Scandinavian countries where anything goes.

On arriving at the house, Moss goes in and showers, as is his habit. I wait and drink a little water because today it is hot. After Moss emerges, dressed and ready to come down to Oristano to meet my father for the first time, there is a knock on the front door.

I go to the door and open it; Moss is just behind me. Vittoria—the girl from school who might have made love to Eugenio before he did something like it to me—is standing on the step. She wears a silly-looking uniform, not one from any school in Nuoro, shorts and blouse, a comical red cap. 'What is it?' I ask her, hoping that she has not come around to take Moss from me, as she might think I did with Eugenio just three months ago. She could know about it if he has written, boastfully told her what I allowed him to do. She is a pretty girl but the cap looks very stupid. I don't expect that Moss will be impressed by her, not by her headwear at the very least.

Vittoria looks over my shoulder at my boyfriend. 'Moss Croft?' she asks.

'Si,' he answers.

'Ho un telegramma,' she tells him.

I start to talk, laugh a little but not unkindly. 'You're a telegram girl,' I say. 'Do you have the funny red bicycle too?'

Nuoro, Sardinia

Vittoria does not want to joke. I think she imagines she is bringing messages about the war dead, like the telegram boys and girls used to when they delivered tragic news to our grandparents' generation. Made known all those casualties of war. I even ask Vittoria what the telegram is about.

She is a little sharp with me, does not answer my question. She asks Moss to sign for it but he doesn't understand her rapidly spoken Italian. I explain what it is that she has said. I also tell him that the girl was in school with me, that she left, although she is younger than I, because she is not so clever. I am worried that he might like seeing her in the uniform. Her legs are more tanned than mine ever become. Wearing shorts which display what my jeans cover. I understand that boys like to gaze upon such distractions.

Moss signs where Vittoria has pointed her finger. I see anxiety in his tightening face. He opens the missive and reads it rapidly. 'It's from Gary,' he tells me. 'My father has died.'

Oh, God, I have not been thinking properly about this. If it had been a more serious looking telegram girl, I might not have been so frivolous. I burst into tears because I am feeling Moss's confused pain. He retains a look that tells me nothing. He might be numb. I even wonder if he guessed what it would say before he opened the letter. Intuition works like that: everybody knows everything about people close to themselves. Deep down they do, I am sure of it. Moss does not like his father but there is a connection between them, nobody wishes members of their family dead.

'Grazie,' he tells Vittoria, and she goes to the side of the property where she has leaned her red bicycle.

Moss and I stand on the step. He is re-reading the short note she delivered. As the girl mounts and starts to ride away, through my tears I also shout, 'Grazie.' Vittoria was always nice to me, not that we were proper friends. I feel a little guilty that I said mean things about her to Moss. I hope to myself that she did not understand my English. I even think I was mean to try to lure Eugenio from her but I never understood his relationship with Vittoria. He asked me on dates before he showed any interest in her. Anyway, he took himself to Cagliari straight after our improvident dalliance. Good riddance to Eugenio; Vittoria has found herself a nice job, and Moss is my only concern today.

I ask if he will need to return for the funeral. I think I might be crying because I know that I could lose him. If he goes to Bury, old Mr Murgia who runs the bakery will doubtless replace him. And breadmaking is not Moss's true vocation. I know he is capable of much more. He does not reply to my question but runs both hands across his face. Pushes them hard into it like he is trying to expunge something from within his cheeks and eyes. I cannot really guess what he is feeling; it is very clear to me that he is in a state of anguish. I take hold of his hand and pull him back inside the house. It is time for me to behave in a manner commensurate with my seventeen years.

I think my tears are also a gift so that he has no need to shed any. His father was never a good one—he has told me this—but death is forever. A bitter pill, leaving no alternative way to end a story.

'It is sad but something you can come to terms with, Moss. You did not wish to get close to him again. It will take time just realising the truth of this new fact: your father no longer lives.'

He nods at my words of comfort, if comfort they are. Then he says, 'Oh Christ.' I wonder why he says it, fear he might be falling back on the Baptist nonsense. People do that in times of distress. He takes an inordinate amount of time to voice his thought. 'Gary will have to do everything,

Nuoro, Sardinia

organise everything. Mum can't.' Then after another long pause, he declares—in a louder voice than needed if it is only me to whom he speaks—'I can't. I can't do it!'

I put my arms around him. I am thinking about my brother Raimondo—who is younger than me but a more thoughtful boy than my older brother, Ercole—he held me closely when my cat, Tigre, died. He never liked that fighting cat, simply understood how much I cared for him, that I grieved the volatile creature's passing. And I decided long before today that I do not like Moss's father. More than a week ago. Ever since Moss told me that he hates everyone who isn't English and most of the people who are, and how he stopped Moss from going to school. But Moss probably loves him, if only in a very confused way. I think that is how I love my own father, and he has abandoned his family although he always tells me that he has not. I love him but not very much when you get to the bottom of it.

'I can't go,' says Moss.

I try not to smile because this is a very sad time, I simply want this boy for myself. If I am not more attractive than a funeral in the north of England, it is a sorry state.

'I live here now.'

This is interesting to me; he may not be the traveller Sperancia surmised.

'I like Nuoro.'

I don't say anything to this. I do not like Nuoro, until I have finished at the technical academy I am stuck here. Much better to be stuck with Moss than without him. That is both kinds of stuck, I think.

Then he strikes a decisive note. 'I will phone my mother tomorrow.'

I don't know much about her and I fear she will insist that he returns to Bury for the funeral. I understand why my boyfriend wishes to make the call. I think I would wish to speak to my mother at such a time although I'd tell her to keep the Catholic bullshit to a minimum. To zero. I could remind Moss to tell his mother not to talk Baptist but maybe I am thinking too intensely my own thoughts and not tuning into his. I remember how he listened to me when I was upset that he wanted to accompany Sperancia—to experience her beloved church service—and I think this is an even greater crisis than mine was on that day. I try to focus upon my boyfriend, recognise what he thinks and feels.

I remind Moss that we are going to meet my father. 'Should I cancel the visit?'

Moss shakes his head. Then he looks directly at me. 'The world is missing a bastard.' I feel jolted by his words and then I smile. Not on my face but inwardly. Dissidente. Moss is stronger than I, and yet I consider myself the revolutionary communist. I can learn many things from this boyfriend. I want to be with him always.

* * *

When Ercole, my brother, arrives in his car, Moss shakes his hand. It is only the second time these two boys have met. Moss has told me that he does not wish Ercole, or my father, to know of his bereavement. 'They would not understand,' he said, and I know that he is right. In Sardinia everybody cries like a baby when they lose a parent or a grandparent. The tears are part of the sombre clothing worn at this time. Taken out of the drawer and put back in it again at a moment's notice. Moss is more reserved, more sincere. Sardinians would not understand him. Not a single one except me. I think it might be that fate made a mistake dumping me on this island. I could be a misplaced Lancashire girl.

We drive to my father's village. I always say that he lives in Oristano because it is the nearest large town. He actually lives in a small village to the north called Cabras. Few in the world know about Cabras and I believe their ignorance a desirable state. It is situated close to the western coast of Sardinia. My father's eldest brother and a great uncle of mine—a dull-witted relative in whom I have no interest—both live in the same village. My father is called Ercole, the name he subsequently inflicted upon his eldest son. The three of them work the family's land. It is a useless corner of a farm, with just enough olive trees to occupy a lazy man. How these three men and the wife and child of Uncle Stefano live off it is a mystery to me. My mother receives nothing from their pitiful harvest. Not a lira. Growing olives is no more a job than is watching the tide go in and out.

The drive is long and Moss does not talk. Not much. He sits alone on the backseat of the car, does so by his own choice. He is thinking and thinking, and I am worried that he might not really wish to be here. I talk a little with Ercole who asks about my studies. I don't like to say too much in front of my boyfriend—not because they are going poorly, I am quite clever actually—I do not wish to remind Moss that I am still a schoolgirl. I feel I am an equal to him, a support in his grief. I know that I sometimes talk very emotionally but I am more substantial than my boyfriend yet seems to think. I need to emphasise my maturity and talking about schoolwork misses the mark.

We arrive at my father's house. I did not explain this to Moss before but it is not really a house at all, just a small studio that he rents, situated on the ground floor of a large house in the centre of the tiny village. My father is not at home. I am livid. He and I spoke by telephone two days ago and arranged to meet at this time. Ercole has driven well for once—arrived at the right hour—and yet my father does not care enough to stay home. It is just before seven in the evening. Still light. Ercole says that our father will be in front of the church. I do not know how he has guessed this but he visits more frequently than I. My father is a dull man, his behaviour quite predictable, I suppose. Except for walking out on us which he may have done at my mother's insistence, so little have I been told about their separation.

* * *

We leave the car outside the house. Ercole leads us a short way and I see the back of the church—the sanctuary of intentional deception—ever prominent in these antiquated backwaters. Ercole takes us around the building. To the front there is a small square with two benches facing each other. Very long benches. Twelve men sit: seven on one, five on the other. Among them sit my father and my Uncle Stefano. Both raise a hand in greeting, neither rises from his bench. My great uncle may be resting from a hard day's olive watching; if he has expired—upped and died—as a means of breaking the monotony of his long and humdrum life, it is no loss to me. Stupid peasants, I think to myself. Stupid fucking peasants. They spend their days pretending to work and it taxes them so much that afterwards they must rest in the square while their wives cook and clean and sow for them. And feed the babies and prepare food for them and for their old folk. The women do everything that must be done under the sun. Everything but watch the olives grow.

My father says something to his fellow villagers. Some nonsense in praise of the exceptional comfort of these wooden-slatted benches, I can imagine. What else do these peasants have to comment upon? His voice is too low for me to hear and I detest the Sard language in which he converses. He comes directly to his three visitors but, looking at me first, says only, 'When does he go back to England?'

I am careful what to say in front of Moss. I know he is feeling on edge, very emotional. To my thinking, the wrong father has died. I am, since meeting and finding true love

Nuoro, Sardinia

with Moss, too mature to say it, but I own this thought. I would sacrifice this old fool to relieve Moss's suffering if such a switch were in my power.

I tell him that Moss is working in the bakery; he is a resident of Nuoro now. I even tell him that Moss is a community citizen and we must all welcome him. My father does not understand what I am saying and I remind him how the European Economic Community works. That we are all welcome in each other's lands. My father waves a dismissive hand. He does not consider Sardinia to be a part of Italy, and so how can such a peasant understand that his daughter loves an Englishman.

After this he turns to Moss, and my boyfriend reaches out a hand to shake. A hand of friendship. My imbecilic father takes it as though it is a trick he barely dares engage with. Afterwards, he looks at his own hand as if struggling to recognise what it is, fearful of the change which an Englishman's touch may have fashioned upon it. He jabbers in Sard with Ercole. I understand and interject a little in Italian. I hate Sard so much. Ercole is being helpful to me. He tells my father that Moss is a good man, works hard in the bakery, likes football as all these men do. This last is a quality that stirs nothing within me but I know Ercole means well. He is trying to win my father over.

Then my father says the stupidest thing and such a simple sentence even Moss can understand this Sard. 'Will you marry him?'

I want to laugh and cry. No, no, no. I am not going to marry him, I haven't even fucked him yet. You think that it works the other way around, ha! What do you really know? You walked out of your marriage just to sit on a bench that sags with peasants, with dumb Sards watching their olives grow. You have no idea how my life works. You might be living in Roman times. Your days have gone, gone, gone. Moss and I don't need a marriage certificate. The permission slip of the regional government of Sardinia. Our love is not a municipal sideshow. And when I have finished school, we are not staying on this wretched island with its all-seeing churches and inexplicable water contamination which slowly turns all the men on the island into donkeys. Look at yourself! Look at your ears! We will be gone from this hopeless corner, beyond the reach of the clawing Sardinian priests. To London, which is an intellectual place with theatres and poetry readings. Or to Berlin because it is a bit East and a bit West. I have yet to talk about this with Moss, concede that he should have a say in the matter. I do not speak these thoughts. I say only that I am young, that I have not seen that far into the future. While I am saying it, Moss takes a hold of my hand. He wishes my father to see that he loves me and I feel taller beside him. The sincerity he exudes must astonish my father. The Sardinian peasantry cannot conduct themselves with a gramme of Moss's dignity.

We walk back to my father's little home. Inside he has prepared a small salad. Mostly items he has grown on the tiny patch of land he tills. There is some cold chicken which he has cut into tiny slices. It is not really enough for four people. The food tastes nice enough but I am embarrassed that this is my family. The fare is worse than modest. It is all that the man who thinks he raised me can muster. In truth, we are all primitive island folk, the indigenous animals of Sardinia nurturing us more closely than we do each other. I might have been raised by the wolf and the rest by the stupid mouflons. The wild sheep of our mountainous isle.

* * *

In the car returning to Nuoro, I sit in the back with Moss. Ercole was happy for me to do this. I think he saw what a difficult visit it has been for us. Our father paid no attention to Moss. He wasn't even rude. Ignored him as he might have done a housefly.

Moss talks in a low voice. I think he is mindful of Ercole because he has also—even before his father died—been sharing great intimacies with me. Things he would not wish me to share with my brother. I assure Moss that he speaks no English. I think I should not have said this because Ercole must have understood. It prompts him to start singing a funny rock song that is on the radio most days of the week. One by the American singer, Johnson Ronson.

> *A hurricane's coming, it was said on the news*
> *That it's all going to get a bit wild*

Moss winces at the singing. Perhaps he is not in the mood for music; my brother sounds very like the man on the record. Like Ronson. It might be the only English Ercole can recite. He is a parrot, has the brain of a parrot. Understands nothing. The language in which the words emerge has no relevance to him.

'I told you about the man in prison...' Moss says this while glancing at Ercole, worried I think that he might understand the word prison. Ercole has stopped singing but that does not mean his brain is engaged in anything more than turning his steering wheel. '...the Berber, Amastan.'

'Stanley?' I ask, and Moss nods. I remember that he was the political prisoner but I had not previously understood that he was a Berber. I say this to Moss, and stupidly I ask, 'Did he have a camel?' Moss giggles and I realise I am still a bit of a schoolgirl while my boyfriend is a graduate of an Algerian prison. This is not a wholly equal relationship; he does not let my idiocy prevent him from telling me more.

'The Arabs don't like the Berbers. I don't understand the cause of this and maybe they get along some of the time. But Amastan told me he was in prison for demonstrating.

A prison guard, who was also a Berber, helped Amastan whenever he could. Gave him cigarettes. I never understood this. Perhaps the guard did it secretly, pretending to be an Arab. I can't tell a Berber from an Arab to this day. I never really understood a fucking thing in Africa. That's why I went to prison.'

Ercole immediately turns his head when Moss says the expletive: it is the one English word which all Sardinian boys understand. 'Not us,' I tell him, reassure Ercole that it was not a request of Moss to me. I hope to myself that this will happen soon, when he has stopped grieving for his father. Not that I shall share the news with Ercole, whenever it comes.

'One day...' Moss took and squeezed my hand as he continued. '...in the exercise yard, a big fat man called for Amastan to go over and speak to him. He and I had been walking together and my friend turned to me and said, "Wait." He really was my only friend in that place. We spoke in English mostly, and Amastan was always patient, always interested in me. He made prison bearable. In response to the call, Amastan crossed the small yard to the fat man and, as soon as he was next to him, I saw the man punch my friend in the stomach. I heard a cry and instinctively started to move toward him but two other prisoners took hold of my arms. They did not hurt me at all, just prevented me from going forward. Stopped me from assisting Amastan, from getting to the fat man. I shouted, "Help!" in English, loudly enough to alert the guards. Quite quickly three of them came into the yard and went towards my friend. The big man—a fat horrible man, I knew a little about him before this incident—who had punched Amastan was already stepping away. One of the guards apprehended him. He did not try to run. He was in prison, so how could he? But, Joanna, Amastan was bleeding terribly, the brute had knifed him in the stomach. While

Nuoro, Sardinia

the other prisoners held me and before I'd understood what had happened, I looked toward the fat man, only to be dazzled by a wink of sunlight reflecting off the blade of the knife the guard was removing from him. That shaft of light confused me, Joanna. It was so bright when my life felt in such a dark place. I thought as I saw it that it might be the flash of my friend's soul departing. I am, like you, not religious at all but I do not like to think that a life can be extinguished without leaving something for us to remember. A guard who was sometimes kind to me confirmed later that Amastan had died of his injuries. In many ways, I hardly knew my cellmate. I could not picture his life beyond the prison wire. The man was so friendly to me in the most difficult of circumstances. I don't know why it happened: his murder. The two men who held on to me were a testament to the fact that it was a plot, not the act of a lone man with a grudge. I have thought back to that day. Thought of nothing else during the two further days I was in prison. Before my unexpected release. The guards had not been in the yard as they normally were. I never heard what happened to the assailant but, honestly, big and fat as he was, I could not pick him out of a line-up of similarly sized people. I don't recall his name although I think Amastan had told me earlier in my prison stay. I don't think the fat man was political but, frankly, I couldn't understand the politics of that country. Not at all. Maybe the killer stayed in prison, or perhaps they moved him to maximum security after such a deed. Or he could just as likely have been set free, the authorities granting his release following the job done on the poor Berber, on Amastan. I never learnt anything more. Still don't know. Amastan was imprisoned by the state and they might have set up his murder while he was in there. I saw it and I understood so little I couldn't help him—Amastan, Stanley—before, during or after his murder.' I see on Moss's face that he is feeling great anguish in telling me this sorry tale. He looks even more distraught than when he described the mugging. 'Sometimes I hate how my life has fumbled along, Joanna. Not my life in Nuoro. My life before I met you; the futility of it all.'

I think we two are the same but I know it is not really the time to say it. I have felt so strongly about the things that I have seen just by living in stupid Nuoro. Moss has been to many places including this cruel prison, but feelings are feelings and we are so very alike. I hope I can make him see that I understand him. I want to tell him that the Berber would have made a better father than his own proved to be. I even think that this is what Moss has been telling me. I just squeeze his hand for fear of getting it wrong, sounding again like a child when I am a woman.

* * *

When we are back in Nuoro, Ercole stops at my uncle's house to let Moss out. It is ten-thirty and I do not wish to leave Moss yet. I start to get out of the car and tell Ercole I will walk home when I have finished talking to my boyfriend. My brother is protective of me in all the stupid Catholic ways. 'What will people think?' he says, and I know for a fact that most people in Sardinia never really think at all. They watch olives grow and confess their sexy thoughts to celibate priests. Sperancia thinks a little and I have hopes for my brother Raimondo—a work in progress—the rest of them can go to hell.

I get out anyway but Moss makes a point of going to the driver's door. 'I will walk her home,' he says to Ercole. His Italian is flawless. With that my brother drives away.

We go into the house. Zirominu is there but at least he wears clothes this time. I start to head into Moss's room— the one that used to be the lounge when my grandparents lived here—but Moss takes my hand. Holds it gently, enough to prevent me from going in there. I guess he is suspicious that I might be trying to seduce him, if I do indeed have any feminine charm with which to do such a thing. He learnt today that he has lost his father, and I am not so sexual as to think this the time to begin that particular adventure. I do not want to pass any time with Zirominu. That is the limit of my reasoning.

Moss says—again, his Italian impresses me—'May we be alone?' Zirominu smiles and agrees. In Sardinia a girl should not enter her boyfriend's bedroom; it happens now and then, a matter of scandal every time. Zirominu goes to his room; I think Moss has won the respect of everyone in the house. His greatly improved Italian has been the key and I have helped him a little with this project. 'I need to speak to my mother,' Moss tells me, using careful English which he knows I will understand.

'Is it not too late at night?'

'She won't be sleeping.' I am impressed that he intuitively knows what is happening in her house and in her mind, from this great distance. Then he says, 'There is no other way. I'm going to reverse the bloody charges.'

I hear the words but he has to explain what they mean. I have never had cause to make a reverse charge telephone call, or even to consider doing so. I speak on the telephone no more than once each month, and my mother always hovers close at hand. She is keen to ensure I am not spending too long on it. Running up a bill. I know nobody who lives so far away as Moss is now going to call. My mother phones my Uncle Andrea who lives at Messina, on Sicily, and I sometimes say hello. Nothing momentous has happened for me to speak further about and he has never mentioned his sister's failed marriage. If I reversed the bloody charges to ask him what he knows, I think he would tell me to hang up, that he cannot or will not shed any light on what has happened between my parents. If I have driven them apart, I am not sorry. I will always support my boyfriend; that he treads ground unknown to me makes it difficult but no less important. I ask if I may come with him to the telephone box and he hugs me. I think I have offered exactly what he wanted.

Moss and I return to the street. We walk briskly to the main thoroughfare where a telephone box is situated. We enter it together and I love how close we are in this funny little upright house. Moss picks up the receiver, he looks at it as though it is an adversary, his lower lip dropping. A deep sigh. Then he asks me if I can tell the operator to connect the call to his mother, reverse charges. He takes out his wallet and from it a card on which there is a phone number. Above it an address with this funny word, Bury, written down. His family home; the corner of the world in which he grew up and to which he might one day return as his father cannot. I don't think that I can picture it, his place of origin may be nothing like the island that has hosted my youth. I would love it if I were able to go back in time and visit his house many years ago. To have seen Moss when he was younger. To have known what he was like before his recent ordeals. Perhaps there was once a more carefree Moss. Imprisoned, mugged, bereaved, these must cause great inner disturbance, and still I think him the noblest boy.

I take the receiver, dial and speak to an operator. She puts me through to another who says, 'Cagliari,' and then another who says, 'Roma.' I am speaking down a cable under the sea. It is a fantastic thing. There are two further changes and then an operator is speaking English to me, asks me which number I want. Moss is holding the card with the phone number on, unfortunately my brain does not translate from the Italian way in which I read the numbers quickly enough. The operator coughs.

Moss takes the telephone from me and speaks his old

Nuoro, Sardinia

home number without even looking at the card. He says, 'Reverse charges, please,' even though I explained that in Italian to a previous operator. Then Moss's face changes. He is listening intently but I cannot hear what he hears. I quickly realise that it is his mother's voice which he listens to. I am party only to my boyfriend's interjections.

'Moss. It's Moss, Mum.'

... ...

I don't know what she is saying to him but I do hope she does not make him go back there. To Bury. He means too much to me.

'I heard today.'

... ...

Moss looks very serious and she might be telling him how his father died. I hope it was not gory; he hates all that.

'Gary.'

... ...

He looks puzzled, I am not sure that Mrs Croft wanted the brother to tell Moss. Very strange. My boyfriend is looking cross and also like he might cry.

'I'm so sorry. Sorry for you.'

... ...

I think Moss is speaking nicely but the voice from England sounds angry, hectoring.

'I don't see what I could have done.'

... ...

This is a very strange conversation. Moss was out of the country and yet it sounds as if his mother is blaming him for his father's death. I'm sure of it. I can read my boyfriend's face, I really can.

'His second heart attack. I didn't know...'

... ...

I didn't know either. Moss said his father was a plasterer which is not a job for a weakling. It is tougher, more honest, than watching olives grow. Both get about the same money,

I think.

'When was the first?'

... ...

Oh God, I think his father has had two heart attacks since Moss last saw him. He will have no more.

'In prison. You think it happened because I was in prison?'

... ...

She's crazy. What she accuses him of doesn't even make sense.

'I don't know anyone called Sir Kinsley. How did he cause the first heart attack?'

... ...

Well at least she realises it wasn't Moss, and she is completely nuts if she really thinks one of King Arthur's knights did it. Moss never said she was a mental lunatic person but maybe this too has happened only because she is grieving for his father. She has lost her husband and she probably liked him more than Moss ever did.

'I didn't ask the men from the Foreign Office to visit. This is the first I've heard about it.'

... ...

My boyfriend still looks like he could cry. I want to tell him his mother is crazy but I think he likes her. He always said his father was the nasty one.

'Mum! I don't even know why they let me out!'

... ...

Not crying but shouting over her. This is going horribly for Moss. I feel for him and also think that if his mother doesn't want him back in England that is actually best for me. I will not lose him to this mad woman. That would humiliate me. I want to see into Moss's face, to know what he is thinking but he has turned away. I think he is confused. Maybe the mother never used to be so crazy.

'What do you mean medicine? Take my medicine...'

Nuoro, Sardinia

… … … … … … …

I don't understand what they are saying now. Moss seems to be listening intently. He is a healthy boy, not on any medicine. His mother talks only nonsense.

'Do you and Gary both think this? That I caused his heart attack?'

… … … … … … …

They think he's a sorcerer

'Him too?'

… … … … … … …

I thought Gary was like Ercole, pretty dumb but on Moss's side. This is really shocking.

'Jesus! Of course I didn't want him to die. I don't know what I can say to that. God, Mum, it's a cruel thing to think. I didn't plan anything.'

… … … … … … …

She really doesn't know her own son. Doesn't deserve him. Moss is not a killer. He is gentler than any man in Sardinia. And he was in prison and then here with me; he has the best alibi.

'I didn't have a plan.'

… … … … … … …

I wish I could understand what the mother is saying. I wonder if she has killed the father and is just trying to blame someone else. Blame Moss. It seems as likely as anything else.

'Well, it happened. I wish I'd never taken the money...'

… … … … … … … … … …

I think she is still telling him off but no longer for killing the husband. She doesn't sound as hectoring as before.

'...and I'd still be there...'

… … … … … … …

It's the prison, she thinks Moss's being in prison gave the father the heart attack. And then she keeps interrupting him. She won't let him explain about the sneaky giant.

'I had to reverse the charges!'

… … … … … … …

'Save your fucking money,' he says, and then he slams down the phone, slams it so hard I think he might have broken it. I know it was his mother he is cross with—more than cross—he isn't deliberately vandalising the phone. Momentarily it reminds me of the stupid Sardinian boys who do exactly that, cause damage because they are frustrated with their lot in life and too stupid to join the Communists and make it better. Then that thought leaves me as I realise that Moss has opened up a rift with his mother, with his brother Gary too. That is what has happened if I have understood the conversation correctly. It is difficult for me to be certain, I heard only my boyfriend's contribution. I don't think he ever expected to be arguing with his mother. I said that Moss looked like he might cry but that is not what he does. He goes inside himself; he is silent. I think of how, just an hour or so ago, he described the fat man knifing Stanley—the Berber—to death. I think that his mother has done this to Moss, stabbed him through the heart. It is a metaphor, I know, but I also feel that I must intervene. Save him from bleeding out everything that is hurting inside him.

I take hold of my boyfriend, very closely and we are already in an intimate position. There can be no other way of sharing the inside of a telephone box. I put my hands inside his clothes, just on the skin of his back, I feel his ribs. I want us to merge together, to be as one. I even think it is happening and we are powerless to stop it. 'We have each other,' I say, and he reciprocates this tight hug around me. I even feel his hand on my flesh, on the side of my midriff. I no longer think my boyfriend to be funny. I think he is mine. And I am all that he has. All that is anchoring him in the world. It comes to me, quite unexpectedly, that love is a heavy responsibility. I know that I must discharge it carefully, help my boyfriend reach the other side of a grief I cannot fully comprehend. It might be grief for his father, or for the Berber. And I have listened closely enough to hear how nauseating it is for him to relive the attack upon him by that nasty brute in Tunis. Now his mother and his brother are leaving him to the world. Only I want him and I want nothing else. I will do whatever it takes for this one. For my floundering Moss. He has me.

Chapter Seven

Heavy Rain in Tunis

1.

On December the fourth, nineteen-fifty-nine my second child was born in the upstairs bedroom of the house on Wolseley Road that Ronald and I still share. We chose the name Moss because it is the same as Ronald's older brother. The two were still quite close at the time of our second son's birth.

Moss Senior came to our church for Moss's dedication ceremony, not that he was a member of that or any other church. I expect he still isn't. A little while after that simple service, Moss Senior went completely off the rails. He even got a divorce from Colleen after I-don't-know-how-many years together. And this was in the nineteen-sixties when that kind of carry-on shouldn't have been happening. I know it's all the rage now. We still exchanged cards at Christmas but I think Ron quickly regretted the name he'd chosen.

Before Moss was born, the church was a source of comfort to our little family. As time went on, we found the behaviour of some of the preachers got barmier and barmier. We—Ronald and I—put it down to Billy Graham. Not just him but he was the ring leader, you could say. There were quite a few shouty American evangelists who tried too hard to excite the faithful. To fire them up with worry about nuclear wars and what not. That kind of fearmongering wasn't for us; Ronald and I are not the sort to bother about nuclear war. Nor were we upping sticks and joining some new upstart religion, although we knew one or two who did just that. And we certainly weren't going to throw our lot in with the Catholics. Moss senior married one, a girl from a large family of Catholics. A woman by the time I first met her. It's not our cup of tea. And if you are so foolish as to marry one, please don't think that divorcing her might put it right. It doesn't work that way. Certainly not when you've kiddies to think about.

In recent years Ronald has been saying that Moss senior is a disgrace, and I think some of those aspersions rubbed off on our own Moss. That's why I think we got his name wrong.

The dedication ceremony for Moss was not our last visit to the Baptist church but I can't say I enjoyed going there after that. I still put it down as my religion if I have to write what it is on a form or at the census which they do every ten years. I suppose I'm set in my ways, and the Baptists have been my way although I don't give it very much thought nowadays. Not in nineteen-eighty, nearly twenty years since Ron and I could call ourselves churchgoers. Fifty since I first got hooked.

* * *

I think I've left Algeria but this is more like no-mans-land than actually being in Tunisia. It is, quite literally, a minefield. The country behind me has been a real eye-opener. Such a mental overload that I feel unsure if I ever had my eyes open at all. I might have dreamt it: three weeks in Algeria, the weirdest place on this Earth.

I arrived in Annaba earlier today—just before eleven—I was pleased with my early start and the morning's hitchhiking. I'm nearing Sicily and the proximity of it feels reassuring. The Algerians have probably been nicer to me than I have to them. Once or twice, I went a little crazy. I've discovered that not understanding what is going on gets more disorienting over time. I thought I would acclimatise but, instead, I just got frustrated. Sorry, Algeria, really sorry. It'll be good to be back in Europe in a day or two.

An early start and a little bit of jumping over my rucksack—the application of my gift—earned me both lifts from Constantine to the coast. Annaba is a seaside resort, so I was expecting tourists and newspapers. I'm desperate to learn what really happened in Tehran; the only copy of Time Magazine on the newsstand was a week out of date. No point in buying that.

On arrival there, I thought to myself how it was only three hours from Tunisia. I became dead keen to go, nearly there and all that. The trouble was, I still had about half of my Algerian currency to get rid of. It's rubbish. It seems like half the hoteliers don't even want it. I won't be smuggling that shit across the border. I'm not completely stupid.

In Fes, in Tétouan, Morocco, I could have given it to the beggars but Algeria is different. I never see any. People are prouder, I think, although it could just be that begging is banned. No one has said it but maybe all the Battypapa posters depict the old guy telling the kids not to hassle foreigners. After all, he's already fleeced them once with his crooked banking. The old despot issues the population with monopoly money and they've all got to pretend it's real or else the police start knocking heads.

When children followed me on the street in Algeria, they never asked for cash like they did in Morocco. They laughed at my hair which annoyed me a bit because, from what I can see, Arab culture could use a few hippies. I didn't fret about it, mind, I do like to bring a smile to kids' faces.

Children back there were always shouting out stuff to me. Shouting but not begging. I've had them ask me about Manchester United before I've so much as opened my

351

mouth to say I'm from a tuppence-ha'penny town close to that city. Either the kids are clairvoyant, or they ask travellers from Marseille and Oslo for the latest gossip about the same football team they do me.

Teenagers in Algeria seemed more orderly, more accepting of their place, than has been the case in Britain since the fifties or maybe before that. Since the black and white movies as far as I can tell. The staring face of President Battypapa on every street corner they walk past may have a stultifying effect on their natural rebelliousness but I've come to think it more ingrained than that. When I remember my friends in Oran, I think how Soufiane was the dutiful geology student, studying what his father wanted him to. I liked his dad too but Soufie was never going to rock the boat. Never ever. And the beautiful Samira, I reckon she would have liked to study like her two friends—maybe lots of her friends, Asia and Soufie were the only two I met—she resigned herself to marrying like her parents demanded. Ha! Unless she's gone hitchhiking to England in search of something more exotic. I do find myself thinking that Samira and I really might be married in another life, another world. One where those obnoxious mediaeval Christians never rampaged on their nasty crusades, then our fathers would see eye to eye. If we all shared the same bigotries, all would be well with the world.

As I said, Annaba is right by the sea. When I got there, I thought I ought to go for a swim. The last time I did that was back in Spain before I ever came to Africa. However, when I walked on to the beach, I could only see mothers paddling in the water with their tiny toddlers. One or two of the little children were naked, some wore swimming costumes. The mothers were all covered up from head to toe in their long shapeless dresses, headscarves too. It's not my place to criticise a culture that I don't really understand but those are not beach clothes. The women would pull their skirts up by about two inches above their ankles to walk into the sea with their little ones. The waves were gentle, still ran on to the hem of their clothing. They seemed okay with that. The important thing for them was not to show the world an unnecessary square centimetre of flesh. One or two of the mothers wore jeans, and they rolled their trouser legs up the same barely discernible few centimetres. It is as President Battypapa has decreed.

I thought young men in North Africa might go swimming. In Blackpool or up in Morecambe they do it even if the weather looks ropey. Showing off is a lads' thing. But in Algeria, the blokes all stay away—sit around coffee shops, drinking, smoking—men with men, boys with boys. I came here to immerse myself in another culture and I find I'm alienated by it. I wouldn't join a snooker club in Lancashire if it was men only. I really wouldn't. I wandered away from the beach without so much as having a paddle.

I have always enjoyed the town centres across Algeria. One way or another there's a kind of buzz there. In Annaba, just a few hours ago, I sat in the square thinking what to do next. Push the money down the lavatory and be gone today, something on those lines. Then I saw two policemen approach a couple of young kids on bicycles. I think the kids were only ten or twelve years old. Children. Their body language—police and kids both—sent a little shudder through me. It's like I have a sixth sense. I doubt if I could have given a voice to it, I just sat still and watched. Knew something was going on. As the policemen were talking to the boys, I noted that one of the young ones was rocking his bike backwards and forwards. He sat astride it; his movement suggested he was itching to go. Not enjoying the conversation one bit. The other kid, the smaller one, was talking a lot, waving his hands. In a split second the bigger kid pushed away on his bike and the gendarme closest to him took two quick steps. Caught him and bundled him over. Bicycle and all. At the same time the other policeman grabbed hold of the little kid—really aggressively—the kid was writhing like this was to be the fight of his life. I could see that he had no chance. A tiny little kid and the policeman was a tough brute. The one on the ground who fell off his bicycle couldn't get up quickly enough. The policeman hovering over him kicked him. Viciously. Looked to be in the nuts from where I was sitting. The smaller boy continued to struggle, so the policeman put him in a headlock. It was the most terrible thing to watch. None of the bystanders in the square did a damned thing. Not one of them. Me neither but how could I have helped? Not from round here and what have you.

The kid on the ground finally stood up but submissively. He held his head bowed forward, the policeman no longer holding him. I guess the lad knew they could catch him if he tried to make off again. By this time the other policeman had let go of the smaller boy. The little one stood up tall as he could make himself, like he was a mouse fighting a cat in a kids' cartoon. The policemen were both saying things—shouting really—I could hear them loud and clear. It was all in Arabic so I don't have a clue what the kids were supposed to have done. The small boy answered a gendarme back in a loud voice, maybe a little insolent. He got smacked across the head for it. The police were really nasty. Shocking to see. The bigger boy gave something to the policeman, it might've been money, I couldn't see. I kept well back just like everyone else on the square. One policeman picked up the fallen bicycle and put the handlebars into the boy's hands. Then the two policemen just turned, walked away. Their shift of duffing up children over for the day.

Across the square, Battypapa wore his smug smile on his sordid little posters. And just ruminating on it now that I've crossed the border—left Algeria—I do wonder if this is the ritual beating of conformity into the very anima of Algerian youth. Had I witnessed the cunning initiation ceremony that underpins Battypapa's reign of tedious terror? The bashing of rebellion from the guts of youngsters before they hit their teenage years. Or were they just currency smugglers like me.

2.

He was not a difficult baby, not at all. I remember Ronald being more taken with him than he ever had been with Gary. I mean by doing some of the handling, the bathing. Even changing him once or twice and I never expected that. Him being a man and everything. Of course, after having Gary we both wanted a girl but that didn't mean Moss was a disappointment. Not then. No one could blame a baby for being what it was, however much having a girl might have been better. And Ronald didn't really blame him but he went on about it—'We were planning to call you Sally,' he used to say—and I had said all along that I didn't know what I was having. Nobody gets to choose. Ron wanted to put me through it again, get a girl next time, so I told him what I thought. The house was too small for us to raise a third child, and if the third was a boy he'd be wanting a fourth, and a tenth, and heaven knows what. I put my foot down and Gary and Moss it was.

He carried on about it a bit, so I stopped talking about it, answering back. I'd decided what I was doing and told him so, there was nothing further to say. And I didn't like arguing with him at all, Ronald would go red in the face and looked a bit ugly when he tried saying I was wrong, that a third was bound to be girl. After having two boys, he said, the odds would be in our favour but I don't think it works like that. I didn't budge but he made me feel it was my fault Moss wasn't a girl. And it wasn't, it was just one of those things. The way he went on about it seemed like he was reaching for someone to blame. As I've grown older, I've noticed it's really just Ron not being able to express himself as clearly as he intends. That's been his problem through and through. He would have liked a girl but didn't get one. Full-stop. He liked the new little one, changed a nappy or two. It was his idea to call him Moss; I never liked the name but didn't say anything. Moss liked his dad; that should have been the end of the story. You would hope.

* * *

After watching the policemen terrorise the two youngsters, I felt awful for having stood by and done nothing. Of course, the police may not have been beyond bashing my head in had I intervened but that is not an excuse if you think through your ethics properly. My not speaking Arabic was the big one for me. I didn't understand or have the tools to really ask. What's done is done, so all I could think to do was go and find the boys after the dreadful incident was over. I had a little plan.

I walked the streets for twenty minutes looking up and down every dusty road and then found them by the seawall. Same kids, same bikes. I put a hand up, like a peace sign—not the hippy one—the universal open palm. One of the kids looked frightened, like I was the police, and I did the sign again. Not near to his head, not like I was going to slap him. That isn't me. Then I dipped into my money belt. I had loads of the dumb Algerian currency left. It's got no value to me, I couldn't take it over the border, it would be pointless. The country's broke. From his thousands of posters, Battypapa's staring eyes hypnotise the Algerians into believing the notes carry a value that they really don't.

I split all I had left in two and put half into each of the kids' hands. Thirty quid each at the Algerian banks fraudulent exchange rate, not the one I got from the cowboy bankers in Oujda. The kids looked at me like I might be a lunatic but then one said an Arabic word that could have been, thanks, and they both spun off on their bikes. I reckon that was the second-best thing I did in Algeria. In first place I'd put consoling Samira when she was upset. The one who was definitely called Samira. Kind of hugged her but not too much. I hope she remembers it as I do.

I took myself straight out of Annaba after that. Rustled up one artistically constructed hitch to the Tunisian border—that's what Rucksack Jumpers do—and I was out of there. Of course, I'm too rational to think I have magical powers but it's sweet to find I sort of do. Lots of my lifts come too quickly to be coincidence. I've got the knack.

The customs check to get out of Algeria was no problem at all and I was grateful for that. I didn't know what to expect but I felt fairly relaxed throughout the ride to the border post. Nothing to smuggle across, thank Christ. The Algerians had guns, of course, which is plain daft in my view. There is no imminent attack. They're just a show of power in the face of nothing whatsoever. No one want's their country.

A customs official took a good long look at my passport, wrote something down on a notepad. This is Battypapa's night-time reading; checking who's come and gone. They didn't look at or ask for any paperwork about where I'd changed money, seems like I miscalculated that. Changed a little more than I should have. Those two beaten-up kids were the beneficiaries of my mistake and I don't begrudge them a penny.

There was an awkward moment when a brash young official, speaking in slow and deliberate English, asked if I knew that taking Algerian currency out of the country is an offence punishable by prison. I think I reddened quite a bit, which is stupid because I had no money on me except travellers' cheques, and they're completely legit. The talk about smuggling, and the guy staring into my face, made me feel exactly as I had done coming into his country three weeks earlier. I think I've worried all along that they might arrest me for the first brouhaha. I remember that I was cock-a-hoop when I got through, after the two customs goons searched and questioned me on the western border. Over time, I have thought it through and I was just plain lucky. Today, the chap saw that I was nervous and asked directly if I had any Algerian currency. I said, 'No,' and started to take off my money belt to show him the travellers' cheques but he waved it aside. He must have seen honesty in my guilt-ridden looks and that rather proves my theory that we of different cultures struggle to read each other's faces. Of course, it is possible that he thought I was carrying hundreds of thousands of dinars and just wanted to get one over on Battypapa. A customs man gone rogue: that's a long shot in my book. Close to maximum improbable. Algerians conform when they hit their twelfth birthday. A couple of kickings from the thuggish cops does it. All except Asia Lellouche. She should be president if they had any sense at all.

As I hoisted my rucksack onto my back, ready to walk through to the Tunisian side, a different customs official smiled at me very strangely. I ignored him—which is generally a good tactic with all figures of authority—but as I was opening the door to leave, he held up a hand. I thought he was going to ask me to take off my shoes but that wasn't it. 'Do you have a car?' he asked in French. That struck me as a stupid question all ways up. If I had a car, they would have searched the damned thing by now. I just shook my head. 'Tunisia, five kilometres,' said the official. That surprised me. It seems like they've built their border post about three miles too soon.

I don't mind walking five kilometres, so I said this to the

border guard. He started to mime as if he was taking a leak—pissing—which was pretty weird behaviour from a stooge of Battypapa. Then he told me not to leave the road if I needed to urinate; uriner is the word he used. The French language just gets easier and easier the more I hear it. I shook my head again because I'm strong-bladdered, I don't tend to need a pee on a sixty-minute walk. The next thing he said was, 'Mines terrestre,' and I figured this French too but it left me cold. Landmines.

I decided that I would stay firmly on the road for five kilometres. It was what he had asked and looked a better prospect than being blown into little pieces. Conform for a little bit. Do so in the circumstances. What is it with these countries, Algeria, Tunisia? They should be friends. They've got their mutual hatred of Israel, what's there to row about? As I dwelt on it, I spotted my own crass reasoning. Twice in the last seventy years, Europe has torn itself apart—countries bombing the shit out of each other like has happened nowhere else on Earth—yet I'm still itching to get back there. It could be that I understand our minefields better than the Arab ones. Neither is better or worse, it's just theirs and ours. The comfort of familiarity. Of course, if we could only think straight, we would admit that we're all the same and open up the borders for ever. Let all our differences cancel each other out. I don't see that happening any time soon. We'll have to keep walking back and forth across minefields until the day we do.

The road is dry and dusty and it's actually very narrow. I'm walking down it as a means to an end, it's not really where I want to be. If cars come in both directions, they have a few passing bays to help them but otherwise they're in trouble. Either a head on collision or they veer onto the minefield. It's flat as far as the eye can see, so I suppose they all use the bays. I hope the no-pissing guy has warned everyone. As I amble along, I find myself like a kid who's scared to tread on the cracks in the pavement. If I'm on the gravel road, I figure that I'm safe. I will not pass even half an inch over the lip of it. Scared of having so much as a single toe blown off. I hear a car coming up behind me and I fear it will push me off the road. It approaches dead slow; the driver probably worries that I'll make him break his own half-inch rule. I see it has French number plates. Instinctively I stick out an optimistic thumb. The driver brakes, smiles, the door opens. Renowned Rucksack Jumper, Moss Croft, only ruddy well does it again. I've pulled up a ride in a minefield. It's outrageous, my thumb is like a magic wand. Bomb factories, minefields, one-eyed prostitutes: it's all too much. I'm ready for Sicily, good and ready. I reckon I'll cadge a lift with the Ayatollah Khomeini if I hitchhike around here any longer. Everything has gone that far round the bend, it really has.

3.

Before Moss started school, I taught him to read and how to say his times-tables. Doing this gives children the best chance, that's what I think. I did much the same with Gary but he was hopeless. The truth is, Gary liked fighting more than he ever did reading. It doesn't matter now because he's doing just that for his country but Moss was better at a young age than his brother ever was. He read library book after library book. He would read aloud to me when he was home from school, Gary playing in the park or kept back for detention. He made me laugh, using lots of funny voices as he told the story. Kids' books but I liked to hear them. Ron too, although he sometimes got a bit fret up. Said they were only silly stories, didn't like Moss being the centre of attention. I think a lot of men blow hot and cold with little ones. Men of Ron's generation, certainly.

Gary and Moss were both card players. I taught them

rummy and cribbage and all the children's games. Later they played whist and something called brag. I never learnt that one. They tried to draw Ronald and I into playing with them but their father was never a fan of games. Except at Christmas time. I always liked to join in. Not for brag which is just a silly betting game although my boys used the Monopoly money. Had that much sense if no more.

Sometimes I'd watch how Moss played his cards, I thought I saw him letting Gary win a bit. Not often but just enough to make sure he didn't lose interest. Moss was about eight years old when I spotted that and Gary is the older by more than two years. I generally like clever but it can be a bit of a curse. Smart ones need a proper outlet, a hobby like Egyptology or something. They can get very frustrated if they have to do exactly the same as everyone else.

If you ask me that was the problem with Moss Senior. He's not stupid even though he married a Roman Catholic. Ronald wouldn't have it, mind you, didn't agree with me when I told him that his brother had a surfeit of frustrated intelligence. I wasn't trying to be clever; I'd read about it in a magazine. The trouble is, Ron's not the sort to accept his own flesh and blood might be cleverer than he is. After I'd said it, I realised that it might have knocked the shine off how he thought I saw him. And I didn't mind the way he was. A bit of a ranter about the trade unions and taxes but I agreed with him about all of that.

* * *

Tabarka, Tunisia, looks much like Annaba did back in Algeria but the feel of it is quite different. A better vibe. The French family which plucked me from the minefield brought me all the way. They even queried if I wanted to try their hotel; they said it has a lido and so I figured it would be too expensive. I'm back on regular currency. No black-market nonsense for me from now on; cheapest possible is my only hotel from here to Bury. If I ever go back to Bury. I hate the place. I might try and find work in Sicily or somewhere like it. We're in the EEC, I'm allowed.

The difference with Annaba is easy to explain. President Battypapa has no jurisdiction here and his face peers out from nowhere whatsoever. He's gone. President Fruitcake runs this country and his face—also white-haired but much less of the stuff—adorns buildings and lampposts across the town. All over the tinpot nation, I expect. Fruitcake looks way cooler because he wears sunglasses. I've not met him, so I can't be sure the impression is on the money. Behind the shades, he might be cross-eyed and angry, the glasses masking the real Fruitcake. He looks like an Arab grandad but I haven't seen how his police treat the kids on the street yet.

At the cheapest hotel I can find, I check into the room and unpack a few things from my rucksack. I've got to seek out a launderette. Think I should return to Europe free of all offensive odours coming from my person or clothing. It looks like a simpler goal than hitching to the Sahara and I cracked that one. I decide to do the necessaries tomorrow morning, before then I'll take a look around town. Make a short visit to the beach. I love the Mediterranean. It calls me from just a couple of hundred yards north of the hotel.

As I walk onto the sand, I quickly feel overdressed. There are many, many people in swimwear. Families, boys, women. Blue sky, warm day, why wouldn't there be? It is still April and I never packed any shorts. There's little call for them in Bury. I make a mental note to buy some, I'll do it in Italy. I think Arab shorts are different—or they don't have any—I only ever see them on youngsters. I decide to sit on the beach, and it may or may not be fair to say that my proximity to a couple of women—young, slim, attractive, both in bathing suits, lying on towels—is more of a co-incidence than an act of deliberation. I try not to look at them, or certainly not to look at them too intently. However, my position is close enough to take in that they are quite dark skinned. Young Tunisians I presume. This surprises me on two counts. They are unaccompanied, no mothers or husbands to fight off the likes of me; and they are showing more flesh to the world than I ever expected to see in North Africa. Liberal-minded person that I am, I feel okay with it. I like the liberation of flesh. Wish I'd brought some shorts.

I sit on the beach, soak in a few sun rays, it's scorching. I'm in my jeans, so have no need of a towel or mat to protect me from the sand. I feel quite self-conscious, probably the most covered up person on the beach. It's a big contrast from Annaba, from the Algerian resort I visited briefly this morning. I extract My Life as a Man from the carrier bag I have brought along with me. I begin reading but from the corner of my eye, I can see that one of the girls is shuffling a bit. She's lying face down on her towel and she's pushed the straps of her swimsuit aside. She rolls it carefully down herself. I think she is doing this to ensure she gets an even tan across the whole of her back. An outrageous thing to do in this country. I never saw topless sunbathing in Spain when I looked around the beaches there, and North Africa is a step change stricter. More than. I think, as I slyly watch—my book obscuring my eyes from the girls—that her breasts must now be outside the costume, face down on the towel. I can't see her precisely but my imagination is like second sight. I find myself hoping that the other girl does not do the same. I hope she talks her friend into rolling her top back up. This is not the way of things here, and breaking the social code might bring out a bunch of violent police. I can't see Fruitcake being pro-boobies. I mean to say, it's quite possible that he's very keen on them in private; these dictators often have a different take on morality for themselves than they do for the masses, the oppressed. I try to read and manage to do so a little but I'm also monitoring the girls' situation. Both are sunbathing, one face up and swim-suited, the other face down and topless. I'll give them a shout if I see the man in the sunglasses coming. President Fruitcake. Then, at a time when I have been contemplating the girls more than my book, the unclothed one turns over. Tummy facing the sun. I look away knowing her breasts are out in the open, on show for everyone. From the corner of my eye, I note that she is lying flat on her back, low down, so it shouldn't let her undressed state be too obvious. Again, my imagination knows what she looks like even as I avert my eyes. In a movement she is sitting upright, I think I saw her naked figure but then, in double-quick time, her shoulder straps are back in place, the dress code restored.

Given that I am a hitchhike-to-the-Sahara type of guy, it is perfectly natural that I should casually stroll across and talk to the girls. Particularly the daring one. I'd like to learn what has prompted this minor outbreak of breast-baring. Work it out even if I don't ask her directly. Leaving my book on top of my carrier bag—to return to when I'm the wiser—I rise and venture towards them.

'Bonjour.' They both reply in well-spoken French and I ask if they are Tunisian.

'Non.' They tell me that they are French, from Paris. That surprises me but, just thinking on it, I recall seeing many dark-skinned men and women in my two brief forays into France. It might just be a deep tan. I'm from Bury and our colour options are pretty much white or lobster red.

I ask what they are doing in Tabarka.

'Vacance.' What else would it be?

I want to tell the girl that she was taking a big risk exposing her breasts but I know I will sound like a voyeur if I say it. Instead, I tell her that it is hot, a comment that is obvious, needs no reply. But the girl, the one I most want to talk to, laughs and says, 'For you!' It's true that I have my jeans on, at least I've left my sweatshirt with the carrier bag and the book. And I need the thin T-shirt or I'll burn. They are darker-skinned, don't get pan-fried like I do. I tell the girls that I've hitchhiked across Algeria, I travel lightly, and I've a well-thumbed copy of The Glass Bead Game if one of them wishes to read it. Make my pack lighter.

'En français?' asks the girl who I fancy.

'Non, anglaise.' I disappoint her. There will be no takers for that dog-eared tome. Then I try to tell them about the dress code in Algeria. The one-eyed women of Nedroma; the tall Tuareg in their blue. They both listen intently, ask questions occasionally, although I'm mixing English and French in order to say it all. When I tell them there were no sunbathers at all on the beaches of Annaba, I think they may realise what I am driving at. That I do not like to think of her—the more adventurous of these two lovely Parisians—getting into trouble during her stay. 'Pour l'amour de Dieu, se couvrir,' I say more loudly than intended and, feeling embarrassed, I turn and leave. For God's sake cover yourself up, I have just shouted at her. I sound like my fucking father.

4.

Moss liked primary school, at least, I presume he did. We weren't ones to talk about what happened every day, whatever went on it was his life and not mine. At parents' evenings the teachers always told me that everything was going smoothly. Not like Gary with his fighting, and he was a bit thick too. And Moss and Gary both went to the Sunday School. To the Baptists. I took them to church for a time although Ronald had stopped going. I can't say if I believed in it or not; I think religion generally stops young ones from going astray. Back then it worked for Moss more than it did Gary but neither stuck to it or ever got baptised. Not like me and Ron did when we were teenagers. I regret it now. If I'd insisted on it, things might have worked out better. I'm not sure what stopped me from insisting but I expect Ronald told them some of his doubts and that can't have helped. I think he is something of an atheist these days and that makes him a lot more certain about it all than me. Ron and I don't really speak about that kind of thing. As I get older and wiser, I see how personal it really is. We don't all think alike and it's no bad thing. I sometimes thought that Moss believed in God a bit, he could be quite idealistic. Stupid with it but at least he thought about these things.

* * *

I get lucky when I hitchhike away from Tabarka. This is just one day after I made a fool of myself on the beach. And the girl had actually read Steppenwolf so we had a lot in common. She pretty much showed me her breasts and then I shouted at her. I can be a right loony sometimes.

My rucksack is full of clean clothes; I read a lot more of the novel in the launderette. It's a weird one; if I really was a literature student, I'd definitely write an essay about it. The ride that I have is with a Tunisian family, it was only the second car to pass. I can stop whichever one I like. The couple who picked me up live in Tunis; they have family in Tabarka. The driver—the man—speaks excellent English. His wife doesn't but nor is she shy. Speaks to me in French. Her face is quite pretty and she wears no headscarf. I want to ask questions about it, to do it without being rude. Appearing rude. This couple remind me a little bit of Mustapha and Khadidja who I stayed with in Oran. Younger than they were, chatty. I'm sure they're okay, my thumb only stops the good ones.

When we have been travelling for a little while the lady,

Heavy Rain in Tunis

who has introduced herself as Myriam—which sounds to me like an upper-class English name but for all I know might be the commonest one there is here in Tunisia—turns to me in the car and starts to talk sternly. I understand her French completely. She uses simple terms, wants to be very clear with me. She says I am foolish to hitchhike. She tells me that it's dangerous to hitchhike in Tunisia, just like it is in America which I must already know if I watch the movies. There are some people who will take advantage of a young hitchhiker. A murderer might pick me up. That seems to be her biggest worry.

I want to tell her that it's different for me. I'm a Rucksack Jumper and that gives me special powers. Immunity, by and large. I know that if I say it, even Wassim, her husband—who understands English impeccably—is unlikely to really grasp my point. Going with the flow, the magic thumb, having karma on your side, these attributes come across as a bit flimsy, pathetic even, when you say them out loud. So I don't; never jinx what's in the bag.

I nod, tell her that I'm staying in Tunis a night or two and then sailing to Italy. This pleases the lady. Myriam meant well. She and her husband make me feel very welcome in their car, and by only talking about Tunisia and America she implies that hitchhiking in Italy will not be so risky. She doesn't say it in as many words but she might as well have. I know that, in Italy, a nod and a smile and a thumbs-up sign will mean what I've always thought them to mean. In Algeria, in Morocco—in Tunisia probably but it's early days—I've never really figured out what on Earth is going on when people gesticulate. I've had to rely on the flow, intuition, karma. My brain is actually pretty useless in Africa. It's all feeling that has got me from Spain to here. All heart. I think it will be better in Italy. In Sicily. I'll turn the brain back on.

This is a good lift; Tunisia looks a little greener than

Algeria. We travel quickly and arrive in its capital city by lunchtime. I haven't visited many of them. I missed Algiers in my circuitous route across that country, and I can't remember which city is the capital of Morocco. I never went to it, it's not Fes. Not Marrakesh or Casablanca either. I smile when it comes to me: anywhere that Good King Bonkers lays his red Fez hat.

5.

Early in Moss's grammar school days, Ronald hit upon an idea that knocked me for six when he confided it. He asked if I thought Moss was queer. Well, I certainly did not and I wondered if he'd only said it because Moss didn't get into fights like Gary. He played football all day every day, tried out for the rugby team. I told Ron that a homosexual would do neither of those things. Ronald seemed relieved by what I said. It was still a funny notion for a father to have about his son. The two of them mostly seemed very close and Ron's not one of them, so it's not as though we've got the heredities for it.

Around this time the two of them began having long-winded arguments. At the beginning I mostly thought it was Ron trying to prove to Moss that he was clever. Talking politics and what have you. Moss had started taking up cranky points of view. 'I'm a communist,' he said once. It got a bit out of hand over the months. Not talking to each other. That.

* * *

I take myself down to the ferry terminal. Checking the escape hatch, you might say. I've decided only to stay the one night in Tunis. I've paid for my hotel room, so I'm hoping the amount of Tunisian money that I have left can buy me the ticket with a little to spare for dinner tonight.

Heavy Rain in Tunis

I've more traveller's cheques to change if it has to be.

The portside building—golden letters of the ferry line, all written in French, across the front—is quite a contrast to most of the shabby buildings I've seen on this continent. It's air-conditioned which I like a lot, no stifling heat inside here. Lots of little booths with a member of staff in each one. I receive an encouraging smile and quickly find myself seated on a comfortable chair across from a friendly lady. She will be happy to answer my questions, tells me exactly that. And she speaks English well. She says that she will find 'the ticket which is right for you.' I like the phrase. On my side, not a shark like Abdul.

The lady is quite old, in her forties I'd guess, but her company uniform is basically western, much like the channel-ferry company employees wear back in England and France. A normal skirt, not the long shapeless stuff many women wear in these parts. I ask her about travelling to Sicily. The cost is near what I expected and, being a bit cautious, I've budgeted for more. Algerian money was weird, nothing cost a damn thing there and I had more of it than I wanted. That was on account of my foolish foray into the black market. I got away with it but won't be trying any of that again. Nothing coming with me onto this boat that isn't allowed. In Tabarka the cost of everything seemed higher than in Algeria. A simple tagine knocked me back about three quid yesterday evening. I may have gone into a more expensive restaurant than I should have. I was hoping to stumble across the French girl and apologise if I'd sounded rude when I warned her about being too western. She was western, so I should have just let it go. There were two young ladies on the far side of the restaurant—probably French—it could have been them but I was very, very unsure. If they'd taken their clothes off, I'd have been able to tell but I wasn't going to ask them to do that. I'm nuts but not that far wide of my home port.

Rucksack Jumper

The lady in the ferry-line uniform asks me if I have family in Sicily. This strikes me as an odd question until I realise that I have not shown her my passport or undergone all the usual paperwork that accompanies border crossings. The tedious leaving and entering of these North African countries. I guess that will occupy me tomorrow. If she thinks I'm Italian that's funny; or then again, why not? Annalise was Italian. I could be an Australian-Italian in her mind although I guess that's just what I'm thinking. She won't be on that wavelength. Never met the girl.

The lady explains that the boat will not set sail until six o'clock tomorrow evening. I'm happy with it, an extra day to look at Tunis. The lady explains that I can have a reclining chair to sleep on inclusive of the ordinary ticket price, or pay extra for a shared or even a single cabin. I'm okay with the recliner. The boat will arrive in Palermo at seven-fifteen in the morning. She then advises that, for just a little extra payment, I can stay on the boat all the way to Cagliari, Sardinia. It will not arrive until after ten o'clock at night and this puts me off. I don't like trying to find somewhere to sleep so late in the evening. I shake my head as she says it. However, the lady is helpful, she wants me to have all the information. Sailing on to Cagliari, which is twice the distance, will only cost me an additional seven and a half dinar. That's what she says. I furrow my brow; it's a cracking price. I tell her that I will take it after all. Then I hesitate, think I might have it wrong. I could be confusing the exchange rate of the Algerian crap with the one for these Tunisian dinars. I'm normally more decisive than this. I ask the lady for a piece of paper and a pen, do the sums and then agree that I will go to Sardinia after all. It really is exceptionally cheap. Flow, flow, flow. Sicily is probably all mafia anyway. Not my crowd.

I like the lady. She has been as helpful to me as she promised at the start. No haggling, no hard sell. It's good to be leaving Africa with a pleasant final transaction. Really good. Her face reminds me of Khadidja, not exactly the same, the thick black hair mostly. She smiles a lot, very interested in me, keen to hear what I want.

6.

We took a two-week family holiday every single summer, unless Ronald's plastering work was slack and we couldn't afford it. Not that we were poor, mind, we always got by. Over the years we tried a lot of different places. Always the same tent. I can't say that many of the destinations suited us. I think we were all after different comforts and there are only so many of those under canvas. Ronald is a Bury man through and through, and Gary is a bit similar. My eldest loved Cleethorpes and nowhere else. Moss, well, I don't know what he made of our holidays. Perhaps they inspired the love of travel which he alone seemed to develop. Not that Ron and I want to take credit for that; it's been more trouble than it's worth, first to last. I am glad we had those times together; they are nice to remember for the most part.

* * *

I have the ticket for tomorrow's sailing in my money belt. Where it belongs. Pretty excited about Sardinia; I don't know much about the place and that makes it more of an adventure. A leap of faith. It is great that I went with the flow. Things always work out when I do that. I also keep thinking about the woman who sold me the ticket. I am sure that she was Tunisian. An Arab. I've been saying that we're all the same deep down and I feel a lot more certain about her than many. In fact, she was more like me than my own dad and mum. She was selling me something and only did it by helping me choose. She made eye contact most of the time but not like a hypnotist. Easy to sit with, I like that. When I asked about my rucksack—which was not with me, I'd left it back in the hotel so she couldn't see how big it was—she laughed lightly. Not at me. Reassuring. 'We had a family who went on board with a fridge, that didn't cost them any extra charge.' That's what she said. Ha! My rucksack won't be a big deal and she had a terrific way of saying it.

I also like to dwell on her little nudge towards Sardinia. I feel like I gave something back by following her suggestion. Perhaps she'll get a bonus for selling me the more expensive ticket but I think it's unlikely. The entire operation was civil, not pushy at all. She's probably on a flat salary, not getting commission or any of that claptrap. They wouldn't get nice people like her in the job if it was all about shaking the money out of our pockets. The Sardinia ticket was such a bargain, there wouldn't be much left over for her anyway. Her thoughtful sales pitch—gentle, letting me make up my own mind—leads me to imagine that the people in Sardinia will be like her. It's not logical but not everything is. Good souls on the island. I have to say, she was a very attractive woman. I don't mean that too strongly, she might have been twice my age. I guess I'm just hoping that Sardinia will be full of easy-to-get-on-with people. Meeting someone my own age would be good. I'll be all right there: it's in Europe.

I puzzle to myself what the lady's name might be, the one who sold me the ticket. I think it's good karma to remember the names of people who have been kind to you. It drops into my mind that she might be the third Samira I've met but then I let that thought go. This one is much too old to be a Samira. I would have preferred it if the second one, the girl in the Constantine hotel, had gone by a different name—just to help distinguish her apart from the first one in my mind and memory—and she was very helpful and obliging towards me. Bandaged up my war wounds. And the first one was the best: prettiest girl on this Earth. As I'm walking down the street, going through all this in my head, to my utter surprise a young man accosts me. 'Fou!' he shouts at me. 'Fou!' This is alarming; he thinks I'm crazy and I don't have the first idea why. I raise a hand, the flat palm, to show I am a man of peace. There is no reason at all for him to say this nastiness.

A woman stands by his side. She wears a headscarf but a very nicely coloured one, green and grey with thin red lines on it, and her face is pleasant although she has a bit of acne. She hisses something under her breath, 'Á qui parlais-tu?' There is something sly about the way she has asked me this: Who were you talking to?

She should know I wasn't talking to anyone, just thinking. I sometimes move my lips when I'm doing that, it can make the thoughts seem a bit more solid. And as I dwell upon it, I suspect that I was saying the words out loud, pondering for all Tunis if the older lady might be another Samira and if I might meet any girls in Sardinia. I suddenly feel embarrassed. I apologise, try to explain that I was only thinking. I won't be doing this in Sardinia where I can make friends more easily. Chat like a normal person, not just to myself. I really can't wait.

7.

Our tent was big; it had a kind of room divider inside. Two separate sleeping compartments as well as the opening where we cooked or sat on our garden chairs. I would like to say we took it to the four corners of the country; the fact is, we didn't. The South East was off limits. Ron says they're all stuck up there. And we only went to the South West the once but I liked it best.

Ronald liked Wales; he had a thing about Anglesey. He

loved crossing the bridge onto the island. He stopped the car on the bridge sometimes just to look backwards and forwards, stand on top of the sea. That was when Moss was five, Gary seven, and once or twice before. I could take it or leave it. And after Gary fell into the stream at the campsite—Red Wharf Bay the place was called—well, I put my foot down. We never went back. The poor boy could have drowned and that would have been no holiday at all.

Ronald still talks about Anglesey but he knows I shan't be going anywhere near the place. Moss could've gone back. After all, it wasn't him who nearly drowned but I don't think Anglesey was fancy enough for him. As he got older, he grew rather headstrong, a bit too keen on his own opinions. That can be all right as far as it goes but I believe life should be more about compromising. Inflating your own ideas can get anyone into a proper muddle.

* * *

I had a little lie down in my hotel room, it's helped me to relax. All okay now. The bust-up on the street was nothing really. I was just feeling excited to be going to Sardinia, not cracking up. I'm hungry, got to get something to eat. It's way past lunchtime, might explain the talking to myself thing. I'll grab a coffee while I'm at it, perk myself up for the rest of the day. I find a bar on what I think is the main street in the centre of Tunis. When I say bar, this is like it was in Annecy and in Madrid. The bars are mostly for diners until later in the evening but you can always get a beer here if you wish. This is another important point to think over when comparing Tunisia to Algeria. In the hermit fiefdom of Battypapa, it all dried up by eight o'clock at night. Unless you got invited to the lock-in, of course but I reckon they are pretty dodgy. If they have them in Annaba, you can bet that the violent police come on in and stop the party. Batons and kicking, all their tricks. I only went to the one

Heavy Rain in Tunis

in Constantine, luckily there were no problems that night. In Tunisia—assuming all of the country follows the same rules I saw in Tabarka last night—they don't stop serving until eleven. Maybe old Fruitcake is more of a party-boy than the killjoy who runs Algeria. They both look as miserable as the measles if you judge them by their posters. I wouldn't vote for either. I don't think anyone votes around here. The fly posters are just to tell them who they're stuck with, not who they can choose.

When I get inside the bar, I find it nice, even plush. It's lined with booths, like an American diner but they're at different angles. Forty-five degrees from each other, not secretive closed little booths like they have in gangster movies. I order a sandwich.

In my head there is a song playing. Another Templeton Ca. number, not the song I hitchhike to. I've no need of that for a couple of days and might try a different tune in Italy.

> ***To paradise - we travel light***
> ***And if we dare - we shall get there***

I think Lewis Taylor is a genius; he writes most of the Ca.'s songs. All the hits.

> ***The road is hard - we must discard***
> ***The tricks and props – this life allots us***

He's written songs about everything under the sun. And then some. One or two love songs but a lot of weird stuff too. Which I like best of all. The sandwich comes, it looks like a good one. I don't eat it straight away because I'm thinking about the song.

> ***The job – the house – the wife – our status***
> ***The car – the kids – our past – all that makes us***
> ***Must be thrown overboard – before the boat can take us…***

Oh Christ. Some girls are laughing and pointing and I wasn't even doing it again, I really wasn't. There are three of them and I stop moving my lips. Give them my best smile. They look Tunisian but it's three more easy-going ones if I can read faces and appearances. Which I generally can, it's just that North Africa demands a pretty intense level of concentration if you are to tune in. To really get people.

I decide to make friends, push through the embarrassment. I pick up my food and go on over to where the three girls are sitting. When the prettiest of them—they are always the most brazen—asks me why I was talking to myself, I explain that I was mouthing lyrics. She says, 'Which song?' so I tell her and she replies, 'Very nice.' She knows it, asks me to carry on singing. I shake my head; I'm not an exhibit whatever else I am. Then she sings a quick snatch of it herself. The spooky thing is she starts at exactly the words I'd got to in my head. It's a kind of chorus.

To the far shore – of that ocean that has no far shore

I tell her she has a great voice, say it because it's true, and start repeating my line about Taylor, the songwriter, that he's a genius. Then I stop. 'Those words weren't written by Lewis,' I say. 'The ones you just sung, he pinched. Plagiarised. Got them from Pablo Neruda.' I'd forgotten it until she sang them. Which is odd too because Neruda is the best poet of the lot. A dozen words from him can mean more than a whole copy of Time Magazine.

'We know that,' she says.

I nod, we're each looking into each other's eyes which is nice. She wears a headscarf but her hair is coming out of it on all sides. I'm impressed these Tunisian girls know Neruda. We really are the same deep down. They ask me where I'm from. When I tell them, they don't ask rubbish

Heavy Rain in Tunis

about Manchester United. I suppose girls aren't interested in it. I quiz them a bit; ask what they're doing here. They are quite easy going. If everyone in Africa was like this, I'd stay. I learn that they are all university students. I decide not to tell them that I'm one too. I'm through with that shit. I ask them what they study and one girl answers—not the one I'd looked to initially, not the pretty talker but the one who sits tallest in the booth, no headscarf—she doesn't actually tell me what they study, she says, 'We're Jews.'

This surprises me enormously. What are they doing in an enemy state? Or have I misunderstood the relationships between their country and this? President Carter has got Begin and Sadat together, stretched some convoluted accord across their many differences. A Nobel peace prize but not enough peace for a picnic on Sinai from what I can gather. And Tunisia never figured in any of that stuff. I thought all the Arab countries except Egypt stood on the side-lines. Booing and booing.

I ask them all what it's like being Jewish in a hostile country and all three girls make different signs to shush me up. I guess that means it's not as great as it could be. A bit of a curate's egg. Shit even. None of them use any of those phrases. Basically, they have never known anything else. I learn that they are Tunisians—Jewish Tunisians—this is their country. I didn't expect that, thought North Africa was all Arabs, save the odd Tuareg. Their parents don't sound rich. The girls seem pretty clever to my way of thinking. All at university. They know everything about Jews. Or a hell of a lot more than me at the very least. They tell me there are Jewish populations all over the Middle East.

'Morocco?' I ask.

'Yes.'

'Egypt?'

'Yes.'

The girl doing most of the talking now—the tall one—

says that there are Jews living in Iran. I enjoy having my preconceptions challenged, it kicks the complacency out of my thinking. Some people die no wiser than when they were twelve years old. It's why I travel: to learn, to find out what it's like on the other side.

The girls would like to know what I study, so I tell them straight. 'I don't.'

8.

We went to Minehead just the once, the year after Gary's mishap in Anglesey. I liked it a lot better, obviously. The town had a genteel quality, not something you can find in Lancashire. This is Ronald's county, the one where we have made our lives. The boys were born here, don't know anything different. I'm not from the north but I get on with those who are well enough.

I grew up in the countryside outside Warwick, my childhood was a different life. Father had the family move up here when I was fifteen. Some crackpot job or other he'd found. Not in Bury, the work was a farm thing. Heywood was the name of the place where his job was at. Anyway, it killed him. An accident, falling from a grain store. That's what Mother said and she didn't talk about it twice.

We were stuck here after that, Mother and I. Ronnie was a member of the congregation at Bury Baptists, as I was too by this time. There would be no more Warwickshire for me once he asked me out. Not after we started going steady. And only the one trip to Minehead. Ronald hated it; Moss was in his element, mucking around on the beach. We even had a day in Butlins. I remember him mostly being a happy kid—more so than Gary—before he started quarrelling with Ron. If you ask me, they each egged the other on. Moss full of daft ideas and Ronald shooting them down when it can be better to let your children imagine the world is like whatever they say it's like. Once they've tried that for a while—run out into the fog—they've nothing left but to come back around to their parents' way of thinking.

* * *

I'm still at the same table, having a second coffee but the girls have gone. They all study at Tunis university which is quite close to here apparently, and I even learnt that this is not the centre of the city. They smashed that previous assumption nicely into pieces, those gentle iconoclasts. The thing that I learnt about being Jewish in Tunisia is that whatever they think about Fruitcake—or God not having anything to do with helicopters crashing in Iran—those girls have resolved never to make waves. To keep their opinions pretty much to themselves. I suspect that the person in the next booth along might have heard that they were Jewish when the tall girl said it in a low voice but one person who overhears something isn't going to make a fuss. Being Jewish isn't being a hoodlum or a bandit, no need to alert the authorities. But then I repeated it a bit loudly which only happened because I've not been having enough proper conversations lately. Become a bit socially awkward, sure it'll mend itself in Sardinia. The volume I spoke at could have made Tunisians share glances. That might have sparked something. A reaction from any Arabs who don't like having Jews in their midst. I'm glad it didn't. With hindsight, I wish I'd been more sensitive toward them. They were pretty affable really, talking to a stranger they'd caught chunnering away to himself.

I only ordered this second cup of coffee so that I can contemplate what I have just heard. Dwell upon it a little longer. I think the Jewish diaspora goes back to the bible but these Tunisian Jews are not one of the lost tribes of the Israelites. At least, I don't think they are. Funny if I've found one. Rewrite the bible someone, Moss has spotted a flaw!

The odd-ball Mormons think that a lost tribe of Israelites made their way up a wagon trail in the wild west. That's just a nutty guess by someone covering up for the truth that the second coming is so overdue, it makes God look rude. Christians seek miracles in the rain running down the faces of statues of the Virgin Mary, and then they think fasting or scuttling off to Mecca is crazy. It's all crazy, so just live and let live. Why don't they? I even think there is something to that effect in the song the Jewish girl and I were singing.

> *The echo we heard – we mistook for the Word*
> *Reason, remorse – riots, religion*
> *Lamentable loves and parochial science*
> *We will reflect – from a different perspective*
> *On the far shore – of that ocean that has no far shore*

Brilliant. I wish I'd written it. All of it, not just the Neruda bit. Those girls must come from a long line of North African Jews. Missed out on the parting of the Red Sea, I expect. Went the wrong way. The Jews in Europe spent donkeys' years in ghettoes, marginalised from the ebb and flow of events. I suppose this horrible segregation happens all over. I sometimes wonder why they don't assimilate more. I shouldn't talk: can't even do it with my own family. The girls looked like Arabs to me until I knew better. It could be that lots of them have assimilated; they wouldn't be the ones to whisper 'We're Jewish' to visitors. If it had happened fifty generations back, they wouldn't even know what they were.

All this trip I've mostly thought about Christianity and Islam. The differences and how to overcome them. But I'm not even a proper Christian, I went to church when I was small but I never really got it, so I'm probably the wrong person to ask. Loads of people take it dead serious but at the bottom of it, religion is just the prejudices of our fathers dressed up as hand-me-down truths. And if those ancient people had really got hold of a decent truth back in biblical times, or whenever it was that Mohammed wrote the Koran, then we wouldn't be in all this shit now. I can't tell people to become atheists—it would be another kind of oppression—but when you let it go, you start to see that we're all the same. That's much better than clinging to ideas that sound daft in sunlight. I think Soufiane and Asia were practicing Muslims of some kind or other but they still treated me like a brother. Farouk and his crazy student friends in Constantine were a different kettle of fish. Took the whole thing up a few levels to the rooftop carpark. Or is that mean of me to think? They always treated me nicely; they weren't nuts and I don't honestly know if their religion is or isn't. And anyhow, I went and told them stupid stories about a make-believe sister. Could be that I'm the crazy one. When they talked about the helicopter crash in Tehran—or thereabouts—and they said God killed the Americans, they weren't trying to wind me up. It was just how they saw it. I don't think they've ever really tried to look at my view of the world but—fair's fair—theirs was new to me. I should have taken the opportunity to discuss it with them. We could have enlightened each other. They were never going to fight me about it. Decent people through and through.

I do wonder what the Jewish girls in Tunisia think of all the goings on. They said that they keep their heads down but they must have opinions. They might be more critical of Israel than your average Jew because they hear more of the Arab perspective. But people who are away from the place they think of as their homeland—Brits in Gibraltar, Marbella even—usually fly the flag like utter nutters. Think they are the true Englanders or true Israelis when they don't even bother to live in the place they bang on about.

The Spanish were really nice people, I'd give them Gibraltar tomorrow. Why not? I've left England and find I hate the place more than ever. And then again, I could murder a bag of chips.

9.

Moss did ever so well in school. One autumn term he did a project about space, the Apollo rockets and everything. I don't know if the teacher set it or if it was all his own idea. Of an evening, long after Moss had gone to bed, Ronald sat down and read it all. And he told me how very well written it was although I already knew it. Moss had stuck a couple of very apt pictures into his booklet. One of them was of the three astronauts who died during the first Apollo rocket launch, and he was too young to have heard about it at the time. He must have learnt about them somehow. Ron took a smashing interest in his son on that one evening, at least. In fact, I remember that space was a thing they had in common, both of them reading and talking about it an awful lot. Back when it mattered. When men were going to the moon, before the Arabs stopped it. Putting up the price of petrol so nobody on Earth could go on such long trips anymore.

I believe Ron was very, very proud of Moss. He didn't mind Gary, I'm not saying that, but we could both see his older brother's marks in school were rubbish. Then the boy started to grow his hair and won a poetry competition and that started up his father's funny suspicions that he might be queer. Moss never did have a boyfriend, so if it was true, at least he restrained himself. And I didn't believe it. I don't think William Wordsworth was one either but if I'm wrong, so be it. Moss could be odd but there was no reason to think he was that way. He went red when I asked him about the girls in his class and boys usually do that because they want one.

* * *

My coffee has gone cold and my contemplation has come to a stop. I'm idling. Sitting still and watching the world go by. A big part of going with the flow is not forcing yourself to draw a rapid conclusion if you haven't figured out the wherefores and whys of all the nonsense that just goes on and on. Everything can wait, everything will come out in the post-match analysis. A couple of guys at a nearby table are waving to me but I'm grateful that this happens while I'm thinking nothing at all. Not so much as a Templeton Ca. song going through my head. It just means they want to talk to my long fair hair. Not telling me to pipe down on the talking-to-myself front. I'm innocent of that one, thank Christ.

I wave them over. I like my table more than theirs, less exposed. It was the Jewish girls' table first off. The two lads greet, shake hands, touch hearts, all is well in the world. Almost before their bums have touched the seat they are saying, 'Margaret Thatcher,' and they are talking a bit too quickly for me. They also say, 'Fou,' say that she is crazy. I think we are all batting for the same team.

I'm feeling just a little flush with money; the ticket for my boat journey tomorrow was an absolute bargain. I ask the lads if they want a drink. I say it casually, I'm good to get them beer, which wasn't cheap last night in Tabarka, so probably won't be here either. I don't say beer in case they're offended by it. I respect everyone's customs but I think it's a bit lame. No one should take offence at being offered something. I would never force anyone to drink anything, not even in England. I'm civilised, not a scumbag.

'Coffee,' they say.

I make that three and as I stand to go and order, the barman catches my eye. I point at my old cup and then signal three, holding up that number of fingers. I reckon this is the most successful non-verbal interchange of my stay in Africa. I've had a few.

The boys start to tell me about President Bourguiba, president for life of this little country dwarfed between Libya and Algeria. President for life: that's a scam. And it's my President Fruitcake they're talking about. I don't tell the boys my analysis of the situation but they tell me he's worse than Thatcher. 'Échanger!' they suggest: Swap! For a moment I think that this is a brilliant idea. Fruitcake would be constrained by the British civil service and distracted by the television too. It could even paralyze him, I don't mean like a stroke-job, just keeping up with the sitcoms and the soaps would probably give him no time for pasting up his posters. I saw some Tunisian tele—Fruitcake's current fare—in the bar in Tabarka last night. It looked woeful. Then I arrest the thought. Give Thatcher the power that Fruitcake has and she'd be a million times worse than she is now. Power can go to anyone's head and she's a bit of a swivel-eyed Ayatollah to start with.

These guys are super-friendly, their names are Mohamed and Taha. Taha is a cracking name. When you say it, it sounds like you've just completed a magic trick. Oh, Christ, my thoughts are rambling now, people take those the wrong way. Whatever else I do, I mustn't tell him about his name. And they want to share a meal tonight. I agree to it; these two are nice kids, teenagers by my estimation. They tell me the name of a good little restaurant they like to use. Mohamed writes the address down. I can find it; I can do anything.

10.

Dr Littlejohn, the Headteacher at Bury Grammar, called Ronald into school after Moss told them he was leaving. He was sixteen, it was all above board. Ronald thought the Head would be a pompous ass before he met him. And when he came home, appointment over, he told me that he'd got that quite right. We weren't against our boy getting an education; the snag was that the subjects he wanted to take would have been a waste of everybody's time. I think sociology is all propaganda. Making excuses for criminals and suchlike.

Dr Littlejohn told Ronald that Moss was very clever. I think so too, which is why Ron and I thought he would get on well in an office job. He could get himself promoted in time; if he did that again and again, he'd become the manager of the place long before he retired. That's got to be better than studying something that's of no use to man or beast.

Ronald put on a pretend southern accent like the one Dr Littlejohn has and announced, 'Your son not coming into the sixth form will squander a bright future.' Apparently, that's what he said when they met. We hooted with laughter at Ronnie's impersonation.

Teachers are always biased in favour of learning but lots of us get through life very nicely, thank you, without knowing what we've no need to know.

* * *

I went back to my hotel for a while, tried to read the Roth but I couldn't really concentrate on it. I'm going to be in Sardinia in forty-eight hours. Half of that time on a boat, so I'll finish it then. Right now, I'm making my way to the Rue de Turquie to meet my new friends. My not-for-long friends because I am doubtful about coming back here. It has been tough. Never say never, it inhibits the flow if you do that. Seriously damages the flow. It's dusk, very warm, hot and dry. I think I last saw rain in Alicante, Spain. Weeks and weeks ago. I wonder where the drinking water comes from.

Rucksack Jumper

I can see the restaurant across the street; I wait for a break in the traffic but this is one busy road, cars just keep coming. I think of going back to the traffic lights which I passed a block ago, crossing there, but then I see there's a gap so I set off over the road. Out of nowhere, I hear the buzz of a moped. The damned thing comes off the pavement and heads straight at me. The rider swerves and I jump the other way. I look at him, his foot touches the ground, not once, not twice. Three times in a jumpy manoeuvre. He's upright, not fallen off, not touched me. Stupid of him, driving off the pavement like that but the lad has some skill in keeping upright. I'll give him that. I run up to him—not fast, not aggressive—just to see that he's okay. He's put his bike back on the pavement and he's just walking round it. Barely putting any weight on his left foot. I apologise and he shrugs: it's just one of those things. He doesn't blame me. I think the poor sod has sprained his ankle, flipped it when he leant too far to the left as he avoided me. I know the feeling; trust me, I nobbled mine in Constantine. This guy might have a broken ankle; I'll let him figure that out for himself. Fingers crossed he hasn't. He doesn't object when I point to the restaurant that I'm going in to. I'm not evading him, we seem to have nothing to do with each other. I had a near miss and he got short shrift for buzzing a moped off the pavement and into the road without looking. He doesn't blame me which I'm glad about; deep down, I blame him. I'd be furious if I'd come off worse.

In the restaurant I don't see Mohamed and Taha immediately, although that's probably because I wasn't expecting to find a whole bunch of other people with them. They are in a group of maybe eight people, maybe nine. I don't take in everybody. I'm leaving tomorrow, so what would be the point? They sit in two lines of young men all ready to eat and they treat me like a guest of honour. I have to say, I feel a bit frustrated by this. I'd have preferred to sit slagging off famous politicians with the two boys. My experience of big groups has always been that the talk is blander, no one wants to offend. It's either football, Thatcher or the Queen. The Jewish girls knew Pablo Neruda, that would have been much better. And I can wish they were here all I want, the Jewish girls wouldn't fit in.

All the other men in this group are older than me—not that much older—enough that I'm no longer looking forward to the meal at all. I expect that some of them are married, might even have children judging by their serious demeanours. I'm good at reading between the lines, seeing the truth in the marks that time has made on people's faces. Quite good, it can be tricky. And I don't care to talk that sort of twaddle tonight, not the domestic lives of people I'll never meet again. And then they'll probably ask me about my mum and dad and Gary, who I never wish ill but they really are as dumb as pig-shit. The conversation could be me saying nice things I don't really believe, or else it will be me silencing people with my gobbiness. I suppose I imagine doing it far more than I permit myself. In fact, I'm more likely to start chuntering some irrelevant nonsense: ask them if they've tuned into the flow, that kind of thing. Taha ushers me into the vacant seat but it isn't next to him, puts me next to an older man who introduces himself.

'Kais.'

We shake hands but I forget to touch my heart. It happens sometimes.

11.

Moss knuckled down in the insurance company. He got his haircut and the paperwork was never a problem. It's just the same as schoolwork really so we knew he would be good at it. He seemed to stop seeing some of his friends and that was a shame. They might have become jealous on account of him getting a wage.

After a year—and without even telling us he was planning it—he left the job but secured another in a local detergent factory. Pipeclean is its name. Moss said all the chemicals they churned out were for breweries and dairies. They didn't make anything for ordinary household cleaning, for a housewife like me. Not a pot of it.

This new job paid better than the old one, which is a good thing I suppose but it didn't seem to have any prospects. Just putting detergent into big boxes that were sold to the industries as could use them. Then he grew his hair long again just as he had in the last couple of years of school. I liked it when he had it shorter and worked in an office.

Ronald said, 'He's probably writing poetry too.' I don't think there's anything wrong with that. If it makes you happy, do it. Just don't expect to make any money from it. That really is a pipedream.

* * *

This is a really brightly lit restaurant. Noisy too. There is Arabic music playing through loudspeakers but it is the talk around all the tables which is making the racket. I think there are only men in here. Loads of them, eight to ten at every table. It could be a rugby club dinner, except that they don't play it in Tunisia.

The meal is nothing special. I have chicken and pretty fancy it looks, but it's really only tomato that it comes with—cooked tomato—and then couscous too, which is nice enough but I'm tired of it. Pizza next, pizza and spaghetti in Sardinia. Can't wait. What's really bugging me is that Mohamed and Taha are both sitting at the far end of the table, nowhere near the place where they shunted me. From what I can see, they just speak to each other, and probably in Arabic. They were so friendly in the afternoon, then they just come here and introduce me to a load of old bores. Turn me into an exhibit—the English boy—it is the last thing I want on my final night in Africa. It's a bit of a shit evening, frankly. The Kais-bloke is making an effort. He keeps talking to me and I try not to be impolite; I think he's an oddball. Confident, brash even. He asks me a lot of questions. I tell him I study literature but don't say any of the long Easter break rubbish. I imagine he might see through it. He's about thirty, dressed up smartly. Well-groomed, hair oil and the closest shave a man can get. All the shit I never do.

He wants to know if I have a girlfriend and I decide to tell him that I do. This is a funny decision on my part because if I really did, I'd probably be travelling across North Africa with her, not leave her behind while I go away for months on end. It is the aggressive nature of his interrogation which makes me choose the affirmative. I imagine Kais is exactly the kind of creep who would take me around Tunis propositioning women in one-eyed veils or to the upstairs room of a prostitute twice my age. For me, making up a nineteen-year-old girlfriend is like taking out an insurance policy. A guarantee that my last night in Africa won't end in humiliation.

Well, the nosy fucker asks a lot of questions about her. About Suzanne, as I have named this fictitious girlfriend. He isn't interested in my family, so she has no need to double as a sister. I tell him that she hopes to be a folk singer, currently she just studies literature like me. The Constantine boys were impressed that the other Suzanne was in a rock band but I'm not trying to impress Kais. Simply imagining something nice for myself. Rock chicks are too brash, I'm a folky at heart.

Kais makes rude gestures, wants to know if Suzanne and I have made love. His words are cruder than that, he even turns to the man next to him—I've not remembered his name but he speaks English pretty well—they whisper for a couple of seconds only and then Kais turns to me, French dropped momentarily. 'You shag in the sack?' he says. I go a little red and he laughs, horrible out-of-control laughter. Points at my blushing face. 'No shag in the sack,' he says to the friend who told him the vulgar English phrase.

12.

Then he was off: hitchhiking. Threw away his job like it was a sweetie wrapper. He told us that he wanted to see the Alps. He hadn't seen as much of England as he could have, none of Scotland except the once when we camped at Pitlochry in April. We went then because it was Easter holidays and Ron's work had gone slack. It turned out to be a mistake. Snow on the tent.

Anyhow, Ronald and I don't see the point of going abroad if you've still some of your own country left to explore; our youngest always did have his own ideas. Wouldn't listen to wiser counsel.

Moss sent a postcard from a place called Annecy which made Ronald very, very cross. You see, it arrived the same day as Gary's Royal Navy presentation. It rubbed his brother's nose in it, we could all see that. One working hard, one slacking. Ronald and I both abhor hitchhiking. If Moss had worked harder, he could have bought a car and gone there in that. Looked at the Alps under his own steam.

* * *

Kais is a twat. I'm sharing a final meal in Africa and the other Tunisians have not been unpleasant to me; I don't want an argument. And I suspect I'd be on my own if I started one. I look up and down the table. We've finished the food now and most of the men have a bottle of beer in

Heavy Rain in Tunis

their hand. A couple are drinking mint tea. Only a couple.

I look for Mohamed, for Taha, they're no longer sitting at the table. I enquire of Kais when they will be back. He shrugs. 'Heure du coucher,' he says: Bedtime. I think he's joking about their youth, so I smile back. Inside I'm seething. I thought those two were okay and then they didn't bother to say goodbye. They're letting all the Arabs down by doing that. Nobody has been this rude to me on my whole trip. I remember back in Nedroma, the chaser of one-eyed whores had the decency to say goodbye.

Kais looks me in the eye, he's got a hard face, looks unpleasant for all his hair oil. 'I wouldn't take your Suzanne from you,' he says. I smile back, it might look friendly but I'm thinking only that he has too little imagination to steal a pretend girlfriend. Twat indeed. Then he follows it up with something I find more sinister. 'I like boys,' he says, 'young boys.' I hate this kind of talk, never think about it really. I know there are people like that out there, thankfully I'm off to Sardinia tomorrow so I'll never see this creep again. Not once I've left the restaurant.

I decide Kais is not really worth debating morals with. I point at my chest. 'Les filles pour moi,' I tell him. I don't want him to have any doubt about what I'm like. Then I say, 'Vieux.' He laughs at this because it means old. I intended to make the point that I wouldn't try to have sex with young girls, this freak probably imagines me shagging in the sack with old Denise or Samira number three from the ferry company. Frankly, I'd much sooner go with either of them than a kid you should go to prison for. Girl or boy. Now isn't my time to say all that; I'm ready for my hotel room. 'Live and let live,' is what I say, do so in English. The French translation evades me. Kais doesn't look like he understands. 'You have who you please but for me only girls,' I say in French, adding, 'Pas jeune,' making my point clear: Not young. He laughs again but I think what I said sounded okay at the second time of asking. I said what I meant, he can laugh or not. I still mean it. And he's still a twat.

13.

When he returned, he looked a state. He'd started tying his hair back like a girl and not even with a proper hairband. He got himself a job, mind, knew that we wouldn't have him scrounging.

At first, he washed up at a foreign restaurant, so I suppose going to the Alps helped in some small way. But it wasn't much of a job if you ask me. Then he went back to Pipeclean. They took him on straight away which means he must have been a half-way decent worker. Maybe better than that, I've no wish to run him down. He said the money was better there than at Pinocchio's, at the restaurant.

I said he should get his hair cut otherwise he might catch it in the machinery. He said this was why he tied it back. An answer for everything had Moss. Not necessarily the best one but always an answer.

He went on a date with Sharon MacDonald. Well, neither Ronald nor I were pleased about that. We wondered what ideas had found their way into his head out in France and Switzerland, amongst our continental cousins, as they are called. Sharon MacDonald is one of those mixed-race girls. Anyone can see that whether you know her father or not. And I certainly do not. Him or any of them. Then our wayward son goes chasing her like she's regular Lancashire.

* * *

The meal needs paying for and because there are several of us, I presume we're all going to chip in. Pay our share, give or take a few centimes. The men show a certain consternation about the bill that I can't fathom properly. I hear one say that Mohamed and Taha have not left any money. Cheeky sods, I thought, but at least that explains why they didn't say goodbye. Kais declares to everyone that he will pay and two or three of the men thank him, shake his hand and go. I'm surprised by this turn-up. I haven't trusted him for a second and then he shows a collegial warmth, footing what will be a big bill if last night in Tabarka is anything to go by. Asking for nothing in return.

He says something to a passing waiter—Arabic, I'm not in on it—the waiter leaves and returns with two more beers. 'For you and I,' says Kais.

I apologise and tell him I wish to return to my hotel. 'Je suis fatigué.'

'Too tired for a new friend?' he says with a smile. I pick up the bottle but my heart isn't in it. This man is not my friend.

The waiter has been standing beside Kai throughout our little exchange. Hovering in the manner of the serving classes since time immemorial, not appearing to listen to us, just waiting to speak without having to interrupt. Kais passes him an unusual banknote, not one which I recognise. The waiter nods and walks back to his station clutching it tightly in his hand. Neither Kais nor I seem to be drinking our beer, he passes the occasional comment to the two others in our party who are still here. I do not listen. They're talking Arabic; I don't attend their words because it's pointless. Find myself imagining being in Sardinia, being among European people whose ways are more familiar to me.

The waiter returns and hands Kais back the same banknote he'd taken as payment. They exchange words and then Kais turns to me. I see as he holds it up, that the note is a one-hundred-dollar bill. American currency.

'I don't have dinar,' he explains. 'Can you pay? I give you the one hundred dollars in exchange.'

I ask how much the meal has cost; I can still do a rough calculation in my head, in the conversion from dinar the entire bill comes to barely twenty pounds, a lot lower than I had expected for so many of us. I think that is around forty dollars, not that I'm up to date with the American exchange rate. I've had no reason to be. No matter what the exact figure is, I'll make a pretty packet if I take his hundred and I think for a second that this is the benefit of going with the flow. Big dosh. I also think—even though it worked out okay—it was a wrong turn back in Oujda. Changing all those pounds into black-market Algerian dinars was unnecessary. The wrong flow altogether. The customs guys would have caught me if they knew how to do their jobs; it really could have ended horribly for me. I nearly crapped my pants that is actually the dictionary definition of bad karma. 'I can pay and I will change the one hundred dollars tomorrow, then give you back what is not mine.'

Kais likes this. 'Thank you.' he says. We calculate some numbers and I try to tell him that I can be precise when I've got the proper information. The accurate exchange rate from the bank. I don't think my French was great on this detail but he trusts me. Why wouldn't he?

I tell him the name of my hotel. I say it with a little hesitation because I don't want this bugger following me there tonight. There is always someone at reception so they wouldn't let him through. Forms to fill out before you get far in a North African hotel. The are-you-a-twat question would catch Kais out. Keep him in the foyer 'til Fruitcake comes.

I pay the bill and put the note in my jeans pocket. Not in my money belt at this point. It's a gut feeling, I don't want him to see me fiddling with it.

14.

I suspected he was seeing more of the little Sharon girl than he let on. He often stayed out late—midnight—without telling us where he'd been. Ronald said Sharon was an easy girl; I don't like that kind of talk whether it's true or it isn't.

If they were seeing more of each other, it didn't come to anything. Sandra at the bakery—who knows Sharon's mother—told me that the girl had only gone and got a job in Manchester. Taken a room there too. This all happened—the girl leaving Bury for good—just a few short weeks before our son went on his big adventure.

Moss didn't tell us that they'd broken up but when I told Ron what I'd heard in the bakery, that they must have, he smirked. 'Barely a break up with a girl like that,' he said.

It wasn't long after I learnt Sharon had gone away that Moss told Ronald and I he'd left Pipeclean for good.

'How do you know it'll be for good when you've still to learn all the twists life has in store?' I was only thinking about how he'd gone back there after he came home from the Alps.

Moss said quite firmly that he was finished with Pipeclean; I don't see how he could have known.

* * *

There are just three of us leaving the restaurant together, all the others went earlier, Mohamed and Taha first. Since those two have left, Kais is the only one whose name I ever learnt. He holds his beer bottle, puts it to his lips, has hardly drunk any of it. I left mine on the table in the restaurant. Untouched and he didn't seem to notice. It comes to me that his lack of concern is because I've paid for everything, my undrunk beer included. His banknote is counterfeit. I want to smile to myself at this. A remarkably warm feeling in my stomach: twenty quid to get out of here and on to Sardinia is a good deal. The penny has dropped through the slot on the top of my head. And I'm relieved that it's only pennies I've flushed away. I say goodbye to the two men, tell Kais that I will see him in the morning although I know he'll not be coming near my hotel. I've worked his game out.

15.

He left our house, our family home on Wolseley Road—the only house he ever lived in and where we'd all enjoyed so many good times together—this was in March. Not close to holiday season really. I should have guessed it would all end like Pitlochry.

He had a full rucksack hoisted up on his back. So full it made me think he wasn't coming back. I wish I hadn't thought it now. I know it makes me sound superstitious but there you are.

I was still looking at him from the upstairs window—looking at the back of his head and the little quickness in his step that the adventure must have brought upon him—when he stuck his thumb out. Asking for a ride, a lift. Fancy doing that on Wolseley Road. No one stops for a hitchhiker here. Why would they do that in Bury? It's not a hitchhiking sort of place. Bury is for workers really. And that's not just hindsight, I thought it at the time. Moss would have been wiser to have knuckled down like the rest of us.

* * *

As I step away from the other two men and walk in the direction that I believe to be towards my hotel—a little uncertain, it has been a long night and I drank a few beers before passing over the last one—I hear footsteps coming up behind me. Kais is back before I've really left him.

'J'habite ici,' he says, pointing in the direction I am walking. I nod. It's plausible: he might live somewhere near my hotel. He puts an arm around my shoulder. 'Moss, Moss,' he says.

I don't like this at all. Soufie never put an arm around me and he was a man I could trust. I retract myself from Kais. I say, 'Thank-you,' then 'Merci.' I only mean, keep your hands to yourself. Can't think of the French quick enough. I'm not really flowing right now.

Then Kais says something that sends a chill through me. 'Il n'y a pas Suzanne.' He tells me confidently that there is no Suzanne.

I don't like lying but I only say things that could easily be true. I could study literature, it's within me, I'm pretty sure. Sometimes I tell people my dad's a decent guy to avoid the more awkward conversation. It's a shame it isn't true. I have no defect that makes having a girlfriend called Suzanne especially improbable, somehow or other Kais has seen through it. He's my karmic opposite, inhibiting the life-force that helps me get a bit of joy from a loveless world. I wonder what I'm even doing here. I don't know any paedophiles in Bury but I've met a few hard-faced bastards before. I really didn't come to Africa just to find more of them. It's no reason to go anywhere.

16.

He told us he was going to Africa but Ronald laughed at that. Told him he wouldn't make it. Ron told me why not but I don't expect he discussed it with Moss. Ronald had figured that it is a long way and as you get nearer—southern Europe or even Africa— the people get poorer. They wouldn't be the sort to give hitchhikers lifts. That was Ronald's thinking and it sounded about right to me. You can't give charity when you've a pressing need for all the money you've got.

I wondered if he would be getting a job to pay his way while he was travelling. Washing dishes most probably, like he had done in the restaurant across town. And if he did that, worked in a restaurant in Paris or the like, then he'd probably meet a waitress there and before you know it, he wouldn't even be wanting to go to Africa. Not if she and he were well suited. Now, with how it's all turned out, I wish he had met a French waitress.

I thought we'd get a postcard if something of that sort had happened but a long time went by without one. I told Ronald, he probably won't send one if he's still in England, at London or Dover. Too embarrassed. For the longest time that's where I imagined he'd got stuck. I guess he must have been more resourceful than I'd given him credit for. He got to where he said he would go and I'm pleased for him. At least he got something that he wanted; a small mercy, I call it.

* * *

Kais suddenly grabs me under the armpits—he's a big man—has me off the ground before I know what's happening. I flail around a bit and he just laughs about it. Does it very nastily, deep and throaty. Nothing is funny; he wants to scare me. I know his sort. My feet are back on the ground now but I'm not in control. Kais pushes me into an alleyway. I hate this.

It's much gloomier down here, just a bit of light from the street we've come off. I feel liquid on my leg and wonder if I've peed myself. As I look down, Kais laughs and shakes his beer bottle at me. He spilled quite a lot of it while lifting me up. How the fuck he kept the bottle in his hand while doing that beats me—I'm five-eight, not titchy-tiny—I'm going to need serious fighting lessons if I keep travelling this haphazardly. Vim Voyager would punch this fucker's lights out, no problem.

Kais tries to kiss me on the lips, succeeds because he's holding the back of my head with both hands. Beer spills onto my hair. I pull my head back, probably because he lets me. I turn and spit; I hate having this man's taste in my mouth. Suddenly I'm stung across the face, he has slapped me harder than I've ever been slapped before. My ears ring—ring or buzz—I can't really hear anything. 'L'argent,' he says. He might have shouted it at me, I can't tell. I'm alert enough to lipread the phrase. No sound has returned. He wants my money. I put a hand on my money belt then before I can take any out, he slaps my face again. Not quite as hard—vicious though—enough for me to feel stunned. I'll give him what money I've got. I want out of here.

I pull the one-hundred-dollar bill from my jeans pocket and offer him that. If he takes it, it's real, but I don't expect he will.

I am confused by how greedily he snatches it. I thought he would want my money belt, now it seems like he doesn't even know I'm wearing one. Very strange that he could figure out there is no such person as Suzanne but doesn't know where a traveller keeps his money. He's not worldly at all, he's just a cunt. I know I've called that right when the nasty shit thumps me in the stomach, winds me, starts trying to kiss me again after I've already given back his fucking banknote.

17.

It was on the same morning that we finally received a postcard when the telephone call came from David Winterbotham. The man from the Foreign Office. The card didn't say much: this is where I am, seemed the gist of it. The picture of the Sahara Desert was quite a surprise. He did it. The franking across the postage stamp had the town's name on it: Ghardaia. I thought it was misspelt but apparently not. When we got the call, Ron and I both thought it was a mistake. He couldn't be in Tunis, he was in Ghardaia. Of course, the post in the desert is slow. Slower than hitchhiking. Camels, I understand.

It was a dreadful call. When it was over and we understood it, Ronald went to pieces.

It's such a shame that the call and the card both came on the same day. I was pleased to see how far he'd managed to travel even though I never liked his methods. The hitchhiking. Getting the bad news turned everything sour.

* * *

I decide to make a run for it, get away from this bastard with as much dignity as I can retain. I'm not doing any of his queer stuff. He's trying to feel me all over, putting his hands into my trousers, that shit. I keep moving— struggling—he makes no progress. I realise how much taller than me he is, and then I figure out how it can help me. I stoop down a little, then suddenly ram the top of my head into his face as he is leaning over me. I ram it hard and he yelps. I hope I've broken his fucking nose. He deserves worse. He starts to fall and I hear the smashing of glass, must have dropped the bottle. I try to run, only to find he has a hold of my leg. Got it in a fierce grip like he's holding on to me for dear life. I think my headbutt must have hurt; a shame I haven't killed him. Moved his nose a little, I expect. He seems able to grip my leg tightly. He brings me down, which is a big reverse for me. Not good at all. As I try to look around, he rises up and then rolls right on top of me. His nose is gushing blood, a flood of the stuff. It's the best sight I've seen all night.

He's tough even with a broken nose. He pushes me down with a knee and I bang the back of my head on the hard ground. I'm okay, I've bashed it worse by accident; I guess it will bruise, could balloon up. I hate fighting and I don't want to land in Europe looking like I've returned from war. I came here in peace, I really did. The bastard has got the bottle in his right hand—I heard it break but he must have kept hold of the neck—he thrusts it into my abdomen, I think he twists it as he does so. It's horrible, so bloody painful I can't speak.

18.

The Winterbotham man meets us at the airport terminal, Heathrow this is. Ronald and I have been to Manchester Airport with the boys; that wasn't to fly anywhere, just for a day out. It's somewhere to go. This feels different, important, because I am meeting a Foreign Office official. David Winterbotham, like I've said. Gary has been given leave by the navy and he is by my side when we meet. He wears his uniform—very smart it is too—and I think that this is a very nice touch. Gary's a good brother to Moss. Even now, after whatever it is he got involved with.

* * *

No, no. This is agony, sheer agony. My sweatshirt rode up my stomach before he pushed the broken bottle into me, even my T-shirt I suspect. I don't know anymore. He's done something worse than just cut my flesh. Something is not right. I've never known this much pain, I don't know what the bastards doing, he might have gone. 'Help,' I shout. Even Kais should help me now—this is too fucking awful—it's not about a hundred dollars anymore. 'Help.' But although I think that I'm shouting, I don't hear myself. Not sure if I am shouting inside or outside my head. I have no consciousness of my mouth, only of the pain in my abdomen. What damage has he done? I need doctors and everything.

I put a hand there and it is not only warm and moist, I realise that I can feel inside myself. The money belt is in ribbons, the cotton is sticking to my insides. I don't really know where my hand is in relation to the flowing blood or the open wound. I hope they can patch me up, someone should come soon.

I remember something my father said to me, something important but although I remember it clearly, it's not the actual words that come to me, not even the look on his face when he said them. It is something else, its essence, its flavour. I know this sounds unlikely—words do have meaning—but it's like I'm in a place where there are no words. Or possibly it is not a place at all. The less here I am, the less I can feel the pain.

19.

Ronald should be with us by rights but he's not. He stopped working when all this happened. The day of the postcard and the telephone call. I'm sorry to say, it has made him very ill. Not himself at all.

In the days between the call and this trip to the airport, he kept changing his mind about it all. At first, he said he wouldn't go because Moss wasn't his son, and then he said he wouldn't go because he couldn't face collecting his son like he was a parcel.

And I said, 'Of course you're Moss's father, I'm not some Sharon MacDonald, am I?' It might not even have been his fault that he was found like that. Nobody has told us what he was up to in Tunis and I don't like to ask Mr Winterbotham.

* * *

The heavens open up: a deluge. Heavy torrential rain, a

cloud burst of it, running like a seasonal river down the Tunis streets. All the drains are overflowing and so are all the gullies. Water runs an inch deep, two inches deep, on every street, down all the side alleys too. An astonishing quantity of rain pummels down onto the city, filling up each hole in the ground, flooding down into basements.

When the police come to examine the body in the morning light—no more than a dozen metres up an alley, off the main thoroughfare on the northside of the city—it must be cleaner than any other found body that has been subject to such a frenzied attack. The blood of the boy has been washed away, carried down the streets, alleys, gutters and drains of Tunis. Some blood from the attacker may have gone that way too. There is little evidence of what has transpired beyond the gruesome wound on the corpse's midriff.

The passport in the pocket of the shredded money belt is saturated, no longer stiff but limp like the linen that formed the belt. It is sufficient to identify the boy. The authorities in Tunis learn that Moss Croft is the name of the deceased. Within the hour they share this cheerless knowledge with the British Embassy.

20.

We, the three of us, walk across the tarmac to meet the aeroplane. It isn't a big one and it seems Mr Winterbotham has chartered it to bring the coffin back from Tunis. It must have cost a small fortune. Mr Winterbotham—he said we were to call him Dave but I don't like to, he dresses smartly like a mister, a sir, even—told us that the state always pays for repatriation. It's very good of them to do that.

I notice that Gary is crying, so I try not to look in his direction after that. We're caring but we're not sentimental people, the Crofts. I think Ronald will miss him most whether he says it or not.

Printed in Great Britain
by Amazon